SONGLIGHT

MOIRA BUFFINI

SONGLIGHT

BOOK ONE OF
THE TORCH TRILOGY

HARPER
An Imprint of HarperCollinsPublishers

For Midie

Ever seeking balance
grant us wisdom
to be shepherds of creation

—Ancient prayer to Gala
Fragment from the *Book of Woe*

PROLOGUE ✳ KAIRA

I'm leaving my bedroom for the last time. I can't take anything with me, as this is supposed to be an ordinary shopping trip. I put my coat on. I haven't had a new one in years and my arms poke out of the sleeves, embarrassing me with their length, like the soft talons of a baby bird. I glance at myself in my little mirror. After today, I'll never stare in it again. I'm seventeen but no one would know. I'm small for my age, thin from illness and plain as a bean. My thick spectacles don't help. I daren't think about what I'm going do. My heart is knocking at my ribs.

Stop thinking, I tell myself. Just go. I close the door behind me.

The smell of ham and cabbage hits me. In the kitchen, my latest mama is cooking. I console myself with the thought that I'll never have to eat her soggy food again.

"I'm going to the market now," I call.

Ishbella looks out of the kitchen. When she first came to our house she was sharp. She wore pointy dresses with pleats like knives and her lips were always painted red. She looks tired and creased around the edges now—and everything I say and do scrapes upon her like a lathe.

"What about your papa's boots?" she demands.

"I've done them." I smile, pointing to a pair of gleaming jackboots.

"Get me a tin of chicken paste," she says.

"I won't," I say to myself. And I leave.

The fresh air hits me. It's dizzying. A wind whips around me as I walk toward the market. But the market's not my destination. I'm going to escape.

I send a thought-frond high into the air, just as Cassandra taught me. A single, solitary note of songlight, aimed keenly. I feel it touch her spirit.

"I'm on my way," I tell her.

I feel Cassandra's presence brighten as she lets me into her consciousness. Momentarily, I see the world through her eyes. She's leaving work, walking down the corridor toward the hospital entrance. She passes a senior doctor and nods to him.

"Good night, Nurse," I hear him say.

Cassandra leaves the building. She walks gracefully, with such an easy spring, so unlike my halting limp. When I'm with her in songlight, I feel a happiness so sudden and acute I find it almost painful. To be held in her light . . . It's like the most perfect summer's day.

When I was in the hospital, Cassandra was the nurse who saved my life. She sensed my songlight before I dared to name it.

"You know what you are, don't you?" she asked. She spoke without using her voice, yet I could hear her very well. I replied the same way.

"An unhuman."

"No," she replied. "Never use that word. You're a Torch."

I see the lights on the esplanade falling in pools ahead of her now. The city's great turbines turn in the breeze, rising above her like a metal forest.

"You know where to meet me?" she asks.

"Yes," I say. "I'm ready."

She senses my raised heartbeat, my trepidation. "Freedom isn't easy. It's dangerous. But it's the right thing."

"Where will we go?" I ask.

"It's safer not to tell you. Don't be scared, Little Bird."

"I'm not."

In my heart, I wish she wouldn't call me Little Bird. I know she does it for safety—we should never say each other's names, not even in songlight, in case a Siren is eavesdropping. But "Little Bird" makes me feel like I'm a kid, just someone she has to look after.

The tram station looms ahead, built in the Brethren's mighty style. I climb to the platform, taking each step slowly. I'm tiring now and I stop to get my breath. I'm getting stronger every day but the wasting fever has left its mark. I tire quickly and my right leg is slightly thinner than the left—some days it aches so bad I need a cane. But I'm luckier than some. I survived.

The platform is crowded. Citizens wait on either side of the tracks. I try not to look at the lone Inquisitor, who stands at the top of the stairs in his dark uniform. I pass him as meekly as I can and walk down the platform. At last, I see Cassandra arrive. She passes the Inquisitor and winks at me. I feel a beam of joy. In truth, I'd follow Cassandra to the moon and back.

I think of the days ahead that I'll spend in her company and the beam becomes a glow that warms my whole body and fills me with strength. My trepidation fades away.

I'm going to be free.

I feel a pang of regret for my papa—but the strain of hiding who I am has grown too much to bear. I know my secret would have broken out sooner or later—and it would cause Papa anguish to destroy me.

I can never be the daughter that he wants.

Cassandra stands apart, as if we're strangers, waiting for our tram. I won't be afraid. I won't have doubts. I will be worthy of her friendship and her care. I allow myself to glance at her, my whole soul shining with gratitude and love.

And then it happens.

I see something flicker in the atmosphere beside her. A male figure, staring at her. A glimmer of a man in cheap suit, a hat pulled over his shaven head. He's one of our kind, a Torch who has been captured and now, in exchange for his life, he must use his songlight to ensnare others.

He's a Siren. And he has my beautiful Cassandra in his sights.

PART 1

✴

1 ✳   ELSA

I know there's something in the lobster pot before I start to lift it. Down there on the seafloor, I can sense the creature I have caught. It's eaten the bait and tried every way to escape, finding its huge claws to be only a hindrance. I do what any good seaworker would do and concentrate on how badly Northaven needs to eat. Food shipments from Brightlinghelm are becoming unreliable and we don't have good farming land round here. Up on the cliffs there is moorland and marshland, not the green and golden wheat fields that you hear of in the south. Our last harvest was shredded by the gales. This runs through my head as I pull the rope up from the sandy floor, bringing the unlucky creature into my boat.

I love the blue melt of the sea and sky, the salt spray, the way I have to balance on the swell, the sun dazzling, the wind lifting my spirits high into the air. I reckon I'm a natural on the water—like my pa. My brother, Piper, is a senior cadet, training for the war. So when Pa died, the boat was left to Ma and me. As a widow, Ma is not supposed to work outside the house, so in those dark years after Pa's death, I taught myself his trade. I think I had it in my bones. Pa knew I liked the water. He'd take me out with him when I was barely old enough to walk. He'd move about the boat, grinning at me, showing me the wonders of the sea. I love the moving waves so much that when I step on solid land, I feel all heavy and bereft.

I look at the lobster, a huge female. I see her egg sacs, held precious under her belly. I admire her blue-black armor, her otherworldly eyes. I'm opening her pot when I realize I'm no longer alone.

I smile with delight and I thrill at the danger. Rye Tern has come.

"How's the catch?" he asks.

I see him then—or sense him, should I say. Songlight can't be described in words. Rye's with me, but he's not. I see him, but I don't. He's here in every sense—but only my sixth one perceives him. He's leaning on a mop, his shirtsleeves rolled up. He'll be somewhere in the barracks, but to me, it seems like he's standing in the stern. The sun still shines through him but as our minds cleave to one another, he grows more solid. "We were parading and I saw your boat. Got myself put on punishment duty so I could come." He brandishes his mop. The way he smiles through his troubles makes my heart flip upside down.

"Reckless idiot." I turn to my work, considering the lobster.

Rye comes closer. "She looks a bit like you."

"I'm better defended." I melt at his grin.

His light is closer still. I've no defenses against Rye at all.

"She's carrying her egg sacs," I tell him. "So she has to go back in the sea."

I lean over the side and let the lobster queen slip back into the water. We watch her disappear down into the blue. Her freedom makes me glad.

Rye comes out to my boat whenever he can. It's the only place that we feel safe, where our love isn't hidden. We can let ourselves go here, high into the air, circling each other like gulls—or we listen to the deep. We can tell when there are herring coming; we sense their sleek glide, all singing the same note. Sometimes there are yellowfins, speeding under us like shooting stars. Always, there are jellyfish, drifting in shoals like the souls of the dead.

His songlight is all I'm aware of now, his presence joining with mine. Desire twists in my guts as I remember the last time I touched him for real. As night was falling, a tap came on my bedroom window. Rye was there in our garden, vulnerable, his jacket ripped from a fight with his pa. I cherish that image of him. It comes into my mind over and over, the way the moonlight fell upon his skin, the hurt that I could sense in him. I climbed out of the window and he caught me in his arms. I held him close, not wanting to speak. The intensity of his body took my breath away. The smell of him, the iron of his arms, his lips on my neck . . . Nothing in songlight could ever come close.

Together we went down to Bailey's Strand and swam. We lay on the sand, under the stars. We heedlessly broke every rule and restraint. Thinking of it now—of being joined with his body as well as his mind—makes me crave it again. I want Rye Tern here, in my boat. I want to smell him, kiss him, explore him with my hands. Rye can tell what I'm thinking of. I feel his longing in every breath.

What we've done is interdicted. According to the Anthems of Purity, which we must learn by heart, I am now tarnished. But how can such a thing be criminal? We are not sex traitors, we are Elsa and Rye.

"I have to see you," I whisper.

"I know," he says. "Something has to change. We have to be together."

"Meet me," I tell him. "Down on Bailey's Strand. Tonight. In the flesh."

"It's dangerous."

"I know."

Our songlight is one keen note of desire. I want his lips on mine, his belly pressing against me, my legs wrapped around him. We hold the note, breathing our need, until the whole ocean feels like it's singing to our tune.

Then I sense him looking over his shoulder. For a second I see the world through his eyes. He's in the refectory, mopping the floor. I hear heavy footsteps approaching him.

"Someone's coming," he says. Instantly, his warmth and vigor fade.

He's gone, leaving me in turmoil.

The quality of the sound all around me changes. I become aware of the breeze, the water lapping against the sides of the boat. I hate it when he vanishes suddenly like this.

I pull in my nets and I turn back toward Northaven. My songlight isn't wanted there. I keep it buried underneath my lungs. I push my songlight down my legs and arms and hide it under my fingernails. If anyone else in our town has songlight, they must keep it well concealed. To my knowledge, it's just Rye and me. In Northaven, songlight is a burden; it's treacherous. Occasionally, I'll sense a note on the air like the colors of the loom, or a sigh like water falling down a drain, or thought-wreathes hanging like the crackling of a fire. And then the singer notices and suddenly it's tight and hard to breathe. I know the feeling. When Great Brother Peregrine took power, back when Ma was a girl, there were culls of all unhumans. Our temple to Gala was closed and locked. Anyone known to have songlight was cuffed around the skull with lead and taken to Brightlinghelm to be enslaved. Every few years, an Inquisitor comes with his Siren to inspect the population. Last time, the Inquisitor took old Ellie Brambling, Mr. Roberts, and Seren Young. I was a junior choirmaiden then. And my songlight had not fully shown itself.

Before the Inquisitor left, he stood with our eldermen and drilled us on how to spot the signs. If we had this mutation, this corruption, it would soon become apparent. If we sensed any signs in ourselves or in others, we were beholden to confess. Did we, when alone, ever feel the presence of another? Did we ever sense what others might be thinking? Did we experience a sensation of floating, of being out of our bodies? Did we ever feel controlled by the will of another? If we suspected an unhuman at work or felt an unhuman stain upon our souls, we had to come forward and speak. If we were honest, no harm would befall us. Our songlight would only be contained. We'd be able to use it in service of the Brethren.

No thanks to that, I thought as my songlight developed in full flow. Night after night I'd wake and find myself high above our house. I would be out in the boat and find myself looking down from the sky, feeling birdsong like a language, or seeing the world through the eyes of the seals that watch me as I work. I felt intensely connected to every living thing. And very, very afraid.

Then one day, Rye Tern showed up in my boat. I'd known Rye all my life—he was one of Piper's friends. He appeared in songlight when I was pulling in my nets. I tried to ignore him, my heart thumping with fear. Unhuman. Unhuman.

"I know you can see me, Elsa."

"Leave me alone, Unhuman," I told him.

"You're unhuman too, fool. What're you going to do about it?" he asked. "Turn me in?"

I had nothing to say. Just a slow tear that fell down my face.

"It's like your worst fucking nightmare, isn't it?" said Rye quietly.

I nodded.

For a while we prowled around each other like cats, claws out, not daring to trust. But it was such a relief to have a friend. I'd been so lonely with my oddness, so scared when it began. It was far worse than my monthlies. The pain and the blood-cloths were nothing compared to the fear I felt when my mind began to leave my body. When I began to glimpse the under-thoughts of others, sensing what they felt when their words said something else, I was full of lonely dread. But Rye and I shared our otherness. It was a solace every time we met. Maybe I'd have loved Rye even if he'd been ugly as a stick, because his hurting, his anger, his raw sweetness, the way he finds humor in the darkest things—all these things are beautiful. But I've watched him grow from boy to man, and Rye Tern isn't ugly, not by any stretch. Rye Tern is a looker. From his long lashes to his gorgeous shoulder blades—every inch of him thrills me.

On land, in person, we make sure to keep apart. Not even Piper, my own brother, knows how we're connected. But we're two songs joined. And there's a word for that.

A harmony.

I sail into harbor quite alone, watching the shadows of the wind turbines move like god-wings over our homes. Our town falls down steep hillsides from the moors above, where our high turbine towers catch the coastal winds. I look at the white houses hugging the cove, our brightly painted front doors. I ignore the barbed wire, the gun placements, and the watch-towers, trying to forget the ugliness of war.

Northaven centers round its natural harbor. The long quay with its seawall protects us on one side and on the other, a mossy headland leads down to Bailey's Strand, our golden-sanded beach. Beyond, to the north, there's nothing but moors and marshes. Only herders live up there. To the east and south of our great island is the vast Greensward, where my mother comes from. It's an impassable, mountainous forest. People live there in traveling tribes, coming out to trade in the markets. It was at such a market that my Greensward ma met my seaworker pa. There's no road through the center of the island, so we're connected to our capital, Bright-linghelm, only by sea. Transport ships come and go, a slow journey of two days through the war-torn Alma Straits, bringing grain if we're lucky, tak-ing fish and all our men.

Northaven is a pretty town, a brave town. We've seen off Aylish raiders more than once. But as I approach the harbor, my breathing constricts and my shoulders tighten. Home.

Mrs. Sweeney is waiting for me. Her husband is our harbormaster—but Mrs. Sweeney does all his work. He's too busy propping up the bar in the Oystercatcher Inn. She's as weatherworn as the wind-whipped Brightling flag that flies above her house. Mrs. Sweeney usually greets me with a good-humored insult. She likes me—rare among the elderwomen, that's for sure. I'm expecting one of her leatherwork smiles, but today, she's agi-tated.

"You're in a lot of trouble, Elsa," she says. "Emissary Wheeler's here." She pulls me off the boat with her big red hands. "He came on the transport ship from Brightlinghelm."

I see the transport ship on the biggest quay, turbines whirring, rust dripping from its bolts, being loaded for its return journey, with iced fish and fruits of the sea. My heart sinks. Emissaries bring news and edicts to the villages. They are our link with Brightlinghelm and have the authority of the Brethren. Everyone here fawns on Emissary Wheeler—and he never brings good news.

"I lost track of time," I say, dismayed.

Songlight is particularly attuned to choral human voices and I can sense our choir, the raw sound tingling down my spine. I should be there.

"I'll see to your catch," says Mrs. Sweeney. "Run."

I'm halfway up the quayside when I realize I'm carrying three mackerel for our supper. Should I go back and dump them in the boat? I'm late enough already. . . .

Beside me, a long, vivid mural runs the whole length of the harbor wall. The colors blur, I'm moving so fast. I see our brave boys and men, in their black-and-red uniforms, repelling an attack from an enemy horde; the Aylish, fiends in dirty shades of blue. Every time I see it, I get a rush of pride, for I hate the Aylish worse than anything alive. Those savage bastards killed my pa.

I trip up the steps and across the town square. It's laundry day and women are cleaning sheets and shirts at our communal laundry while their children play. There seem to be pregnant women wherever I look. First Wives, Second Wives, widows dressed in gray.

The Elders' Hall, looking small but mighty, is draped with Brightling flags and banners: our black-and-white bird of prey, soaring on a red background. As I draw closer, I hear my fellow choirmaidens, singing our anthem. The words and tune are so familiar they're ingrained. I pick up my part of the harmony before I get to the door:

"Brightland, Brightland, ever human, ever true,
Brightland our home, our noble Elderland,
The Brethren have remade us,
In purity we stand . . ."

I press against the heavy doors and hurry into the space without thinking.

"Brightland our pride, our enemies we smite,
The Brethren victorious—for liberty we fight . . ."

The door slams shut behind me as the anthem ends. I find myself exposed in front of the whole assembled company. I see a flash of anger from Hoopoe Guinea, our choirmother. She's responsible for all Northaven's choirmaidens of marriageable age. A tongue-lashing will follow, that's for sure. All eyes are on me as I make my way to the back of the choir stand. To one side of me I see a blur of disapproving black: the eldermen. That luxurious coat belongs to Emissary Wheeler. I daren't look him in the face.

My friend Gailee Roberts makes room for me. She looks down at the mackerel I'm holding in dismay. Chaffinch Greening and Tinamou Haines turn round to stare, as if I'm some alien creature. Chaffinch, dressed in pink, with perfect, sculpted hair, looks at my seaworker's boots with a sneer. My eyes stare straight ahead—as if what I've just done is perfectly acceptable.

Wheeler walks forward, inspecting us. He saves a special disapproving glare for me. He's tall and he projects strength, but when he opens his mouth, his voice is high and weak.

"The time has come for you to prove yourselves as women. Northaven has raised you in virtue. It's now your privilege to sacrifice your purity on the altar of marriage."

What is he saying? I try to decipher his bombast. Marriage?

I feel like I've been sleepwalking. This has been our fate since girlhood—but the reality of it hits me only now.

"The senior cadets are leaving. Soon after, Northaven's long-serving heroes will be coming home on their wedding leave. You'll be gifted to your husband by the town and it's your duty to serve him by bearing him sons."

I can't unpack what he's saying. *The senior cadets are leaving.* Does he mean Rye and Piper? Leaving when? I look at Gailee, wanting her to translate. Our brothers are leaving? And a bunch of men we haven't seen since we were tiny little girls are going to come home and take us to their beds? I've always known this was going to happen, but it's felt far-off, unreal.

"At last . . . ," whispers Chaffinch Greening. She is on her tiptoes in excitement. Am I the only one who is appalled?

"Your training as choirmaidens is almost complete," says the Emissary. "It only remains for your choirmother to teach you the mysteries of the marriage bed."

He glances at Hoopoe Guinea and she gives us all a sticky smile. Nela Lane snickers. Uta Malting tries to hide her grin. Tinamou Haines nudges Chaffinch Greening. We've been training for our wedding day for years. I always thought I'd get out of it, that I'd invent some acceptable reason not to be a bride. How can I marry a stranger? I'm in love with Rye Tern. These thoughts are whirring through my head as Wheeler looks us over.

"You are Brightland's Hope and Beauty. You are all Emblems of Victory. Over the coming days," he rasps, "lists will be drawn up. Those not gifted as a man's First Wife may yet be chosen as his Second."

I'm clenching my fists in dread. I'll be married. Rye will be gone.

"Our heroic fighting men have earned you as their brides. Your every thought must be on them."

Ely Greening steps up. He's our lickspittle mayor.

"Northaven's choirmaidens have been very well trained—my own daughter, Chaffinch, among them. I can assure you of their loyalty and devotion."

He directs Wheeler's gaze toward Chaffinch. From behind, I see her do a coy sway, reveling in her status. Wheeler appraises her, approving. Then his eyes fall on me. He pauses. His eyes take in my sea-salt dress, the sweat under my arms, the mess of my hair, the mackerel in my fist.

"I'm only sorry that one of you sees fit to arrive late, dragging her supper."

"Apologize, Elsa Crane," barks Hoopoe in frustration.

"I'm very sorry."

I suppose I should call him "sir" or "Emissary." Or do a coy sway. But in truth, I despise Wheeler like pissweed. He glares at me, waiting for more.

"Some girls need a firm hand and I hope you get it," he says. "You'll not be going out to sea once you're a wife."

That's the last straw. I have to see Rye Tern.

I slip away the moment we're given permission to leave. I take in lungfuls of air outside the Elders' Hall. Gailee Roberts hurries loyally after me.

"Did you forget our inspection was today?"

"Yes."

"Go back. Make your peace with Hoopoe Guinea. Tell her the wind was against you."

"I've used that excuse too many times."

Chaffinch catches up with us. "How dare you come and stand in our choir, stinking of old cod guts."

"They're mackerel," I tell her.

"D'you think you'll get on the list for First Wife, going around behaving like that?"

"I've got a job, Chaffinch. I'm out every day, providing food, while your head's full of bog moss."

I don't realize that Hoopoe Guinea is behind me.

"Elsa, marriage is your first duty."

I fall silent in dismay. My time of reckoning has come. And Chaffinch is going to enjoy it.

"You let me down in front of Emissary Wheeler. You let every choir-maiden down."

I don't dislike Hoopoe. When we got the news that my father was dead, she was very kind to me. I've disappointed her ever since.

"The wind was against me," I say sheepishly. It sounds so feeble.

"I know your mother needs you. I know you have to work. But marriage training must come first."

"I'm sorry."

"What would your father think to see you getting chastised?" she asks. "Do you think he'd be proud?"

I shake my head, my gaze on the ground.

"Gwyn Crane died doing his duty. When are you going to start doing yours?"

This hits home.

Hoopoe walks away, the choirmaidens following in her wake. Chaffinch Greening turns, giving me a sly glance. Only Gailee remains.

Gailee Roberts will never be a First Wife. The only person who can't see it is the girl herself. Her family has an unhuman stain. When Mr. Roberts was taken to the Chrysalid House, the whole family lost their standing. Gailee and her siblings struggle now. Her mother works through the night, taking laundry, doing piles of mending. She doesn't have a pension like a war widow, so Gailee acts as mother to the little ones. Gailee has no songlight—but sometimes I think she can read me like a book.

"Shall I call for you tonight?" she asks. "Let's walk down to practice together. You still haven't chosen your special skill."

"Nothing I'm good at counts."

"Elsa," she pleads. "You could get First Wife. Your pa died a hero, which is bound to give you points."

She doesn't mention her own pa.

"I'll come round later and help you style your hair," she offers.

Gailee's own hair is already fixed in a plaited sculpt that looks like it won't move for several days. I see that she's been practicing with makeup too. There's red on her lips and cheeks; her eyelids blackened with a wobbly hand.

"I'll show you needlework too, if you like. That'd be a fine special skill. And it can't be so different from mending fishing nets. . . ."

It should impress me, how hopeful Gailee is. She watches others, like Chaffinch or Tinamou, who are both First Wife material. They puzzle her, as if their privileged behavior is a subject she can learn. Gailee has attached herself to me because I stop the others being cruel. They bully her. But sometimes I lose patience and I'm cruel to her myself. She can be a proper irritation. Her whole purpose, her every waking thought, is set on how to please the elders. She doesn't give up. Partly my heart breaks for her because of her unhuman pa. We've never talked about him being taken, not once ever. Gailee's ma and her sisters were all examined by the Inquisitor and his Siren, but apparently her pa had kept his songlight to himself.

"What about dancing?" she says as we start walking up the hill. "I bet you could dance. That's a special skill a man is sure to like. I wanted to choose dancing but Chaffinch said I'd make myself a spectacle."

"Chaffinch is a stinging wasp." I hold out two of the mackerel.

"I caught these for your ma," I say. "We've got plenty at home."

Gailee takes them with such a gush of gratitude that I'm annoyed all over again.

3 ✳

The shadows are long as I pass our row of shops, though there's never much in any of them. The only busy time is early in the morning—the queue for bread in Malting's Bakery begins before it's bright. The day's work is over at the quayside; all the fishing boats are moored and the sea barrier is pulled across the harbor mouth. This is in case the Aylish should attack at night. It hasn't happened since I was tiny but the edict's still in place.

By the harbor, I walk past the bronze statue of Great Brother Peregrine. It's Elder Greening's pride. He raised a whack of money for it, insisting on donations from every single family. Our Great Brother looks wisely out to sea, as if he's gazing at a vision of our future. There's a slogan written underneath—but girls aren't schooled in letters, so I can't tell what it says. Piper told me it reads *The Human Will Prevail*, which, for obvious reasons, I find horribly disturbing.

No one talks about the days before Peregrine anymore, but Ma told me that when she was a child, each town used to be led by a council, drawn from all its citizens, some with songlight, some without. These councils are now known as malign rings. We're taught that the malign rings were petty and corrupt, controlled by mind-twisting unhumans who were trying to hold us back. Great Brother Peregrine raised a citizen's army, destroyed the malign rings, and united us. He has made us a great nation aided by his ten lieutenants, the Brethren. We hear about them on *Sister Swan's Daily Address*.

Northaven has two radiobines now. One is in the Elders' Hall; the other is owned by Ely Greening. Chaffinch guards it jealously, and only her closest friends are allowed round to listen to *Berney Grebe's Music Hour* and *Soldier of the Week*.

The radiobine is just one of the Brethren's innovations. They began a program of building, they brought us turbine power, and Brother

Peregrine reintroduced the use of money. Ma told me that people resisted this at first. Money was a lost idea from the Light People time and many felt nothing from those days should be revived. Hadn't the Light People virtually destroyed us? But Great Brother Peregrine said that some ideas from the Age of Light shouldn't be rejected out of hand. Money, he said, would lift us out of poverty. And Northaven got richer, that's for sure. The harbor has its new wall, the Elders' Hall has alabaster pillars, and the transport ships go daily now to Brightlinghelm. But the war with the Aylish is a drain on our nation. The wealth that we had is disappearing.

There's one innovation that I won't ever think about. The Chrysalid House.

I pass Mr. Aboa, arm in arm with his heavily pregnant First Wife. His Second Wife follows behind, plainly dressed to accessorize the First, chivvying their children. She carries a heavy bag of potatoes. Mr. Aboa is a veteran. He walks with a crutch and he can no longer fight, but, as far as I can see, he's got things all sewn up. He's got his pension from the Brethren and I bet he never lifts a finger. His Second Wife looks tired. Maybe she is pregnant too. I watch her go, thinking of my looming fate. The war. Marriage.

I have to see Rye.

Opposite our house is a large mural of Sister Swan, the Flower of Brightland. Her eyes are lowered and her arms are held out, as if she's giving us her blessing. We're supposed to revere her as an example of perfect womanhood. Personally, I don't like the smug look of her. My stomach growls angrily, as if my hunger's giving voice to the way I feel.

I approach our little house with its yellow door, a color chosen in happier times, now peeling, pale, and weatherworn. Inside, my mother is chopping up vegetables. Curlew Crane, or "Curl," as Pa always called her. Her face is framed by her widow's veil. She's been wearing it since he died, when I was ten years old.

"Mrs. Sweeney came by," says Ma as I walk in. "She said you missed choir."

"Not all of it," I say. "Sorry."

The word withers in the air from overuse. Ma at looks me with weary disappointment. I put the one remaining mackerel down, trying to placate her.

"Is that it?" she asks.

"I gave the rest to Gailee."

She doesn't disapprove.

"Well. There's enough."

She sweeps the veg into a pot. Her head is bowed. Something's paining her. She's heard the news. . . .

"Go see your brother," she says, her voice low. "He's in the garden."

Great Brother Peregrine tells us that boys must rely on each other, not their families. So Piper, Rye, and the other cadets have lived in the barracks since they were eleven. Home visits are usually only on a Sunday, so Piper's appearance on a Tuesday night is rare. The cadets are going to the front. I'm going to lose Rye—and I don't know what to do.

I watch Piper for a while before he sees me. He's planting spuds, covering them with soil, making sure that when he goes, we have enough to eat. He's full-grown now, muscular and lithe. I'm glad to see his strength, although no man's body can keep him safe in war. And unlike me, Piper belongs. He's cadet captain, senior rank in his year. He wants to fight for Brightland, like our father did. I imagine him in ten years, when it's his time to marry. He'll be standing on the deck of a transport ship, leading the returning men, proud to have served, free to take his wives.

Or there'll be a carved stone bearing his name, in a neat row with all the other carved stones, line after line of them, up by the turbine towers. Pa has a stone. *Gwyn Crane*, it reads, and the date he died. I can make out those letters well enough. But there is no body buried there. *Missing In Action*, it says. For years I thought that this meant he might still be alive, that the Aylish might have him in a far-flung prison camp. But Rye put me right. *Missing in Action* is what they write when you're blown to pieces and your comrades can't find the bits.

A quiet fell on our house when Pa died. We were so young when he went to war, but the hope of his return was like a light. Pa was huge and warm-hearted. His spirit was made of the sun on the sea. When we got the news, Ma's grief was like a tidal flood that slowly rose above us all. She tried to keep it from us but she was underwater, moving through a blue-gray world, hardly taking breaths. She made every effort to be strong, but I'd catch her staring at his empty chair, her shoulders hunched in disbelief. Ma still has her looks—her dark, flawless skin, her cheekbones—but her eyes are like windows to her loss.

Piper keeps digging. I want to remember him like this, the way his hair won't lie down flat, his fine brows frowning, his determination to do a good job.

A memory of him comes to me. I was on Bailey's Strand soon after Pa died, leaping the waves on a very windy day, jumping up, each one rearing like a monstrous head. I fought them, body and soul—but when I couldn't feel the ground, I realized I was out too far. The sea was taking me. The tide had turned and every wave that crashed pulled me even farther out. Piper heard my cries. He swam in and dragged me out, risking his life— then he railed at me for being such a fool. I held him fiercely. That feeling, that feeling of each wave sucking me farther from the shore, of struggling against a massive force, that's what I'm feeling now. This war is like a tide that can't be stopped.

Piper sees me.

"Is it true the cadets are shipping out?" I ask.

"We leave on Thalday. The transport comes at dawn." His words hang in an odd silence that no words of mine can fill. He carries on digging the neat row of spuds.

It's strange that my brother has no songlight. Then again, apart from our looks, we don't have much in common. Piper likes things to be in straight lines. Rules and routines make him feel safe, whereas I long to kick at them. He likes to make things with his hands, and I am all fingers and thumbs. Piper can take a piece of paper and turn it into a swan. His old bedroom is full of paper birds and delicate model gliders made out of card and whittled wood. I remember how he'd sit with Ma as she carved her animals, making his planes, studying a pamphlet his sergeant had given him on the principles of flight. He'd never let me play with them.

When my songlight came, in the height of my confusion I kept reaching out to Piper, trying my notes in a whisper, stroking him with thought-fronds, to see if he would answer. He never did. Piper has always been private. Sometimes I feel he's annoyed with me for being born. Before I came along he had our parents to himself. I pushed him off Ma's breast and I suppose our father always made a favorite of me. When Pa died, I never saw him cry. I saw him shaking with emotion, but his tears stayed closed inside. Overnight, he took on the role of the man in the family. Ma kept coaxing him to be a boy—to play, to run, to be carefree. But Piper carries things alone. He's looking at me now with his deep brown eyes as if I am another of his burdens.

"When I go," he says, "you'll have to take care of Ma."

"I will, you know I will. And Ma can take care of herself."

"Make sure you're on the list for First Wife."

"You know that isn't up to me."

"Yes it is. And all I hear is how sullen and disinclined you are."

"Who told you that?"

"Conrad Haines."

"That's his horrid sister Tinamou besmirching my name. She knows I can't stand her."

Piper approaches me. He's serious. "I want to be a pilot. You know how hard I've worked for it. It'll lower my standing if you're Second Wife."

I look at him askance. "So my marriage is for your benefit?"

"It's for Brightland's benefit and your own. How can you bear not being the best? Don't you feel Pa's eyes on you?"

I'm taken aback. For a moment I feel the pressure that Piper feels, his exhausting drive to be as good as Pa. It makes me sad.

"I'll try harder," I say.

"Promise," he insists.

I don't want to promise. My promise won't be true.

"Elsa, promise."

"I promise," I say.

Piper turns away, putting on his jacket, stamping soil from his boots. "We've got leave to eat with our families tomorrow. A farewell meal. I'll see you then."

As he reaches the gate, he gives me a fleeting smile. And then he's gone.

My mother's at her shrine when I go back in. Her goddess is Gala—Creation, the life force; Gala, the mother. All Gala's temples are closed since Great Brother Peregrine took power, as so many of her priests and priestesses were unhuman—but people are still permitted to worship her at home. Gala is the restorer, the great grower and healer, whose slow work on the scars and toxins of the Light People is bringing our Earth back to life. After thousands of years, the storms have receded, and the great deserts have begun to shrink. In my mother's mind, Gala is the force of life on Earth.

If only Ma had more children to console her. But Piper and I were as much as she could bear. She suffered through both pregnancies with grievous sickness. She survived my delivery—but her womb did not. That's why she wasn't pressured to marry again. Most young widows must remarry so they can keep on bearing sons. Ma helps new mothers through their labors now. But our tiny family is another thing that makes us an oddity in Northaven. No wonder Piper tries so hard to belong.

Ma wants to sit outside when we've eaten, catching the last rays of the sun. She's distracting herself by carving. Ma has got a way with making things.

She sees a piece of wood and can bring a creature out of it. I have a dolphin that sits on my windowsill, his tail in an ocean spray of gnarls. Piper has a tiny fawn. Tonight, she's carving a heron. It's bringing her no comfort.

"Eleven years old, our boys are taken to that barracks," she says, airing deep-felt grievances. "A day here, a night there—that's all we've seen of Piper since. What wisdom is it, to keep us separate from our sons? Men should grow in the company of women."

"Piper's the best cadet they have, Ma. Everyone says so."

"It doesn't make him any less likely to—" She checks herself. She breathes.

I try to find something that will comfort her.

"I know we lost Pa . . . but it doesn't mean we'll lose Piper. . . ." I'm just making it worse. "I heard that since Montsan Beach, our forces are making good progress. . . ."

Ma smiles wryly, as if I'm very young. "When Heron Mikane won the battle of Montsan Beach, they said we'd be in Reem by first snow. That was two years ago, and Reem still stands."

I cannot bear this suffocating war. Curse the Aylish for everything they've done. I have to see Rye. I have to be with him before this agitation kills me. Recklessly, I send my songlight like a beam and I search for his presence. Instantly, he senses me. He draws me toward him, aware of the risk. We will not hold this link for long. It's as if I'm outside his dormitory, staring in through a misty window. He's packing a kit bag with his comrades.

"Bailey's Strand," I say in songlight. "Come now."

Rye senses my urgency. He wants this. He'll be there. He doesn't have to say a word. We separate.

In our garden I stand, acting a calmness I don't feel. I look at Ma, carving her bird.

"Why don't I pick some samphire for tomorrow night?" I suggest. "You know how Piper loves it."

"It'll soon be dark."

"It tastes best when you pick it at dusk. It gets the evening dew." I kiss her cheek and go before she can protest.

I run across the headland, a small grassy promontory, with rocks and cliffs around three sides of it. Bailey's Strand lies beyond. I never spend long up here. It's where the town gibbets stand.

A horrible sight awaits me. Two adulterers from the south, caught a month ago, are still hanging there. I stop, my knees weak, looking at what's left of a man and a woman, now rotting in the wind. Sex traitors, running for the north. I turn away—but the image is burned on the inside of my eyes. And in their place, I see Rye and me. The choirmaidens say this place is haunted and I don't doubt it. Adulterers, degenerates, runaways, and thieves—their bodies are left where all the town can see. It's not only people with songlight who fear for their existence.

I pull myself together and make my way down the cliff path. Huge sand dunes rise up to meet the headland. It's where the best samphire grows. I look down and see Rye in the distance, close to the cliffs, keeping out of sight, making for the far end of the beach. He stops by the Cormorant Rock, skimming stones across the waves. I start gathering samphire, so I have a reason to be out in case anybody sees me. Then I send my songlight to meet him.

"Rye," I say.

He senses me. "Why aren't you here in person?" His disappointment makes him speak aloud, not using his songlight.

"I was going to come. But I saw the gallows."

I show him the picture: the couple hanging in rags, their faces picked by crows and kites. Rye takes it in.

"We should be struck down for what we've done to those people," he says. "What did they ever do to us? Nothing. Northaven's cursed, I swear it."

I know Rye's anger. It burns in him, rising to the surface far more frequently than mine. He's angry with his father, the eldermen, Emissary Wheeler, and every other prideful hypocrite who walks about like he owns the place. Usually, I can calm him, bringing his mind to one of our imagined havens. We've made an island in our reveries, where we live in a hut made out of driftwood and other such nonsense. But today, there's no mental escape.

"I know you're shipping out," I say. "Wheeler told us—and that's not all. He said the returning men will soon be home. My wedding day is coming."

Rye senses my foreboding. I feel the hot coals of his frustration glow.

"We're faced with a choice then, aren't we?"

I nod. This choice has been coming for a long time.

"Once you're forced to marry, how long will you be able to hide what you are?" he asks.

I shake my head. "I would have to make myself a ghost to endure it."

"Then we have to run away." Rye says it simply, making it sound easy.

"Like that couple on the gallows?"

"Come down here," he urges. "We should go now, without hesitation. Over the rocks while the tide's out—then up across the moors. We're way beyond the watchtowers. Nobody would see us."

Even as he says it, I realize that it's been down in my underthoughts all day. What other option do we have?

"We're risking our lives," I say.

"We're risking them more if we stay. . . ." He sighs deeply. "You'll get found out—and I don't want to die in a war I don't believe in."

This troubles me. No one hates the war more than I do, but there's no doubting that it must be fought.

"Of course you believe in the war." He shakes his head.

"Rye, the Aylish are our enemy. They'd murder us all if they could."

"How do we know? Great Brother Peregrine has lied about songlight. We know we're human, like everybody else. And we know those people on the gallows have done nothing wrong. What else have the Brethren lied about? What if they're lying about the war?"

"The Aylish killed my pa; they killed your brother. They're *monsters*."

A wave of pain floods Rye, as I knew it would. He feels it every time he hears his brother's name. Daniel Tern was twenty-one. His body came home in a sealed coffin—meaning the mess was too horrific for anyone to see. When the pain passes, Rye looks up at me.

"Who's your real enemy?" he asks. "The Aylish might be savage, but if the Brethren found out what we were, they'd take us to the Chrysalid House and cut the songlight out of our brains. That's monstrous enough for me. It's not the Aylish we must fight against. It's Peregrine; it's the Brethren."

I fall silent, taking this in. He's never voiced such mutiny before. Up on the headland where I'm searching for samphire, the ground seems to shift beneath my feet. I look far out to sea. I take in my breath. And I rejoin him on the beach.

"Rye, they'll chase us down and that's a fact."

"Come on," he begs. "We'll be well into the Wastes by dawn. We could head south for the shelter of the Greensward."

An ache fills my body, worse than I can bear. I want to be with him under the stars. I want to be free. I'm about to tell him so when I sense something. Perhaps I'm mistaken. It's the weird noise of the cormorants, the tumble of the waves.

"Were you followed?" I ask.

"No."

"Are you sure?"

"Yes." He gestures impatiently at the huge, empty beach. "Don't you think there must be others like us, who want things to be different? Not all runaways get hanged. I heard there's people with songlight, hiding in the Greensward. We could join them."

My heart is tearing in two.

"What about my mother? If I leave, she'll have no one."

"If she loves you, she'll want you to be free."

I see the passion in Rye's eyes. I want to kiss him again and again. I want to fall into the sand with him and find a different kind of harmony. But my seaworker's mind is ever-pragmatic.

"We'll have a better chance in my boat. If we leave now, we'll have nothing. We'll need food and money to survive. I'll get my earnings. And you can't be seen as a cadet. I'll bring some old clothes of Pa's."

"When?"

"The harbor barrier is already set. Nightfall tomorrow. I'll meet you here."

I feel his relief. We hold one another in a bond of silence.

"Nightfall, tomorrow," he whispers. And our pact is made.

At last, I slip away from him. Caressing him with songlight, I rise up with the gulls.

I will go with him.

I will fight with him.

I will lie with him and be his wife.

I will live with him.

Or die.

After she's gone, I stare out at the sea. My feet are in the sand but my heart is in our future. Joy, excitement, I don't care what it's called. We're leaving Northaven. Elsa Crane will come with me. Her radiance lingers in my every cell. Elsa. I skim a smooth stone over the foam and count eight before it sinks into the sea. That's a record even for me and I will take it as an omen of good fortune. Eight. We will leave this place behind and I will be better than my pa.

I think of him now, Pa, rank with stale whiskey, shabby bastard in his elderman's suit, holding court nightly in his tavern. I think of my ma, his Second Wife, her life of toil, raising us all, doing the dirty work. I think how Pa uses her, how he speaks to her. *Woman this, Woman that, Woman, fill my glass.* Ma must obey him, even when he's drunk. And when he's drunk, he's nasty. Once, when I was about seven, the ball that I was throwing fell into his beer. He looked at me and snarled: *Come here, you little turd* . . . and he belted me. My pa, Mozen Tern. I will not be like that. I'll try to make Elsa's life better every day.

The cormorants are settling on their rock as I turn toward the town. I have to sneak back into the dormitory. If I'm caught, my excuse is ready. I'll say I went up to my brother's grave on the clifftop, to pay Dan my last respects. They know I might be joining that poor fucker soon. That should do it—

And then everything changes.

A figure steps out in front of me, neat and slick in his cadet captain's uniform. I have been followed.

"Piper."

He looks pale, and then he starts to speak.

"I heard what you said. Who were you speaking to? You said Brother Peregrine was your enemy. The Brethren are your enemy." He points at me. "Unhuman!"

That accusation flays me like a whip. I've dreaded it for years. Now that it's finally come, it seems unreal.

"Unhuman," he repeats, his voice tight with the pain of betrayal. I look at Piper, making my plan. It's over. I must run, now, immediately. But my eyes are locked on his and before I can move my body into action, Piper throws himself on me. He's lightning quick, full of outrage. He's livid with my treachery; it's pouring off him like a heat. I resist the force of him, fighting him away. I feel the years of our now broken friendship grasping hold of me. We fall, crushing seashells beneath our weight. He writhes with me, down on the ground. We twist like scorpions, kicking up the sand. Piper's strong, but he's not built like me. He's athletic, whereas I am all muscle—and I'm fighting for my life. What do I do; do I knock him out? Do I kill him?

This lad was once my closest friend. We were boys together. We still sleep in the same bunk. I know the sound of his snoring; I know how hard he pushes himself. I see him striving every day to be something that none of us should be: a hero, a hero in this hollow war, fodder for the battlefield.

I get him on his back like an upturned scarab. "I don't want to hurt you," I tell him.

"You've always hurt me," he yells. "You pushed me away. Now I know why—Unhuman!"

I won't break this bastard's arm. He's Elsa's brother, my boyhood friend, and I love him.

"I tried to tell you when my songlight came," I say. "I wanted to tell you so many times, but—"

Piper shuts me up with a knife at my throat. I release my grip on him, the metal cold against my flesh. I should've broken his fucking arm.

"Who were you with?" he asks.

"Fuck's sake, Piper!"

"I saw you talking. I heard one half of your coward's plan. You're a deserter. Who were you with?"

His knife hand is shaking. This boy is no murderer. In Piper's true nature, he sits on his bunk making fucking paper birds. He spends every waking hour trying to fill the boots of the soldier that he wants to be—but at night he dreams of being himself. From my bed above his, I feel the ache of his dreams, like smoke wreathes surrounding him. I never pry but I can't help knowing. Poor bastard. Like every cadet, he longs for love—but Piper wants a kind of love he cannot ever have.

"It was a choirmaiden, wasn't it," he presses. "Who?"

"Put the knife down; I won't fight you."

"Give me her name!" he cries.

"Fuck you."

Some survival instinct propels me. I shove his knife out of the way and get him underneath me. I let my full weight slam down on him. It winds him. For a moment, I see Elsa in his face. His wide mouth, his deep-drawing irises.

"Yield and I'll release you," I tell him. "Just like when we were boys."

"Unhuman," he says with gritted teeth. "Traitor . . ." He's struggling to breathe.

"Yield and let me run. You'll never have to look at me again. Yield!"

"Unhuman!"

I'll crush this fucker's windpipe if he doesn't yield.

Piper yields. I release him. I stand and get my breath back, preparing to run. I might make it as far as the scars on the moors before he gets back to the barracks and has them set the hounds on me. But suddenly, I feel like I'm a boy again. Whenever Piper and I fought, we'd feel the pain of it afterward in hot tears, the shame of having grieved each other. I want to cry now and I can see that he does too.

"Piper," I say. "I'm sorry."

It breaks my heart that Piper can't be free. Sometimes, I think his prison's worse than mine.

"Curse your lying, unhuman soul," he says, and his voice cracks.

"I wish that things were different," I tell him simply. I wish I could have told you everything about me. I wish we'd talked openly, without fear. I wish I could have loved you the way that you love me."

Piper comes at me. For a flying second, I think that he'll embrace me. Then I see the rock he's clutching.

I hear the thud as it hits my skull—but it takes a few seconds to feel the pain. I look at Piper, shocked. As blood runs into my eye, I take a few steps away toward the cliffs—but my legs won't run. My knees give—and the ground rushes up to meet me.

I come round to a thumping pain in my head and a horrible ringing sound in my ears. My neck is cramped so bad that I can't lift it. My head is lolling to one side. I slowly straighten up, waiting for the blurred world to come into focus. My arms are pinned. No part of me can move. I am tied to a chair. The first thing I do is try to reach Elsa, to warn her, to tell her. But it's as if there's a thick blanket over my songlight—not just because of the blow to my head. I realize where I am. Underground, where songlight can't travel.

Our jailhouse has a room for this very purpose, a dungeon for suspected unhumans, an interrogation room. I see slippery stairs leading up to the light. It's morning. It's already tomorrow and Elsa will be preparing her boat, secreting money and supplies. How do I warn her?

As I blink, a shadow falls over me. It's Emissary Wheeler, the biggest fish in our little pond. This is very bad.

"Unhuman," he begins.

My body starts to shudder. *Don't let me cry. Gala, please don't let me cry.*

"Your cadet captain heard you communing with a choirmaiden. I want her name."

I twist with horror at what Piper has done. Piper Crane, you bootlicking, treacherous fool. You are risking your own sister.

"Give us your accomplice," orders Wheeler, "and it will go better for you at your trial."

I exhale, coming to terms with what I must endure. I'm fucked. That's for certain. Gala, what a waste, what a fucking stupid waste. . . . But they can cut my balls off before I give them Elsa.

"You face the destruction of your mind in the Chrysalid House," explains Wheeler, with mock patience. "The procedure isn't subtle. Your skull will be drilled, here and here." He puts a finger on each of my temples. "If you tell me everything, I'll send a favorable report and the judges might accept you as a Siren. You'll remain sentient, how about that? But if you hold back, you'll most certainly be made a chrysalid."

I say nothing, staring at the floor. Wheeler grabs my hair and lifts my face.

"The pain will start very soon," he warns. "And like it or not, I will get that name. Do you understand?"

Elsa. I must warn Elsa.

Everything turns white with the strength of Wheeler's blow.

Perhaps I pass out because the next thing I'm aware of is someone putting a cool cloth on my pounding head. I hear a voice, whispering.

"Give him a name. Give Wheeler a name and you could save yourself."

Piper Fucking Crane.

"Rye, cooperate with them. They might make you a Siren."

That backstabbing bastard is trying to give me water, ministering to me like a nurse.

"One day," I tell him, "you'll know what you have done."

"Who were you with?" he presses. "I'm trying to make things easier for you. Wheeler needs a name."

"Fuck you, Piper."

"I want to help you. Was it Gailee Roberts? Her pa was unhuman."

My contempt flies out.

"You're a pitiful *rat*."

Piper steps back, as if I've slapped him.

My shuddering body is turning hot with outrage. I want this bullshit over. I yell for Wheeler. He appears by my chair with Ely Greening.

"I'm ready to talk. I'll tell you everything."

I see the excitement in their eyes. Wheeler nods his thanks to Piper.

"Her name?"

Piper stands in my periphery. I'm going to fuck the little bastard up.

"Not *her* name," I say. " His."

Piper quails and I realize immediately that I can't go through with it. No matter what he's done to me, I can't knife him so meanly. He's in enough torment as it is.

"His?" questions Wheeler, his lip curled in disgust.

"I've been communing with an Aylishman," I say.

"What Aylishman?" Wheeler scowls, skeptical.

"I am in love with him," I say. I can feel the emotion in Piper build but I don't even glance at him. My lie runs on, growing, taking color.

"He wouldn't give me his real name. His ship lies off the coast."

"Where?" yells Greening in excitement. "Where?"

"I sensed his songlight on the breeze and I called him to Northaven. He said I must call him Cormorant. He's in love with me too."

"You expect us to believe that?" sneers Wheeler.

I grin, baring my teeth. It's better to go down fighting. At least I won't be fucking crying.

"My strong, beautiful Aylish lover said he'd bring his ship to take me to Ayland. He said he'd set this town on fire."

Wheeler slams me with a punch. I taste the blood.

"You're an aberration in every way," he yells.

"And yet I exist!" I spit my blood. It spatters on his boots.

Wheeler beats me till I'm purple. He beats me till I'm beyond pain. He beats me till I rise up off the chair and look at him from high above. I see the sweat on the back of his neck. I see Greening salivating. Piper's standing at the filthy sink, rigid, knowing he can't turn away. Wheeler doesn't stop until his knuckles are red raw.

"Cuff his mind," he orders. And arms come to pull me from the chair.

Elsa. I must reach Elsa. They drag me up the slippery steps. As soon as the daylight hits my eyes, I send my songlight up. My girl is on her boat. I see her graceful arms fling out a fishing rod. Her hair blows around her in the wind. She's as dazzling as the sunlit sea.

"Elsa!"

Immediately, my pain smites her. I'm not strong enough to hold it back. She physically crumples with the shock.

"Rye!"

She has to know what's being done to me. She has to prepare herself. I let her see how Wheeler pummeled me. I feel distress pouring out of her, her songlight more radiant than I have ever seen, the whole rainbow of her spirit stricken.

"Rye!"

On the parade ground, in front of all my peers, my tormentors force me to my knees. Elsa cleaves to me in her light. I feel her knees buckle. She says "No," over and over.

"Don't let them get you," I tell her in songlight. "Don't let them see you. Please!"

Wheeler is telling my comrades what I am, while Elsa clings to me.

"There's an unhuman in your midst," he declares. "He has confessed his powers and he is collaborating with the Aylish to destroy us all." Wheeler holds a lead band in his hand, and while he speaks, he's forcing it onto my skull. I curse him seven shades of blue and Elsa feels what's happening to me.

"No, no, no!"

Her love is the most precious thing in this whole sorry universe.

"Save yourself," I beg her. "Promise me. Save yourself."

Wheeler tightens the band around my skull. I feel it smothering my songlight.

"I love you. I love you." Her words beat through me. My heart is going to shatter.

Wheeler screws tighter and he locks the lead band. My songlight is a suffocating whirlwind, trying to tell her my love, bursting out of my skull. Dear Gala, my head will split and my eyeballs will fall out. Elsa's cries are muffled. I can't hear her anymore. Her light is fading.

"Rye . . ."

"Save yourself!" I beg—but my songlight deadens into sickening quiet and my words sink back into a hueless fog. She's gone.

I'm leaning on the side of the boat, horror trembling through me. Rye. Our harmony's been broken and he's gone. Like a machine, I pull in the nets. I reel in the lines. I turn the turbine back toward Northaven.

That didn't happen. It didn't happen. It was a nightmare and I'm still asleep. I will wake and find myself stretching in my bed. Rye will be free. I'll meet him on the strand and I'll say, "Let's run, let's go without delay."

Sickness seizes me. I turn and vomit into the sea.

I let my body steer the boat. My mind is too numb.

Save yourself, he said. *Save yourself.*

I have a stash of food under the seats. I took Pa's shirt and jacket that Ma keeps wrapped in paper in the bottom of a drawer. I took my little roll of money. I left when it was barely bright, like it was an ordinary day. It hurt me sore to part from Ma without a single word. But if she knew, she'd be in danger too. Knowingly harboring an unhuman is a grave offense.

Save yourself.

A desperation grows in me, a wild hope that somehow I'm mistaken, that what I saw was a mirage, like the ships and islands that I sometimes see, floating in the hot sea haze. But as the turbine drives me in toward the town, I sense an atmosphere, a buzzing like a host of wasps. A crowd is forming.

Ma is on the quayside. Her expression tells me all I need to know. She grabs my rope and pulls me in, her eyes dull with consternation.

"There's a Shaming," she says. "We've all been summoned."

When there's a Shaming, the whole town must go.

"Elsa, are you ill?"

Save yourself.

"My monthlies have come early," I tell her. She looks at me and nods, unsure if this is true. Mrs. Sweeney comes hurrying past.

"Leave your catch where it is," she says, pained. "They've found an unhuman among our cadets."

Ma takes my arm and helps me out. We pass a group of seaworkers' wives, washing fish guts off their hands.

"We've raised a snake among our lambs . . . ," one of them tells us, as she hurries off to the town square.

I falter, lightheaded.

"I'm sure that we could watch from here, if you're unwell?" suggests Ma.

"No," I say.

I have to see this. Even if it kills me. I won't let Rye go through this all alone. Besides, you're only allowed to miss a Shaming if you're dying or in labor. I force myself to approach. There's a figure tied to the shaming post. He looks so small.

"It's Rye Tern," says Ma, a flatness in her voice.

Rye is trying to stand tall but he can't lift his head. It keeps falling forward, the lead band cruelly tight around his skull. His songlight is encased. It can't penetrate the lead. His face is lurid with welts and bruising. His shirt is stained with blood.

A pang lacerates me. If I'd gone with him last night, without hesitation, we'd be running through the hinterland. Rye forces his head up, peering at the crowd. His family is there. His mothers are both weeping but his pa stands like a rod. It's obvious he's drunk and scared.

When Rye's eyes finally find mine, all I see in them is love. I stop breathing, held in a moment of stillness, wanting time to stop.

Let time end now.

But it flows on. I realize Wheeler is speaking.

"The evidence is irrefutable. He was witnessed communing with another unhuman. When we interrogated him, he confessed he was luring the Aylish to our shores. . . ." There are shocked cries from some of the townspeople.

Rye's eyes are still locked on mine. I don't need songlight to know that he told this lie to protect me. I am humbled by his courage. Then he breaks his eyes away, looking at the sky, as if his very gaze might endanger me.

Save yourself.

"He's a traitor," continues Wheeler, his whip curled at his side. "From this moment, he is no longer Rye Tern. His name is stripped from him and with it, his humanity. He's revealed for what he is: a mind-twisting unhuman. His boyish face might tempt you to pity him, but this miscreation cares nothing for you, your sons, or his country. He would betray us all to Ayland."

"Unhuman," screams Ely Greening, unable to restrain himself. "We cast you out!"

This gives some of the townspeople the excuse they want.

"Unhuman!"

"Treacherous bastard!"

"Mind-twisting devil!"

The yells come thick and fast. But among the two thousand souls of Northaven, many remain silent. Not everyone likes watching the destruction of a boy. I see Piper standing with the senior cadets, his shoulders taut, his face a mask of duty.

Wheeler steps forward and puts a gauze over Rye's face. This is symbolic of our rejection. His human features are lost to us and Rye is now a thing.

"This unhuman will go to the Chrysalid House. Judgment will be passed. Then its skull will be pierced, its powers cleft. It will neither speak nor mind-twist us again. This creature must never breed. In the Chrysalid House it will be reborn, to serve Brightland with its labor."

I am gripping Ma tightly.

"Hide what you feel," she hisses. "Hide it."

We don't see many chrysalids in Northaven. It strikes me what a dreadful word that is. Chrysalids labor at the hardest jobs, the ones that humans never want: sewers, slaughterhouses. They're used to clear toxins and they're sent into minefields. Once, there was a band of them who came here with their masters to dig metal from the moors, buried since the Light People time. They dug up huge rusted plates of ancient industry and long metal bars, which they dragged down onto salvage ships. The men had gauze over their faces and when one of them drowned in a corrosive pool, his masters left him where he lay.

They are men and women. I will never call them chrysalids again.

Wheeler walks into the crowd, watching us all like hawks.

"A mind-twister rarely works alone. Who else would betray their neighbors to the Aylish enemy?"

I shrink away into myself.

"We will find you. You'll reveal yourself. And we will purge you from the human race."

Wheeler turns to Rye's father. "Mozen Tern, this is your son. What do you say to him now?"

Everyone looks to see what Mozen does. He walks forward, attempting dignity. He's memorized the words that he must speak.

"In the name of the Brethren, I cast you out. I curse the womb and the egg that made you. Like a cuckoo, you grew in our nest. Your name will never be heard again." Mozen's hands tremble and shake. He picks up a handful of dirt.

"Unhuman," he says.

He throws the dirt like he's supposed to. Rye stares at his father, unflinching.

Rye's mothers must follow, then his little brothers and sisters. Each must take a handful of dirt and throw it, saying the word "unhuman." Wheeler stands by with his hand resting casually on his whip. Those who can't do it, like Mozen's Second Wife, are helped by the others. I see how broken up she is. And this hurts Rye more than anything. His shoulders sag.

Please don't cry. Please don't cry. You are so brave. I love you.

The crowd lines up. Some can't wait to throw their dirt, but others just want this ordeal to end. Mr. Malting, our baker, looks furious. Sergeant

Redshank looks full of pain. For every vicious pelting that Rye gets, there's someone who'll throw short or to one side. But no one speaks up, no one says Rye's just a boy, no one yells for this to stop. My mind is screaming the injustice of it all. But I too remain silent. What a town of cowards we are. When there's a Shaming, we're told we must be as one in our rejection, in our condemnation—and we all go along with it.

"Unhuman."

"Unhuman."

Piper leads the cadets. He throws his handful of dirt with just the right amount of force, not too hard, not too soft, with accurate precision. No feelings show, as if my brother's hollowed out inside.

Rye is sinking to his knees now, slumped at the foot of the shaming post, covered in dirt, hunched in the mud. Rye has always been braver than me. He hated having to hide what he was. Ma and me are moving up the line. I pass the elders, forcing my features to stay calm. I let out a silent cry. But Rye can't hear my awful, discordant soul-song of despair. His gaze is on me again. I can feel it through the gauze. I want to help him. I want to free him. Tears of love are pouring from my eyes.

Save yourself.

I am a coward. I scoop up a handful of dirt.

"Unhuman," I murmur.

I throw it.

And turning my back, I walk away.

I keep walking. I'm going to burst into a run and sprint until I fall down in a heap—but I feel Ma put her arm through mine. I must walk. To run would be to reveal too much. She walks me in the direction of the harbor. I feel her willing me to keep my feelings checked. Has she guessed? Does she know that I'm in love with Rye?

She knows.

Ahead, I see the choirmaidens gathering. Their talk is all about Rye Tern. Who would have suspected him? How horrible to have one in the midst of all their brothers, a vile unhuman, communing with the Aylish. Gailee is with her little sisters, comforting them. I know they must be thinking of their pa. Ma calls her aside.

"Gailee, my love, would you tell Hoopoe I need Elsa at the harbor? She won't be at marriage training. We got a big catch in today and it all needs sorting."

Gailee nods, looking at me in concern.

Ma gets me in the boat and we set to work on the fish I caught—not a big catch at all. Mrs. Sweeney is talking further up the quay with some of the sea-wives. Sad business, sad for his family, terrible how it happens. Was he really communing with the enemy?

"You never know with a mind-twister," says one of the wives. "They can't be trusted. Best to catch them young, before they do any real damage. . . ."

Behind us, the Shaming is over. Rye is picked up off the shaming post. I feel my shoulders hunch into a sob. Ma grips my hand.

"I want you to weigh the fish. Weigh each one and count them. When you finish, do it again."

One. Two. Three. Four. The dead fish accuse me with their lidless eyes. *Coward. Coward.*

"Now there's a sorry sight," Mrs. Sweeney says. "They're taking him back to the barracks."

"They should hang him on the gallows," says the sea-wife.

"He'll be on that ship to Meadeville with the new recruits. There's a holding camp for unhumans there," Mrs. Sweeney informs her. "Then they'll take him upriver to the Chrysalid House."

"Best place for him," says another sea-wife.

I look up—and wish that I hadn't. The cadets are dragging Rye like a rag doll. Wheeler and Greening follow behind, satisfied their job has been done. Ma stands with me. A silence falls. Everyone in the harbor looks on. Some look defiant, righteous; others are shaking their heads as Rye's broken body is taken inside.

"Look, my love," says Ma. "I think you've missed these mackerel here. Will you weigh them for me?"

I weigh them for the third time. One. Two. Three. Four.

As the sun begins to set, Ma releases me. I think she senses my need to be alone.

"I'll take this lobster up for Piper," she informs me. "I want to give him something special for his parting meal."

I had forgotten all about it. I nod noiselessly.

"Why don't you take a walk along the strand?"

She's telling me I must recover myself. I have to act normal in front of my brother. I have to send him off in the way that he deserves. I nod again and go. I have still not said a single word.

How was Rye caught? What gave him away? Did another cadet betray him? Maybe Piper will know.

I pass some of the elders. They pontificate to one another, commending themselves, as if what they've done is law-keeping, not torture. I want to vomit on their feet.

The sobs don't come until I'm halfway down the strand. I smother them as best I can, sending my songlight to the Cormorant Rock. I let my songlight cry out my grief, my rage, my sorrow. As my flesh-body stands in stillness, facing the sea, my songlight body is unconstrained. In songlight, I roar with white, inchoate pain. If someone passes, they'll only see a girl, standing at the water's edge, staring numbly at the waves. But the cormorants must sense my unloosed songlight, for they take off from their rock, scattering, wheeling up, then diving down into the sea.

How I hate this town. I hate these mean people with their tight lips and empty smiles. I hate Wheeler and Greening. I hate the Brethren in Brightlinghelm. I hate that metal statue of Great Brother Peregrine. Worst of all, I hate myself. I lash myself for missing my moment in time, for being too gutless to slip away with Rye. We should have gone last night, as soon as we had the idea. I held us back. This is my fault.

At last, I am exhausted. I could walk the cliffs like a ghost, until my body pines and dies. I turn, wiping my eyes.

A girl is staring at me. I start with shock and I breathe my songlight back into my body. But this girl is unhuman. It's only her songlight that I see.

She walks toward me. She's small, maybe younger than I am. But her eyes look old. A neat dress, bony knees, spectacles. Her walk is ungainly. Fear begins to beat my heart.

"I'm sorry," she says. "For your pain."

I back away.

"I felt your cries from far away."

She's not from Northaven. Her accent is strange, something like Wheeler's. She gestures behind her, down the coast toward the south.

"I'm from—"

"Get away" is all I say. And then I start to run.

Duty is hard. There are losses. They must be borne. This is a soldier's life. A soldier must keep going. He must not show he's affected. Bear it.

Sky looks very blue today. Blue in a whole different way. Can't take my eyes off how blue it looks. They are carrying the unhuman past. Look at the shape of the barracks as it meets the sky. Never quite noticed the shape.

Bundle of rags. Filthy. Dragging him.

Thal, god of war and invention, Thal have mercy on his unhuman soul.

Wheeler orders him to be put under a hose. Wash him clean. See him, unhuman, writhing like a worm. Sky is such a cobalt weight of blue. Blue, pressing on our town.

Thal, guide my hand so I may serve.

I notice Sergeant Redshank at my side. This man is my rock. Ever since Pa died, he has been there. Hand on my shoulder.

"The junior cadets are ready for your speech, my lad."

A cobalt weight falls into my belly. I had forgotten.

"Shall I stand them down?" asks Redshank. His quiet, gruff voice, his graying eyebrows, like an owl. "Given the unexpected events—"

"No," I say. "I'm ready."

Make myself useful. Sky blurring. Weight of blue, turning liquid. That must be stopped. This blurring of the sky, this liquid in my eyes. Push it back from whence it came. Walk with Redshank. He will lead the way. Junior cadets, standing to attention at the sight of me, giving me their full respect. See their eyes. Shock. They are afraid. Unhuman, writhing like a worm. Cleansed. We are all cleansed.

Breathe. Be their example. Show them duty. Make your voice work. Throat tight. Stop this fucking nonsense, Piper Crane. These boys need you. The Shaming has shocked them and they must be bolstered. Speech, prepared and learned days ago. Need to pull it from my brain. The juniors loved Rye. Don't use his name. The unhuman had that easy strength, that open grin, hint of mischief round his eyes. Got me into trouble, time and time again. Had a look that said, "Don't worry about those orders. We can break them, no one's going to mind. . . ."

Like being hit with a tidal wave, sucked, submerged into a lethal force of water, realizing that all along, all along, the charming, grinning Rye was lying to us all. Fuck's sake, don't use his name. Think of him as dead. Loss. Shock. Get used to it—because what you did was right. He was treacherous.

Sergeant Redshank clears his throat. These boys await. Grasp the nettle, Piper Crane.

"The senior cadet you knew as Rye Tern . . . He was an illusion," I say. I swallow down a lump. "The thing that sits in Rye Tern's body. It is ugly. And deadly. What we did to that unhuman—it is right. When an unhuman is found, mind-twisting among us, Our Great Brother tells us that we must disempower it. The creature that we knew as Rye can no longer reach his evil Aylish masters."

Even as I say this, I know it's an untruth. I know that Rye was talking to a girl. He was talking to a choirmaiden, one of our own. But now that the story has been publicly told, it seems wrong to contradict it.

"The unhuman must be cast out," I say. "You know this. And it's hard. But if we continue to be vigilant, this corrupting mutation will soon be bred out of our race."

Their faces. Thirteen, fourteen years old. Some eager in agreement, others still showing their shock and dismay.

Why did Wheeler have to beat him so bad?

Don't think that.

He'd already confessed.

Don't think.

How could I have stopped it?

Quash these fucking thoughts and carry on.

". . . For, as our Great Brother tells us, the unhuman has weakened us for long enough."

Rye.

Find the words. Short trousers, wooden rifles at their sides, our insignia on their chests. Inspire these junior cadets. Rouse them, that's what Heron Mikane would do. That's what my father would have done.

"We seniors are leaving for the front. We have our battle orders and we're proud to go. But if the Aylish attack, Northaven now relies on you. You must step up," I continue, finding my flow. "You must stand with our elders as our brave defense. You'll give those wooden rifles to the smaller boys and you will learn to use real guns. You're becoming men—true, human, Brightling men—and there is nothing finer in this world. Are you ready to fight for Northaven?"

"Yes, Captain Crane," they cry.

"Will you fight to the death to protect our town? Your mothers and your sisters now depend on you."

"Yes, Captain!"

They are turning their thoughts from the Shaming. They are thinking of the future. So must I. I'm going to war and this is what it's like. I will lose better men than Rye.

"Sergeant Redshank will instruct you—and he's the best there is. He taught Heron Mikane his battle craft and he taught my father. You're blessed by Thal, god of war and invention, to have such a fine instructor."

"Follow Piper Crane's example, lads," says Redshank gruffly.

I lead a cheer: "Victory to Brightland!"

The junior cadets repeat it, over and over, until Redshank sends them all away.

When Pa died, Sergeant Redshank, he was there—not in any girlish way with hugs and handkerchiefs. He never said a word about Pa once he'd given Ma condolences. But he taught me to be strong. Action would heal, he said. Endeavor. He gave me a program of exercise. He kept me busy from morn till night. He knew that I loved airships and gliders and he brought me news sheets from Brightlinghelm, with pictures of all the advancements in aerial flight. He brought me a pamphlet on how the wings were made.

He too is a victim of the unhuman's charm. Perhaps he also feels this cobalt in his guts—I will ask. But when I turn to follow him, Emissary Wheeler stands in front of me. He must have listened to my speech. I salute him but he brushes my formality away.

"I hear that the unhuman was your friend?" he asks.

"From childhood, Emissary."

"Did you know he was a double aberration?"

I am puzzled by the expression. "No."

Wheeler picks up my perplexity. "In Great Brother Peregrine's *Definition of a Human Male*, our desire must be for women only."

I feel as if I'm falling.

"Yes, indeed," I say. "How else are we to repopulate the Earth?"

"The unhuman admitted that he loved another man. He was a traitor and a deviant."

"Yes," I say. I am clinging to the sides of the hollowness inside. "The lads and I, we can't wait to get into a Pink House. We're hoping it's the first thing laid on for us, when we arrive in Meadeville. We know we're there for training but there's a rumor that we get Third Wives. . . ." I look up.

Wheeler smiles indulgently. "It's the right of each new soldier to visit a Pink House and learn to sow his seed."

"It's pretty much all we talk about, sir."

"I'm glad to hear it. That is healthy, Crane."

He moves a little closer. Cologne. He wears a lot of cologne. I smell damp wood and tangerines. Don't look at his raw fists.

"Tell me, did the unhuman, even in boyhood, debauch himself with another cadet?"

"Not to my knowledge, sir."

"If he did, you must give that cadet up."

My fingers are slipping on the hollowness inside. "I never saw anything of that kind," I say.

Wheeler looks into my eyes. I cling on tighter. Of course I am hollow. Of course I am empty. I am a vessel, put on Earth to serve Thal. Thal and my country. Aberration. I am not an aberration.

Wheeler seems satisfied. He walks, gesturing for me to follow. The blue is sinking into heavy dusk.

"Sergeant Redshank tells me you've applied to be an airman—a role for the elite. What makes you think you're worthy?"

I don't even need to think before I reply.

"I've devoted myself to the study of flight. I wish I could show you my childhood bedroom, sir. It's all birds and planes hanging from the ceiling—models that I made. I've studied the design of all the latest gliders. I watch the kestrels on the moor, how they swoop and kill. I see how the seabirds rise on currents of the air. I know I could fly. I dream of it. And I'd harry the Aylish from the sky."

Wheeler looks at me some more, as if he wants something that I have.

"Today must have been hard for you. You showed your loyalty at every turn."

He puts a pin in my shirtfront. On it is a pair of wings.

"This is your commission. Congratulations, Airman Crane."

I don't stop running till I'm almost home. I feel followed all the way.

Who was that girl? Is she still watching me somehow? Her bright songlight . . . where did it come from?

I get a grip on myself. I wash my face at the pump, under the mural of Sister Swan. I look up at her, the white and perfect Flower of Brightland. She offers me no comfort. I settle my nerves and open our door.

I see Piper, sitting with Ma at the table. They've both eaten.

"Sorry," I say. "I walked farther than I realized."

"Don't you worry," says Ma. She stands and gets a plate of food from the stove while I pour myself a long drink of water. I stand and glug it, putting off the moment when I must look my brother in the face. Ma puts the food down in front of me. She's gone to great efforts. The lobster meat, the samphire—it all looks delicious. But my belly's full of rocks. I start to cut the white meat, wondering how I'll swallow it.

"How was marriage training?" asks Piper.

"I didn't go."

"That's my fault," says Ma quickly. "I kept Elsa with me. The catch was very big today."

Piper disapproves. "It's important that she goes, Ma."

"Like I say, it's my fault."

My knife grates upon the plate. I hate it when Piper talks to Ma as if she's a child. Silence pools around us.

"What's that?" I ask, noticing a pair of red enamel wings.

"My commission," says Piper, with a flush of pride. "I've been chosen for an airman."

"It's an honor." Ma smiles. "Reserved for the best."

"That's good," I manage to say. "No one's worked harder."

He swallows, almost bashful.

In a flash, I see Piper, falling from the sky, wings twisting round him, broken in a plume of fire. Why is every thought dragging me into a dreadful pit?

It's not Piper; it is me. I am burning. I am falling from the sky.

"You two sit and talk awhile," says Ma, keeping her voice lighthearted. She touches Piper's shoulder. "I'll go and pack some of your things."

She goes into the bedroom. The Shaming sits between us, as if Rye's broken body is at the table too.

"He was your best friend," I say.

"Yes. But losses must be borne." Piper drinks, as if his throat is dry. "I'm glad that he was caught."

I take in my breath. I let it out slowly. I must not be angry at his blind and stupid ignorance. He has no songlight. Why shouldn't he believe what the Brethren say? We're told from infancy that songlight is an evil.

"How was he caught?" I ask. "Who betrayed him?"

This surprises Piper. "Rye betrayed himself," he says.

"But how was he found out? Who turned him in?"

"Does it matter?"

"Of course it matters."

"Whoever it was," says Piper, "you should shake his hand."

"Why would I do that?"

"Because he did the right thing."

Piper doesn't meet my eye and horror creeps up me like a licking flame.

"The unhuman was seen on the beach," he continues. "He was communing, talking to some invisible presence, full of illicit passion. He uttered treasonable words, have no doubt."

The flame leaps out of me. "It was you."

He looks at me, superior, defiant. "What if it was?"

I breathe my disbelief. "You loved him, Piper, from when you were a boy. . . ."

Piper swallows again. "That unhuman withdrew from me years ago. I always thought it was something I'd done that made me lose his friendship.

Now it seems obvious. He had a secret to hide. If you doubt his treachery, he said that his war was with the Brethren. I had to report him. I did what was right."

This town is a sinkhole and my brother is a rat.

"Rye was always your friend," I cry. "He loved you and he was loyal."

"How would you know?"

I am burning, falling, burning. I want Piper to know what he has done.

"Because I was there."

Piper recoils from me, standing. His breathing has risen. And now my fate is in his hands. I should be afraid, I know I should. But I'm a plummeting white flame.

"Rye asked me to run," I tell him. "We should have gone, over the rocks, over the moors. I told him to wait. And it cost him everything." My voice cracks.

I feel the shock running through Piper. We stand, staring at one another. He is my mirror image in so many ways: our slim height, our hair, our dark skin and eyes. But our characters have always been like chalk and cheese. Now we are different in another way. He is a human. And in his eyes, I am not.

He speaks in a low tone. "How didn't I see it?" he asks.

"I always hoped you would. . . ."

"If it wasn't for our mother, I would turn you in."

That shakes me to the core. There's nothing more to say.

We hold each other's gaze till Ma comes back. She can sense the broken atmosphere, the rift.

"I've made an apple cake," she says. "Let's eat a bit together."

Piper shakes his head. "I'm going to the barracks. There's drinking to be done."

Suddenly I remember he's being sent to war. Ma pulls him into a hug and doesn't let him go. Piper buries his head in her widow's veil and I see him shaking with a single, dreadful sob. He swallows again, as if his throat is choked.

Whatever he's done, he's still my brother and he's leaving on the transport ship at dawn. That plane, falling through the air . . . I pray to Gala that it won't be him.

"You'll be in my thoughts," says Ma. "Every minute of the day . . ."

Piper lets her go. He gathers his things.

"May Gala keep you safe," I say.

He gives me one final look. "My god is Thal. You know that."

When he's gone, Ma stoops, leaning on the table, holding herself up.

"I hate this war," she says.

I take her in my arms.

I have to keep hope. I mustn't despair. Rye is shackled, somewhere in the barracks, his body and mind marred by his ordeal. What can I do? There has to be some way I can help him. I pace my room long into the night, uselessly watching the moon rise and fall. There's a nightingale singing nearby, loud and passionate. Maybe Rye can hear it. . . . Maybe that bird, with its song of love and yearning, will help him keep his hope alive.

I stop pacing. I have to save him. If it was the other way round, if I was caught, he would do anything—anything—to free me. I will act. I have to stop this dreadful thing from happening. I'll mend the ill that Piper's done. I'm dressing in the moonlight. I picture myself cutting wire, stealing keys, opening locked doors.

I climb out of my window, running down into the town, avoiding pools of pale turbine light where some sleepless worrier might see me from a window. As I approach the barracks, something makes me pause. Piper knows what I am. . . . He might be expecting this. I would get caught for sure. Perhaps his disgust is so great that he's already spilled the truth and *they* are coming to get *me*. But all is quiet. The barracks looks deserted. That nightingale is closer now, splitting the darkness with its desperate song.

I climb on a water barrel and, using a drainpipe, I pull myself onto the roof of the junior cadet house. I could drop from here into the parade ground. My eyes scan each door, wondering where it leads.

I send my songlight up like a bright beam. Maybe, just maybe, Rye will sense me through the lead. I must keep hope. I won't let them destroy his mind.

"Rye," I cry in songlight. "Rye."

The nightingale falls silent. Weirdly silent. Suddenly, I get the feeling that I'm not alone. And I hear a small voice.

"I'm very sorry for your loss."

I turn, startled. She's back, standing on the apex of the roof, her songlight bright and vivid. The girl.

She's in a nightgown hand-embroidered with trailing flowers. Her hair is tied in two tight plaits. Who is she?

"What do you want?" I ask. I'm ready to run.

"I heard your cries on the beach," she replies in brightening songlight. "I could feel what you were feeling. I'm so sorry about your Rye."

Where is this girl? What does she want? Her spectacles reflect a small, plain bedroom.

"How long have you been watching me?" I ask suspiciously.

"I heard your cry. It made me so sad." Her voice is tentative but her presence gains in radiance. "Please don't run away."

"I'm not going to run," I tell her mistrustfully. "I'd fall off the roof, wouldn't I."

The girl looks around, seeing the barracks, seeing the smudge of gray dawn on the horizon. I put out a thought-frond, trying to get the feeling of her songlight. I sense no harm from her. She's even more nervous than I am. Somehow, I feel that she's sincere.

But I'm losing time. I cannot let this girl distract me. I crawl forward on my belly, peering down into the parade ground. Would it injure me to jump?

"What will you do?" she asks, coming closer.

"Rye was taken as unhuman," I tell her. "They've put a lead band around his skull."

"Yes," she says. "They do that. So he can't use his songlight."

"Is that what you call it too, songlight?"

She nods. The nightingale starts singing again.

"You can't rescue him," she warns. "Please don't try. You're one girl against the tide. They'd catch you straightaway. And they'll destroy you too."

Something in me falters. I mustn't let her shake me. I will jump. I will free my Rye—and if they come at me, I'll throw myself on their bayonets. I ready myself—

And I feel myself bathed in her songlight. She is holding me. It's such a curious sensation. It feels . . . as if I know her. It feels as if I'm loved.

"Please don't let them take you. Your friend would want you to survive." *Save yourself.*

I put my head down on my hands and let the grief run through me. That nightingale, it's singing how I feel. Then I feel a harmony of pain, coming from the girl, straight from her heart, and instinctively I know that she's lost someone too. We hold this chord of songlight. And when I can move again, I look at her more closely. Lonely, vulnerable, but a bright power in her small frame. The nightingale's song seems to pierce right through her. Is she a vision, sent by the Aylish to confound me? Is she a Siren, sent by Wheeler to expose me?

"No," she says, as if she has read me. "I'm just ordinary. I'm nothing special, nothing at all."

There is nothing ordinary about this whole encounter.

"Where are you?" I ask.

"In my room, in Brightlinghelm."

I'm instantly full of doubt.

"That's not possible. Brightlinghelm's two hundred miles from here. Rye found it hard enough to reach me when I was out at sea. . . ."

The girl nods. "Not everybody's songlight is the same. Yours is very strong. I heard you. And I think I have strong songlight too. It's safer that you're far away. I'd never connect with anyone close. I know how dangerous it is."

56

We're sitting now, opposite each other. I glance down at her feet. She's wearing dainty crocheted slippers. It looks like she made them herself. Perhaps crochet is her special skill. The relentless nightingale sings on.

"There have always been people like us," she says. "As far back as time goes. The Light People had a word for us. They called us telepaths."

"Telepaths? How do you know?"

"My friend Cassandra told me."

Her songlight changes when she speaks the name. I know that this is who she lost.

Suddenly she tenses.

"Hide yourself!"

I fall on my belly. There are doors opening. A floodlight comes on, shining over the parade ground. I peer down from the parapet and see the senior cadets, carrying their kit bags, rifles on their shoulders, led by my brother, marching to the harbor. Their backs are stiff, their sleep-torn eyes ahead. A barred door opens. A figure is dragged out by two guards. Rye. He can walk—just. But he's slow, bent like an old man.

"Do people ever escape?" I ask.

"I hope so," the girl replies.

She watches with me, as the troops march down the quayside and line up to board the transport ship. As the last of them gets on board, Rye reaches the quay. The guards are getting fed up with his slow, painful steps. They pick him up and drag him. His comrades are standing on the deck in formation. The guards take Rye and throw him in the hold. The girl was right. If I had leaped down into that parade ground, they'd be tying me to the shaming post by now.

I make a pledge.

"I will not rest until I'm with him," I say.

The girl holds me tighter, feeling my pain. We watch until the boat leaves the harbor and disappears into the fog. Then I turn and look at her. Gala, there's such sadness in her eyes.

"What's your name?" I ask her.

She twists nervously. "We shouldn't say our real names. Where I'm from, in Brightlinghelm, there are Sirens everywhere."

"Why haven't you been caught?"

She goes quiet. "Cassandra protected me. She taught me the best ways to keep safe. She told me to send my songlight further and further. It took a long time. I can go right up into the firmament now."

"Could I?"

"Maybe. If you try."

She is a small, extraordinary force. I didn't know it was possible for songlight to be so strong.

"You hear that bird?" I say to her. "A little bird with a big song. I'll call you Nightingale."

Nightingale seems to like this. She comes a little closer, looking at me, choosing me a name.

"You're heartsore, striving. You're Lark."

I hold her gaze and smile, accepting my name. As if a pact has been made.

Later that morning, I take my boat out and I turn it north. The coast is wild up here, with ragged, spiking cliffs. The fog lingers; the sky is thick and lowering. Only the seals like this part of the coast. I don't set my lines and I don't throw in my nets. Damned if I catch a single fish today. I don't want to feed that town. Why should I? They'd kick me like a dog if they knew what I was. They'd bury me in dirt. I lie on my bench in the boat, watching the gulls wheel. I won't lift a finger, not for anyone.

I think I must have fallen asleep, for when I wake, the clouds have lifted and Nightingale is there, sitting in the prow, polishing her spectacles.

"I like your boat," she says.

"It was my pa's."

She puts out her small, translucent hand as if she's laying it on the wood. "It's beautiful here," she says.

I look around at the cliffs and screeching gulls, wondering what on Earth she sees.

"They're taking Rye to a holding camp in Meadeville," I tell her. "How might he escape?"

"I think it must be very hard. I don't want to raise your hopes, Lark. It wouldn't be fair."

I'm thankful for her honesty. Truly. It's best to know.

"But there are people who help," she says. Other Torches, like Cassandra. She never used the word unhuman. Not once. She told me there had always been Torches in the human race. She said we were part of humanity's great diversity and that the word unhuman was simply a lie. She said the Brethren's time would pass."

I look at Nightingale, struck. "The Brethren's time will pass?"

"She believed it," says Nightingale firmly. "Cassandra was going to help me. She told me I was not alone. She said there was a place...."

"What place? Where?" I ask.

"Somewhere safe. She wouldn't tell me where but she was helping me to escape. Now she's gone. They took her." Nightingale pauses, breathing her loss. "But I believe it's there, Lark, her haven. And maybe your Rye will find his way. Somewhere, there are others like us. And they're free."

I feel an ember of hope kindling. Rye will escape.

Nightingale starts to sing after that, a song from the radiobine, with the sweetest tune I ever heard. She doesn't know all the lyrics but it expresses exactly how it feels to be in love. Nightingale's voice floats over the waves, brightening the air. Occasionally, I put in a humming note, where I think another voice should go. We drift, building a harmony. She stays with me all day. And I am not alone.

PART 2

I'm conscious of him all the time, chained down in the hold, that band on his skull. I know the smell of his sweat, the sound of his snores, the way his eyelashes look when he's asleep. I know him. Or thought I did. When we were boys, if we got into trouble, he'd always take the worst of it. He stood up to people. Now I realize what his fire and vigor was. Why do they call it songlight? It's a dark and frightening thing.

Elsa. It's taken hold in her, corrupting her.

I look down at the black waves passing, trying to breathe through the nausea, as our ship plows through the dark. Seasick. I'm just seasick.

I did what was right.

I pace the deck, fighting the sickness. The mutancy of songlight is one of the mysteries of science. I imagine it clinging to each cell, embedding itself in every nerve, like mistletoe, slowly corrupting its host. I must cut this unhuman off and sear the wound. I take two clean breaths—then Rye's false tale about spying for the Aylish jumps into my mind. Protecting Elsa. How noble, how villainous. His double, triple treachery.

The shock is still congealing in my guts. The pair of them, ensorcelled together on the beach. They've excluded me from their golden songlight, as if I'm the one who's cursed, not they.

She's blighted. A cancer in our family. What would my father think? Would he still swing her up and put her on his shoulders and carry her to the shore, to take her on his boat? Would he still have her on his knee, holding her lovingly as she slept? Gwyn Crane would have done his duty, I know that. And I have failed in mine. I've left her there, corrupting Ma. . . .

But how could I have told Ma? It would break her.

Elsa. Her mistletoe smile, mistletoe arms, stealing into my parents' hearts. Ma doesn't know the malignancy growing in her house.

But it's hard to think of my little sister at the shaming post. I stare up at the night sky, watching the clouds scud over the stars.

That dream I had. Holding Rye, feeling his arms around me, comforting him. He understood. I tended to his wounds. He loved me. Awoken by it. Woken, moaning, drenched in sticky shame. Briggs and Vine laughing at me in their bunks. Shrugged it off. Told them I had Sister Swan exactly where I wanted her. Told them she was gasping.

"Pink House." Vine grinned. "This lad needs a Pink House."

"Don't we fucking all?" I said and everybody laughed.

Rye's not dangerous to me now. His powers have been encased in lead. I'm going to tell him what I think.

I volunteer to feed him.

There are two chrysalids down here in the hold, gauze over their faces, greasing the turbines, dealing with our waste, doing all the menial tasks unfit for us humans. Perhaps Rye has watched them, considering his fate.

I see him, curled up, chained to a beam, facing the wall. I address him as I should. He no longer has a name.

"Unhuman."

He turns toward me like his whole body aches. He's ripped the gauze off his face. It is in shreds around his neck. His face shocks me, purple and yellow with bruising. A cut has split his lip. I stand there, holding his bowl. I put it down.

"Your rations."

The silence grows taut. As if this creature has the right to resent me.

"I know it was Elsa you were with," I say. "She confessed it."

All the anger drains out of him then, like blood from a stuck pig.

"Have you thrown her to the hounds, like you threw me?"

His quiet, bloodless voice unsettles me. His bruises disturb me. I won't give him a reply.

"So you drew the line at ruining your sister?"

"You ruined her," I charge him. "You seduced and corrupted her."

"We fell in love."

I suddenly hear a voice trapped in my skull like a mosquito's high-pitched hum: *I am living the wrong life.*

I accuse him immediately.

"Are you trying to mind-twist me, even with that band upon your head?"

He looks at me as if my question makes no sense. "I'm allowed water," he says.

I give him a ladle of water from a bucket. I hold it to his mouth. It hurts his lips but I see how it revives him. He drinks thirstily. I look at how tightly the lead band is fastened to his skull. The skin has weltered up on either side.

"Please, may I have more?"

Has no one let him have water? That's a needless cruelty. I refill the ladle and he drinks. I put the bucket down within his reach.

"I don't blame you, Piper, for doing what you did," he says. "It's what we're taught to do."

"I did what was right," I assure him.

"I don't hate you. I can see you're caught. Your wings are stuck to their web."

"Be very careful what you say to me," I warn.

"Why?" he asks. "Is there worse punishment than this?" I see something like that old grin of his. Wry Rye. He speaks slowly, as if it hurts his mouth to talk. "We hear only one creed, Piper. It's Peregrine's creed. It's become our reality. But there's a world beyond it that we have to find. A world where there's true liberty."

"This is mind-twisting, proof of your treachery."

"Elsa and I did nothing wrong. We're not evil or dangerous to anyone. We're in love and that is beautiful and good."

I can't listen to any more of this. I turn to go.

"Piper, wait...," he cries. "Your sister is in danger. She's in grave danger and you know it. This ship has lifeboats. We could take one, you and me."

"This is desperate."

"We could rescue her. We could all of us be free. . . ."

I look at him in disbelief. "I'm strong against your poison. I feel nothing for you, unhuman."

Rye holds my gaze. "Then why are you here?"

Out on the deck, there is a punching bag. I work till I'm exhausted.

Nightingale comes to my boat the next day and the day after. She's reticent at first. We're so unused to trusting. She watches me work and wants to know all about the turbine and the sail, how I use the lines and nets, and what all the different fish are called. She turns away when they come up in the nets because she can't bear to see them suffer.

"You'd make a terrible seaworker," I say. "People have to be fed."

"I know," she says. "And I like to eat fish, but . . ." I can feel the compassion pouring from her as she looks at their huge eyes and heaving gills.

She begins to open up about herself. I'm surprised to hear that she's seventeen. She looks younger. She tells me that she lives in a flat, three stories off the ground, near Peregrine Park, wherever that is. Her mother died when she was born. "My papa's been unlucky with his wives. His current wife, Ishbella—who makes me call her Mama—hasn't given him any children. When they argue, Papa calls her barren."

To be barren is a horrible fate in Brightland.

"Papa's applied for a Second Wife so I suppose I'll have two mothers soon," she says.

"Is he a veteran?" I ask.

"No," she says, her eyes sliding away from mine. "He's in a protected profession."

I'm not sure what this means but I don't want to appear ignorant by asking and Nightingale quickly changes the subject.

"You're so lucky to have all this space. From my window, all I can see is one spindly tree."

"The city must be amazing, though," I say.

"The sea is amazing."

Nightingale asks me to put my hand in the water and she cleaves to me, getting a tingling sense of the cold. The shock of it makes her laugh. I wish

I could share her delight. But the ever-constant pain of Rye is like a leaded band around my heart. Nightingale takes off her spectacles and closes her eyes, letting the sun and the breeze suffuse her.

Through her joy, I glimpse her loneliness. This girl kind of breaks my heart. I don't think she has any friends. Rye knew me to the core—but Nightingale carries her songlight alone.

"How long have you known you were a Torch?" I ask her.

"Since I was twelve. I've been hiding it for years, so scared sometimes that I can hardly eat."

This girl might look frail, but I wonder if her full power would wrench my innards out. She tells me she's a choirmaiden like me and when she's feeling well enough, she goes to marriage training.

"But when I speak with the other girls," she confesses, "I keep sensing what they think. I try to block it out but it makes things very hard. How do you cope with that?" she asks.

"It isn't like that for me . . . ," I tell her, puzzled.

I reckon Nightingale needs some respite. She looks eaten up with strain. I start to sing a sea-song as I work, a carefree, meandering tune, and she listens, adding a note here or there.

Soon, she's lying on my bench, joining in. We sing, getting to trust each other's voices. Then Nightingale takes the lead, making up a tune and lyrics of her own. We sing them over and over, until they become true:

> *"There is a place that we will find,*
> *a place where we'll be free . . ."*

I don't know what it is about the simple act of singing that brings us so much closer but I know by the time we have finished that this girl is going to be a true friend to me.

"I need to find the courage to escape," I confide in her. "And I need to do it soon."

I feel her concern.

"I can't stay here like a useless coward," I tell her. "I have to get to Rye while he's still at the transit camp."

"One girl in a boat, turning up at Camp Meadeville? Even if you made it that far, they'd arrest you straightaway." Her eyes are big with trepidation.

I know she's right—but it's eating me up.

"Why do they persecute us, Nightingale?"

"You know why," she replies. "Because of the malign rings."

"The old citizens' councils?" I ask.

"They were dominated by People of Song. And they abused their power. The malign rings held us back from progress, shunning every advancement, keeping us in ignorance."

"Do you believe that?" I ask her.

"My papa does," she replies. "He told me how Great Brother Peregrine raised a citizens' army. With his trusted Brethren, he swept the power of the malign rings away."

There is a mural of Northaven's old council on the back of our barracks. The senior cadets use it for target practice.

"Were they as evil as everyone says?" I ask.

Nightingale considers. "I think they probably had power for too long. I expect they were corrupt. My papa was just a boy when Great Brother Peregrine liberated us. He immediately signed up to serve the Brethren. He says that with Great Brother Peregrine came the era of the human."

There's so much I want to ask this girl. I want to ask her what Brightlinghelm is like. Do they have gallows there? Do they hang adulterers? Has she ever seen a Pink House? Does she miss her dead mother? How must it be, knowing that her birth caused her mother's death? How does she carry that burden? Nightingale is looking at the coast, humming one of her songs, while all my questions swirl in my underthoughts. Finally, I ask:

"Have you ever seen the Chrysalid House?"

Nightingale turns to me. "I see it every day. It's down by the river."

"What does it look like?"

"Low-set. Hardly any windows. It's mostly underground."

"So people can't use their song?"

She nods, her eyes downcast.

I press her. "How do they kill songlight?"

She answers slowly. "They take needles and skewer the brain. They kill a person's will and take their light. We see chrysalids leaving, with gauze over their faces. Women's wombs are taken, the men are made eunuchs. All their hope is gone. The mutation mustn't be allowed to—"

"Stop," I beg her. "How do we save Rye?"

Nightingale has no reply. She looks at me as if she's desperately sad that I'm still hoping.

I stare at the horizon, despair seeping into me like the tide. Minutes pass and the darkness grows. Rye is gone. This will shatter me, it will break me apart. Suddenly, Nightingale envelops me in her openhearted glow. I tell her I have to find the strength to leave here and follow Rye but I know in my heart that the journey is not survivable—and death is a fearful thing. Nightingale understands. She is with me. She holds me like a small and kindly light of hope, until the tide of pain begins to ebb.

Then she distracts me.

"What's it like underwater?" she asks. Without waiting for an answer, she leaps into the sea, drawing my songlight in after her.

Of course we're not really in the sea. We're not wet and drowning and unable to breathe. We move our songlight through the water like a pair of ghostly seals. Nightingale is thrilled by everything she sees. She seems to have no fear. She looks at the scallops, laughing at the way they swim. She imitates the dour faces of the cod. She marvels at a silvery shoal, moving in unison, safe from my nets.

And then I show her something in the seabed. It looks like a vast metal bird. Its head is bent and buried, rusted deep in the seafloor. Nightingale walks on its wide, barnacled wings, weeds swaying around it, home to eels.

"It's from the Light People time," I tell her. "It flew in the air and crashed there." Nightingale looks at the long row of windows.

"What were they flying away from?" she asks. "How did it fall?"

Neither of us knows, so the questions hang in the water.

Back in the boat, Nightingale is thoughtful.

"Have you ever seen a whale?" she asks. "There's the skeleton of one in our museum. It stretches the whole length of the great hall."

"I've seen orca," I tell her. "They scare me half to death. I once saw an orca flip a seal into the air and tear it clean in half. But no one's seen a whale for years. I expect they all went, in the Age of Woe, like the tall oxen that ate the tops of trees."

Nightingale says she thinks that the whales are far away, not dead. She sends out a loud greeting, a love song to all whales, wherever they may be. Her lightness dances; her good humor is relentless. She seems so excited to be on my boat, as if she's drinking in the freedom. Her song is so pure, sometimes it can hurt. As if all the particles that make me are vibrating with her notes.

I'm going to marriage training, as I should. We know the returning men are expected any day and we're busy making decorations for our nuptials. We've been told, by a blushing Hoopoe Guinea, what to expect in our wedding beds.

"The man's penile mast will harden and he will put it into your most secret parts."

Tinamou and Chaffinch are convulsed with giggles as Hoopoe describes us opening like blooms. She makes it sound so awful. I want to tell Gailee it's nothing like that. It's something wonderful. It's bliss.

And then I realize I'm approaching this wedding like a sleepwalker. I'm trudging slowly toward disaster. How can I go through with it?

I sit with Gailee and the choirmaidens, sewing *WELCOME HOME HEROES* on a banner. We'll hang it on the choir stand, which the eldermen and seaworkers are building on the quay. We must be on full view when their transport ship arrives. Personally, I wish our banner said *FUCK OFF BACK TO BRIGHTLINGHELM* but I keep my head down. Although my heart is itching to run, my feet have succumbed to a fearful dread. The shaming post is always in my sight.

I miss Rye's swearing. He'd drop swears into his language like salt and hot pepper. He'd smile and say "That's a load of fucking bollocks," or "Fuck that for starters." Only Rye could swear and make it sound funny and clever and full of light. . . . I will swear now on Rye's behalf: I will never ever forgive that bastard Wheeler and that creeping bollocks Greening and my stupid fucking brother for what they did to him.

I try to not think of Piper at all. But Ma feels his absence. Her anxiety for him eats away at her. I see her standing in Piper's room, staring at the birds and flying machines. She works hard to keep herself from grieving. If she's not seeing one of the wives through childbirth, she's out all day, helping the new mothers. She volunteers for Hoopoe too and helps us finish the dreadful banner. I know she wants to be with me—yet I can't talk with her. If I confide, I worry that the floodgates will open and the whole truth might come tumbling out. Ma will then be knowingly harboring an unhuman. And I can't do that to her.

I live for the hours I snatch with Nightingale, the freedom to be who I am, to say what I think. One afternoon, I drop my anchor down near Bailey's Strand. I have a pile of fish to gut. Nightingale amuses herself, balancing along the edge of the boat. I am desperate for distraction from the gnawing ache. Will Rye still be in Meadeville? Will he be on his way upriver? I'm not aware of voicing this but Nightingale seems to hear.

"Come and see where I live," she says. "Try and reach me." Then she smiles bashfully. "My apartment's not much. It's not beautiful, like here."

It amuses me that anyone could think my town is beautiful.

"What are you doing now?" I ask. "In your physical body. Where are you?"

"I'm sitting in the kitchen, peeling vegetables."

"Isn't that a risk?"

"Well, I might cut my thumb, I suppose."

"I mean using your songlight."

"I'm using my very innermost voice. And Ishbella never notices me. She keeps the radiobine on so we don't have to talk."

"You have a radiobine?"

"Can't you hear? It's *Sister Swan's Daily Address*."

I strain my ears. "What's she saying?"

"Listen." Nightingale grabs my hand. She closes her eyes and draws me toward her. I feel myself staying still, yet hurtling through space, a thrilling, disconcerting feeling. I draw in my breath and close my eyes, and when I open them, a small kitchen is coming into focus. I'm so utterly amazed that I can't organize my vision. Nightingale has brought me here as if it's easy for her. Light is streaming through my mind, dazzling my consciousness. Nightingale tells me to steady my breathing, to breathe in and out with her. As my breath settles into her rhythm, I begin to calm. I see that everything is painted cream. Nightingale is at a table, peeling carrots. A woman, who must be Ishbella, is chopping spuds at the sink. All around us, there's a velvet voice. It's coming from a radiobine on a shelf. Sister Swan . . .

"She's at the harbor," Nightingale tells me. "Seeing off our ships."

"Sons of Brightland, you are fortunate," says Sister Swan. "You're part of a revolution. No longer are you like the Aylish, prey to power-hungry unhumans. You're men we can look up to, men we can revere. . . ."

Her voice is like music, soft as crushed roses.

"The Aylish move without free will, for their minds belong to their unhumans. But with your strength, with your free will, their power will be destroyed. We will liberate the Aylish from their unhuman overlords and they will join our civilized land. We will bring them the future!"

I hear a roar of patriotic cheers. Ishbella looks up at the window, as if proud to be a Brightling.

"I speak for every woman," continues Sister Swan, "when I offer you my thanks, my prayers, my love. Long live Brightland!" The radiobine fizzles and crackles into a chant and, under it, a rousing piece of music.

My concentration strains. The kitchen spins and dazzles—and I find myself back in the boat.

"That was unbelievable!" I cry, exhilarated.

Nightingale is laughing. "You did it, Lark, you came—all the way to Brightlinghelm."

"I heard Sister Swan on the radiobine!"

"Well, that's what we get every day," says Nightingale with a wry smile. "Personally, I'd rather be here on the sea with you."

"You have such powerful songlight," I tell her. "It's incredible. You just seemed to pick me up and take me with you. How do you do that?"

"Cassandra once said . . ." Nightingale stops herself. She stands and moves across the boat. Her image shimmers as she stands in the full sun. "Cassandra told me my songlight had rare power. She was trying to teach me how to control it. There was one time when I hurt her. And in truth, I'm afraid of it."

"How?"

"I once injured someone."

Who?"

"A Siren. He had his sights on Cassandra. I was trying to save her. It was an instinct. I just threw all my power at him and . . . he collapsed."

"You hurt a man—with your songlight?" I ask, amazed.

Nightingale nods.

"I didn't know that was possible."

"Neither did I," she says.

"What happened?"

"Cassandra had told me to meet her at a tram station. She was going to take me out of Brightlinghelm. I saw a Siren, in songlight, following her. The Inquisitors were closing in. As soon as I perceived him, I tore into him with the full force of my songlight. I— He collapsed. He lost consciousness. But I noticed him too late." She exhales, her breath shaking with regret. "The Inquisitors forced Cassandra to her knees. I watched them cuff her skull with lead. The only reason I'm still here is that the Siren was dazed by what I had done. I'd hurt him so badly he couldn't discern me. Cassandra was begging me to save myself. . . ."

I know there's nothing I can say that will take her pain away. I hold her, as she held me.

"Tell me about Cassandra," I urge, hoping it might help her to talk. "How did you meet?"

Nightingale pauses for a while and lets me share her memory.

"The wasting fever got me hard," she begins. "It came on suddenly. I collapsed in the street and by the time my papa carried me to the hospital, I was delirious. I don't know how long I was there, but the first thing I was conscious of was waking to find myself lying in an iron lung."

Taking my hand, Nightingale shows me the scene. I see a hospital ward in the dead of night, neat rows of beds, most containing children. It's as if she's outside her own body, floating in songlight, looking down at herself. Her face is pale and ghostly, her eyes closed fast, and her body is encased from the neck down in a huge breathing machine. I can hear the slow and steady pump of the machine, inward, outward, imitating human breath.

"You must have been so frightened," I say.

"I was. But I would have died without it. It was the strangest feeling, floating there, above myself. I was looking down on two doctors and a nurse standing at my bed."

I see a young woman in a blue-and-white uniform cooling Nightingale's forehead with an ice-cold cloth.

"Cassandra?" I ask.

Nightingale nods. "She had the kindest eyes I had ever seen." She pauses for a while as if she's drinking in the image, then she carries on her tale. "One of the doctors had a waxed mustache. He was the senior of the two.

And I could hear them talking."

I see the figures just as Nightingale describes.

"He was saying, 'This child won't survive.' He said there were worthier candidates for the machine. He told the other doctor to give me a big dose of morphine to send me on my way."

"To death?" I am appalled.

"He thought I wasn't worth saving. And I could see immediately that Cassandra thought it was dreadful."

"What did you do?" I ask.

"I screamed at the doctor to stop. I begged him not to do it. But he couldn't see me or hear me. He wasn't aware of me at all. I tried to shake the younger doctor but he carried on filling a syringe. I turned to Cassandra and said: "You have to save me—please!"

"And I realized she was hunched, her eyes closed in pain, as if I was blinding her. My songlight was hurting her; my songlight, which I'd kept hidden right down in the depths of me. My songlight, which I never till that moment admitted to myself. Cassandra felt my desperation like a pain.

"Please help me!" I cried. The doctors were oblivious, they couldn't sense me—but Cassandra could. She pretended she was overcome with sadness.

"'It's hard,' she said, 'to see so many children die. I've sat with this girl all day. She's a fighter. May we please give her a chance?'

"And the mustached doctor looked at her, as if she was very silly and sentimental but also pretty, and he said: 'It's sad, but there we are. This fever's been burning through the city and we must prioritize boys and men.'

"And I was yelling 'No, NO,' and begging her to save me.

"Cassandra said: 'Her father . . . Her father is a loyal servant to the state. And it would grieve him to see her perish.'

"That carried weight. And the senior doctor stopped the other doctor, who was about to inject me in the neck, and he said: 'Let's see if she rallies. We'll review her case at dawn.'"

"Cassandra saved you?"

"Yes," says Nightingale. "But my pleading had taken the last of my strength. I fell unconscious again. And that night, I think that I came very close to death."

She shows me herself, lying in the darkness of the breathing machine. There's a haunted look in her eyes as she recalls it.

"What happened?" I ask.

"Cassandra came. . . ."

I see the darkness around Nightingale starting to dissolve. A woman's bright arms curl around her, capable arms, arms made of songlight.

"I felt the strength of her light all night long, willing me to rally."

"She was healing you?"

"I don't know. She made me want to heal myself. I wanted to live so badly, just so I could thank her. Every time I took in a breath, it felt a little easier. The darkness went from black to gray. It went from gray to blue. And finally, it felt like I was lying in blue sky. Next time I awoke, the breathing machine was gone and Cassandra was sitting by my bed. Her eyes were singing me a question, very quietly, like the bubbling of a pan on the stove. She asked me if I knew what I was. 'I'm unhuman,' I said. She told me never to say that word again. She told me I was a very powerful Torch. . . ." Nightingale closes her eyes, despairing. "But for all my power, I couldn't save her."

I don't know what to say. I try to comfort her as best I can, and, for a while, silence is our harmony.

At last I wipe the tears off my face. The shadows are lengthening. I've done no work. The fish still need gutting.

"I must go," says Nightingale. "I love it here, Lark, but I get so tired. Papa will be home soon and he likes me to be lively. He gets upset when I keep falling asleep. . . ."

I know just what she means. Songlight is exhausting. I have been sluggish every night since Nightingale has been coming.

"What's a protected profession?" I ask, wondering about her papa.

Nightingale bites her lip. She gazes down the coast toward my village. She sees only its quaint and sleepy beauty. She smiles.

"Listen," she says. "I think the sea maidens are singing to us. . . ."

And then I hear it. My choir.

10 ✷

The choirmaidens are on the quayside as I bring in my boat, standing on their new choir stand, practicing under the unwelcome banner. Half the town is watching. Ma helps me out and I can tell that she is sore with frustration. I'm late again.

The choirmaidens are halfway through the anthem that Hoopoe has been teaching us, a filigree of voices interweaving joyfully. My heart sinks as I join them.

"Welcome home, our brave and valiant men
I sing my joy, as you return again.
For ten long years, you've fought to make us free
And now in thanks, I give myself to thee . . ."

I stand next to Gailee, finding my place in the harmony. Hoopoe is conducting, glaring at me. Emissary Wheeler is pacing up and down the quay, absorbed in his own self-importance. I feel Gailee singing her heart out by my side. We've been learning this tune for months, but today, I really listen to the words. I find them chilling.

"My pure heart I place in your strong hand,
In loving you, I know I serve my land.
Thal bless this day and bless our valiant men,
We sing our joy as you return again."

"It's tomorrow," Gailee whispers to me. "Our bridegrooms are coming on tomorrow's transport."

I'm not ready. It can't happen. "Tomorrow?" I ask in dismay.

Wheeler clears his throat. He is halfway through directing a rehearsal. "By this point," he says, "the men will have disembarked. Commander

Mikane will be standing at my side, the mighty hero who has burned like a comet through the battlefields of Ayland. On the orders of Great Brother Peregrine himself, I have been tasked with honoring Heron Mikane with the highest decoration in Brightland, the Star of Thal." Wheeler is about to burst with vanity. "In a short verbal tribute, I will enumerate and eulogize his most celebrated achievements. . . ." He blows on like a bag of wind. "At the glorious battle of Montsan Beach, Heron Mikane led a force that was outnumbered three to one. His epic victory has made him a Brightling hero like no other." He pauses for effect. "When he has received his decoration, the commander may choose to thank me. Not until I give the signal will you cheer. You'll then proceed past him, past all your bridegrooms up to the Elders' Hall, giving the returning men a chance to appreciate your grace and comeliness. You must behave at all times as Northaven's finest flowers."

If this man dropped dead right now, I'd cheer.

When he's said his piece, Hoopoe comes to his side.

"Choirmaidens," she enthuses. "We've gone through every detail of the ceremony. You know what's expected of you at the banquet and on your wedding night. Now go home and get ready to give your bridegrooms a wedding to remember."

A thrill of excitement rips through the choir.

Chaffinch Greening is ecstatic. "I've dreamed of Heron Mikane all my life!"

Tinamou Haines swoons: "I'd be Second Wife for Heron Mikane. . . ."

"I'd be Third Wife," squeals Nela.

"And Gailee would be his little dog." Chaffinch laughs and the other girls join in. "Gailee, sit!"

Gailee reddens, hurt. And Hoopoe does nothing to stop them. I have had enough. I stride up the hill and Ma strides after me.

"Elsa, you don't help yourself. You know the elderwomen are drawing up the lists for First and Second Wife. You deserve to be First."

My anger comes pouring out. "Why must I marry at all? Lying down in service to some stranger? It sounds disgusting—and I can't believe you'd make me."

Ma is shocked by my vehemence. "I'm worried for you, that's all. These last few days you've been so distant. Elsa, talk to me. . . ."

It's wrong of me to take my anger out on Ma. It's not her idea to marry us to men we've never met.

"I'm sorry," I say. "I just need time to clear my head. I'll see you back at home. . . ."

"I'm sorry too," she says. And I feel the weight of everything unsaid.

I decide to go and visit my pa. On my way to the graveyard I see some kids playing. I take their ball and throw it against a mural of Commander Mikane. He's standing on a pile of Aylish dead, the flames of Montsan Beach high in the sky behind him, his dark hair falling over his shoulders, a weapon held in his hand like a toy. I aim the ball at his big warrior bollocks.

"You should watch out, Elsa. You'll go too far one day."

Gailee has followed me. I bounce the ball back to the little kids.

"Probably."

She asks where I am going and she walks with me. We look at Pa's memorial stone and the jumble of letters. *Missing In Action*. His bones lie in bits, somewhere on an Aylish field. Ma used to leave him flowers every week but she stopped coming up here long ago. Her grief is in a different place. She isn't underwater anymore. Maybe I will reach that place with Rye. I pull some weeds out of the grave, thinking what to do. I can't get married, that's all I know.

Gailee is looking down at the harbor. Chaffinch Greening is sitting down there on the seawall, giggling with Nela Lane, Sambee James, Uta Malting, and Tinamou Haines, their talk no doubt bent on who will be the Mrs. Mikanes. Heron Mikane has the highest rank, the best pension, and no doubt the biggest muscles to go with it. Two lucky girls will get to bathe his smelly feet and rub him down with aromatic oils. His First Wife will prepare him for his marriage bed and then lie down and wait, giving herself in gratitude, a living present from the Brethren and our town. Then his Second Wife will get a turn. Excitement ripples between the girls, thrilled to be putting their opening blooms into use. To me they look like livestock, curling their hair to be slaughtered.

"I know I'll never get First Wife," says Gailee in a low voice. "Chaffinch says there's a stain on my family. She calls me unhuman spawn."

"Chaffinch Greening is as thick as bread," I tell her in frustration. "You'll get a good husband . . . if that's what you want."

"D'you mean that?"

"Course I do." I nudge her, trying to cheer her. "You might even get Mikane."

"Huh . . ." She smiles bashfully. "Now I know you're lying."

We watch a family group at another grave. The Second Wife has a big toddler tied on her back with a yellowing scarf. A pack of barefoot kids stands in the grass as the First Wife lays her flowers. This war is eating men.

It occurs to me that Gailee's pa has no memorial. She's lost him, just as I lost mine, but maybe Mr. Roberts isn't dead. His name has been taken, like Rye's, but he's probably alive, a chrysalid somewhere. Does he still have memories? Have they taken all his will? Does he still have power of speech? What remains of his mind? Gailee must have asked herself these things a thousand times. What must that be like for her?

"My mother spent all day up at the Mikane house today," she chats as we walk back down the hill. "Your ma was there too, with the rest of the townswomen. They were mending windows, whitewashing. It'll look perfect when the commander arrives."

"Gailee," I ask her. "When they took your father—"

She cuts me off straightaway. "I don't want to talk about it."

I persist. "Did you ever discover what happened to him? How long was it before he got to the Chrys—"

"Please, just stop!"

Gailee walks away. I feel bad for upsetting her.

Tomorrow.

A husband I don't want.

Tomorrow.

What will I do? I will certainly die if I leave. But if I stay, I'm in peril too. Alone, I reach out for Nightingale. I have to tell her. But how do I reach her? She has always come to me. Without her guidance, how do I find her? How do I get my songlight all the way to Brightlinghelm?

I make Nightingale my point of concentration. I don't think of the physical distance between us. I try to sing myself toward her. She spoke of rising up into the firmament and this is the sensation that suddenly I feel. I let myself go up into the lightness . . . and I fall from a height, landing back in my own body.

I try again. And again, concentrating harder and harder on Nightingale, listening for her.

No luck.

I try until nightfall creeps across the town.

"Nightingale!"

I am about to give up. I sit, cross-legged, too tired to strain. One last attempt. I rise as slowly as I can, my mind empty of all thoughts. I feel a sense of weightlessness . . . then suddenly I feel as if I am moving very fast—and staying very still—that most curious sensation. I sense her. I move toward her like a flare—and I find myself in an opalescent bedroom, shimmery as mist. There she is, looking at me, ironing a pile of shirts. Nightingale. I'm so amazed I can hardly speak.

"I did it," I say, thrilled at my achievement. "I got to you."

Nightingale's room takes on a firmer glow as she speaks.

"Lark," she says. "You can't be here."

"I have to tell you. It's tomorrow—"

"Don't come here in the evenings. It's dangerous."

She looks so thin in the flesh. I see dark rings under her eyes. I notice how her nails are bitten to stumps. Her dress, beautifully pressed and embroidered, looks too big on her.

"You have to go."

"But I need you!" I press. "My wedding day—"

"Go now—just go!"

She's pushing me away, with real and present fear. Disappointment courses through me.

Then I hear a man's voice. "Kaira?"

Footsteps are approaching Nightingale's door.

"I'm ironing, Papa," she desperately cries. Her door swings open.

"Leave that," says the man. His uniform is black. "Come and sit with me."

My heart turns upside down with fear. He is an Inquisitor.

"It's *Music Hour* and I know you like it. Come and pull my boots off. . . ."

Her papa, standing in her doorway, black boots, a bottle of ale in his hand. An Inquisitor.

I step backward into blackness. I feel the body-shock as my songlight rejoins me. I sit on the headland, dizzy.

Now I know why Nightingale said his profession was protected. I know why she's so thin and anxious. No wonder she loves the freedom of the sea. An Inquisitor.

Her life is in danger every day.

11 ✳

Later, in the low light of a turbine lamp, Ma fits the wedding dress she has been making me. I've ignored this hated garment since she started work on it. Now it's almost finished. I'm standing on the table while she marks the hem.

"Is there anything you want to talk to me about?" she asks when the silence between us has stretched to an ache.

"No."

Holding pins in her mouth, she works her way around the dress. Then, when the last pin is in, she breaks the silence again.

"Do you want to ask me anything?"

"I know what he'll do to me, if that's what you mean."

"It was different for me," Ma says. "I chose your pa. Or we chose each other, I should say. We met at Borgas Market—and there was lightning between us. Your brother was the result. You came along twelve months later."

I don't want to think about my brother. Or my pa.

"The war has taken all our choice," says Curl sadly. "But a lot of the women I tend have found contentment. They didn't choose their husbands, but their homes are full of love."

"You sound like Hoopoe Guinea." This silences her.

I jump down and pull the unwanted dress off. Ma takes it and threads her needle. She seems determined to talk.

"I was up at the Mikane house today."

"Gailee told me."

"I remember Heron Mikane when he was younger than Piper. He used to hang around your pa like a lost dog."

"Did he?"

"Used to hang around me too. You were only a baby. He was shy, a bit gawky . . . No one would have guessed he'd turn out to be a commander. But then, war changes people."

I'm not much interested in Heron Mikane, but I'm glad Ma is filling the silence.

"They were a troubled family, the Mikanes," she goes on. "An Aylish ship raided Northaven, early in the war. You were a newborn in my arms; Piper was just walking. The Aylish came ashore at night to steal supplies. Most of us were in our beds but Mrs. Mikane always rose early. She worked at Malting's Bakery and was up before the dawn. Anyway, they stabbed her, as she tried to raise an alarm. The Mikane boys went wild after that. Heron was the only one who turned out well. The other two are dead, I think. Your pa treated Heron like a little brother. Took him out on the boat. You're too young to remember him, I suppose."

It's strange that she remembers Mikane from when he was just ordinary. It's only to us choirmaidens that he's a big heroic beast. Unreal.

"There was a sweetness to him," says Ma wistfully. "I expect that's long gone now. . . ."

I get a flash of Rye, his sweetness, how my flesh would feel on fire when he was near. I feel a hot flare of pain for all the things we never got a chance to do. Ma seems to sense my mood.

"Elsa," she says, "I don't know how to fight this. Everybody has to be a wife."

She's trying to make tomorrow easier for me. "Our soldiers aren't monsters; they're your father's friends and comrades."

"They're old men."

I cross the room.

"Like I say, I wish you had a choice."

My voice comes out small. "I chose Rye Tern."

I see the wedding dress falling from Ma's hands. I see the ache of her compassion. If she hugs me, I will cry. I go into my room and shut the door.

I can't rest. I send my songlight up above the roof, hoping Nightingale will come. But the stars travel across the night sky and still I am alone. I think of Rye, staring at the same sky. . . .

As first light saturates the world with gray, I'm still restless and awake. I walk into our kitchen, hopelessness misting my brain. Nightingale can't help me. Nobody can. Out of the window, a thick fog lies over the town. I see my dress, beautifully finished, laid on the table like a dainty corpse. I put it on. Curl has done me proud. In our pitted mirror, I am an elegant and lovely ghost.

I can't do this. I won't be this silent, unprotesting bride. Suddenly, my course is clear. I'm going to do what I should have done days ago. I put Pa's thick coat on over my dress and slip my feet into my seaworker's boots. I cut a lock of hair off and leave it on the table for my ma. I hope she understands what I must do. Without another thought, I sneak out of the house.

In my mind's eye, I see Rye disembarking from a ship, shuffling into the Chrysalid House. I see him resisting; being whipped, hanged, shot, destroyed. Then I create a better image; Rye is running, a fugitive, looking for me. I made a pledge to live with him or die. And that is what I'll do. I head down to the harbor, ignoring Sister Swan's painted eyes. No one is about. Mrs. Sweeney's curtains are still closed but the barrier is open. I leap into my boat and loosen the moorings. Before I know it I am out at sea. The fog will hide me.

"Rye. Rye. Rye." I say his name aloud, louder and louder. "I am coming."

With all the force of my songlight I repeat it. This fog. Curse this fog for hampering my boat. I will find my way through. I will find you, Rye. I am wearing this wedding dress for you.

Then I realize Nightingale is here. She's staring at me in concern.

"Your wedding day?" she asks, looking at the dress.

"I tried to tell you last night. That's why I searched you out."

"What are you doing? Why aren't you with your mother?"

"Because I'm going to rescue Rye or die trying."

I turn my back on her, seeing to my turbine. In truth, I'm angry with her. She should have told me about her pa. She picks up on my mood.

"I'm sorry," she says. "I didn't know how to tell you."

"You put us both at risk."

I feel her raw loneliness.

"I thought if you knew my papa was an Inquisitor, you'd never want to see me again." She looks so forlorn.

"Does he know about you?"

"Of course not. And I'm careful, Lark."

The turbine will hardly turn. This damned fog has killed the breeze. Nightingale hangs her head.

"Papa is not a bad person," she says.

I almost laugh at this but Nightingale defends him. "Sometimes good people do bad things. . . ."

"Like sending us to the Chrysalid House?"

She looks as if she's going to cry. "He believes in things that are false. But we're told they're true. You can't blame him for believing them."

I acknowledge this. The whole country's swept up in those lies. My brother believes them too.

"I know I'm in danger," says Nightingale. "I'm not stupid. I come here every day to be with you and it just puts off the inevitable. They will find me out." Her tears fall then. Tears of fear and helplessness. All my frustration with her goes.

"Nightingale, you have to escape," I say.

"I tried. And Cassandra was taken. . . ."

"Try again now. I'm going to find Rye. You should run too. Where was Cassandra going to take you?"

"She never told me. She said it was safer if I didn't know."

"She must have mentioned something."

Nightingale thinks. "She once told me her people were from the mountains, out east, near the Tenmoth Zone."

"The Tenmoth Zone?"

"It's one of the irradiated places from the Light People time. Cassandra said nature had no balance in there. She said that every spring, an abundance of moths would hatch. Most of them would be eaten by the colonies of bats that nested deep in the corrupted zone. The moths that survived would blow over the hills in great clouds. They would flutter and flap to the ground and eventually they'd die. She said no one went outside for days when these moth clouds were in the air. And when the hatching ended, her people would sweep up the fallen moths and bury them in the ground. . . ."

I take this strange story in. "Do you think that's where she was taking you, the Tenmoth Zone?"

"I don't know. Maybe the Greensward somewhere."

"Rye thought there were people like us hiding in the Greensward. How would we get to them?"

"We?" asks Nightingale, her eyes wide.

"You, me, Rye," I persist. "How would we find them?"

Nightingale realizes I'm serious. "You really think you can rescue him?"

"I've wasted too many days already. I'm going to sail to Meadeville."

"That's foolhardy, Lark." Her eyes are full of fear for me.

"What's foolhardy is marrying a man I've never met who's almost as old as my ma. I'm running, Nightingale. And there's nowhere I can go, except toward you and Rye."

There's a silence. Then she says, "I'll help you all I can. I'll send my songlight toward Meadeville, to see if I—"

She's cut off by a deafening BOOM, a rumbling explosion, somewhere down the coast. The noise vibrates right through us, distorted by the fog. It dies away.

"What was that?" she asks.

"I don't know," I tell her. "But I don't like it."

Nightingale clutches her chest. "I can hear screams," she says.

I listen—but all I can hear are the startled gulls.

There's a brand-new Listening Station on the coast near here. It's scientific, military. There's a big metal dome on its flat roof, with an antenna in the middle. Sometimes, when I'm fishing, I see the dome facing up toward the sky; other times, I see it pointed at Ayland, a hundred miles across the sea. Before the Listening Station, there were just telegram machines. We can communicate with Brightlinghelm by radiobine now.

"Men screaming. Skin burning. Fire!" Nightingale's eyes are closed, as if she is there with them. I try to see what she sees, but there is only fog.

"The roof's collapsing. Help. Help. Get us out!"

I see her twisting with panic and pain. She's fading, as if her light is being pulled into the dreadful suffering.

"Nightingale!" I cry. "Nightingale!" I surround her with songlight, making her stay with me.

"Can't you hear them?" she asks, her eyes filling with tears. "They're dying. A missile, straight from the sky. The roof caved in on them. Oh, Lark . . ."

A missile. What could have fired it?

And suddenly, looming out of the fog in front of us, comes a huge Aylish battleship.

There's a knock on my door. I'm lying on my chaise, with mashed cucumber all over my face. Before I can arrange myself, a man is standing in the middle of the room. That senseless idiot Lady Orion has let him in. I barely have my wig on. I rapidly stand with my back to him, wiping pale green slime off my face, laughing with embarrassment. It's Starling Beech, Kite's lackey who sports a shock of upright hair.

"You've caught me at my ablutions. . . ."

"Sister, forgive me," he stammers. "Brother Kite has asked for you. You're wanted in the war room."

I stiffen, sensing an opportunity. Keeping my face averted, I ask the lackey to wait outside for one tiny moment. As soon as he's gone, I hit Lady Orion as hard as I can. She doesn't react so I kick her too.

"Stupid, silly bitch. Why did you let him in?"

She doesn't reply, of course.

I wash the rest of the mess off my face. Lady Lyra stands ready with a towel to pat me dry.

"Light makeup. Top speed," I say, enunciating clearly so that the dumb creatures understand. My ladies apply corrector, blush, and kohl. I won't leave my rooms without this paltry minimum, not even if the palace is burning to the ground. Whatever Kite wants, he won't get it till I'm perfect.

"Come," I tell the chrysalids.

They move into formation like silent cygnets, white-clad, veiled in organza, all unsung products of the Chrysalid House. They never speak, or smile, or cry. They have no feelings, no opinions. They are there to obey simple orders—and their orders are to follow me. I have made them part of my myth.

Starling leads us from my rooms to the Brethren's center of military power. We walk along the ladies' corridor (of which I am the only resident of note), through the long gallery with its ancient art and artifacts, past the banqueting hall with its high, stained glass windows, over the carousing rooms, across the cloistered courtyard, where Great Brother Peregrine has his library, and into the great hall. This was built in the days when the malign rings held power. It's a perfect circle, under an impressive dome. There is now a memorial in the center, dedicated to the fall of the old councils and Peregrine's Great Liberation. Peregrine stands in marble, his rod of state held over a cuffed unhuman.

Sometimes I muse upon the days of the malign rings. Songlight was a trait that people longed for in their children then.

We hurry in formation, dressed from head to toe in white. Everyone gives way to us. Flunkies and councillors bow and scrape. In spite of our speed, I must exude calm. This too is part of my myth. I must be a constant emblem of the womanly virtues of patience, love, and grace in this ruthless place of power. My dress has white chiffon trimmings that float behind me as I walk. My wig is styled with diamonds, glinting in the morning sun. My ladies and I always make a splash.

As we approach the war room, Starling halts. "Brother Kite wants you alone."

"So my visit is clandestine?" It would profit me to make this man my spaniel. "Starling," I say, using his name like a caress. "You'd better tell me what you know."

"I . . . I don't have clearance, Sister."

I smile at him as if he's the only man I've ever cared about.

"You have clearance from *me*. . . ."

He swallows, his big Adam's apple bobbing up and down his neck. "Forgive me."

"One day," I whisper, "you'll stop being afraid. Then, who knows what might happen?"

He blushes to the roots of his startling hair.

I enter a dark mezzanine, leaving my ladies with the bashful emissary.

Below me, military personnel communicate with our armed forces, wearing heavy headphones, glued to radiobine machines. A huge map makes up one wall, showing our long, green Island of Brightland. It lies beside the continental promontory of Ayland, separated from our enemy, at the narrowest point, only by the Alma Straits. There are battle markers everywhere, dots showing the locations of our ships. There are lines drawn and redrawn over Ayland, showing our proud advancements and the shame of our inglorious retreats. There are no lines on Brightland. The Aylish pigs have never kept a single foothold on our shores.

The slim window, floor to ceiling, gives a glimpse of Kite's brand-new landing strip. I pause, distracted, as one of his experimental firefuel planes comes in to land. I feel the roar of its engine vibrating through my viscera as it touches down. It leaves in its path a firefuel haze.

These planes, known as Fireflies, are controversial. They are the brainchild of my possessor, Kite. But Peregrine has not yet approved their use. The planes break the First Law and the Council of Brethren is deeply divided on their use. But, Gala, they are magnificent.

The First Law was the pillar of the Age of Woe, the thin thread our ancestors clung on to. It probably saved life on Earth from total destruction and for thousands of years it has been obeyed by all. *Mankind shall nevermore use firefuel, in any of its forms.*

I watch the heat haze pumping from the Firefly's engine. The propeller whirrs ten times as fast as any turbine could. It halts on the airstrip like Thal's own chariot.

My possessor is approaching me, fervor in his eyes. Niccolas Kite, Peregrine's most ardent disciple. He has risen in the years that I have known him from a humble Inquisitor to director of the Chrysalid House and then beyond, to chief military adviser. I know I've played my part, rising with him, smoothing his way, inculcating people with all his agendas. I've oiled his wheels to make him strategist in chief, and Kite's ambition continues to propel him. He is set on being Peregrine's heir.

It's been six years since Kite picked me from the wreckage of my home. I was a girl of sixteen. I feel a familiar emotion as I see him. I used to think that it was awe. Now I call it by its proper name. Fear.

A motion of Kite's hand warns me to halt, to stay where I am, out of sight from the main floor. He wastes no time pushing me into the shadows. No one must see that this great supremo needs my help.

"An Aylish battleship has destroyed our Listening Station in the north," he tells me. "One missile—a direct hit."

This is a blow. The Listening Station is brand-new radiobine technology and cost almost as much as his Fireflies.

"Only an unhuman could have been so accurate in thick coastal fog. Find him," orders Kite. "So I can destroy his ship."

All Aylish ships have a Torch on board. I know immediately what I have to do.

"Peregrine has given me the war room," says Kite. "And I want the best possible result."

I must be loving, loyal, intelligent, desirable, and keen.

"Unbind me. Let me serve." My survival depends on being exactly what he needs. I turn away, taking off my wig. When I turn back, I feel naked in his gaze. I don't raise my eyes. Kite sees my own hair cropped and shorn around his most enduring gift to me, a Siren's lead band.

He takes out the key, which he wears on a hidden chain. I am a little taller than he is, which I know he dislikes. I very slightly bend my knees so he doesn't have to reach. He puts the key in the band's subtle lock. I feel the click running through my cortices as he turns it. He removes my hated burden. I am not just the Flower of Brightland; I am Kite's secret Torch.

I see the need in his eyes. He wants to find a way to ingratiate himself with our Great Brother. Relations between them have not been good of late.

"Let me tell Peregrine the Aylish ship has been destroyed."

My songlight rushes, unchained—and I feel a lightness so euphoric that for a moment I forget to breathe. Kite wastes no time. He gives me the location of the Listening Station and my energies turn north. I'm looking for an Aylish vessel, somewhere off the coast. I pour my songlight into the task. My body tenses with exertion—but after that first rush of elation, my powers feel vaporous and slow. It was the same last time he released me, and the time before. My powers used to soar effortlessly. Now I have to force my songlight to bend to my will. An agony of anxiety begins in me. It takes every particle of energy I have to send my songlight so far. I curse myself, as seconds tick by. The Listening Station can't be hard to find. It should be a hot spot of human agony.

"What's keeping you? Where are you?" Kite's impatience doesn't help.

At last, I hear a distant conflagration, men panicking, others screaming. I home in on it. Yes, I can sense them. Their torment allows me vision. I pass over their blistered bodies as quickly as I can. Beyond, I hear the sea. All is white with a thick mist. There's nothing to cling on to, nothing but the gulls and the deadening fog. I'm floundering.

This is what happens when songlight's kept entrapped. It starts to lose its power. A few years ago I would have seared my way onto that Aylish ship like a comet. Now I'm straining to my limit and this anxiety won't help. I concentrate on the sound of the waves, forcing myself to find my old brilliance. Few Torches can travel this far.

"Well? The coordinates?"

"The distance is great," I say. I grip a nearby desk, forcing my mind onward with everything I've got. I sense the human souls on board an old Brightling transport ship. I catch the thought-wreathes of battle-weary soldiers, drifting up like smoke. They're our own men, making their way back to a little coastal town.

"There's a transport ship close by," I say to Kite. "Our men. They're troubled by the conflagration. . . ."

"Find the Aylish!"

I leave the transport ship behind and listen.

I sense a potent male energy, a bright, curious intelligence. An Aylish-man, the Torch. My prayers are answered as I see him on the prow of a magnificent battleship. Relief pours over me. His energy draws me closer, like a magnet. He is staring out to sea, his gaze pinned on something in the water.

"I've got them," I say to Kite.

I rise up, using the Listening Station to triangulate the position of the ship. Kite takes the coordinates and on a nearby radiobine machine, he barks an order to an underling. "Wire the captain of the Brightling transport ship."

"Kite," I say as I hold myself over the waves, "that transport is old, ill-equipped—"

"Then the Aylish won't expect it to destroy them."

I hear Kite speaking on his comms unit to the Brightling ship's captain. I should retreat now, back into my flesh. Kite has what he wants. He's giving an order to fire without warning. I should tell him that's a mistake—but I am relishing the last of my freedom. My songlight will soon be encased again. I'll cherish every moment that I have, strengthening myself.

I'm drawn toward the thought-scape of the Aylish Torch. I rein in my instinctive hate. I cannot let him sense me or he'll pounce. I balance myself on the deck, my songlight focused on him, and I feel my presence stabilize. He's younger than me, his hair in a ponytail, a bright jewel round his neck, the usual azure shirt. This man knows his own allure. I flex my songlight, moving closer, careful to keep myself concealed. He's inexperienced and feels his responsibility as keenly as a blade. I see the skin on the back of his neck, his slim hands resting on the rail, the potency in his gaze. Dare I steal his thoughts? It would please Kite if I discovered where this battleship was sailing from and what its mission is. The Torch is beaming all his light down toward the waves. Why?

Then out of the mist I see it. A tiny boat, a peasant fishing boat, a young woman in it. Gala, she's a bride. And she's not alone. . . .

In my other reality I'm dimly aware of Kite, his orders given, coming at me with the metal band.

"Wait!" I say.

He covets my powers and so he envies them. He likes it best when my skull is bound in lead.

"What is it?" he asks impatiently. "What can you see?"

"A small boat. Another Torch," I say. "I hear two songs together, like a harmony.... One is uncanny. I swear it's coming from—"

And suddenly, I'm choking.

I have let down my guard. The Aylish Torch is attacking me, in songlight.

"I have you, spy," he hisses.

I feel his energy wrap itself round mine, a potent force. I inhale, rigid. This is an attack, an attack upon my person. I try to struggle free. I fight back. He's wrestling my songlight. This Aylishman has me locked, locked. I'm unprepared. It is too long since I was in combat. He will tear my spirit from my body—or I will tear his.

"Who are you?" he asks. "Who's sent you, spy?"

I feel his atoms grasping mine more fully—and suddenly we are both on the mezzanine, looking down over the war room. This is unthinkable. The Aylish Torch has outstripped me. Kite cannot perceive him. I am contorted, unable to breathe.

"Woman, what do you see?" he barks.

The Aylishman looks at him. I feel his body shudder with disgust. "Sister Swan," he says. "Chained by your master."

This Aylishman has discovered my secret. He knows I am a Torch. I am confounded.

Suddenly, the war room fills with an engine's roar. Outside, another firefuel plane comes in to land. I fight harder to release myself, trying not to let the Aylishman see. But he stares, drinking it in, the soaring design of the wings, the light frame, the tiny mirrors to catch the sun's power, *the firefuel engine*. I struggle against him, trying to free myself. I feel like a fish in the mouth of a bird.

In a flash, I see an image of a boy, diving into a mountain lake. That's it. I have his name.

"Kingfisher." I turn on him. "Kingfisher . . ."

He loosens his grip, unnerved that I pried out his true name. He lets me go. He stands in his songlight, his Aylish eyes locked on mine, the insult of his uniform an iridescent blue. For a second, I see him fully. I pull out a whirl of images from his life, barbed wire, ravening hunger, diving into a cold lake, making love, salvation. I feel something tear inside. Has this bastard just pried the same from me?

"Zara," he whispers.

Then, in his reality, there comes a great explosion. He stumbles as his ship takes the impact. I feel a shock wave—and his songlight vanishes. The Brightling transport ship; they've fired. I fall to my knees, my breath heaving.

"He attacked you, didn't he," accuses Kite. "Their Torch saw you coming."

"We hit their ship," I say in my defense. "We've incapacitated them."

I think this will please him, but Kite is cold with fury.

"You let him beat you."

"I was distracted—"

"You brought him here. Did he see this room, our planes?"

My silence is his answer.

Kite controls his urge to hit me. He reaches for the lead band and roughly locks it to my skull.

"Useless," he says.

My humiliation is complete.

We are screaming, screaming. The battleship is going to plow through my boat and rip us into splinters. Gala save us—I can almost touch its steel side. It takes every ounce of skill and all my store of battery power to veer to one side of the monstrous prow. My boat is dancing dangerously in the furrowing waves. I throw my weight from one side to the other, trying to steady her. If they notice me, surely all they'll see is a solitary girl? I'm small fry, I'm a minnow, not worth the kill.

"Lark," says Nightingale, pointing up to their ship's rail. I see an Aylishman, staring down at me. He's walking toward the prow to get a better look, his long hair tied back. Gala, we've heard what the Aylish do to Brightling girls. . . .

I sense his low chord, studying our harmony. He has songlight.

"A Torch . . ." Nightingale can sense it too. "He wants to commune with you."

I block him out with a wall of hate. But he persists. I feel the rhythm and thrum of his songlight, like wingbeats all around me. Lying snake; he's trying to tell me that I needn't be afraid.

"Aylish bastard," I say under my breath. "You killed my pa. . . ."

I can tell that Nightingale is startled by my swear. It's interdicted for a Brightling girl to swear. A Brightling girl shouldn't even know such words. But Rye Tern taught me well.

How much can the Torch sense of Nightingale? Can he perceive her physically, as I do? Or are we a confusion of two different songs? How much does he sense of her extraordinary light? Then suddenly, the Aylishman is not alone. We see a ghostly figure on the deck behind him. A woman . . . a woman in songlight. Cropped hair. A white gown. Torch. She has the bearing of some kind of goddess and she's staring right at me.

Then the Aylishman runs at her in songlight and she vanishes from sight.

"What was *that?*" asks Nightingale, dumbfounded.

I shake my head. I turn my thoughts on putting as much distance as I can between that Aylish Torch and me. Nightingale is with me all the way, gazing into the fog ahead. I think how exhausting this must be for her. I was wiped out by sending my songlight to her in Brightlinghelm. I think of all the emotion she's expended, all the effort to support me, all that light . . .

"There's another ship," she says. She points. "Brightling men . . ."

"How can you tell?" I ask.

"Can't you hear them?" she asks. "All the voices?"

I strain my songlight but I don't hear a thing. She could hear the men in the Listening Station too.

"Do you hear everyone?" I ask.

Nightingale is puzzled. "Don't you?"

I can only sense other Torches. It's a dreadful burden for Nightingale if she can hear everyone.

BOOM.

Cannon fire sends me to the floor. I cower, hands over my ears, as something shoots over us. Half a second later, the main turbine on the Aylish ship explodes. It collapses on their bridge, burning in a ball of flame. A klaxon starts blaring. We see Aylish, rushing like ants. The Torch at the prow turns and runs toward the fire.

"The Brightling ship," says Nightingale. "It fired on them."

I can hear cries coming from the Aylish deck. A man on fire leaps into the water. Nightingale turns away.

At last the fog is lifting. My sail puffs out in the rising wind and my turbine starts to turn. Then I see it, an old Brightling transport ship, coming out of the haze, heading for the Aylish. Great welts of rust are dripping down the sides and a ragged line of soldiers is cheering on the deck, rejoicing at the sight of the burning battleship. Are these our men, Northaven's men? A cannon sparks and flares. A boom of smoke. A deafening woosh.

"Get down!" cries Nightingale.

I feel the heat as the missile soars over us. Nightingale is covering me with her songlight, as if that could protect me. . . . The missile hits the stern of the Aylish battleship. I realize, daunted, that my boat is right between these two warring vessels. Where do I go? Do I continue with my plan to run? I meant to be miles out to sea by now but the fog has disoriented me. As the mist burns off, I see familiar cliffs. My attempt to evade the Aylish battleship has taken me back north. Northaven's turbine towers are looming.

Suddenly, we're aware of something shooting through the water, coming from the Aylish ship. Torpedoes go under my boat at extraordinary speed, cutting through the water, rocking us dangerously. Seconds later, the whole lower side of the Brightling transport ship explodes. It lists immediately, a hole in the keel. Of course the Aylish would retaliate. Of course they would. Brightling men scramble on the decks, dragging the launchers into position. Will they notice me? Will they avoid my boat? From the Aylish ship, another round of torpedoes fires. This time, there's a dreadful underwater boom as the keel of the Brightling vessel is hit. The shock waves threaten to upturn my boat.

"You're right in the firing line," cries Nightingale.

I look up at our ship. But what I see grievously dismays me.

"I think the battle's over. . . ."

The rusty old transport ship is tilting to one side, fatally wounded. Men are sliding down the decks. Their comrades try to aid them. I'm still too far away to discern faces, voices, but Nightingale is there with them, feeling all their panic and their pain. I turn round to see the Aylish. Plumes of black smoke rise above their ship but they are still intact. I realize they are in retreat. Wounded, they're returning to their lair.

The transport ship is sitting lower in the water, listing dangerously now. It's going to sink, without a shadow of a doubt. Men are scrambling to lower lifeboats but they only get two in the water before the sea begins to suck down the ship. I twist my sail and use the last of my battery to kick my speed.

"I have to help them," I say. I steer my boat toward the floundering men. Nightingale grips me.

"The men in the hold," she says, her face haunted. "They can't get out. . . ."

"Come away from them, Nightingale. There's nothing you can do."

I'm stern with her. I hold her in my light, forcing her away from their pain. I wonder what it must be like to have suffering draw you like a magnet. Is that what drew her toward me? She picks up on my thoughts.

"Cassandra was teaching me how to control it. She was teaching me how to make barriers so I could protect myself. I'm getting better at it. I can try to block it out. . . ."

"I'll help you," I say. "I'm with you. We'll rescue as many as we can and then they won't be suffering."

This seems to relieve her.

Then suddenly she stiffens. "Ishbella's trying to get in my room. She's shouting at me."

"Go."

"I don't want to leave you—"

"I'll be all right."

"She's banging on my door."

"Go!"

My friend vanishes. I realize how much she has buoyed me, how her presence has helped me keep afloat. I'm alone now, in a sea of drowning men.

I power toward them. I'm close enough to hear their shouts and swears. They are clinging to the lifeboats, holding on to flotsam—or sinking. The transport ship upends itself and with a horrible sound of rushing water and breaking metal, it goes under, sucking I don't know how many men down with it. I'm glad Nightingale is spared this. I know the waters here are deep, shelving down from the coastal cliffs. I see men, like insects in a sink, eddying toward a dreadful swirling hole.

"Here!" I cry. "Here! Make for the nets!"

I throw my fishing nets into the water, thinking the men can use them to clamber in. I hold out my hand and it's grasped tight. A man almost pulls me into the sea. He lands on the floor of my boat, soaking, breathless, a face like a stoat.

"A bride," he says. "What the fuck?" He gives me an almost accusatory glance. "Are there no men left in Northaven?" He reaches into the water.

"Forbe!" he yells. And he pulls in a shaven-headed soldier.

"Syker," says Forbe as he flops into the boat. "Thank fuck. . . ."

More men are scrambling up the nets on the other side. I watch as the sea closes over the wreck.

"Here," I yell to the men in the water. "Here!"

Another survivor clambers in, bare-chested, covered in tattoos.

"Wright," cries Syker. "Where's Mikane?"

"He went down to the hold," says Wright, coughing.

"Fucking what?"

"He was looking for John Jenkins."

"Wasting his life for that shitwit Jenkins?" Syker is incredulous. "Fuck's sake!"

"Syker," says Wright, glancing at me. "There's a young lady."

I don't like being called a young lady. It makes me feel useless. "I'm a seaworker," I say. "This is my boat."

Syker doesn't seem to hear me. He's grabbing the tiller as if my boat now belongs to him.

"Hamid!" he yells. "Use the fucking net!" A man who must be Hamid scrambles in.

I'm now acutely aware of myself as a girl, as a bride. These are the men who will be our husbands. I find myself feeling small and ashamed—and I don't know why. I turn away, searching for more men—and I see a figure floating face down. I lean over the side and grab his rough shirt.

"Here," I cry. I try to pull him in and I'm horrified to see he has gauze on his face. Like Rye.

"Not that one," shouts Syker. "He's a fucking chrysalid."

I pull harder, determined to save him. Syker moves up the boat. He pries my hand off the man and kicks him back into the sea.

"He's a fucking unhuman. Save the men."

I stand, looking at Syker, shocked.

"Hamid, take the tiller," he commands. "Head for that flotsam."

Two more men heave themselves in, soaked, coughing up brine.

"Fuck!" one of them yells. "Fucking Aylish fucks!"

Syker stands in the stern. He is the captain now.

"How many more before this crate sinks?" asks Forbe.

My boat is heavy, sluggish in the water.

"Chuck this shit out," orders Syker. And all my fishing equipment goes in the sea. It's not that I mind. I know the men are more important. It's just . . .

Wright sees a man clinging to a wooden box. "There's John Jenkins!" he yells.

"Not fucking Jenkins," urges Syker. "Where's Mikane?"

Wright throws a rope to Jenkins, determined. "Mikane told me to look after Jenkins."

Jenkins clings to the rope. Hamid and Wright pull him in. Jenkins starts wailing when he gets in the boat, rocking back and forth.

"Hel. Hel. Hel. Hel." He repeats it over and over. There's something badly wrong with him.

"The commander!" yells Forbe. I look where he is pointing.

There's a huge man in the water, sinking in a greatcoat. Forbe dives straight in, bringing him to the surface.

"Get him on board!" orders Syker.

Wright and the others grab him. The boat tips dangerously as they pull their commander face down onto the deck. His head is at my feet. He looks dead. Hamid comes to his side and turns him on his back. I see that half his hair is missing and his head is gnarled with scars. This can't be the warrior from our murals.

"Mikane! Mikane!" cry his men.

Wright is pumping his chest up and down. He must have been taught this in their battlefield training but they should have him on his side—that's what you do with drowning men, you put them on their sides. Why am I so scared to speak? He might die while I am silent.

"Turn him on his side," I quietly say to Wright. "Press his back. Then the water can run out." Hamid and Wright heave the heavy man over.

"Commander, come on!"

Wright pumps his back. The commander suddenly convulses, vomiting up water at my feet. His whole body contorts as the retches go through him. He vomits again, a stinking salt mess. At last, he breathes. The scars have taken half his face. He only has one eye. Oh, Gala, the smell of his sick is churning my guts.

As the last of the fog blows away, more Northaven boats arrive. Our seaworkers take on the rescue, but, to my dismay, there are few men left alive in the water. Some are floating, faces down. The waves have taken all the rest.

Wright is praying in relief. "Thank you, Lord Thal. For saving him this day . . ."

"I don't need your prayers," cuts in Mikane. The great legend lies back, looking at the sky. He breathes, in and out. Alive.

"So," he says. "On it goes."

By the time we enter the harbor, Mikane is fit to stand, the seasoned leader wearily preparing himself. His back is to me as he takes in his childhood home.

"Northaven . . . ," I hear him say, with something like disbelief.

I suppose he hasn't seen this dump for over fifteen years. And there it is, the whole town. The citizens stand on the shore, tense and silent. Hoopoe, Wheeler, Greening, the stiff-backed eldermen, the little welcoming committee of wives and mothers, the junior cadets' marching band, the choirmaidens under their hopeful banner. Everyone looks ashen, watching the survivors.

"Look at those lush little bits," says Forbe, eyeing the choirmaidens. "They must be for us."

Did he just call us *bits*?

"We'll have two of them each by tonight." Syker grins. "Think of that, Jenkins. Two sweet girlies to warm your bed." He shoves Jenkins between the shoulders, trying to get a reaction.

"Fucking wasted on him," says Forbe.

John Jenkins is lost in his own world. He damns Hel over and over, under his breath. As if all that's left of him is his swearing.

Heron Mikane says nothing, his one remaining eye trained on the approaching coast.

The elders meet us on the quay, by a group of little children holding limp Brightland flags. The junior cadets stand ready with their tuneless band. Behind them, shopkeepers, citizens, and wives have all assembled to welcome home their men. Now they watch in silent shock as the survivors disembark. Only one of them, Wright, turns to me:

"Thank you, miss," he says.

That's when Mikane notices me. I'm crouching, my knees up by my chin.

"Huh," he growls. And he climbs out.

Another boat is coming in behind us. Mikane and his men go to the survivors. I'm left in my bedraggled wedding dress, looking at Hoopoe Guinea, Mrs. Sweeney, and my ma.

"Elsa . . ."

She pulls me into her arms. It isn't until I feel her heat that I realize how cold I am. I'm drenched in seawater, shivering with shock. Mrs. Sweeney hands Ma a blanket and she wraps it around me.

But Hoopoe has no mercy. She starts the grilling of a lifetime.

"Why on earth were you out on the sea?" she asks. "What were you doing?"

I clutch at an excuse. "I thought I'd get some scallops for the wedding feast."

"Who asked you to?"

"No one. I thought that fishing could be my special skill. . . ." This sounds dangerously feeble.

Ma leaps to my defense. "What does it matter why she went out? She saved all those men."

To my relief, Mrs. Sweeney backs her. "This girl should get the Brethren's medal," she says, touching my cheek with her rough hand. "She brought back Heron Mikane. . . ."

"I'm taking her home," says Ma, putting her arm through mine. "If you don't object."

"I most certainly object," cries Hoopoe. "Go and stand with the brides, where you belong."

"She's soaking wet," insists Ma.

"I'm fine," I say.

I'm glad of Ma's support as we walk toward the choirmaidens, but my heart is aching. Did she find the lock of hair? Does she realize I was trying to run away?

"Talk to me when you're ready," she says, her eyes full of concern.

"I'm sorry about the dress," I say meekly.

"Elsa, I don't care about the dress."

I go to stand with my fellow brides, the blanket wrapped around me. "What have you been up to?" asks Tinamou Haines, accusing me with a jealous glare.

I say nothing. I have spectacularly failed to escape.

"She went out man-hunting in her boat," Chaffinch tells everyone.

"Flaunting herself in front of our bridegrooms, before the rest of us could get a chance."

Gailee slips her hand in mine. "How did you know they were out there in the fog?" I pretend I'm shivering so much that I can't answer. "You saved them," she whispers.

That much is true. But in saving them, I have trapped myself. I should be miles from here. And now, by tonight, one of those wet, slippery men will have his hands on me.

"Which one of them is Commander Mikane?" asks Uta Malting, her eyes wide.

They watch as Syker strips off his wet shirt.

"He looks a commanding type," says Chaffinch.

I watch Mozen Tern scurrying from his tavern, giving whiskey to the surviving men. I bet he'll charge them for it later. I close my eyes, farther than ever from my Rye.

"You're freezing," says Gailee, and she puts her arms round me, embracing me with warmth.

More fishing boats arrive with a cargo of corpses. Heron and his men help unload them on the quay. I see my mother and some of the other widows tending to the dead, laying them out, giving them dignity. The Second Mrs. Aboa has found her son and her keening wail of loss is horrible to hear. The group of the bereaved grows bigger. Nela Lane runs from the choir stand, distraught. Her eldest brother, Otin, has been found. She was just a little girl when he went away to fight. To have him die so close to home . . . the cruelty is harsh.

Commander Mikane pauses in his work. He has his eye fixed on the women. I realize he's staring past Mrs. Aboa, past Nela and her family—to my mother.

He's staring at my mother as she lays out a dead sailor.

She doesn't notice him. Heron remains, gazing in stillness. Maybe he remembers her. Perhaps he's thinking of my pa.

Most of these men have served ten years. Mikane has served far longer. He can't be many years off forty. His hair, so lush and dark in all our murals, is graying at his unscarred temple.

The survivors are knocking back old Mozen's whiskey. Brute bodies, sinewy, all of them tattooed, scarred inside and out. John Jenkins . . . His mother's trying to greet him. He turns away from her and curls himself into a ball.

"So many dead," says Sambee James.

We choirmaidens have always known that marriageable veterans will be in scant supply. That's why each man gets two brides.

"There's too many of us . . . ," whispers Uta Malting.

She has voiced what we're all thinking.

Wheeler must have written books on how to be a pompous fart. I see him stepping over the corpses to greet Mikane. It's as if he can't bear to abandon his carefully rehearsed ceremony.

"Commander, this is not the welcome you deserve."

"That can't possibly be Heron Mikane," says Chaffinch, crestfallen.

The choirmaidens stare at his gray hairs and his ruined eye, unable to conceal their dismay.

Wheeler doesn't lift a finger to help with the dead. "May the Aylish die screaming for what they did to us today," he says. Is this puffball really going to choose this moment to give Mikane the Star of Thal?

The commander turns to him. There's no warmth in his face and his voice is raised. "Maybe you can tell me why our betters in Brightlinghelm ordered an ill-equipped transporter to take on an Aylish battleship?" he asks. "My men survived years of war and have died senselessly on their way home."

A hush falls over the harbor and Wheeler is taken aback. For once, he doesn't know what to say.

Greening joins them, trying to conciliate.

"Our women have prepared food for you all, Commander. And your brides are waiting to offer you consolation." He indicates us, the choir-maidens, with an ingratiating smile.

Heron looks at us in disdain. He points at the corpses.

"Their only bride is death."

His voice booms out, a man used to giving battlefield orders. The harbor falls silent. The grieving women look up at him.

"There'll be no marriages today," he cries. "Today, we bury these men."

Kite looks away, pacing in disgust, while I replace my wig. The fight with the Aylish Torch has left me flat with exhaustion. All I want to do is sink into a sleep but I force myself to stay strong.

Kite. I owe him everything. He holds my chains. I have made him what he is. He could end me with a word. The complexities of our relationship churn in me as I do my best to restore my beauty without my ladies, without a mirror. I look at my reflection in the window glass. My brilliance is diminishing, confined inside my skull. If I weren't so weary, I would weep.

But the mask is soon complete. I am once more the woman of serenity, the lovely flower of Brightland.

"Is your vanity such a distraction?" he asks.

I turn to look at him and see his lust. He desires me, even now. Or rather, he would like to punish me with sex. It took me a while to realize that Kite wants my body because my mind eludes him. So I've learned how to feed his fire. If my songlight is waning, my beauty might soon be the only power I have.

The comms officer appears. He gives Kite the news the transport ship has sunk and that Commander Mikane was on board. He has no other information.

"Peregrine must know as soon as possible," I advise Kite. "Don't let him hear the news from anybody else."

Kite grips my arm and takes me with him.

"Our Listening Station is rubble," he hisses as he walks me through the palace. "A ship carrying a national hero has sunk and an Aylish Torch now knows we've broken the First Law." Kite's voice is clipped. "I needed a victory. And you handed me defeat."

I feel my failure like ashes in my throat. *Think*, I tell myself. *Think through the exhaustion, get a plan of action. He's growing tired of you. The only thing that keeps him tied to you is sex. And that's as fragile as a spider's web.*

All my endeavors to make myself useful, to make myself loved, to be an essential feature of Peregrine's rule, to instill his ideas and bolster morale, everything I've done to ensure that I'm adored and needed and revered could be swept away with one word from Kite: Unhuman.

"Kite," I say, stopping him in the courtyard, outside Peregrine's library. "You can turn this to your advantage. . . ."

He looks at me as if I've lost my senses. But when I tell him what he should say, he nods begrudgingly.

Gala, sometimes I am brilliant.

Our Great Brother is sitting at his desk with ink-stained fingers, involved in the great task of writing down his life. I feel a vague sense of dread every time I meet him, and not just because he is all-powerful. Peregrine reminds me of my father. He has the same waves of silver hair, the same air of righteous wisdom. He rises as we approach.

"Dear Zara," he says. He is the only person who uses my childhood name and he always greets me first. I'm sure it's just good manners but it never fails to unsettle me. Today, however, I'm grateful for Peregrine's courtesy. I know he respects my tireless campaigning and my universal usefulness, but it would be a presumption to mistake his politeness for fondness or goodwill. His eyes, beneath his twinkling smile, are always steely with mistrust.

He takes us into his sanctuary, a room that feels cozy in spite of its great size. Floor-to-ceiling mahogany shelves host his collection of ancient books and artifacts. It smells of old paper, incense, pepper, and time. This is Peregrine's laboratory, where he tries to resurrect one ancient relic after another. He takes us to his worktable, an organized array of scientific instruments, magnifying glasses, and timeworn cogs.

"Look at this," he enthuses. "A science expedition returned with it, from the caves beneath the Tenmoth Zone."

He shows us his latest acquisition: an antique electrical device, once white, now yellowed, cracked with age.

"I've spent some hours trying to fathom what it's for. At first I thought it was a weapon; these blades on its base were once razor sharp. But this hydrocarbon dome protects them. I believe it might be a kitchen device. It was found surrounded by ancient glassware. My latest speculation is that it was once used for liquefying food."

"Ingenious," remarks Kite politely.

With his wrinkled eyes and silver hair, Peregrine projects humility. He once said, *It is not a leader who is great, it is his men.* Such mottoes are underneath his statues everywhere. *A Brotherhood is Stronger than a King; Woman Makes the Home. We Must Multiply to Prosper.* Most famous of all: *The Human Will Prevail.*

Enterprise Will Heal the World—that was the motto underneath Peregrine's statue in Fort Abundance, the Brightling colony where I grew up, the place where the Aylish murdered my family. My father, before they slit his throat in front of me, used to read us the wisdoms of Great Brother Peregrine every single day.

Even after all his years in power, Peregrine still beams intellectual curiosity and a warm, self-deprecating interest in others. But underneath it all, there is a ruthless core. Peregrine got here by force. And I must make no mistake: he's still an affable killer.

"The Northern Listening Station is destroyed," begins Kite.

"I know. What else?"

Peregrine moves away from his artifacts as Kite efficiently reports the day's events, briefly describing the unfortunate destruction of the transport ship.

"We dealt a significant blow to the Aylish vessel. Quite possibly destroying it."

"But our ship sank?"

"Unfortunately, yes."

"What news of Mikane?" asks Peregrine.

"None as yet."

"It was a reckless, ill-considered attack." Even without my songlight I can sense our Great Brother's wrath. This is where Kite should sink. He gave the order for our transport ship to fire, heedless of the men he put at risk. But I watch him deliver the argument I've given him.

"If our new planes had been commissioned, I could have had a swarm of them bombing that Aylish vessel within half an hour. There would have been no need to involve our ships."

Peregrine regards him with surprise. "Are you turning this into a plea for your planes?"

"We could have them protecting our coast tomorrow. That Aylish ship would have gotten nowhere near."

I feel sure that Kite is going to get what he wants. And I will be to thank. But Peregrine confounds me.

"You might as well know now," he says, holding Kite's expectant gaze. "I've made my decision on your planes. No."

Kite thinks he has misheard. "Pardon?"

"I won't commission any further development. A clear 'no' is best. We won't be investing anymore."

This comes as a bolt from the blue to Kite and to me.

"Why?" he questions, aggrieved. "You've seen the trials. The Fireflies are the innovation we've been looking for."

"I've been uneasy from the start."

"They will change the game."

"Only a fanatic would break the First Law."

This comes out of Peregrine with force. Kite gets his breath, still struggling with disbelief.

"But the engine was inspired by discoveries you made in your own laboratory."

"The First Law, Kite: *No firefuel in any of its forms.* That moratorium once saved us from extinction. I can't break it. I don't want that as my legacy, do you understand?"

"Your legacy would be victory." Kite urges his case. "Great Brother, we have an advantage and we must press it home. Let me arm the planes. We're already training pilots. We could strike at Reem within a month."

Kite should hide his ambition better. Peregrine runs his finger over an old flat keyboard machine, a mysterious meld of rust and plastic. They have been dug up in the thousands and their use? Unknown.

"If we revive illicit technology, so too will Ayland. If we attack them with firefuel, they will retaliate—and on the slaughter goes."

Kite needs to stop speaking now. There is a way around this. He needs to be cleverer. We need to retrench. I touch his arm—but he is plowing on:

"We could destroy Reem. We could raze their capital to the ground."

"Kite," says Peregrine, with weary patience. "What if this war of attrition cannot be won?"

I'm shocked. Peregrine has voiced something unthinkable: a doubt. I feel it jolt Kite like an electric shock. He must retreat and think. He mustn't say another—

"Voiced by anyone else," says Kite, his eyes blazing, "that would be treason."

Peregrine exhales. The silence is full of shifting power. I take a step forward, trying to catch Peregrine's eye, as if to say, "Kite doesn't mean it. He's just angry at the losses of the day. He feels responsibility as your strategist in chief. He feels the weight of Brightland's victory pressing down on him."

But the two men are locked on one another. I am an irrelevance, a decoration.

"Have I heard you correctly, Great Brother?" asks Kite. "Are you saying that you think we will lose?"

"I'm saying," explains Peregrine with deadly patience, "it is possible that neither side can win."

I press a hand of warning on Kite's arm, but he shrugs me off like an irritating gnat. He's determined to play his losing card.

"Firefuel will give us everything we dreamed of fifteen years ago. Ground our planes and you ground our hope."

Anger glows in Peregrine.

"Dear Brothers," I cut in. "It pains me to see my favorite men at odds." I try to make light of it, a lovely vapid flower.

"Forgive us, Zara," says the courteous Peregrine. "Perhaps I've not been clear enough." He pierces Kite with eyes as terrifying as my father's. "I've done many ruthless things in the name of our country. I've returned the human to his rightful place. I've given man his freedom and ascendancy. The cost has been great—and I've never faltered. But this crosses a line. Our forebears poisoned our globe because of firefuel. Forests burned, deserts grew. Men starved and fought. We died to the point of extinction. The First Law saved us and I will not break it. We have evolved, Kite."

Kite finally perceives that he has pushed too far.

"Thank you, Great Brother. I cherish your wisdom, as always."

"Our gliders and airships are second to none. Perhaps with better strategy, they'll win."

With this dig at his strategist in chief, Peregrine kisses my hand. It's the sign that we're dismissed.

Kite walks fast, ignoring me. I put my arm through his, trying to console him.

"It's a setback. We have to—" I begin.

"I don't want to hear a word. You're a failure."

Again, he's blaming me. All the fault is mine. I feel another wave of fatigue. My cortex is thumping and I must sleep soon. I try to find my clarity. Advice. He needs advice.

"You can fight this in the council," I tell him as he pulls me down the ladies' corridor. "I'll help you. Let me use my powers; I can influence Peregrine's favorites."

Why did I say that? Why did I imply that Kite is not a favorite? His hand grips my arm so tight that I know it will be encircled with a welt.

"Let me go to Peregrine tomorrow," I plead. "Let me talk to him."

"You've done enough damage, unhuman." Kite is full of scorn. "You let that Aylish Torch beat you. You were weak. Because of you, they know about my planes. Because of you, we've lost all element of surprise."

"My songlight would be stronger if you let me use it freely," I retort.

"So you can try your influence on me?"

I cry out in frustration: "What must I do to prove my loyalty to you?" We're at my rooms. He puts me inside. He's going to leave.

"Come in with me," I entreat. "Let me calm you. This is just a setback, Niccolas. . . ."

Fool. Never use his name. *Never let him see your desperation.*

His lips are a thin line, drawn across his teeth. "I knew, when I was an Inquisitor, that Sirens don't last long. Songlight burns brightest in the young. . . ." He comes closer. "Never forget how my last Flower lost her crown."

I swallow.

"Let me down again and you will share her fate."

He leaves.

In my white and lonely rooms, my hated ladies are standing blankly, gauze over their faces, waiting for an order. How these creatures haunt me.

"Get out of my sight!"

I throw whatever is at hand. My wig brush hits Lady Orion. She hardly reacts. She picks the brush up, walks toward me, and silently replaces it. The chrysalids retreat, their spirits crushed, their songlight dead.

Mikane and his men work tirelessly, digging graves in our cemetery up by the turbine towers. The women of the town enshroud the dead. Instead of wedding hymns, we choirmaidens sing a searing funeral dirge.

The sun is setting as the drowned are laid to rest. Some are strangers to our town—the crew of the ship was from all over Brightland—but many are grieved by mothers, fathers, sisters, friends. Nela doesn't stand with us; she's sobbing with her ma. Sergeant Redshank knew many of the dead as boys and he stands, bowed with timeworn grief. Year after year, he sends them off to war. How many of the boys he trained are rotting underground? As we sing, our faces are all wet with tears. We're such a backwater here. The war is something that happens far away. The events of the day have brought it home.

My thoughts fall silent as Commander Mikane addresses the town.

"We soldiers all know Death," he booms. "Death has long been our companion. She comes to take our comrades and our foes. We hear her, we feel her—Dame Slaughter. We soldiers feed her with our exploits. She comes in our dreams at night, reminding us what we did by day. Hers is the blast of blood hitting our faces; hers, the taste of another man's gore. Death shows us her power. Today, we have brought her to Northaven."

Wheeler meets Greening's shocked eyes. This is not the speech they want.

Mikane continues: "We all play a waiting game with Death. How will she strike? Who will she take? What other convulsions will she put us through before we join her in a winding sheet?"

I look at Mikane's men. Wright would follow him anywhere. Jenkins is shuddering, his eyes on the graves. Syker looks uncomfortable, his stoaty face in a grimace.

"Death's taken my eye and half my face. She's marked me as her own. . . ." Mikane points to the graves. "Now these men lie in her marriage bed. More lie at the bottom of the sea." He stops, his shoulders heaving. "A transport ship is not made for battles, as our leaders have just proven."

He's not holding anything back. His words fall like snow, melting into us with cold truth.

"Once again, the mistakes of generals, with their orders from afar, are filling a mass grave with Brightling flesh."

Wheeler steps in. Clearly he thinks this cannot go on.

"They died as heroes, fighting for Thal," he cries. "They died for Brightland, and for Glory!"

These platitudes are empty. Mikane looks aggrieved, as if he can't bear to hear them.

"Glory will not bring them back. The best we can do is to respect them with our silence."

Wheeler stops. To say another word would be an insult to the dead. Silence falls. No one moves. Death blows around us on the breeze, feasting, caressing us. Maybe Jenkins senses it because he collapses on top of a grave, hugging the soil, distressed.

Syker is furious.

"Get up, you mad bastard," he hisses.

"Leave him be," orders Mikane.

"That grave should be his," cries Syker in frustration.

Mikane's eye glints. "Just be thankful it's not yours."

Mikane goes to Jenkins. He lifts him.

"You're home now, John," he says gently. "There'll be no more death today."

Mikane walks with Jenkins onto the headland, away from the town.

When he's out of earshot, Wheeler takes charge.

"May Thal, god of war and invention, take them into his hallowed halls, where they will be heroes forever."

He drones on for a while about how great it is to be dead. I'm not listening anymore.

Gailee and I walk back to town, arm in arm. Sambee James comes to our side. She's one of the youngest choirmaidens.

"Have you done the sums?" she asks.

"What are you talking about?" I reply.

"There's only nine bridegrooms left," she says. "There's twenty-six of us. Work it out."

"I've been thinking about it the whole while," says Gailee. "Some of us will be Third Wives."

Immediately, I know that this will be my fate.

Hoopoe calls an informal gathering in the Elders' Hall, for us choirmaidens and our mothers. Chaffinch sits with her pouting ma, who wears a sleek funereal dress. Gailee's nearby, gripping her mother's small, careworn hand. Ma is by my side, waiting to hear what Hoopoe has to say. Nela and her ma sit looking numb with loss.

"As you know," begins Hoopoe, "when there's an excess of young women, the Brethren need your service in a different way. . . ."

She takes a deep breath. As if this is difficult to sell.

"It's an honor to be a Third Wife. Those of you not chosen for First or Second will leave for Brightlinghelm, where you'll aid our great nation by comforting our troops."

There's a silence. There have never been any Third Wives taken from Northaven.

"In Pink Houses?" I ask, seeing as no one else is speaking.

"Yes, Elsa, Third Wives are votaries of Thal and they reside in Pink Houses. They receive medals of service from the Brethren."

Uta Malting's mother looks thunderously angry.

"I won't have that for my child," she declares.

Mrs. Greening turns on her, knowing that Chaffinch, as an elderman's daughter, is safe. "Refusing an edict is treason, as you know."

There are hushed mutterings of discontent. Hoopoe tries for calm.

"Ladies, please, in this time of war, Third Wives are married to

Brightland. The Brethren take good care of you. You'll have better rations, finer clothes—"

"What about babies?" interjects Sambee. "If we have babies, what becomes of them?"

Hoopoe looks uncomfortable. There's no way to sweeten this pill.

"The Brethren have decided not to burden Third Wives with motherhood. . . ."

Uta's mother leaps on this. "So it's true? A Third Wife has her womb cut out?"

This causes consternation among the choirmaidens. Hoopoe start to lose her patience.

"No one wants this situation," she cries. "It's a result of the tragic events of today."

Mrs. Greening slices through her words with a loud cry: "It's Ayland's fault; the evil, mind-twisting Aylish! They have taken the lives of too many men. Death to the Aylish!"

Like well-trained parrots, everyone joins in—"Death to the Aylish! Death to the Aylish!"—turning their fear and fury on our hated enemy. By doing so, they're forgetting, even absolving, those who would cut out our wombs.

"We must do our duty," cries Hoopoe, buoyed up on this patriotic wave, "until this war is won."

As the meeting ends, Hoopoe and the elderwomen gather around a table. The matchmakers. They'll be deciding which nine girls are going to be the lucky First Wives. The rest of us will be in the pool to be chosen by the men as their Second Wife, showing off our special skills. Gailee is quiet and drawn. She seems to have lost hope. Her mother looks as if her small frame can't take another blow. Nela is crying as she leaves. Even Tinamou Haines looks full of dread.

Ma tells me to wait outside in the square. Instantly, I know she's going to plead on my behalf.

"No," I say. But she insists.

I stay in the shadows by the door. I watch as she approaches Hoopoe. Hoopoe is at a refreshment table, making herself a calming herbal tea. Ma brings a small carving out of her bag. It's an owl.

"A wise bird for a wise woman. . . ."

Hoopoe immediately knows it's a bribe. "It's lovely. But you know I can't take it."

"My husband gave his life for Brightland," begins Ma, "and you can see his spirit in Elsa. She's strong and hardworking. She'd make a wonderful First Wife."

I'm dismayed to see pity in Hoopoe's eyes. "Curl . . ." She leans in confidentially. "I like Elsa. She's clever and full of fire. But the Brethren state that the five wifely qualities to be rewarded are beauty, obedience, modesty, thriftiness, and grace. Elsa is . . . unruly."

"She's passionate. What man doesn't like some passion?"

Mrs. Greening has walked over. "A most desired quality in a Third Wife," she says, pouring herself a glass of water. "I'm sure Elsa will do very well."

Ma bites her tongue as Mrs. Greening goes back to her seat.

"How can you be part of this?" she hisses to Hoopoe. "Sending our children to be army whores? If we all stood together, Wheeler couldn't take them."

Hoopoe glances over at Mrs. Greening. She gives Ma a warning. "Some people would call that seditious, Curl."

Ma takes stock and holds back her reply. She leaves. I sneak out after her and put my arm through hers, grateful that she tried.

I go to bed as soon as I can, leaving Ma to resurrect my dress. But as soon as my head hits the pillow, my mind starts racing and I lie restlessly. My gut claws with an ache for Rye. I send my songlight out to him and feel an empty loneliness I cannot bear. How expendable men are. How easily they die. Images of the day crowd in. The sea swallowing the transport ship; the gauzed man drowning; the Aylish Torch, his songlight like feathers beating round my mind; the soldiers in my boat, the harshness of their swears; Mikane puking at my feet; John Jenkins, frightened of his ma. And Nightingale . . . her small, bright presence in my boat giving me strength, feeling things so keenly. Precious bird, Nightingale.

Perhaps she hears me because the next thing I know, she's lying next to me, the merest hint of her, in faintest songlight, like she's very far away. There are shadows under her eyes.

"Are you all right?" I ask her.

"When my songlight burns bright, it makes me so tired. . . ."

"Thank you," I say. "For being with me."

"I was scared you'd die in the sea."

I smile at her then. "I'm harder to get rid of than you think."

She smiles back and fades into sleep. I cannot trouble her with what tomorrow brings.

I watch Ma through the crack in my bedroom door, cleaning my wedding dress, setting it by the stove to dry, then praying, a candle lit at her shrine to Gala.

16 ✴

I walk at the rear of the bridal procession, next to Gailee. She has made every effort with her appearance. Every ringlet is set rigidly in place, her face a mask of makeup. She looks like a brightly colored doll. We each hold a posy of lilies in our hands as symbols of our purity.

The cadets accompany us with pipes and drums, leading us past the townsfolk, who have all come out to watch. The junior choirmaidens, who now process behind us, acting as our flower girls, will be the next to go. Maybe the war will be over by then. Maybe dogs might fly.

Chaffinch and Tinamou are up at the front, undaunted by yesterday's events. They have lived for this day for years and nothing's going to spoil their glow. Death? That was yesterday. Today is for life.

There's another transport ship in the bay. I see Wheeler walking up to the town square with two more Emissaries. They're not just here to pick over yesterday's events. They've come to take the Third Wives.

As we reach the town square, we see the soldiers waiting. Our bridegrooms. Nine of them, twenty-six of us. They've made an effort to clean themselves up but most of their kit has gone in the sea. They're dressed in borrowed shirts and whatever they have left. Heron Mikane is wearing his damp greatcoat. His arm is on John Jenkins, who is staring at the ground. Perhaps he's trying to stop poor John from running for the hills. Syker and Forbe are looking us over, like we're already naked. By tonight, each of these men will have a house and two wives. And the rest of us . . . Don't think.

Wheeler approaches Mikane and makes his puffed-up speech, delayed from yesterday, determined not to be robbed of his moment. I, Leland Wheeler, am ordained by Great Brother Peregrine to blah, blah highest honor in Brightland, blah, blah, courage and valor, blah, blah, I decorate you bollocks. He pins the Star of Thal on Mikane's sea-soaked greatcoat.

Mikane is inscrutable as Wheeler asks him if he'd like to speak. The town is silent in anticipation.

"I thank Great Brother Peregrine for this honor." He takes the medal off his chest and holds it aloft.

"I dedicate this medal to the dead."

He puts it in his pocket without another word.

Wheeler, somewhat peeved, walks into the center of the square. "Here in the sight of Thal," he announces, with all the solemnity of a man with a broom stuck up his arse, "let this wedding day begin."

We sing our anthem as we lead the way into the Elders' Hall.

"Welcome home, our brave and valiant men
I sing my joy as you return again.
For ten long years, you've fought to make us free
And now in thanks, I give myself to thee. . . ."

The soldiers follow us. Then Emissaries, eldermen, and townspeople. The hall is soon packed. Sun pours through the high windows as we take our places. I feel each note of the joyful tune diminishing me further. The soldiers stand opposite. Between us—underneath the mural of Mikane, hero of Montsan—are benches where, by the end of the ceremony, the married triples will sit.

Hoopoe Guinea is nervously in charge, looking at her list of family emblems. Emissary Wheeler is standing sternly at her side, preparing to give her the name of each surviving soldier. Anxious parents look on. I'm worried that Ma won't have found her way in and my eyes scan the crowd. At last I see her, squeezing in at the back next to Mrs. Sweeney. I should have eaten something. I couldn't get anything down first thing and now I am lightheaded.

"Marcus Wright," begins Wheeler. And Wright steps into the center. I can almost smell his cologne from here.

I know I'm not on Hoopoe's list. There's no way I'll be a First Wife. I'm the least deserving here. I'll be in the mix for Second, when girls have to perform, to show off their special skills. And I have no special skill. I'm going to be taken by those Emissaries and put on that transport ship. Beyond that, I know nothing. I can sense Gailee's heart thumping next to me. I find her hand and squeeze it. I will not think about her fate.

I find myself rising up instinctively. I'm trying to reach Nightingale. And then I realize what I'm doing and draw myself back down. There's no escape in mind or body from what will happen here.

They say that a frog will jump out of a pan of boiling water, but if you start with the water cold and heat it slowly, the frog won't save himself. He'll stay in there until he boils. We've been in our pan since we started marriage training.

It feels like another trick the Brethren are playing on our town, like the shaming of Rye, where we were told we must accept a senseless, cruel, abhorrent thing—and everybody did—like we were under an enchantment. Today, we sit in front of our whole town, being slowly boiled to death.

I close my eyes and see Rye so clearly, standing under my window in our garden, raw from fighting with his pa.

Come to the beach. Let's be together.

I lose myself in the memory. I climb out of the window and jump. He catches me in his arms. I cling to him. I go with him. We love each other on that beach, Rye Tern and I.

I'm dimly aware that I'm supposed to be singing. By the time I open my eyes, six men have their First Wives. Six wedding bands have been clamped on six wrists. Six brides sit by six strangers. It's happening so fast—as though they have to do this before anyone can yell for it to stop.

Hoopoe prepares for the next couple. "Gyles Syker . . ."

Syker stands, hair slicked back. He walks to the center of the hall, full of himself, his eyes wandering over our breasts, a man who doesn't doubt his sturdy appeal. Hoopoe continues:

"It's our privilege to give you, as a gift to cherish, your First Wife, Tina-mou Haines. . . ."

I hear Tinamou exhale, as if her breath has been held for the whole ser-vice. Is it relief she feels? Syker eyes her in carnal anticipation as she walks toward him. We choirmaidens sing our harmony, calling on Gala to bless them with fertility. As we sing, Syker snaps a wedding band on Tinamou's wrist and kisses her proprietorially. She flushes with excitement. They sit with the other couples under the mural of Brightland's greatest son.

"John Jenkins . . . ," calls Hoopoe.

Jenkins doesn't move. He's muttering.

"Hel. Hel. Hel. Hel . . ."

Mikane helps him to his feet. They pass close by me and I see Mikane's melted ear.

"Here, John," says Mikane in a low voice. "The Brethren, in their wis-dom, say you must be wed." Mikane leaves Jenkins in place. And Hoopoe continues.

"John Jenkins, it's our privilege to give you, as a gift to cherish, your First Wife . . ." Hoopoe consults her list, making sure she's got it right. "Nela Lane."

Nela looks at her ma in a confusion of relief and dread. Her ma urges her on. We sing about the joy of making babies as she goes to Jenkins. I see the bewilderment on her face. She's marrying a man who's clearly lost his mind. Hoopoe helps Jenkins snap the wedding band on Nela's wrist.

"Hel," says Jenkins.

Syker lets out a hysterical laugh. Nela turns red with shame. Her angry mother looks at Hoopoe Guinea. Hoopoe directs us to sing and we lift our voices, drowning out John Jenkins's ungovernable swears.

Suddenly, I sense a flash of songlight in him, jangling, discordant, atonal. As the music lifts, he listens. His swearing falls silent. His eyes meet mine and I know beyond a shadow of doubt that Jenkins is a Torch, a broken Torch. I'm filled with apprehension. Can he sense me? I smother my songlight and close my eyes. When I open them, Jenkins is looking at the windows, lost in the music. Is our singing helping him get his wisps of discordant songlight under control? As it disappears, his low, desperate mutter begins again. "Hel, hel, hel . . ." I am filled with pity. My heart is hammering.

There's only one man left.

"Commander Heron Mikane . . ."

We all watch as Mikane walks into place. The mural of his youth and beauty mocks him from behind.

"Hero of Montsan, pride of Northaven, it's our privilege to give you, as a gift to cherish, your First Wife . . ."

Why is she pausing? We all know it's Chaffinch Greening.

"Chaffinch Greening."

Chaffinch smiles, trying to look delighted, as she's been trained. But her smile turns more and more frozen as she walks toward her husband as if she'd rather be marrying the mural. Mikane glares angrily at Wheeler as he puts on the wedding band. He doesn't look at Chaffinch. They sit.

In front of me, Uta Malting starts to panic. She hasn't been chosen and she's horrified. Her father is an elderman, our baker. Surely she should have been on the list? Gailee's hand sweats in mine. Her head is bent. She knew that this was coming.

"Choirmaidens," instructs Hoopoe, "please take your seats."

We obey her as one. Hoopoe's voice is calm and measured as she addresses the bridegrooms.

"A First Wife is gifted for the service you've done. Your Second Wife is yours to choose. Each remaining girl will now share her special skill."

"Those not chosen," rasps Wheeler, "will have the honor of serving our army as Third Wives."

There is consternation among the girls. My teeth are clenched as I prepare myself. Uta starts quietly weeping with fear.

"We'll start with Gailee Robers," says Hoopoe in a jaunty tone. "Her special skill is traditional singing. . . ."

They have put Gailee first. That's so cruel. I can almost hear her heart, fluttering with terror. She stands—and I stand with her.

"Elsa Crane, sit down," barks Hoopoe.

I stare at her in protest.

"Sit down until your name is called."

"I have no special skill!" It comes out of me as a shout. I look at Gailee. She's shaking her head, silently begging me to sit. But it's too late. I have already jumped out of the pan. I walk away from the newlyweds and push my way through the crowd toward the door. It is the hardest thing I've ever done. Ma rises to her feet as I exit.

I cross the square, not knowing where I am going or what's coming next. Any second those Emissaries will catch up with me and bring me down into the dust for daring to protest. But at least they know; they know that one of us objects. I turn, waiting for Wheeler and his henchmen.

But nobody comes out. I hear Gailee's shaky voice begin to sing.

Crestfallen, I realize my own insignificance. They don't think me worthy of pursuit. The remainder of the ceremony is of greater interest than me. They can punish me later, when all the fun has been had. A horrible feeling of shame consumes me. My protest is trifling. I find myself climbing the branches of a nearby tree.

"What are you doing, Elsa?"

Only Ma has followed me out. I see her down below and her expression guts me.

"Some of us'll be Third Wife," I say. "I can cope with that life. Others can't."

"Please, try to be chosen. . . ." She is almost in tears.

"Gailee won't survive it, Ma. It'll kill her."

Ma stares at me, holding my gaze. A resolve seems to form in her, and, to my surprise, she climbs the tree. She climbs it like a Greensward girl, straddling a branch nearby. She looks me in the eye.

"If you want to run, I'm with you."

I couldn't be more amazed. "What d'you mean?"

"Your pa's dead and Piper's gone. I've tried to fit in this town but I don't. And I won't let them take you for Third Wife."

Her eyes are on fire. Was she planning this as she prayed to Gala during the night? I feel a rolling blue wave of love for my mother. The tightness in my chest eases. Ma means it.

"There's cloud coming in over the moors. We can pass the sentries in the dark," she says. We grasp each other, conspirators. "Go and pack what you need," she instructs. "I'll tell them you're sick."

"Curl," I say, using her name. "If they catch us, they'll hang us."

Ma nods. We both understand. The risk, the real likelihood of death is best left unspoken. She climbs down the tree with feline grace and goes back into the hall.

I look down over Northaven. I take in the turbines and their unending toil, the boats, our houses in their hopeful colors, the light dancing on the sea. I imprint it on my core, bidding it farewell.

I listen to the efforts coming from the hall. Uta Malting is playing her violka now. She must be nervous. She's a good player, but today, her bow scrapes the strings. I cringe for her.

I'm crossing the square when someone else walks out: Heron Mikane.

How dare he leave.

I watch him as he rolls a smoke. He represents the only hope my sisters have. To be performing and he leaves? Their humiliation is complete.

"My sisters are singing for their lives in there."

I say it loudly but he doesn't look at me. His eyes are on the sea as he lights his smoke.

"I've heard enough," he states, exhaling a tobacco ring.

We're nothing to him, we choirmaidens. We're an irritation, mayflies to be swept away. I'm going to make this bastard look at me.

"Why did you fry your face?" I ask. Mikane slowly turns. "I heard men chop their own feet off so they don't have to fight. A bit of frying oil would do the trick."

I have his attention now. He draws on his smoke, regarding me.

"You know a lot about it," he says.

"You'd be crab food if it wasn't for my boat," I tell him. "And we're invisible to you, all of us."

He nods slowly in agreement.

"Have you chosen your Second Wife?"

"No."

"Choose Gailee Roberts. She's gentle and she's not a whore."

"What about you," he asks. "Are you a whore?"

"I'd rather run off a cliff than marry one of you."

Mikane takes the insult. He steps toward me, glowering. I've poked the old wolf and now he will pounce.

Hoopoe Guinea comes out, nervous. "Commander?" she enquires.

"I'm weary," he replies. "My men are weary." There's a finality in his voice.

"You could view the Second Wives tomorrow?" placates Hoopoe. "I'm sure Emissary Wheeler would allow a day's grace."

"Has John Jenkins made his choice?"

"No. May I suggest—"

"He chooses Gailee Roberts."

I look at him, surprised. So does Hoopoe.

"Gailee Roberts, yes, of course. . . . And you, Commander? Have none of our choirmaidens caught your eye?"

Heron glints at her. "My *eye*?"

"I beg your pardon—captured your interest? We'll reconvene tomorrow."

"No need," says Mikane. "I'll take that one."

He points right at me.

"You can send my wives up to the house."

He turns on his heel and walks away, leaving us both staring.

PART 3

As my ladies dress me in an evening gown, I see that Lady Scorpio is standing close by. I tread hard on her foot as I pass.

"Bitch," I say.

She shuffles her weight and keeps staring ahead. If these creatures reacted, I wouldn't be so cruel, but they just stand there, watching me. I hate Lady Scorpio with every atom of my being. Of course, she doesn't hate me back. She's not jealous, obsequious, contemptuous, or loyal. She'll never feel dread or lust again. She has no attitude, outlook, taste, or opinions. She's there only to obey.

Like all my ladies, she was a gift from Kite. These gifts are here as a warning. Lady Scorpio once had a different name. Before I appeared, she was Kite's lover, his secret Torch. Now her purpose is to be my constant threat. *Let me down again and you will share her fate. . . .* Sometimes I catch Kite looking at her, through her gauzy veil, trying to gauge if there's expression in her eyes. But the woman who she used to be is dead. I wonder if he misses her.

No. He is not capable of love. And I am. Inside my burning heart, I know that there is love, because this loneliness is consuming me. Kite makes sure I cannot see beyond him. He makes sure he is the only thing that matters. He is a cancer, eating me.

I have spent hours on my appearance, in case I should run into him. Everything is plucked, scented, styled, shaded, oiled. I have changed my nail color seven times. I have chosen my gown with care, opting for white layers of tulle that make me look insouciant. My lipstick is a shade that Third Wives use. I think they call it *Ready for Bed*. I leave my chamber for my radiobine address. My ladies trail behind me like a white, vaporous mist.

Kite.

My survival has depended on him since I was sixteen. As I make my way through the half-deserted corridors, I remember the moment I first met him. He was still an Inquisitor back then. His face was so smooth, so startlingly neat. I knelt before him in Fort Abundance, cold, wet, bedraggled.

The Aylish had attacked us by surprise. It was a massacre.

My father, an elderman, had his throat cut in the street and my mother and sisters drowned trying to escape by sea. I alone survived. Kite found me, hiding in an underground water tank. I cowered in my white petticoat, shivering like a half-drowned cat.

"You're Elderman Swan's daughter, aren't you?"

"Yes, sir."

"Zara . . ."

Kite took me to his quarters. He wrapped me in a blanket and warmed me by his fire. He gave me food. At first I thought that he was kind, a kind, handsome hero. Then I felt his cold fingers on my face. He turned me to look at him.

"Why were you down in that water tank?" he asked.

"I . . . I heard the Aylish coming. And I hid."

"I want you to stop lying, Zara."

At that moment, I realized he knew.

"Tell me why you were in the water tank."

"My father . . ."

"Your father what?"

I said nothing, too terrified to speak.

"He locked you in there, didn't he?"

"He . . . No . . ."

"Don't lie to me." Kite abruptly let me go. "I received a telegram from Elderman Swan, two days ago. Shall I read it to you?"

He drew a neatly folded paper out of his pocket and read my father's note:

"'*Tragedy has struck. My eldest, Zara, is unhuman. She must be removed without delay. I am keeping the girl in a water tank, underground, where I believe that her songlight can do no harm. If she should drown, I hope it will be swift. It will spare her from the fate that all unhumans must endure. I believe in the quest for a pure human race. And I curse the egg that engendered such a miscreant. Awaiting your swift arrival, William Swan.'"*

Kite saw my consternation. And I swear he smiled.

My father discovered I was unhuman when I poured myself into my little sister's ordinary human mind and planted an urge to say bad words there. I got her into dreadful trouble and thought it a fine joke. But when my sister saw me laughing, she pieced together what I'd done and went straight to my father. He was ashen, I remember that, as all his love for me seeped away. He called me an evil influencer, a mind-twister. His rejection was sudden and complete. I was sixteen. I hardly knew what my songlight was or how to use it.

I tried to defend myself in front of Kite but my words were all inadequate. His questions kept coming until all I was clinging to was a tattered plea for mercy. Yes, I had invaded my sister's mind. Yes, I could sense the thoughts of others.

"Can you sense my thoughts?" asked Kite. "What am I seeing?"

I tried. But all I could see was a dark pool. I told him so.

"Interesting," said Kite. "That dark pool is the mental image I use to prevent unhumans reading me. It's rare," he continued, "for a Torch to be able to read and influence human minds. Songlight, in general, can only connect with other songlight. We may call you mind-twisters, but, in truth, few have the skill. You are most unusual."

I didn't know what to say to this.

"You know what happens to unhumans, don't you?

I fell to my knees, begging him to spare me. I was sobbing, crying.

"Tears are nothing but a noxious irritation."

The blanket that covered me had fallen to the ground, and I noticed the way he looked up and down my body. At once, I saw a way to survive. I promised him my loyalty, my nakedness, anything, if he would spare my life.

Kite pulled me to my feet. "Stop crying."

It was an order formed in ice. I forced myself to stop. I made a dark pool of my own and submerged all my distress. Once more, I felt Kite's fingers manipulate my face.

"Quite a little beauty."

Those are the words that changed my life. Sometimes I wonder what my fate would have been if my features hadn't pleased him.

"Maybe there's a use for you," he said.

Kite took my body then and there. No one knew. No one helped me afterward. This was my new reality. Kite had spared me. He was saving me. I was now his. How could I object to what he did?

The next morning, Kite had me walk a line of Aylish prisoners. I had to nod at any who were Torches. It wasn't hard to find one. My diligence seemed to impress Kite. That night, after he had taken me again, he took scissors to my hair and cut it all off. He put a band of lead around my skull, so tight I thought my eyes would burst.

"You'll get used to it," he said.

I never have. I chafe under it still. That hated metal, shackling my spirit. I think the lead will slowly poison me.

Kite gave me a white mourning veil to cover my cropped scalp, to hide my Siren status. On the voyage back to Brightlinghelm, the crew treated me with tenderness, as one touched by tragedy. They knew nothing of my songlight. To them, I was the sole survivor of a dreadful massacre. My losses gave me a special standing. They called me "little flower." Kite noticed how my presence inspired their valiant behavior.

When we returned to Brightlinghelm, Kite brought me an expensive wig and a choirmaiden's dress. He put me before Great Brother Peregrine and told me to describe the attack on Fort Abundance. But Peregrine's resemblance to my father undid me. At first, I couldn't meet his eye; I couldn't find the words. But this mighty man showed patience. He made me feel at ease. Soon I was telling him all about my family, my loss. I described, vividly, what I witnessed from the low grille in the water tank: how the Aylish had blown up our walls and ridden in, savages on horses. Kite had already taught me that crying was an irritant, so all the grief I had came tearlessly out of my dark pool.

"We should get her to speak in front of the people," said Peregrine, hatching my future. "Her looks have a kind of radiance. Her resilience has dignity. When people hear her tragedy, it would remove any doubts they might have about the war."

Peregrine smiled at me then, with his deadly, twinkling eyes, not knowing what I was. "I want you to be useful to our cause, my dear," he said.

And I have been, ever since. I have carved myself a position of respect. I am the only woman on the Council of Brethren. My position there is decorative, of course—I'm there to ensure gallant behavior and a standard of manners—but my presence matters. Kite releases me from the lead cuff whenever he wants information from a rival, or he needs me to plant an opinion in a tractable head. We choose our victims carefully. Men already corrupt are most open to my influence. I take every precaution not to be discovered. And with me at his side, Kite has risen. His ambition still soars.

If my powers wane, he'll replace me—because nothing will stop him getting what he wants. He wants to be Peregrine's heir and he'll do anything it takes. I know he's going to the Chrysalid House, observing the arrivals, waiting for the right beauty with the right skills. Eventually, he'll find her, then he'll strike. And I will be like Lady Scorpio.

I have carefully planned my radiobine address. I sit behind the huge arachnid-like microphone in the wood-paneled chamber and begin.

"The Light People thought it nothing to cross the globe by air. They crossed continents and oceans; they went to the bright moon and farther than the planet Mars. . . . We live with the mistakes they made: the deserts and the storms that they unleashed on us, the irradiated zones, where we may never safely go. They burned so much firefuel, they lit the whole planet up at night. But in their genius, they took us to the stars. . . ." I talk about flight for a full half hour.

When it's done, I set out upon my mission. My task this evening involves no songlight. How can it? The Siren's band is locked beneath my wig.

I arrive outside our Great Brother's rooms, my ladies around me like a halo of white. Peregrine's guards tell me to wait. I have never visited him alone. He may refuse to see me.

A moment later, a man walks out. Brother Harrier, man of the people, Kite's chief rival. He walks with a cane from an old war wound and he's grinning at me through his beard.

"Swan?" He doesn't call me "Sister" like everybody else.

"Good evening, Brother."

I've never attempted to twist Harrier's mind. He isn't politic like the rest of them. He says exactly what he thinks and he doesn't care who hears it. If I had freedom, I'd find him powerfully attractive, but I never allow myself such dangerous thoughts. I drown them all in my dark pool.

"I liked your radiobine address." He grins. "A clever bedtime story, condemning firefuel, yet making us all yearn for an age of flight."

"I'm glad you enjoyed it, Brother."

He leans back, surveying me. "I wish you'd come into the city with me, Swan."

Why's he suggesting this? What does he want?

"I'm often in the city," I coolly reply.

"Not with any freedom. Your time's arranged to the last second."

That much is true. Each day is filled with functions and appearances. I'm escorted through a carefully orchestrated series of events, meeting widows, choirmaidens, veterans, Inquisitors, cadets, matchmakers, eldermen, little children, anyone who might benefit from my tireless crusade.

"I'd like to see you walk in freedom through the market and the streets." His eyes are so piercing, cornered with laugh lines.

"What on earth for?" I ask him, bemused.

"To talk to people, to see how they live. People feel close to you. They love you because of the radiobine. Do you realize the influence you have? You could use it for some good."

"I use my influence in the best cause possible: the triumph of Brightland."

This man is making the ground slide beneath me.

"Our Brethren are caught up with winning the war," he says. "But I worry we're neglecting people's basic needs. They see you as their ally. You should come with me, into the city. We could effect some positive change."

"My agenda's quite full."

"Kite's agenda," he states, his keen eyes boring into me.

He steps far too close, his untidy hair and bearlike look only making him more sensual.

"Kite would be nothing and nowhere without you."

Harrier breathes me in. Then he walks on, leaving me turned upside down.

When I am finally shown in, I leave my ladies at the door. I am taken aback to be led right into Peregrine's private bathroom. I can see immediately that everything here is reproduced from the Light People time. An enamel suite was found quite recently, perfectly preserved, in one of the Peat Bog Houses on Gabarus Moor. It was stained a remarkable shade of green and it has led to quite a fashion in the palace for installing flushing toilets and deep enamel baths.

"Forgive me, Zara. My back is troubling me. This is the only thing that gives it ease."

He's up to his waist in milky foam, grinning like a crocodile. He's trying to unsettle me with a camaraderie I cannot trust. I thank Gala for the bubbles.

"I'm sorry to hear our Great Brother is in pain," I say in my most caring tone.

"I've just had Harrier in here, cracking my spine like a bone doctor."

I squirrel this fact away. Harrier is close enough to manipulate Peregrine's aching back. Peregrine wouldn't dream of letting Kite that near.

"Let me read your mind," he says, his steely eyes sparkling. "It isn't hard. You've come to plead for Kite's planes. . . ."

"Yes," I say, slightly unsettled by his turn of phrase.

"Your loyalty does you credit."

"Kite doesn't know I'm here," I assure him, ignoring the thick, damp fuzz on the old man's chest.

"Tell me how I can help you, Zara."

"Great Brother," I soothe, "I am here to help you."

He raises his eyebrows and waits.

"We know that there are spies at large," I begin. "Some are unhuman. . . ."

"Yes?"

"Do you agree there's a strong possibility that Ayland is already aware of our Firefly planes?"

I hope this covers me. Peregrine need never know about the ponytailed bastard I let into our war room. His eyes narrow.

"Are you saying it's too late? We've started on this illicit path, so now we must continue?"

"If we abandon firefuel now, Ayland may outmaneuver us. What if they have firefuel of their own?"

Peregrine sighs a deep sigh.

"This is why my back aches. My neck has been killing me all afternoon." He sits up. "Help me out."

To my consternation, Great Brother Peregrine holds out his veiny hand. I search for a towel and I hand it to him. The old man grasps hold of me and pulls himself up, using me to balance. He climbs out, water sloshing onto my lily-white tulle. I keep my eyes averted as he drips on the mat. It's bizarre. I don't sense carnality in him, not like the constant scorpion dance with Kite. It's more like I'm his mother and he's a little boy. No, it's not that either. He's treating me like I'm another man, almost his equal, like Harrier. I'm disarmed by such intimacy.

"I hope the bath has eased your pain," I say.

"Your frankness has."

When I'm sure the towel is safely wrapped around his waist, I face him. I see the shape of the youth he used to be. His frame still has strength in it. He's thoughtful as he puts his ring of state back on.

"What's your counsel?" he asks.

This is a trap. It is well known that Peregrine holds women in contempt. He never sees or speaks to any female if he can help it. He has no wives and to my knowledge, he never goes near a Pink House. I mustn't be deceived by his geniality. This wily old crocodile could be about to snap his jaws on me.

"It would be unbecoming to voice my opinion," I tell him, with just the right amount of self-deprecating grace.

Peregrine regards me, sucking in his cheeks. I will show him I am wily too.

He pads into his bedchamber and puts on an old gown. He hasn't dismissed me so I follow him. There are books and scrolls in piles around his bed—the room of a man who never stops working, a man beyond all claims of physical love.

"When I was a girl in Fort Abundance," I say, "I used to massage my father's neck. He always said I had just the way to relieve his pain. May I?" I ask.

Great Brother Peregrine sits in his old robe and lets me put my fingers on his neck. I feel his bony spine, the lumps of tension that he holds. I see how thin his hair is at the back. He's tender. I apply some force and after a few minutes, knots in his muscles loosen and, as he moves his head, I feel his tendons click. He sighs with some relief.

"Harrier thinks we should destroy the planes, publicly enough for the news to reach our enemies," he confides. "The Aylish would understand that we have experimented with firefuel and thought better of it."

"They'd never believe it," I say at once. "The Aylish are no fools."

A deeper, longer sigh.

"My thoughts exactly." He pauses. "Solitude is a cliché of power, Zara. Every decision carries monumental weight."

"We stand with you, Great Brother. I stand with you. You are so well loved. . . ."

"Send Kite to me. I'll talk to him. Although I fear his Fireflies might be our undoing."

A win. A win. My heart leaps.

As I hurry to Kite's chambers I find myself unaccountably moved. I should be full of joy at my success and yet my heart feels raw with a strange and poignant pain. What is it that I'm feeling?

Suddenly, I understand the brilliance of our Great Brother. He has shown me his soft belly and made me his friend. In his vulnerable humility, he's drawn out my love. The clever old reptile sensed my solitude and offered me the very thing I crave—companionship. Does he want me to love him like my cruel, beloved father? Why? What does he need me for? I have no answers to these questions and yet all I want is to go back to his rooms and sleep like a lapdog, curled up at his feet.

I slow my pace, taking deep breaths to settle the rush of hot emotion I am feeling. Not until I reach Kite's rooms can I focus my mind on my cold possessor.

Starling Beech lets me in and I smile at him, *Ready for Bed*. Flushing with pink, he brings me before his master. My ladies follow and we stand like ghosts while Kite practices the martial art of Thal. He is shirtless and oiled, barefoot, a salamander of a man. He makes me wait while he puts his body through an iron routine of torturous positions. I'm sure I'm meant to be impressed with his prowess, but I find myself fighting an urge to smile. I am twenty-two years old. This man has held my reins for six long years. Compared to Harrier's easy masculinity, there's something almost ridiculous in Kite. How have I never seen it?

At last he turns to his shrine of Thal and bows his head. Finally, he looks at me.

"Peregrine's going to let you have your planes," I say.

He gives nothing away. But as he dresses, I see resentment in his eyes. I have undermined him, interfered.

"Clever little spider."

"I got you what you wanted," I exclaim in frustration.

"It's impressive to watch you spin your web," he continues. "But you forget—I could turn it all to dust with a fingertip."

I'm sick of this, of being bullied, used, and threatened. I am sick of being afraid. A flame of fury erupts in me like firefuel.

"It takes one spider to see another," I tell him. "And your own web is hanging, full of holes."

"What do you mean?" he asks.

I look at him. I see his insecurity, his need.

"Read my mind," I say. And turning on my heel, I go.

The days crawl by. When I first got to Meadeville, there were only five of us. Now there are fifteen. Transports come and go, bringing troops to train. They also bring prisoners, manacled and cuffed around the head. Unhuman, so they say. Meadeville is the final holding camp before we're taken upriver into the jaws of the Chrysalid House. For days I have paced in my chains or sat with my back against the wire. We get rations twice a day and there's a modicum of shelter. They don't want us to die of cold or starvation. They're investing in our bodies. We are going to slave for Brightland.

We don't talk to each other much. There doesn't seem much point. Why get to know someone? It's only going to cause more pain. Beyond the politeness of saying my name and where I'm from, I try to keep silent. But these people can't help going through their trauma. They talk in circles, all day long. My eyes go round the fence, trying not to listen as they pour out their woe. The inner fence, the outer fence, the barbed wire, the watchtowers. I scan the gate. I scan the training camp beyond. No one is escaping from this dump.

Fear has sunken into me. I make myself face what lies ahead so that when it comes, I won't shit my fucking pants. A barge will arrive to take us all upriver and we'll be drugged to keep us quiet for our journey to the Chrysalid House. When we get there, we face the farce they call a trial. Our crimes are read out before a panel of Inquisitors, who act as our judges. We're all given the same sentence. Some will be reprieved, picked out and trained as Sirens. But most will be sent for their appointment with the surgeons. Those surgeons are the peak of Brightling medical achievement—the best training, the most experience, our most advanced equipment—all bent on killing songlight. They damage our capacity to think, to imagine, to resist, to be ourselves, but they kindly leave us our capacity to work. Our balls or wombs are taken and our tongues cut out. Once these delicate procedures have been done, we're cocooned in bandages. We are the chrysalids then. And we emerge transformed, without spirit, will, or bollocks, as laborers for the Brightling cause.

I am determined to die on the way. I'll run at the fence and let them hammer me with bullets. I won't become their dummy. And yet, another dawn rises and I am still here. Something holds me back. A false hope of escape? I bet each one of us is harboring the same hopeless dream.

Don't think. Don't think of Elsa. Don't think of holding her. Don't think of that night on Bailey's Strand. Stop thinking now, or you will fucking break.

I watch the soldiers and the sailors on parade. These boys will soon be shipping out, on their way to the Aylish coast. It must be good for their morale to see us unhumans, all chained and shuffling here. I'm sure that we remind them why they fight.

Farther up the riverbank, my view is of some low wooden buildings. Two or three of them are painted pink. Occasionally I see girls outside, hanging laundry or sweeping dirt. They have pink ribbons sewn around their necks. There are taverns down there too, and at dusk they spring to life with little strings of turbine light. The soldiers' carousing keeps us sleepless, long into the night. At last these boys have got their chance to fuck.

All day long, I watch the planes and gliders taking off and landing. The pilots get no respite. Someone wants them trained fast. They go up in gliders first and then, when they have gotten the hang of the controls, they put them into Fireflies. These planes are on everybody's lips. Our guards look up with pride every time a Firefly soars. The noise of them tears through the sky. They're faster than seems possible and when they land, they leave a trail of chemical fumes. On my second day, I see one hit the runway and explode.

Piper?

All day, I envisage his death. I feel nothing, neither grief nor satisfaction.

Only a dull ache for what we used to be. Poor bastard, striving all his life to get up in the air, then immediately hurtling down to death. So fucking pointless that I want to laugh.

Then, this evening, I see him. He's in a brand-new uniform with a crowd of airmen, singing drinking songs outside a Pink House. They slap each other on the back and, one by one, they all file in. Piper Crane in a Pink House? That's a fucking laugh. I stand till it grows dark, my eyes trained on the pink door. How long will he last in there?

I'm distracted by the boy who's sitting near my feet. His name is Freed Atheson and he's from Want's Cove. He's fifteen years of age. I've tried to avoid this bleating boy ever since I've been in here but he follows me around. He picks and scratches at his lead band until his skull bleeds and at night he lies there, whimpering for his ma. Fuck Freed Atheson; he tears my fucking heart out. I wish he'd leave me be. But he has attached himself to me, as if I can protect him. Fool.

"The guards say that the barge is coming later," he informs me. "To take us up to Brightlinghelm. They say it has a flat roof so they can put us all on show."

"Shut up, Freed." But he goes on.

"They arrange it so we get to Brightlinghelm when all the citizens are on their way to work."

"Fuck that," I say. "I'll take my chances and jump in the river. You should too."

I shouldn't put hope in this kid's head.

"You can't," he tells me. "You won't be able."

"Why not?"

And then I see the guards. They're outside the inner fence, tooled up with their nightsticks. They're prepared for trouble. One is filling a tray of syringes from a bottle full of dope. Gala . . . It's time to run at that fence. Grasp it with your chained hands and try to climb. The higher you get, the quicker they will shoot you. Time to end this fucking—

My eyes meet Piper Crane's. He's out of the Pink House, staring right at me.

He approaches, wearing his authority as one of the elite. The airmen are revered round here. I see him calling to the guards. One of them goes to the gate. I don't know what Piper says, but the guard lets him in. Meanwhile, they're starting with the syringes. Mrs. Kitt, the adulteress, gets it first. She puts up a good fight but they hold her down and push the syringe into her arm. She goes limp, a curse dying on her lips. Freed Atherson joins the other prisoners, running to the corners. The guards are going to enjoy a game of snatch and grab. I remain where I am, my eyes fixed on Piper.

He has a syringe in his hand as he slowly walks toward me.

"I told them you were my catch," he says. "They've given me the honor." He looks down at the syringe. "It'll spare you some pain."

I have nothing to say to him. Not a word.

"I'm here to help," he says, approaching. "There's a way you can survive."

I think of that Firefly, blowing up in flames.

"There's a way to stop the surgeons drilling needles into your head. At your trial, you can plead to be a Siren. You must convince the judges of your willingness. That's how it works. You must beg them to let you train."

I laugh in disbelief. Only a special kind of coward becomes a Siren.

"I'm not saying it's an easy choice, but you'll keep your faculties," he assures me. "You'll keep your spirit."

"Do you think so little of me?"

Piper falls silent.

I don't blame anyone who begs the panel of Inquisitors at their trial to make them a Siren. Who knows? Maybe when the crunch comes, I'll be on my knees, roaring for mercy with the best. But my fellow prisoners have told me this much: Sirens are not reprieved until they have found a Torch, hunted them down, and ensured that they are caught. Not many can go through with it. Faced with the reality of destroying another, most will end up in the Chrysalid House. The constant gossip in this holding pen has taught me that Sirens don't last long. Mrs. Kitt told us of the Siren in her village who went ten shades of mad, attacked her Inquisitor, and then stabbed herself in the guts with his knife. Others says that only true cold-hearted bastards can succeed.

"I'm trying to help you," says Piper. "Train as a Siren. You could survive this, Rye." Behind him, I see a barge arriving, a low black barge with a flat roof.

"Fuck your help."

And he comes at me with the syringe.

I hold him off. We wrestle. It's as intense as an embrace. But I'm still weak with the broken ribs that Wheeler gave me. Piper has been training hard. His arms feel like steel. He soon gets me on my back.

"You called me a rat," he says. "I'm not a rat. I did what was *right*."

One by one, my unfortunate neighbors are succumbing to the guards. Two of them are holding Freed Atheson. He's squealing like a piglet as they get him on the ground. I've blocked out all their suffering, these people. And yet I know their stories, every one.

"Look around you, Piper," I say. I'm going to tell this rat-faced bastard what I've learned in here. "Here's the truth. Most of these people aren't unhuman." I draw his eyes to Mrs. Kitt. "That woman is an adulterer. That man is a thief. That girl ran from a Pink House. And that boy there . . ." I turn so Piper can see Freed. "That boy loves another boy."

The guards plunge the syringe into Freed's back. Slowly, he goes limp. Piper's eyes remain on him.

"Anyone can be called unhuman. The Chrysalid House is there for all. I pray you never see it."

Piper stares down at me. My warning has hit home. I stop resisting him. What's the fucking point?

"You win," I say. "I yield. Why don't you ease my fucking pain?"

Time seems to slow down as Piper puts the needle next to my flesh. But I don't feel it pierce my skin. What's the bastard waiting for?

Piper lets the contents of the syringe dribble harmlessly down the outside of my arm.

I meet his eyes. The old pull of boyhood. We fight, we cry.

"I did what was *right*," he says.

I close my eyes, pretending that I'm floating on the wings of dope. I close my eyes in stillness. Piper remains for a second too long, holding me in the wrestling embrace. Then he releases me and goes.

Instead of packing our things and running for the moors, Ma and I try to fathom what has happened. I'm Commander Mikane's Second Wife.

Ma walks me home from the Elders' Hall, as bewildered as I am. "Why did he pick you?"

"I don't know. I insulted him. I asked him why he'd fried his face."

"Oh, Elsa . . ."

"But he saved Gailee Roberts, just because I said he should."

Ma takes this in. "I wonder if he realized who you were? Your pa was kind to Heron. And maybe he remembers me?"

"He doesn't care a fig for who I am," I tell her. "He didn't even wait to hear my name. He knows he's old as Hel and griddled like a chop. Perhaps he's done this just to punish me."

"Don't be so cruel," cries Ma. "Those burns must cause him pain." She's leaped to his defense and in truth, I'm not proud of my flippancy. It's not the commander's appearance that troubles me.

"Someone else will be a Third Wife in my place," I say. "That's what I call cruel."

Ma is silent then. As soon as we get inside, she brings out Pa's old whiskey and she pours us both a glass. She hands me one. I feel its fire travel down my throat. I voice the question that's hanging between us.

"What about running away?"

Ma looks away. "Elsa, everything is different. You're the wife of a great commander—even Second Wife is no small thing. And you know what it means if we run."

I see the gibbet in my mind, the dead swinging side by side. Ma tries to sweeten the pill.

"If Heron Mikane is anything like the boy I once knew, there are worse husbands you could have."

I gulp back the rest of my whiskey. Ma does the same. She refills our glasses.

"That speech he gave when he buried his men," she ponders. "About Death. I can't bear to think what that man must have seen. He's suffering."

"So are we."

She looks directly at me. "I don't know what to tell you. I wish I could marry him for you. If you can't stomach him, I'm still prepared to run. But you'll have standing as the wife of a commander." I sense her desperation. "You'll be safe."

It's on my lips to tell her, *Ma, I'm unhuman. I can never be safe. What if Mikane finds out?* But I pack my things into a bundle, ready for my wedding night.

As we leave the house, I see a small crowd gathered at the harbor, lit by the transport ship's great turbine lights. The little group of Third Wives is waiting to board. Wheeler and his fellow Emissaries corral them, separating them from their homes, their families. Their heads are bowed. Immediately I run down the hill.

"Elsa!" cries Ma.

I don't answer. Fuck Mikane, he can wait.

Ma catches me up and we join the small crowd, mostly family and neighbors of the eight leftover girls. I'm surprised to see that Uta Malting's there—none of the soldiers have chosen her. I can feel the red heat of her humiliation. Francine Merrin and Stacee Shrike are clinging to each other in fear and disbelief. Rhea Vine and Molla Quail look like they're waiting to be shot. No pomp and pride for them, no band or choir to see them off. These girls are being whipped away before the shock sinks in.

How can we all allow this? Why are we all frozen? How can we be standing here, letting these Emissaries take our girls for *rape*?

As I watch, one man steps forward. Uta Malting's pa, our mild-mannered baker, kind and decent, respected in the town. On Uta's sixteenth birthday he gave a cake to every girl in the choir. He's standing firm now. We can't hear what he says but Wheeler shakes his head, implacable. Mr. Malting raises his voice. Then, when he is still rebuffed, he shouts an insult. Others join in. Ma grips my hand, moving forward.

Wheeler and the Emissaries take out their whips. Wheeler raises his palm as if, in his benevolence, he understands that this is hard. This enrages Mr. Malting even more. He breaks his stance and makes to hit. Who'd have thought he had it in him? Uta cries out his name. Her distress brings out that of all the other girls. They become hysterical. And the families erupt. We all erupt. I find swears flying out of my mouth, stinging Wheeler. Ma forcefully holds me back.

"Don't, Elsa. They will take you too!"

Mr. Malting grabs his Uta. Rhea Vine runs to her grandmother. The guards from the ship fire a warning volley over our heads. Girls scream. People fall onto their bellies. All three Emissaries crack their whips. The crowd cowers. One by one, the girls are taken on board. The Emissaries pry Uta away from Mr. Malting and the eldermen arrest him. Stacee Shrike breaks free, running—and it looks like she will throw herself right off the quay. Her mother is shrieking her name. One of the Emissaries grabs Stacee, lifting her like a rag doll. He carries her over his shoulder. Wheeler boards with them. I bet this is one journey he doesn't want to miss. He'll be comforting the helpless girls, telling them how much the Brethren care for them. No doubt trying the goods. Bastard. Bastard. How I hate him.

"You shouldn't watch," says Ma, holding me. "There's nothing you can do."

I'm hot with guilt and shame. I wipe my angry tears away.

"It should be me," I say.

"It shouldn't be any of you," she replies.

The eldermen—none of whom have lost their daughters—soon disperse the crowd. Mr. Malting is taken to the jailhouse. Ma and I watch until the ship rounds the headland and disappears from sight.

"Mikane could have stopped this if he'd wanted to," I growl. "He could have come down here and stood up for those girls. His troops could have taken on those Emissaries."

"Why would Mikane or his troops have a problem with Third Wives?" asks Ma. "They've spent ten years and more at war. Pink Houses are normal to them."

Anger is still surging through me as we reach Mikane's front door. He'll have probably taken full ownership of Wife Number One by now. My first task as Second Wife, according to Hoopoe's instructions, is to feed them both and re-prepare the wedding bed. We know the rules and procedures by rote. And if our husband swerves from them, we're meant to gently coax him back. Ma knocks on the door.

"Heron's only three years younger than me," she says, almost to herself. "And now he gets my daughter. . . ."

Mrs. Chaffinch Mikane lets us in with a slightly bewildered look. I can tell immediately that she's still a virgin. She whispers to Ma, anxious.

"He might throw you out. My ma came with me and he told her to go. It's permitted for our mothers to prepare us for our marriage night, but he threw her from the house."

"That's very unmannerly," says Ma politely.

"Where is he?" I ask, dumping my stuff on a chair.

"In there." Chaffinch points at the bedroom. "Can you believe? When I tried to enter, he shouted, 'Get out.'"

"I expect the man's bone weary and he just wants to sleep," says Ma wisely. "He's fresh from the battlefront, Chaffinch."

"I'd be grateful if you'd observe my married name," says Chaffinch, looking at my mother down her pert, pink nose.

"Beg your pardon, Mrs. Mikane . . ."

How will I live with this obnoxious minx?

Ma puts a small carved bird that she has made on the mantelpiece; her gift to the house. Then she pulls up her sleeves and starts clearing the table, where a huge hog obviously ate its food. Chaffinch doesn't lift a finger. She points at my small pile of stuff.

"Don't leave your clutter there," she says. "Go and put it in the back room."

I can feel her readying herself for a lifetime of bossing me around. Her hands will stay soft while I work every hour, looking after her and the hog. From this day forward, I'll need permission to do everything, permission to go out on the sea. How will I ever see Nightingale?

I take my things to the Second Wife's room. Poky, plain, dark. I stand in the tiny space and the desire to leave Northaven overwhelms me. Rye . . . Rye . . . he feels farther away than ever. Ma and I could be running over the moors by now. Twice, people who loved me have said we should run. And twice, I have stayed, like the coward that I am. I look at my drab future. I think of Heron Mikane, owning me. What have I done?

I'm not the only one feeling trapped. When I come back in, Chaffinch is fluttering. She's scared, like a bird stuck in a glasshouse. She's wringing her hands, talking quietly to my mother.

"He wouldn't let me bathe him. I had the oil for his feet all prepared and ready but he wouldn't let me take his boots off. He's still got them on. Why's he sleeping with his boots on?"

"Maybe he's got foot rot," I suggest.

"Elsa, shush," calms my ma.

"I'm serious," I say. "Maybe all his toes will come off with the boot."

"Why did I get you?" snaps Chaffinch. "Mikane should have chosen Uta or Rhea. Any girl is more deserving. My mother's saying Elsa Crane's gameplay is the talk of the town."

"I'd be grateful," I say, "if you'd observe my married name."

"My friends are down there on that boat," cries Chaffinch. "I wish to Hel that you were on it too."

Ma cuts her off firmly. "It'll be harder for you both if there's conflict in this house."

"Too damn right." A growl.

Mikane is in the bedroom doorway, king of grime in his underwear and boots. What a sight. What's left of his hair is standing up; his scarred torso is salted from the sea and crusted with dirt. He strikes a match, loud on the stone wall. He uses it to light a stinking tobacco smoke. Then he seems to realize who my mother is. His voice changes.

"Curlew Crane . . ." He goes into his room and returns with a shirt. He seems bashful. "Gwyn's wife," he says.

"Yes. And this is his girl, Elsa."

He glances at me fresh, seeing my father in my features. Then he gazes at my mother, taking in her widow's veil.

"He was a good man."

"Yes."

"I'm sorry for your loss."

My ma is looking at him strange. Like she's seeing something I am not.

"It's long ago, Heron," she says.

A silence falls. But their gaze holds.

"I wish you peace and harmony with your young wives," says Ma.

I do believe there's a warning in this. Mikane half smiles. Ma politely bows her head and leaves.

Our husband looks at us.

"I want a bath," he says. "And pour it without any yapping."

Heron goes back into the bedroom, leaving the door open. He lies on the bed, pulling his boots up with him.

Chaffinch and I look at one another.

I boil up pans of water while Chaffinch frets and our husband snores. A sign of all our blissful days ahead. When the bath is ready, Chaffinch puts in oils and herbs. She lays out clean clothes and lights candles. We look at the huge, sleeping form.

"You're First Wife," I say. "You wake him up."

Chaffinch approaches the bed. She looks at me, unsure. She puts a fingertip on Heron's unburned shoulder—and he springs awake, a battle-front reflex, grabbing Chaffinch's wrist so tight that she yelps. Heron seems to realize where he is.

"Next time you wake me . . . do it with your voice."

When she offers to undress him he refuses her assistance. Not only that, he puts us outside the house and closes all the shutters. We sit on a bench under the front window, waiting, while he cleans himself. Chaffinch plays with her wedding band, twisting it round and round her wrist. Neither of us has a thing to say.

The land feels so flat, so heavy. I'm desperate to be on the sea. I want to feel buoyed by the waves; I want the breeze on my face, rising and plunging, my hand in the water. I want Nightingale. She'd find it so odd that Commander Mikane sleeps in his boots. She'd be shocked that I asked him if he fried his face. What will she make of this joyless union? I'm on the point of recklessly reaching up to her when Chaffinch asks me to loosen her hair. It's still pinned into its wedding sculpt. I gently tease it out.

"He's supposed to have taken me by now. He's hardly looked at me."

"He's probably drunk a barrel load of beer," I say. "I doubt you're even in focus."

"Tinamou Haines . . . Her husband, Gyles Syker, he couldn't keep his hands off her. I thought he was about to get going right there in the Elders' Hall. She's got Sambee James as her Second Wife. Sambee's a dote. I wish I had Sambee James."

"I wish I had Sambee too. But I got you. And you got me."

I take a risk, deciding to be honest.

"I didn't throw myself at Mikane," I confide. "I left the hall so as not to get chosen. I was going to run away."

Chaffinch is shocked. "Why?"

I shrug. "I probably wouldn't have lasted long."

"You were seriously going to run away, rather than be Third Wife?"

"I'm surprised no one else had the same idea."

"My ma says Third Wives get money. Third Wives are rich. They live in fine houses. She says the Brethren look after them."

"I don't fancy having my womb cut out."

"The Brethren care for us, Elsa. They'd never ask such a sacrifice without some consolation."

We can hear our husband splashing. The next thing Chaffinch says sounds very small and true.

"I'm scared of him."

The admittance seems to do her good. Her anxiety comes tumbling out.

"That speech he did at the funerals. . . that's not how a hero's supposed to speak. And why's he so angry with everyone? Why's he so rude and churlish to my pa and to Emissary Wheeler?"

"I expect we'll find out," I say.

"It's my duty to ease his cares. But what if he won't let me?"

I run my fingers through the tangles in her hair, fluffing it into a haze. I can feel the tension running through her body. I give her shoulders and skull a massage, how we've been taught to relax our man.

"None of this is going to be how Hoopoe Guinea said," I tell her. "We have a choice, Chaffie. We can be at each other's throats, you laying down the law like a yapping dog and me resenting every word. Or we can work together. In public, I'll be as meek as cheese. But in private, treat me as your equal and I will be your friend."

Chaffinch weighs this up. I want to reach out to her, to open the door and let the trapped bird fly. But I fear that Chaffinch is the kind who likes the safety of a glasshouse. She'll soon be hopping around, eating aphids and tomato flies, while I break my beak, flapping at the windowpanes.

We hear someone approaching. Gailee is coming up the hill at a half run. She's clearly on her way to fetch her ma.

"Our husband's crying," she says breathlessly. "We don't know what to do. He's using awful, awful swears and when his mother left, he started to wail. We don't know how to talk to him. He seems so lost." She's close to tears.

I get to my feet. "Oh, Gailee."

Gailee wrings her hands.

"I know I'm lucky," she says. "I know I'm one of the lucky ones. . . ."

I try to think of how to comfort her. "Perhaps you should sing to him, you and Nela."

"Sing?"

"I think you should try to stay very calm when you're around him and sing. I think you have to try to bring him into harmony."

"How do you know that?" asks Gailee, surprised.

"His face when the choir sang. Didn't you notice him? I think there might be peace in music for him."

Gailee looks at me strangely. She nods. She runs on. I think Chaffinch and I are thinking the same thing. Perhaps we haven't got it so bad.

The splashing stops. We hear a cascade of water as our husband climbs out of his bath.

"How do I look?" asks Chaffinch, nervously arranging her hair around her shoulders.

I eye her up and down. "If I was a soldier, I'd fuck you."

Chaffinch doesn't know whether to admonish me or laugh. I take that as a step forward and smile at her.

When we go in, Mikane is dressed in workingman's trousers and a vest, standing at the mantelpiece, looking at my mother's carving of the bird. His uninjured side is to us. He has thick, dark hair, graying only at the temple, a fine-chiseled face, a perfect, muscular physique. It completely takes us both aback. He's gleaming, all the way down to his well-shaped feet.

"What's this?" he asks, holding up the bird. As he turns, I see how far the scarring travels down his body. His left shoulder and arm, his chest. I wonder if my ma is right. Perhaps it gives him constant pain.

"One of the villagers made it," Chaffinch says, trying not to show her apprehension. "Everyone contributed to this house. I made the curtains, see?"

She runs to the window and proudly shows off her work. "I embroidered them specially, so that when you pull them closed, you see the Aylish, burning at Montsan Beach. You're there. . . . And the brave two hundred . . ."

Mikane makes just the slightest of nods, as if he might have known.

"We're so proud of you in the village," Chaffinch chirrups on. "You made a new foothold on Ayland's shore. With only two hundred men, you fought the Aylish back, and by the time reinforcements arrived, the whole of Montsan was in flames and three of their ships were burning on the sea. I know all your battles by heart," she boasts.

Chaffinch waits eagerly to hear Heron tell his story. We've been taught that men like it when you heap praise upon their exploits. But Heron remains silent.

"My mother carved the bird," I say, proud of my ma's skill.

He looks at it again. Ma has captured the heron's energized stillness.

"Curlew Crane . . ." He turns the tiny bird in his massive hands. Then he puts it back.

"I want more food," he says. "And plenty to drink."

Chaffinch keeps bravely trying to get Heron to talk. When he just keeps on eating, she starts telling him all about her boring life, all the prizes she's won for singing, all the wonderful things that her father's bought for her. Near midnight, Heron gets to his feet.

"I need a piss," he says, and goes outside. Chaffinch takes in an expectant breath. It's time for her big moment. Her hymen is going to be history. And now that her husband's all cleaned up, he's not quite such a horrible prospect. When he comes back in, she kneels down in front of him, like she's supposed to, and humbly asks him what he'd like.

"This is how it's going to be," he says. He points at the tiny back bedroom. "I sleep in there. Alone." He points to the big marriage bed. "You two sleep in that. And if anyone asks, you can tell them what you like."

He goes into the back bedroom, kicking shut the door.

I get into bed next to Chaffinch. She's mortified.

"He doesn't like me," she says. "How can he not like me?"

"I don't think he likes anyone," I say.

Chaffinch turns away, scooping all the blankets.

In the middle of the night, I hear something. A man's muffled cry; the sound of a nightmare. I get up out of bed, consumed with curiosity. I creep across the floor. His door is open, just a crack. Heron lies in a troubled sleep. Ministering to him is the elegant figure of Death. Her bony fingers caress his face, lingering in the contours of his scars. Then she senses me. Her black sockets peer at me, angry at being disturbed. She rushes at me with her hateful grin—and I wake.

This is my nightmare, not Heron Mikane's.

I'm sweating. Chaffinch is puppy-snoring at my side. I sit up, trying to get my breath back. I go to the window, wanting the reassurance of first light. I see my husband standing in the garden. He's looking at the town. He has a smoke in his hand but he doesn't light it. He doesn't do anything. He stands, looking at his birthplace, looking at the sea.

It's the dead of night. There are two turbine lights pointing down on us as we lie drugged on the flat deck of the barge. All around us is a thick white river mist. I peer through the gauze that has been replaced over my face: two guards, the skipper, two enslaved engine men. I've been twice blessed: Piper didn't drug me and mist shrouds the river.

My fellow prisoners lie like corpses. I force myself to a similar stillness, although my mind is racing. Sergeant Redshank taught us what to do if the Aylish ever made us prisoners of war. A man might slip through his bonds if he dislocates his thumb. The pain is almost intolerable—but what does it matter if freedom is gained? Redshank never thought I'd be using his trick on Brightland's own guards. Slowly, imperceptibly, I force my left thumb out of its joint. I might ruin my hand forever but I'd crunch every bone to get myself free. I grit my teeth against the searing pain—and I feel something give. I pull my hand through the cuff and I lie, sweating out the agony. But now, when I need to, I can use my arms to swim.

I have to unchain my feet and I don't have long. We'll be in Brightling-helm by dawn.

It feels like the mist is filling my mind and I think, desperate for a plan. If there's no other way, I'll hurl myself, feet bound, into the river. I know the chains and the lead band will drag me down—but I will drown a free man.

Life's short. It's fucking short and I'm so angry.

The two guards up at the front are armed with crossbows. I watch their body language. An argument. One of them raises his voice. I can't hear what they're saying. The other guard walks away from him, kicking each prisoner, checking that we live. I hope he doesn't see my wrecked left hand; I try to hide it with my torso. His kick lands at the base of my spine and pain shoots from my arse to my eyeballs. He checks that I am breathing and moves on. He approaches the rear of the barge. He sits three feet away from me and starts to roll a smoke.

I allow myself to think of Elsa, her sun-kissed skin, her magnificent hair, her radiant songlight, her smile. I see the grace in her shoulders; I remember her laughter, her tenderness as she whispers my name. I see her eyes. I feel her touch, her body. She loves me. Elsa will live. She'll live for both of us. If I die now, I have loved her, and that has to be enough. I've got to take my chance.

The guard at the front stares ahead into the mist; his colleague nearby is smoking with his back to me. I spring forward. My arms go around this guard's neck and I pull with all my might. I'm like an animal, teeth in a snarl. I won't release my grip until he's dead. He struggles and he's strong. My injured hand is screaming but I have the advantage. The turbine and the churning water drown out the sounds of the guard's feet scraping on the deck, desperate to free himself. I twist hard. His neck snaps. I wait until he's limp, cradling him like a child.

My first murder. My first kill as a soldier—one of my own countrymen. I force my unbroken hand into his pockets. If he doesn't have keys for these shackles, I am dead. I'm dead and I have killed a man for nothing.

Sweet Gala, I find them. On the third attempt, the key fits.

"Hey!" The guard at the front has seen me. "Hey!"

He reaches for his crossbow. The shackles are open. An arrow sticks into my leg. Before the pain hits my brain, I leap into the water.

It's cold. My body shocks; my lungs freeze. I must stay down. I must stay hidden. If I come up for air they'll kill me. Gala, the lead band is heavy. I hear arrows landing in the water all around me. My lungs are screaming, desperate to rise. But I move down, deep into the murk. I swim as we were taught, my legs moving like a frog's. I'm starting to rise. I have to take a breath or my brain will burst. My head breaks the water. I see the remaining guard and the skipper, crossbows raised. I take in a lungful of air and a host of arrows flies toward me. One of them gets me in the shoulder but the water slows it and I feel nothing, nothing. If it weren't for the darkness and the mist, a trail of blood would give me away. I dive down like a cormorant, forcing my dislocated hand to work, saving all the pain for later. I thank Sergeant Redshank for teaching us cadets so well. Something slimy brushes my arms, weeds, fronds. I put out my good hand and grasp them. An arrow, slowed by the water, glances off the lead band.

Perhaps the bastard thing just saved my life.

I feel my way through the weeds. I flow downstream with the ebbing tide. The pain is beginning to wrack me. An explosion of lights in my brain tells me I need oxygen. I must rise. I must breathe. I let my face break through the surface.

And I see the barge farther away. Another arrow flies. But they can't see me anymore and it lands wide. I try to feel the arrow in my leg. It hasn't gone deep but it hurts like hell. I pull the fucker out. Free, I'm free as the stars. I turn and float on my back. I give myself up to the tide and drift away from the barge, down toward the river's mouth.

During the night, I hear a *BOOM* on the edge of a dream and imagine it's the sea battle. But I'm soon woken by one of Papa's men rapping on our door. I hear hushed, urgent voices and rise to see Papa pulling on his boots.

"Go back to bed, Kaira," he says.

"What was that noise?" I ask.

"An incendiary device."

"Where?"

He hesitates to tell me. "Our Inquisitor Station."

My face crumples into worry. He could have been there. He could have been hurt. His man stands at the door, breathless in his uniform.

"I'll be back soon," says Papa, reassuring me. "Go to bed."

Ishbella and I sit up, listening for news on the radiobine. We know it's insurgents. They have attacked the city's forces several times and their attacks are becoming more frequent. I'm torn about these people. I know there must be Torches among them, fighting for their freedom—but they are attacking law-keepers like Papa. When news finally comes, a tinny man with a quack-like voice tells us that two Inquisitors and a Siren have died of wounds sustained in the blast. Insurgents are at fault, terrorists, traitors. There's a house-to-house search underway. Every Siren in Brightlinghelm has been commandeered to hunt them. The law will be swift. He says that the dead Inquisitors, heroes in the fight against the unhuman threat, will be avenged.

When Papa comes back in the middle of the morning he looks haggard. He brings a thin man to the apartment with him, wearing a gray, shabby suit, thick with mortar dust. I feel the blood drain from my skin. A Siren.

I hide my songlight in the deepest recesses of my heart and pray that Lark doesn't try to reach me.

"This is Keynes," says Papa. "He's going to help me for a while."

A long, retractable steel leash binds Keynes to my pa, waist to waist, in case the Siren has ideas of personal escape. Pa locks our door from the inside, pockets the key, and unchains himself from the Siren. "Keynes has lost his master in the bomb."

"Evans is dead?" asks Ishbella, shocked.

Evans is Papa's station leader.

Papa nods. He sits, clearly shaken.

"Oh, Papa," I say. I can see he wants comfort and I put my arms around him, not knowing what to say. I am forcing calm on my thumping heart, as I did the day they took Cassandra. *Don't think of her*, I tell myself. *Don't think.* I know the Siren has a lead band on his head but he's a predator, right here in our house.

"Where are your manners, hound?" Papa barks at Keynes. "This is my daughter."

"Good morning, miss," says the Siren.

"Good morning, Keynes," I reply.

Sirens aren't supposed to interact with proper humans but today is clearly an exception. Papa tells Keynes to sit on a stool by the door. He can't share our table; that would be too much. I make hot tea. Ishbella fries up bacon scraps and potato cakes.

I have to warn Lark. She mustn't come to me today. But I must keep my mind pristine and blank, in case a stray beam of this Siren's songlight penetrates his leaden cuff. Keynes . . . His cropped hair is greased in spikes, his skin pitted with cuts and thick with dust from the bomb. I see that he is shaking and upset.

"May I get him a blanket, Papa?"

But Papa doesn't hear. He's talking to Ishbella.

"We've lost the compound," he says. "We dug Evans out from the rubble. Sanchay got his leg blown off. He's still alive but not for long. The female Siren took the full force." Papa nods at Keynes. "This hound was lucky to survive. He's going to be sleeping in our cellar for a while."

Gala. Gala. I must be polite to him, kind and polite, then he won't suspect me. I reassure myself: with that lead band on, he can't sense me. I am safe. I bring him a basin of water and a blanket. When his hands and face are clean, I pour him tea and serve him a plate of food.

"What are you doing?" screeches Ishbella. "Don't waste bacon on the likes of him."

I take the bacon scraps away from Keynes but I slip him another potato cake.

"Thank you, miss," he says.

I meet his gaze—and nod with a smile. It will look suspicious if I'm nervous.

"Keynes is a good hound," says Papa. "He can have a treat today."

I put the bacon back on the Siren's plate.

I can sense Lark, thrumming her wings in my mind. I know she has news but I'm holding her back. I'm desperate to hear from her. But not here. Not here. Keynes is too close.

"Thank you, miss," he says again.

I'll walk to the park. I'll find a quiet spot and make sure our meeting's brief. Lark, my brave Lark. Is she on her way to Brightlinghelm to be a Third Wife?

Sister Swan comes on the radiobine for her morning address. Her voice is low with respect for the dead. She tells us that a second Inquisitor has now died of his wounds. Papa hangs his head. Sanchay was his friend. Sister Swan talks about the vital patriotic work that Inquisitors do. She talks about the enemy within, unhuman insurgents, more treacherous than the Aylish. I put my arms around Papa's neck. Dylan Sanchay would bring beers and they would play dominoes long into the night. I think of my papa being blown to smithereens by people who hate him. By our own Brightling people. Traitors.

I am one of them.

Sister Swan tells us that the Brethren, in their concern for our safety, are imposing a curfew. House-to-house searches will continue. We must stay in our homes from nightfall to sunrise, unless we have a stamp of permission. The gates to the city are remaining closed and all road and river traffic will be searched.

"It's going to be a busy day," says Papa grimly.

"Can't you rest awhile?" I ask.

"I'm station leader now," he says. "It's up to me and this hound Keynes to catch the scum that did this."

When they go, I waste no time. I take my coat and put it on. I'm in the hallway and Lark is flittering, flickering all around me. She's desperate to speak.

"Where d'you think you're going?" cries Ishbella. "Your papa will be using this apartment as the Inquisitor Station now. I want your help to organize the parlor."

My face falls. "Let me go to the market for you," I offer. "You'll need bread and cheese and meat. Papa and his men must be fed."

"You're too much of a weakling to carry it all."

"No, I'm not. I'll prove it to you." I grab some bags, our ration books, and go.

The outside air smells of rain. The sun is weak and watery but it feels good on my skin. The pain in my hip isn't bad today. I watch a line of little boys marching to the junior cadet huts. My mouth waters as I pass the queue for bread. Not yet, Lark, not yet.

I hurry through the market, as fast as my leg will go. There are armed soldiers with Inquisitors searching the taverns and the cafés, pulling people out. I'll go to the park and find a quiet spot. I'll get the food on my way back. Great Brother Peregrine looks down with benign eyes from a large mural above the long queue for vegetables: *The Brethren Will Provide*.

I think about the day I lost Cassandra. I was ill afterward. A fever gripped me and I thought that it would burn me clean away. As my body grew hotter, I rose up, unloosing my songlight from my body as if I was sending it beyond the blue firmament, into the midnight of limitless space. I sent Cassandra's name, an airburst of booming songlight, loving her, thanking her. If she was anywhere on Earth, I wanted her to hear me. I sent her name high above the clouds to where the atmosphere meets space.

"CASSANDRA . . ."

I wanted Gala to hear me. I wanted to be heard right out into the starlit deep. I cried her name with all my being:

"CASSANDRA . . ." As far into the distance as my mind would go. My consciousness hovered as I breathed, listening to see if she might reply. And then almost inaudible, I felt a voice, far distant, an almost childlike hint of song, a curling question I could hardly decipher.

". . . ?"

Perhaps it was Gala. Perhaps it was one of the star-men from the Light People time. The legend goes that when they set the Earth on fire, they tried to escape it, running like castaways for the vast, dead reaches of interstellar space. The question came again, clearer, more pointed.

". . . ?" cried the voice.

I thought it might be a distant Siren's trick and I fell back into myself without replying. For a while, I lost all sense of what was real. The fever carried me aloft. During that time, I had a dream. Perhaps it was a vision or message, I don't know. I saw a ship, out in a spiral of the blue—a huge ship floating in the air and behind it a beautiful city with domed houses and glistening domed towers. Somebody there had noticed me. They had heard my cry. Somebody was looking.

"Where?" came the question.

It might be nothing but a figment but I cherish my city, my fever dream, with its slow-flying ships and great glass domes, gardens growing inside them. I've drawn it in my sketchbook. I don't know what makes me think of it today but it comforts me. Perhaps one day, Lark and I will find this place. Perhaps one day, we'll meet. I think how wonderful that will be and I forget how tired I am.

I'm nearing the park. It's cold and windy and the sky is heavy with approaching rain. There's nobody about. Lark comes to me in a rush of songlight, bringing the breeze of lovely Northaven. She's pleased to see that I'm outside.

"It's good to see you with fresh air on your face," she says.

She surrounds me with her news. It comes in such a rush I have to ask her to slow down. I'm not sure I've understood. She's the Second Wife of Commander Mikane?

She shares the events, her feelings, showing me image after image. He's smoking in his sea-stained uniform; he's holding a carving of a heron; he's sleeping in a tiny room, a figure of Death caressing his brow.

I know immediately this is fate; this is meant to be. Something will happen because of this union. Mikane is a great hero and so, to me, is Lark. The shadows that have weighed on me all morning loosen their hold.

"This has happened for a reason," I tell her.

"I knew you'd say something like that." She laughs.

Lark shows me how ruined Mikane is, how broken. She shows me how he drinks. She paints a picture of a man defeated.

"And yet," she says, "he keeps surprising me. He hasn't taken us; he barely looks at us. His mind's elsewhere, on other things. I thought I'd hate him. But I don't."

I should break my news. I should tell her my fears. But something holds me back. I am enjoying Lark so much as she takes in the sights of Peregrine Park. Her strength and beauty lift me. She sees the view below us, the sweep of the city's turbine towers and I take her to the edge of the palisade. We look down over Brightlinghelm. She's flexing her songlight. I swear it's getting brighter and more potent.

"It's funny when you see a place in songlight," says Lark. "The whole city shimmers and moves."

"That's how Northaven seems to me," I tell her. "Vivid and glimmerous."

Lark falls silent. Her thoughts turn dark. "Which of those buildings is the Chrysalid House?"

I show her a low building near the river—stark, virtually windowless. A barge is moored nearby and men are unloading unconscious figures. I feel Lark craving for Rye, just as she knows I am grieving for Cassandra. We stand, mourning them, our shared songlight a golden solace.

Then we both sense it together. Another presence.

Songlight.

Somebody is watching us.

"Go," I say.

Lark vanishes.

I turn. In the distance, near the fountain, my papa is with Keynes. My heart skips a beat as I realize Papa is holding the lead cuff. The Siren's powers have been unlocked.

I draw my coat around me, feeling bare. I make my way toward them, a smile stuck on my face. I cram my songlight into an acorn, into a hard, impenetrable nut. I hide it in my spleen. Did he sense me? Did he sense Lark? Even these questions are dangerous. I stop thinking and concentrate on the sound of water, flowing from the hands of our fountain. Until last year it was a figure of Gala, big-bellied, big-breasted. Then they replaced it with a marble Sister Swan.

"I'm on my way to the market," I say to my papa. "To buy you heroes some lunch."

I smile at him with nothing inside.

"How are you feeling?" asks Papa. "No pain in your leg?"

"No, I'm fine." I'm a big sunny cloud of nothing. "Why are you in the park?" I ask.

"Keynes is working. He says he gets clarity here. He's going to find me a terrorist."

I smile as widely as I can. I quash every single thought. I'm a sunbeam, a bubble, a silly grinning flower.

Then I feel someone's dirty fingernails opening my head. Someone's trying to pry their way in. I force down barriers. I mustn't look at him. I won't. My breathing tightens as I feel him pick and slither, looking for an entrance.

"What's the matter?" asks Papa in concern.

"Nothing," I smile. "Nothing." But I sense my smile is a grimace.

I won't be attacked like this. I won't be violated by this creeping creature. I exhale as powerfully as I can and with all the power of my being, I imagine a gale forcing him away.

Keynes crumples backward onto a bench. I see the strength go from his legs. And he releases me. He knows. There's no two ways about it. The Siren knows.

"I have to go to the market, Papa. I promised Ishbella."

"Don't overdo it, my lovely."

We part. Papa turns and sees Keynes, sitting on the bench, winded.

"Who told you you could sit?" he barks. "You're here to work. So do what you were spared for."

Keynes looks at me, his expression weird. "Good day to you, miss," he says.

"Good day to you, Keynes."

I smile as if nothing in the world is wrong.

By the time I get home from the market, carrying a big ham and bread and milk and cheese, the exhaustion has hit me. What did I do to Keynes? How did I get him to release me? It's like the roar of songlight I sent out to the Siren who was following Cassandra. Whatever it is, it has wiped me out. My head is fuzzy and my legs are heavy with fatigue. Climbing the stairs to our apartment takes an age, yet I feel a terrible urgency. I must tell Lark. The unthinkable has happened. *Keynes knows.* The house is quiet. Ishbella has cleared our parlor for Papa's men. She gives me a list of tasks but I tell her I'm dizzy and I go to my room, my refuge. I close the door.

With my last strength, I rise up to the blue, as high and far as I can, like Cassandra taught me: *The farther you go, the harder it is for anyone to track you.* But now I hardly have the strength to get to Northaven. I force my songlight, using the last of my energy. My head is aching, fit to break.

I find Lark alone, scrubbing her husband's kitchen. Wordlessly, I share with her. *Keynes knows, he knows.* Lark leaves her work and walks into her garden, thinking what to do.

"Nightingale," she says, "leave now. Take some money and just go."

The thought of leaving Papa wrenches me with sadness. But I know she's right. For Lark, it would be simple. She'd fling some things in a bag and sprint down the stairs. She'd run through the streets until she came to the city gates and then she'd come up with a marvelous plan of climbing walls and sliding over rooftops. I wish I had her easy strength. But my body is shaking with exertion.

"They've closed the city gates," I tell her. "Where will I go?"

Lark looks at me, undaunted.

"We're going to find a way. Your friend Cassandra knew people. I bet there are Torches who help other Torches."

"The terrorists?"

"Your father and his Siren are the terrorists," says Lark quietly. "You need to find Cassandra's friends."

"But what about Keynes? I can't use my songlight."

"I'll help you."

I feel such relief at this. Lark will help me. Strong, brilliant, vibrant Lark. She'll give me the courage.

"There's a curfew," I tell her. "If I'm out after dark, they'll arrest me."

"Then get as far as you can while it's bright. Find a hiding place and stay there."

I look at Lark, overwhelmed. But she is right.

I leave her, fading back into my flesh. The sounds of the day come back in my consciousness: children playing in the yard. I take my precious drawing book from under the bed. For the second time, I look around my little room, leaving it forever. I must sit, just for five minutes, five minutes to get my energy back. I rest on my bed, fighting the pull of my terrible fatigue.

I want to leave something for my papa, so that he knows how much I love him. I want him to try to understand. I decide that a picture will do better than words. I begin a drawing of us both—but soon my tears are blurring the paper. I brush them away and start again. I draw myself as a child floating in the air. He's holding my hand, smiling at me, about to let me go.

When it's finished, I tear it out of my sketchbook. I lie back for a moment, my whole body aching. Within seconds, I'm asleep.

"Where's Heron?" I ask Chaffinch. She's lying in the tin bath in our room. The water stinks of perfume.

"He went up to the graveyard," she complains. "Get me some more hot water."

I pour a kettle into her bath and set off after Heron. I don't know how to talk to him. But I don't know who else I can ask for help. Nightingale's situation is desperate and Heron's the only person I know, apart from that shit-cake Wheeler, who's ever even been to Brightlinghelm. Maybe I can glean some information. Where can Nightingale be safe?

But how can I ask him? What can I say? To voice anything is to put myself in peril . . . yet something spurs me on. Heron is the man to ask. He despises Emissary Wheeler. I could see that at the funeral. He despises Ely Greening too. He looked up to my father. He respects my mother. He's kind to John Jenkins. Perhaps he has compassion. But he's been fighting for the Brethren since the start of the war. If he knew I was unhuman, he'd be implacable against me.

As I reach the top of the path, I see Heron in the distance, standing at the new graves, talking to one of the widows. To my surprise, I realize it's my ma. Perhaps she's been up here, visiting my pa. Heron's looking down at her and she is talking. Whatever they're discussing, there's an atmosphere between them, a taut closeness in their stance.

Weird.

Heron sees me and breaks away from Ma. Instead of greeting me, she turns and kneels, laying long-stemmed flowers on the new graves. It's like she's trying to collect herself, like she doesn't want me to see her face. Heron approaches, taking the moorland path. His eye is looking past me like he doesn't want to be disturbed.

"Husband?" I begin.

"I'm going to buy a horse," he says, and he walks on, ignoring me.

"May I talk to you?"

I see a horse trader waiting on the edge of the moors. I follow Heron toward him.

"I have something to ask you."

"Ask it, then."

I stand there uselessly, trying to find my words. Heron shakes the trader's weathered hand and looks over his beasts. I bite my lips while he chooses his horse. A mare, a sturdy plodder. No proud cavalry stallion this; she's a beast of burden, made for the moors. He makes the deal and the horse is his.

He gives her a carrot.

"Heron?"

He waits for me to speak. I don't know how to begin so I stroke the horse, putting my hand on her soft gray muzzle. I reject a host of dull remarks. The only thing to do is to get straight to the point.

"I must ask you about Brightlinghelm."

He waits for more.

"We hear so little here. Only rumors . . ."

"What's your question?"

His eye is scanning the horizon. He wants to be riding. I can't tell him about Nightingale—so I tell him about Rye.

"I had a friend," I begin. "He was my brother's friend, Rye. A cadet. I knew him all my life. Anyway, he was Shamed and beaten. They found out he was . . ."

I can't say the word.

"An unhuman?"

"He was taken to Brightlinghelm and I wondered if . . . if you knew what might happen to him there, if—"

"He'll go to the Chrysalid House. If he begs loud enough, they'll train him for a Siren. Most likely he'll be made a chrysalid; I'm sure you know that."

"But I mean what would happen if he escaped? Do any of them ever escape?"

He glances at me then. "Why would I know that?"

I'm on dangerous ground. But it's too late to go back. Nightingale needs me.

"I've heard there are insurgents. I've heard they help unhumans."

"Insurgents? You mean traitors?"

"Do you know anything about them?"

"Why would you think I know anything?"

And suddenly, everything falls apart. My desperation becomes clear. "Do you know where they are? Do you know how somebody would find them?" My distress is pouring through the cracks. But I can't let Nightingale be taken.

Heron greets my questions with a silence. He regards me with his piercing eye. With each word, I have dug myself a grave.

"Sorry," I say, turning back toward the town. "I don't know why I spoke of such a thing. . . ."

I walk away. My cheeks are burning. Heron has risked his life a thousand times fighting for the Brethren's cause. What was I thinking? I'm a stupid, stupid fool.

I get to the top of the lane that leads down into the town when I hear his mare behind me.

"Elsa."

I turn, surprised to hear him say my name. So far, he's only called us "you two" or "girl." I look up, dreading what he's going to say.

"I don't know much about it, as I'm not cursed with that affliction," says Mikane.

He's rolling a smoke as he sits in the saddle. "But your friend, should he escape, might share his troubles in a Pink House."

Something about the way he says this makes me realize there's more to it than face value.

"Which Pink House?" I ask.

He leaves my question hanging while he lights his smoke.

"I'm told a man might find respite from anything on Maiden Lane. Sign of the Blue Rose . . ." He turns the mare and goes. I watch him heading for the moors.

Something has passed between us, more valuable than any information. Trust.

I try to contact Nightingale straightaway but I get no sense of her. I feel a rising panic. This is how it feels when she's sleeping. I'm dismayed. Why is she sleeping? She should be leaving her house. She has no time to lose. I try and try but my songlight isn't strong enough to break into her dreams.

I head for my new home and when I get there, Chaffinch is sitting on the doorstep in a sulk.

"Where were you?" she asks.

While I've been gone she has had visitors, Hoopoe Guinea and Chaffinch's nasty, frilly mother. She had to make them tea and she's fuming that I wasn't there to do it for her.

"You can't go out unless I say."

"Sorry," I mutter.

"No you're not. You say you want to work together but you don't have enough respect for me. You have to ask me before you can leave."

I can't be bothered with this.

"I saw our husband," I tell her. "He's just bought a horse."

This changes the subject, puzzling her. "What does he want a horse for?"

"Maybe so he can get away from us."

"I suppose you think that's funny."

I swallow my smile.

"I had to lie for him," she tells me. "Hoopoe and my ma were grilling me. Has he taken us both? How many times? Is everything in order?"

"What did you say?"

"How could I tell them my own husband doesn't want me?"

I sit next to her, trying to find some sympathy. "I'm sure he just needs time."

"Tinamou came round this morning, gloating. She told me all the things that Gyles Syker's done to her. I want those things done to me."

"He'll soon fall for your charms, Chaffie."

"But it's not manly. A man should take his wives the minute they're given. I want to be swept off my feet and pinned on the table."

This is so wearisome. "Shall I clean the stable out for his horse?" I ask.

"No. There are spuds to peel and all the tea things to wash."

"What are you going to do?"

Chaffinch is determined. "When Heron Mikane gets home, I'm going to be irresistible." She flounces off to our bedroom and shuts the door.

I reach out for Nightingale over and over. All afternoon there is silence. My anxiety worsens. What if it's too late? What if they've cuffed her mind already? It happened so fast when they came for Rye. I hide my dread in hard work. I wash up, prepare our meal, clean out the stable, and by the time Heron rides in, I've washed the salt and grime out of his greatcoat and I'm hanging it outside to dry. He watches me. I look at him warily.

"Has your mare got a name?" I ask.

"Horses don't need names." He dismounts.

"She's called Erix," I tell him, plucking a name from one of my ma's Greensward stories. Erix is a woodland girl who marries the King of the Underworld. Heron looks at me. He nods, accepting the name. He goes into the house. The trust holds.

A few minutes later, I hear him shout: "Get out of my bed."

23 ✳ NIGHTINGALE

It's dark when I awake. My head is still pounding. I hear Papa and his men in our parlor and the low hum of the radiobine. How long have I been sleeping? I sit up and rub my eyes. And when I open them I jolt back into my pillows. Keynes, the Siren, is sitting on my bed. He's looking through my sketchbook.

"Hello, Kaira," he says. "Songlight is so tiring, isn't it?"

Oh dear Gala.

"Your father's been using mine all day, searching for the evil scum who planted that incendiary device. I feel like I could sleep now for a week."

"Keynes," I say.

"I was most impressed when you forced me from your mind. I've never experienced anything quite like it. It must have taken all your energy."

Gala, help me.

"I felt it like a turbine bolt," continues Keynes. "And I can see that it's exhausted you."

"What do you want?" I whisper.

"I'd like us to be friends, Kaira. But you've deceived your papa, haven't you?"

I feel like I am falling off a burning ship. "Please don't tell him."

"You've been very cunning. Poor papa. When he finds out, think how it will ruin him."

Keynes smiles, as if he's enjoying the thought.

Think of how to fight him. Fight.

"It would tear his heart to shreds to send his darling to the Chrysalid House. It's obvious that you're the only thing he cares about."

I realize how much Keynes hates my father. He'll serve me up as an unhuman, just to see my papa's face.

"He'll never believe you," I tell him.

"Maybe not." Keynes grins. "But the doubt will be there. And it will grow. In truth, Kaira, I hate your papa like a plague and it would give me joy to cause him pain."

Waves of anguish shudder through me. I am such a crybaby. Lark would never cry. She'd hold this Siren in her gaze and think of something strong to say.

"You have no evidence," I say.

"The girl you were communing with in the park . . . I think you've drawn her in this book." Keynes darts his poison in a pleasant, friendly voice. He lifts my sketchbook. Not Lark. I will not give him Lark.

"This is her, isn't it?" He shows me one of my portraits. Lark stares back at me with deep charcoal eyes. In my hours of loneliness, I've put her on the paper. How I could I have been so careless and so stupid?

"I couldn't really see her in the park this morning. She was just a shapely shimmer," Keynes calmly tells me, as if this is an ordinary chat. "But her songlight left a strong impression. This lovely hair, blowing in the wind . . . She's beautiful, isn't she? I like her seaworker's boots."

Not Lark. You will not come for Lark.

"These turbine towers—that pretty little village in the background. It won't be hard to find out where she—"

"Get out of my room or I'll tell my papa."

Keynes smiles then. "Shall I tell your papa? Shall I reveal how treacherous you are?"

His question sinks into a yawning hole.

"Poor Kaira . . . I was once a frightened child, like you."

I swallow, trying to present a courage I don't feel. "Tell me what you want."

Keynes holds me in his gaze. "You're going to set me free."

I close my eyes. The room is spinning. He has me trapped, like a beetle on a pin.

"I work hard," complains Keynes. "I exhaust myself, cleansing my country every day. And at night, I'm locked in a cell without thanks, without praise. We Sirens should be lauded for what we do, but we're abused. We're trampled and insulted by the men we work for. Your father, he treats us like dogs. Well, I am not his hound." He's betraying his emotion now. I can smell the bitterness in this man's sweat. "I'll spare you, Kaira. You can carry on living your happy little life. But in return, I want my liberty."

I curse myself for falling asleep. I've missed my chance of freedom. I missed it.

"What must I do?" I ask.

Keynes pushes back the lank tufts of his hair, revealing the cruel keyhole in his skull. "Your papa is wearing the key around his neck. Steal it."

I know immediately that I won't be able to. I'll fail. And the act of trying will betray me anyway.

"What if he catches me?"

"That's a risk you have to take. You'll steal the key tonight or I will tell him what you are."

One way or the other, I am lost.

"Where will you go?" I ask, playing for time. "Will you join with the insurgents?"

His smile stretches to a sore grimace. Like something I have said has wounded him. He rocks forward, pulling his jacket tight around his ribs. His head is bowed.

"Radika Helms . . ." He says the name and then he can't go on. He commands himself before he speaks. "She was my fellow Siren. Her cell was next to mine. The bomb left her guts hanging from the bars." Keynes pauses, choked.

"I'm sorry," I say. "I'm so sorry that you lost her. I'm sorry." And it is true. I feel a knife-twist of compassion for this wretched man. He will never join the insurgents. He hates them with every atom.

"What I do with my freedom is none of your business," says Keynes. "But vengeance will belong to me."

I realize how much he is made of hate. He's dangerous. So dangerous.

"I'll do what you ask," I say.

He looks at me, wondering if he can trust. "Before dawn, you'll release me from the cellar and give me that key."

I nod. He stands to go. With my sketchbook.

"Give me my book."

He shakes his head. "It's my evidence—just in case you fail me." He leafs through, devouring its pages. "It's wonderful, you know. At first I thought you must have drawn all these things from your imagination. Then I realized that you've seen them. That city you've drawn, with glass domes and hanging gardens . . . Where is that?"

"It isn't real," I say. "I just made it up."

"You saw it. Like you saw these huge airships and this girl with the seaworker's boots. You're not just any unhuman, Kaira. Your songlight knocked me off my feet." He puts my book in his gray, dusty jacket. "If you let me down, you'll be the greatest prize I ever caught."

"What are you doing in here, runt?" My papa's at the door. He grabs Keynes by the back of the neck and turfs him into the corridor. "Filthy hound. You stay away from my daughter!"

This won't help. It'll enrage Keynes. It'll make him hate my papa more. I follow, trying to placate.

"It's my fault," I assure Papa. "I wanted my window closed. I asked Keynes to help me."

"Don't speak to him, Kaira. Sirens are all dogs." Papa helps Keynes on his way with an angry kick.

"Papa, don't be cruel!"

"There's only one way to treat his sort. . . ."

"He was helping me. He hasn't done anything wrong."

"He'll wheedle and manipulate, trying to get his freedom." Papa pulls Keynes up by the lapels. "My daughter might be kind but she's not daft, hound. She knows you're unhuman scum."

Keynes turns round, his eyes upon me, nursing his wounds.

"I told you not to look at her," cries Papa. "You can forget about your supper now."

He marches Keynes out of the apartment and down the stairwell. I hear the heavy cellar door slam closed.

It's an agony waiting for Papa to sleep. I serve him beers while he complains about the day.

"Sometimes, I want to jack it all in," he says.

"No you don't," counters Ishbella. "You're the station leader." She talks about how our lives will improve. Evans, as station leader, had a house with a garden. He was on a better wage; he had a better pension. "This could set us up for life."

"It isn't what it used to be," sighs Papa, looking bleak.

And at last, he slopes off to bed.

The curfew lasts till dawn. I can't run till then. I can't go outside. I try to connect with Lark but it's the dead of night and she's asleep. I sit on my bed, thinking about Keynes, locked in the cellar down below. No food, no water, not even a blanket.

Your father . . . he treats us all like animals.

I have always loved my papa. He has spoiled me since the day that I was born. He has lavished me with care. He sat by my bed when he thought I was dying and I could hear him whimper like a wounded bear. But I have to face the truth. Being an Inquisitor has made him mean, in spirit and in soul. It has diminished him. Papa doesn't even notice his own cruelty.

I think of what we've done to Keynes, all of us, every Brightling. I think of him, kicked and called a hound, watching what's left of Radika Helms sliding down the bars of her cage.

With a sinking heart, I know what I must do. I have to set the Siren free.

In the hour before dawn, when Papa's in his deepest sleep, I creep into his room. Ishbella's nearest to me and I have to make my way around their bed. Papa's back is to me and I see the keychain around his neck. I have my sewing scissors and I try to cut through it—but it's made of strong, tensile stuff.

Papa wakes. "What are you doing?"

He sees my shocked face, the scissors in my hand—and he knows. He takes me into the kitchen.

"You'd better tell me what you're up to, Kaira."

I decide to make it seem like my own idea, a compassionate act.

"Papa, you should free Keynes. It's cruel to keep him like that."

Papa looks at me, bewildered. Then his face changes. "I know what's happened here," he says. "That bastard's mind-twisted you."

He grabs his whip and he's going to go down to the cellar. I pull him back. I beg him not to go.

"Freeing Keynes is my idea alone. He's so unhappy, Papa. I can't bear to see it."

"Unhappy?" Papa is shocked. "He's lucky he's alive." He sits me down as if he's explaining something to a child. "You've got to understand something, Kaira. Sirens hate us. I have to treat him like that or he'd kill us in our beds. Trust me, Keynes is a viper."

"But we've done that to him, Papa. All of us . . ."

Papa snaps into a rage. "What are you talking about? D'you want us overrun with mind-twisting unhuman scum? Is that what you're saying?"

"No."

"Are you saying you don't approve of what I do? Because I put food on this table." He swears under his breath and tears bite my eyes. Papa marches me to my room.

"You don't have a clue what I deal with every day. And I hope that little viper has messed with your mind—because your disloyalty would break my fucking heart."

And with that, Papa slams my door. He has never sworn at me before and I am shaking with distress.

I have failed, as I knew I would. And Papa will find out the truth.

I toss and turn, thinking of the barge by the Isis, bodies being unloaded into the Chrysalid House. I wake breathless—dreaming of Wheeler pulling black gauze over my face. I pace the house; I listen to Heron's moans as he fights off the Aylish in his own troubled dreams. I sit at the kitchen table, watching clouds scud across the stars. It's turning bright before I sense Nightingale. Her anxiety comes pouring out:

"I couldn't get the key!"

I try to calm her but she's too distressed. Her songlight blinds me, desperate and uncontrolled. It's almost painful.

"What key?" I ask.

"I went into Papa's room. I tried to cut the keychain but he woke up." To my utter dismay, Nightingale tells me she was trying to free a Siren.

"Are you mad?" I ask. "A Siren's only purpose is to catch you in a trap."

I try to slow her down but she tells me the whole story in a rush of painful images. Her fear is overwhelming. I try to imagine what it must be like, being so scared of your only parent. She has to get away from him. This is a disaster.

"He's locked you in?"

Nightingale is so pained and panicking that she hasn't checked the door. To her surprise and relief, it opens.

"I should have known he wouldn't be so cruel. He'd never lock me in."

I wish Nightingale wouldn't make excuses for this man. But along with the fear, I feel her powerful love. It's complicated, that's for sure.

"Where's your papa now?" I ask.

She peers down the corridor. "He's washing. Ishbella's getting dressed."

"Don't waste a moment. Run."

"I promised Keynes I'd help him."

"Nightingale, you tried. Run now, I beg you. Rye missed his chance. Don't you dare miss yours."

As she grabs her coat, I show her my conversation with Mikane.

"You put yourself in danger for me . . . ," she whispers, moved. She heads for the door.

"Heron said we should look for a Pink House with a blue rose on the door," I tell her. "Go there now. It's on Maiden Lane."

I hear her father splashing in the bathroom. I see her stepmother slouched on the bed, wearily pulling on her skirt. I'm terrified we are too late. Nightingale unbolts the apartment door as quietly as she can. She closes it behind her, praying it won't creak. Her heart is pounding.

"I'm with you," I say. "I'm with you all the way."

She hurries down the stairwell, past the door to Keynes' cellar. I see her hesitate.

"Keep moving, as fast as you can!"

Nightingale hurries across the courtyard, the pain in her hip making her slow. If anyone should see her . . .

Then I hear my name.

"Elsa, are you deaf?"

I turn from Nightingale's reality and I am in my own.

Chaffinch is shaking my shoulder. I'm at the kitchen table, staring into space. She's up and dressed.

"Our husband wants his breakfast."

Heron is standing in his bedroom door, pulling on his shirt, staring at me curiously. I'm still in my nightdress, my feet cold and bare.

"Sorry," I say. "I've had a restless night. . . ."

I put the kettle on the stove and go to dress myself. In my room, I connect with Nightingale. She's laboring down the street. She's already out of breath.

"I'll get on a tram," she says. "The tram will take me right into the city. It will preserve my energy."

The tram stop seems a million miles away. She keeps looking behind her for the sound of pounding feet. *Hurry, Nightingale, hurry.*

"Elsa!" calls Chaffinch. "Where's our tea?"

"Go," says Nightingale. "Keep yourself safe."

"I'll come again as soon as I can!"

Chaffinch is wearing a dress as low cut as she dares. Her breasts stick over the top like little moons. I quickly make a pot of tea and she leans over Heron, pouring him a cup. Then she reaches across him for the jug of milk, making sure he gets the full lunar view.

"Say when," she offers.

"I'll have it black," murmurs Heron without looking up. I put bread and butter on the table and organize a plate of smoked fish and cheese. Chaffinch drapes herself on her chair, every limb arranged to entice him.

"I was thinking I might bathe myself today," she says, her voice all silky.

Heron makes no comment. His eye is on his food, which disappears quicker than a blink. That's a soldier's way, I suppose: stuff it in while you've got the chance.

Chaffinch picks up a pot of ointment. She offers it to Heron.

"I got you this gift."

"What is it?"

"I hope you don't mind, but it's balm for your scars." She runs her tongue across the tip of her teeth. "Would you like me to apply it?"

"Is there a problem with my scars?"

Chaffinch has no answer. Heron wipes his mouth with the back of his hand.

"I'll be out till nightfall," he informs us.

"But it's your honeymoon," coos Chaffinch. "You could stay at home with me."

Heron finishes his tea. He takes his smokes and he goes outside.

"Well, *fuck*," exclaims Chaffinch. "How long will this nonsense carry on?" She is finally losing her patience. "When will he do his duty? It's his *duty*."

"Maybe his manhood was shot off," I suggest.

"I've seen him pee and he pisses like a man. Why won't he take me like a man?"

I have to get out of here. I have to be with Nightingale.

"Chaffie, may I have permission to—"

"No! This is a problem for both of us. By the time he goes back to war, we should both be pregnant." Chaffinch is relentless. "I'm desperate to tell my ma what a big washout he is," she complains. "All those battle tales? I'm beginning to wonder if they're even true."

"Don't tell your mother. If Heron finds out you're disloyal, he'll be even harder to get into bed."

"He isn't natural," huffs Chaffinch.

I suddenly see a way to get out. "Maybe he needs oysters," I suggest. "I've heard an old wives' tale that oysters make a man's juices flow."

Chaffinch is curious. She'll try anything.

"May I go on the sea?" I ask her like a good Second Wife. "I know where to find the very best. I'm sure once Heron's tasted them, he'll be at it like a ram."

I take her giggle as approval and I run from the house. I find Heron saddling his mare. I ask him if he's partial to oysters.

"I'd rather eat worms," he says.

My heart sinks. "Scallops, then," I say, trying to keep the desperation from my voice. "I know all the best scallop beds. I could catch you some."

"Why are you so anxious to get out on the sea?" That strange, curious look from him again.

I clutch at something. "For my mother. She gets seasick badly. She's all alone now with the boat—and I want to help."

He looks down the hill. Ma is leaving for the harbor, wearing Pa's old seaworker's boots. They are several sizes too big for her.

"Go tell Curl that you'll sail the boat." He uses the diminutive of her name. Not "Mrs. Crane" or "your mother."

"Catch a tunny," he says. "I like nothing better than a tunny steak."

My heart leaps. "For tunny I must go out far. I might be out all day."

"I have Erix here for company." He pats his mare like the King of the Underworld.

Ma is looking up at us. The wind is blowing her hair out of its widow's veil. She looks different somehow, like one of the weights she carries has been lifted off. Heron regards her.

"Invite your mother to eat with us," he says. This is generous but problematic.

"Should I invite Chaffie's mother too?"

"No." He sets off.

I run down to Ma and tell her that Heron has asked me to take out the boat. She's grateful.

"It was a rough sea yesterday," she says. "I thought I wouldn't have any guts left . . . and I didn't catch half as much as you."

"He's invited you to eat with us."

She's surprised. And pleased. She looks as if she wants to talk—but I must be with Nightingale. I run on down the hill, leaving puzzlement on my mother's face.

At the entrance to the harbor, I almost fall over Mr. Malting. He's tied to a post, kneeling in his own piss. This must be his punishment for standing up to Wheeler. Elder Haines is guarding him.

"Don't speak to him," he barks. "He's being punished."

I meet Mr. Malting's gaze and let him know, as best I can, that I think he's an absolute hero.

At first, Mrs. Sweeney doesn't want to let me have my boat.

"Newlyweds don't sail; it's unlucky," she says. "Sidon doesn't like it." Mrs. Sweeney's house is virtually a shrine to the sea god.

"My husband wants me to go," I tell her. "Ask him, if you think I'm lying."

She relents and helps me with the nets, her eyes alive at the prospect of gossip.

"How is he?" she asks with a smutty wink.

"None of your business, Mrs. Sweeney," I say with mock shock.

"He's a big, gorgeous beast, you lucky little minx. I wouldn't mind those scars. I think he's all man."

I give a sigh, like someone whose body aches with pleasure.

"So tell me," she asks. "How did you snare him? I heard you climbed a tree so he could see your private goods."

This is getting wearisome. "Wouldn't you have done the same?"

She cackles with laughter, like we're two girls together. I can't wait to get away.

I rejoice to be on the waves again. I raise the sail, using the breeze to leave the coast behind.

"Nightingale. Nightingale!"

Am I too late? Has she been apprehended? As the wind blows my boat out into the deep, she connects with me—giving me a glimpse of where she is. I find myself in a tram, approaching central Brightlinghelm. Nightingale is sweating her relief to see me. The tram is huge and magnificent, clanging and roaring like a mythical beast. The doors open in a glassy shimmer and it vomits people onto the platform. Nightingale climbs out. I sense she's near the river and she heads along a narrow street toward the Pink District.

"I've never been in this part of the city," she says. "It's got a fearsome reputation."

"Look for Maiden Lane," I remind her. "A Pink House, a sign with a blue rose."

The distance between us is so great. With the motion of the waves, it's exhausting to stay with her. Nightingale makes it seem easy when she comes here. Her songlight is such a powerful beam. Mine is stretched to its limit. I see her flicker in a blur of streets. The sunlight on the sea is dazzling and my two realities collide in my mind. I rest on the waves for a moment, taking in slow breaths of air. When my head has stopped spinning, I rejoin Nightingale, feeling that peculiar sensation of traveling through space yet remaining where I am.

I'm with her on a crowded street, very, very far from my body. She grasps my songlight with her own, strengthening it. I hear a cacophony of voices, the shouts of market traders; the hum of the great city. Close to Nightingale, music can be heard. A radiobine blares out a patriotic song from a nearby soldiers' bar.

In the boat, I bait the big hooks of my tunny lines with sprats. I drop them into the deep. Tunny are difficult to catch. They're just about the fastest swimmers in the ocean and it's hard to pull them in. I sail farther into the deep, and, as I ready the lines, Nightingale comes to a stop, bewildered.

"I'm lost," she says.

The street scintillates, coming in and out of focus. I sit very still and breathe slowly, pouring my focus into her reality. We're on a narrow twisting lane, crowded with market stalls.

"A Pink House. A sign with a blue rose," I remind her.

"Almost every other house is pink," she says. "But none of the streets are named. It's like a maze."

She's right. One nameless alley runs into another. There are traders and beggars, veterans missing limbs, raggedy children. I try to rise up, to see the lay of the land but Nightingale pulls me back down.

"Nobody must sense you," she whispers. "Keep your harmony in mine so we're just singing on a single note. . . ."

I walk with her, in her shoes, feeling the painful effort in my knee and hip. Our breathing is one breath, our songlight one muted song. We pass street sellers, pickpockets, a frightening preacher from the church of Thal. We walk on, searching. Everywhere there are soldiers, sailors, military personnel, fragments of Brightlinghelm's vast army on their rare days of leave. The shimmer of distance gives me vivid, bright colors and soft, ragged shadows. We pass a statue of Peregrine. *The Human Will Prevail.*

"Can you sense Keynes?" I ask her. "Is he looking for you yet?"

"Don't mention him. Even to think of him is a danger."

"A blue rose. Keep your mind fixed on a blue rose."

Each house is painted in different shades of pink. Some have young women sitting in the windows, wearing very little, dark rings under their eyes. Others have women posing in doorways, standing in haloes of tobacco smoke. They all have pink bands around their necks. Nightingale is too sheltered for this place. Truly, so am I. Hoopoe said that Third Wives lived in fine houses and dressed in fine clothes. Not true. These girls look hardened, underfed.

A group of servicemen passes. I see the weird shape of baggy trousers and fur-lined coats. They have big goggles slung round their necks.

"Airmen," says Nightingale in answer to my puzzlement.

Immediately, I think of Piper. I have banished all thought of him for the longest while. Piper. I push the thought down into the hole where my brother used to be.

"Hey, girlie," cries one of them. "We're all heroes, don't you know? Give us a kiss." To my horror, one of them slaps Nightingale with a drunken kiss.

"Go on, kiss him back," the airmen cry. Nightingale struggles but they hold her fast. "What's wrong with you? He's a fucking hero."

I pour all my strength into Nightingale. "Knee him in the bollocks," I say.

Nightingale slams her good leg up into the airman's groin.

"I don't want to kiss you."

The airmen fall about, laughing. Their comrade is clutching his balls.

"Little slut. Look at her, she's like a plucked chicken." The airmen let Nightingale go, clucking and squawking at her like hens. Nightingale stands by the gutter, recovering her dignity.

"Stay calm," I warn her. "Emotion might reveal us."

I can feel how hot she is. Her heart is clanging with fatigue. We pass a stall selling offal and the smell sickens her. She stops, leaning on a rusting turbine mast. I wish that Heron Mikane had songlight so I could ask him where this blasted Pink House is. A huge dog starts barking and snarling at her, pulling on its chain. Nightingale stumbles backward. She flees down a narrow passage and comes out on another street, her weak leg aching.

"It's no good," she says. "I need to rest."

Suddenly I see something. At the end of the passage behind her is a half-hidden door. Dirty pink, with a faded blue rose on it.

"Look behind you. . . ."

She sees the flower. Relief fills her—then trepidation. "What if it's a trap? What if they keep me there and make me a Third Wife?" Our paper-thin plan is blowing in the wind.

Somehow, my trust in Heron holds. "What's the alternative?" I ask. "Knock."

Nightingale puts out her hand to knock on the door—

—and suddenly I feel a dreadful rush. Pain—PAIN—

I lurch back—

My body—my body isn't there—

The worst choking feeling—a terrifying panic—where am I?—

I'm crying out—it's agony—

A precipitous fall—a fall into a white abyss—

"NIGHTINGALE," I scream—

I fall forever, guts churning—

I see my boat below. My flesh-body's lying there. I'm not breathing. Gala, what's happening to me? I can't get back into my body. I need to breathe—

The boat is shooting fast across the waves, bouncing hard against the crests. A speed I can't fathom. A second later, Nightingale is in songlight with me, her arms around me.

"I've got you."

With her help, I rejoin myself and fill my lungs with oxygen. For a moment I just breathe, my breath harsh against the wind.

"The boat's moving too fast," she says. "I think your songlight . . . it lost connection with your body. . . ."

She's right. I find my limbs again, glad to be whole. Then I see my tunny lines; two of them, taut as violka strings. A tunny couldn't pull the boat like this. Not even two. I'm still so breathless and disjointed I can hardly speak.

"What's pulling us?" I ask.

Nightingale concentrates her songlight. She peers into the water.

"An enormous black-and-white fish!" she squeals. Then I see a beast rising out of the waves and plunging back beneath, my lines in its mouth.

"It's not a fish," I say. "Orca."

I'm awry, dizzy, fumbling; I can't operate my arms and legs. I'm looking for my knife.

"Lark," says Nightingale, fascinated. "It has song. . . ."

And then she tunes me to the creature's overwhelming song. My body cannot take it; the vibration is too great. It's maddened by the lines. I have to cut them and free the thing. Where's my knife? I grasp it in my hand.

"Now," cries Nightingale. "It's diving!"

The creature's rearing downward, taking the side of the boat with it. I fall over. I cling on to a rope but my hands won't grip.

"Lark, hold on. Hold on for your life!"

A thud. A flip. The boat capsizes. I feel the shock of the water. There's nothing to hold on to. My limbs flail. And finally, the tunny lines snap. I feel something more powerful than Sidon, turning, coming at me through the water. It finds my thrashing leg. I feel the bite of its teeth as it pulls me down into the dark.

25 ✳ NIGHTINGALE

I'm screaming:

"LARK, LARK!"

With every heartbeat, her name thunders from my frame. I fall to my knees on the pavement outside the pink door with the blue rose. I scream:

"LARK, LARK!"

I scream with every outward breath and all the power of my song until my throat's in rags—and still I keep on crying out. I feel people cluster round me. A man with sharp fingers shakes me, but I'm in the sea.

"LARK!"

I shriek underwater like a Hel god, deafening the whale—and it spits her out. I try to draw her back up to the surface light.

"LARK!"

The sharp-fingered man is crying my name.

"Kaira, Kaira, stop. You're hurting me!"

Keynes has found me.

I can't lose her. I can't be alone.

"LARK!"

Her lungs are full of water—

A young voice. A desperate, heartfelt cry. Who, where?

"*LARK!*"

I'm at the council table. Kite has got his Fireflies in the air, but Peregrine won't arm them and Harrier is on his side. My lead band is off underneath my perfect wig. My master has given me my instructions. I'm to mind-twist Brother Drake—a libertine and toad. He must cast his vote in Kite's favor. The argument is crucial, deadly earnest, a growing rift between Peregrine and Kite—but I cannot concentrate. In my mind, there's an explosion of sound and light.

"*LARK!*"

While Peregrine is speaking, I'm forced to stand.

"What is it, Sister?" he asks.

I realize by his puzzled face that the cry's been heard by me alone. I know it would be fatal to explain.

"I am unwell."

"*LARK!*"

Pain confounds me. A blinding songlight takes my strength.

"Sister," cries Peregrine, coming toward me, in fatherly concern. "Are you hurt?"

"*LARK!*"

My legs give way. In a pretense of chivalry, Kite supports me out. The pain is sickening.

"What are you doing?" he hisses, as soon as we're alone.

I cling to the wall, dropping to my knees. He lifts me, turning me.

"Explain yourself!"

"*LARK!*"

A shower of anguished sparks go convulsing through my head.

To my horror, I vomit. I cover Kite in hot spew.

He steps back, roaring in disgust.

27 ✳ NIGHTINGALE

My body's writhing, the effort of holding her is so great.

I'm weakening. I call on Gala; I call on Sidon, the god of the sea.

"*Lark . . .*"

I hear a voice far away, a strange accent, a faint: "Where are you?"

I hear my papa cry my name. "Kaira. Kaira . . ."

I try to move my lips but I can't make them work.

"Give her space," Papa cries to the crowd. "Get back."

I need to hold Lark in my songlight. I cannot bear for her to drown.

"*Lark . . .*"

I feel a cloth pressed down upon my face. Liquid Sleep, an Inquisitor's best tool. I resist until I have to take a breath.

Then everything goes black.

PART 4

Flight is natural to me. It's natural, as if I'm a bird. Why was I named for a sandpiper? Pa should've named me for a swift. For here in the air, climbing and falling in my plane, turning in the wind, that's how I feel. I want to do this every day for the rest of my life—and if that means my life's short, then so be it.

My teeth were clamped with fear, first time I went up. But almost straightaway, the fear became a soaring joy. I can forget everything here in the air, my mind only on the task, becoming part of the machine. I let Thal guide my hands. After only days of practice, I can land my plane without a bump. Other lads haven't been so lucky. We've had two fatalities already, may Thal exalt their souls. One lad overshot the runway, his plane turning over and over. Another had a faulty engine and his plane exploded in a ball of fire. Wing Commander Axby has been shaken by each loss. We feel how deeply he cares for us, how much he wants us to succeed. We're learning how to cope with the incredible speed and there's a legion of engineers constantly refining, redesigning, making our engines safer, more efficient. Thal praise them.

"You're flying with the gods now," says Wing Commander Axby. "The risks are great. The air is not a natural place for mortal men to be. But war requires everything we have."

We've been assigned gunners who sit in the cockpits with us. The gunners are all smaller lads who can fit in the tiny front seats, aiming our firepower. My gunner is called Tombean Finch, a wiry fellow from Whitecliffe. His grin is infectious. Finch and I have called our plane *Curlew*. It has long, delicate wings, covered in tiny mirrorlike plates to catch and store the solar. Its battery backs up the firefuel engine. My cockpit is a mass of dials, and every day we've been drilled in the function of each one. We've been taught to preserve fuel by using air currents and we've learned what different formations of clouds might mean. I'm getting a sense of my new element, the air.

Finch has sharp, smiling eyes and a laugh that makes me feel as if I haven't got a care. I'm glad that Axby put us together. Finch and I are hitting every target and we're flying at the head of the formation now. The sky, the light, my glittering plane, my friend Finch, the world's horizon. These things have lifted me. My future is magnificent.

I never need to think about the past.

When we first arrived, Brother Kite paid our squadron a special visit. We stood in line as he inspected us and I was struck by his fine features. He looks like an icon of Thal.

"Thal sent me a dream," he told us. "I saw a plane flying like a comet, powered with firefuel. Thal himself has shown me the means by which you, Brightland's airmen, will vanquish Ayland forever."

Brother Kite reminded us that the Aylish are riven with corruption. He inspired us, telling us that Brightland's fighting men were the vanguard of the human race. He has filled me with desire for conquest and for glory. When we had tattoos of the war god inked into our arms, I made sure mine had the face of Kite.

Today, we have our first long mission, to test the stamina of our planes. From Meadeville, we're heading up to Brightlinghelm, then over the Greensward to the Tenmoth Zone. We're aiming for the ruined city of Tenmoth, which the Light People built. It falls into the Great Palantic Ocean, which nobody in recent times has crossed. The Tenmoth Zone is still full of irradiance, like the humanless desert continent that lies to the south. Axby has told us we must imagine that Tenmoth is Reem, Ayland's capital. We won't be armed with bombs—our missiles will be filled with paint so that we can test our accuracy. I reckon my gunner has got a good eye.

We set off at daybreak. The firefuel engine takes us high into the air and in less than half an hour, we're flying over Brightlinghelm—a trip that takes all night by barge. We peer down at the turbine towers and apartment blocks, a glorious sight. The Isis flows through it like a ribbon of blue.

"That's the Brethren's Palace," Finch informs me.

I see lawns and fine buildings—but before I can properly admire their magnificence, the city is behind us and we're flying over villages, towns, and fields. After a while, Finch leans round and passes me a breadcake. We follow the river over miles of farmland, then over a great deforested plain, where mud and tree stumps form a dismal landscape. Finch teases me about my Northaven accent. He tells jokes into the listening device, good jokes that make me laugh, jokes about how scared he'd be if he was locked in a bedroom with Sister Swan. It's a release to be so disrespectful.

Finch shares stories about his family. With both his father's wives, he has seventeen siblings. I can't imagine what such a family is like. No wonder he never shuts up. He must have fought hard to get heard. His older brothers are all serving Brightland. Cormack, the eldest, is dead. He has four married sisters and his youngest siblings are still kids and little babies. He has nieces and nephews, cousins everywhere.

"There's always washing hanging on the line," he said. "I never see my mothers without babies tied upon their backs."

I reckon everyone in Whitecliffe must be a relative of Tombean Finch.

He hands me a bag of toffee. I resolve to buy something delicious next time, something to share with him.

"What about you then, Crane? What's your family like?"

It's easy to talk about Ma and Pa. My love for them comes pouring out. Finch is full of sympathy about my pa. Then he asks about my sister. Such a welt of confusion comes up in me that I fall silent. I can't bear to think of her despoiling Pa's boat with her unhuman hands. She's an affront to Thal. But I don't say this. I just tell Finch that she's a pain in the arse. I can't think what else to say.

Why did Pa squander his love on Elsa and not me? Unhuman cuckoo in our nest, pushing me out from the day she was born. I squirm with disquiet.

Finch is pointing downward at a long green scar running under the land.

"That must be one of the great roads of the Light People," he tells me. "They used to call them freeways, imagine that."

I'm glad this boy is here to distract me. It's hard to sink in gloom in the sunshine of his presence.

"They were mighty people," I agree, shaking my head at their folly. "Mighty men. And yet there they lie, under the green."

"What do you think of this firefuel, then?" Finch asks.

"I think it's sent from Thal," I say, thinking of Brother Kite.

"Doesn't it make you uneasy? It was lust for firefuel that killed off the Light People. Those fools went to war over it, with bombs bigger than this plane. They blew themselves to fuck. And here we are, a thousand feet in the air, in a flimsy piece of tin, with a tank of firefuel under our arses—"

"This plane is a miracle of Thal," I say firmly.

As the ranking airman, I'm not going to have seditious talk. But I don't like the way that Finch's words unsettle me.

He falls silent, but not for long. Finch soon starts to hum a song he's heard on the radiobine, a song with an irresistible tune. I find myself joining in the chorus. I repay Finch with a Greensward song that my ma used to sing when we were small. It makes me sore in the heart to think of my ma and I think of my own Greensward blood as we approach the vast canopy of trees. I will make her proud.

For over an hour we fly above an immense tangle of green. The mountains rise and fall in their glory and the living canopy of trees goes on as far as the eye can see. Ruined towers and spires of the Light People give us further landmarks, and by the time the sun is at its height, we see the northeast coast approaching. Far in the distance, over to the west, I can see moorland. Northaven lies in that direction. I get a pang of homesickness, for Ma, for the sandy streets, for my life as cadet, for—

I won't ever think his name.

The landscape beneath us begins to change. Scrubland. The greenery falls away. We're flying over an ugly, stunted desert of twisting concrete ruins. They're overgrown with creeping things, but none of it looks healthy.

"Tenmoth," says Finch.

We become aware of our fellow pilots, flying alongside us, their planes glinting in the sun like jeweled birds. We hear Wing Commander Axby up ahead, speaking in our radiobine earpieces, another innovation in our Fireflies.

"Keep formation. You'll see an ancient avenue of towers. Use it to guide you. At the top lie your targets."

We see the grid of the ancient city, square blocks, as if a giant child had drawn it on the land. We head for the alleyway of ancient towers.

"Prepare to fire." We hear Axby's voice crackle in our ears. "I'm dropping white paint to make your marks. Each of you has your own color paint so you can see how accurate you are."

One gunner fires too early and hits one of the ancient towers. Another gunner leaves it too late and his color bombs land in the sea. Finch hits Axby's white marks with ease. His bombs explode in colored blooms on streets and rooftops. I think how it will look when there are Aylish, swarming out of their homes like woodlice from a rock. I don't much like the way it makes me feel.

"Good work," said Axby when our task is complete. "Pilots, it's up to you to navigate your way back. I'm going to take up the rear. I want you back in Meadeville by sundown."

Finch and I keep to the coast. The ruins of Tenmoth go under the sea for quite some while. We see the grid of streets continue underwater, seaweed clinging to the ancient concrete. It's a fearful place. At night, by all accounts, the moths and bats come swarming out, clouds of them rising like a pestilential fog. Such a cloud could bring down any plane. I'm filled with a chilling distaste for the place. But Finch says:

"Life is invading the zone again. It'll bury the toxins eventually." He believes that everything's progressing toward a better future. "In a hundred thousand years," he says, "people might live in Tenmoth again."

This thought's not much of a consolation as we leave the forbidding place behind.

High on our returning, I'm distracted by little plumes of smoke rising above the canopy of the Greensward. Once more I start thinking of my mother's people.

"What's that?" I ask.

I veer off our route. Finch peers down, as intrigued as I am. He has the best view. His windows go right under his cockpit, to ensure he finds his targets.

"I see people down there," he cries. "There's a clearing. . . ."

Sure enough, we're over a settlement. The plumes of smoke are from illegal campfires. We see tiny figures scurrying, darting for cover. It's impossible to gauge their numbers. Their encampment winds under the trees. I descend lower, curious. There's an old creeper-covered temple nearby, rising above the canopy. I see some men emerge onto the roof, staring up at us. Are these my mother's tribe, the Greensward people?

"Nomads," says Finch. "They probably think we're gods."

When we're not flying, we are learning geography and map-reading in class. Our instructor tells us that the Greenswardians have held themselves aloof from the Brethren, persisting in the old ways of the Traveling Time. We know they're being courted by Great Brother Peregrine and encouraged to unite, but they're fiercely independent. There's a rumor that in these remote communities, unhumans still wield power. There's also a rumor that the Greensward is used by all manner of undesirables to escape from righteous justice. They're staring up at Finch and me. I circle again and fly in lower. I know time is of the essence but I want these remote tribes to see what modern Brightland can offer them—the miracle of flight.

"I don't like the expression on their faces," observes Finch. "They look pretty hostile to me."

"They're probably afraid. They need to see what the Brethren can do for them."

I take the plane as low as I dare and salute the people. I see they're dressed in green fatigues, armed with powerful crossbows. Finch takes my lead and salutes them too. Then one man raises his crossbow.

I rapidly ascend—but an arrow whistles up. We feel it thud into the fire-proof textile that makes the lightweight undercarriage. I try to shrug it off but I am disappointed, in them and in myself. I have been foolishly naive.

"They misinterpreted our gesture," I say.

"Bastards," exclaims Finch. "Do you think they're insurrectionists?"

I say nothing, curving our plane back toward Brightlinghelm.

We're still flying over the forest when the engine starts sputtering. It momentarily cuts out. I look at the fuel gauge. We're near the bottom of our reserve.

"I don't understand," I say, dismayed. "Axby told us there was plenty of firefuel for the journey. Can you see the engine? Is there a fault?" I ask Finch.

He twists round and, crouching in his seat, looks at the underside of the plane.

"I can see fuel dripping down the arrow," he says. "Those savage fuckers shot a leak into our tank."

I try to reach Axby, but our detour over the settlement has left us far behind. We've lost contact. My hands are slippery with sweat as they grip the controls. The plane coughs, sputters, then cuts out. Thal. Thal. I don't know what to do. I'm not experienced enough for this. We begin to plummet.

"Solar power," yells Finch. "Switch to solar!"

I click to solar. A fierce juddering, the plane is twisting, falling—and at last the battery kicks in. Using all my strength, teeth gritted, I bring *Curlew* steady. My whole body is drenched in sweat. I try to glide from cloud to cloud as we've been taught, but conditions are against us. The sky is endless blue and the wind is in our nose. Our planes have battery power for maybe thirty minutes. As we make our way over the landscape of stumps, I realize that we won't make it back to Meadeville. I watch the battery run down by each percentage point.

"What's the plan, Crane?" yells Finch.

It rushes before me—my life till this point—my sister, my mother—Pa—Rye. Rye. I close my eyes. Is this no more than I deserve? I betrayed him—

I feel a stinging slap. Finch has unbuckled himself. He's leaning on his seat, staring right into my face.

"Fly this plane, you fucker." His eyes are full of determination. "If you don't get us back alive, I'll fucking kill you."

I don't question Tombean's logic. I'll get him back. I won't be responsible for this boy's death.

"We're not going to die," I promise him.

I remember in a flash my mother's face when Wheeler came with the news that Pa was missing in action. Her mouth fell slowly open; her eyes fell slowly closed. I remember how I ran into her arms, holding her so that I couldn't see her grief.

"I won't die on a training exercise," I say. "My ma will be proud of me. My pa will be proud."

We can see Brightlinghelm ahead. I use the Isis to guide me, flying in a line over its meanders.

"Get back in your seat," I order Finch. "Buckle up. Sit fucking tight. I know what we have to do."

Our speed is terrific as we reach the outskirts. The battery is dead. We're a few hundred feet above the land. I'm going to use the Isis as a runway. I see another flash—Rye, skimming stones near Cormorant Rock. I realize I can skim the plane. I don't know for sure if it will float. It might hit the water and disintegrate. But even if it sinks, we might just have time to get out alive. A single obstacle will see us spinning out of control. If we hit a rock or a boat, we'll be done for. Thal give us strength.

"Gala," prays Tombean. "Gala, help us."

I hear him breathing fear through my earpiece. I see his knuckles, curling round his seat.

"Bring us down safe and I'll buy you a fucking bucket of beer," he cries. He manages to hide the crack in his voice.

"Sing one of your fuckwit songs," I shout to him.

He begins a crude Pink House song. His voice is shaky but it grows stronger. It's exactly what I need.

The kestrels over the moor, the seabirds, the swallows of summer. I give my body over to its instincts. I feel the plane become a living creature, no longer a frail construction of wood and tin. I feel myself become the plane.

"There's a bridge ahead," yells Tombean. "There's a fucking bridge!"

Breathe. Swoop. Use the panic as power. Streets and buildings fly by in a blur. I pass low over a tugboat, sending its crew screaming to the deck. The bridge is right ahead. I gauge the length of my wingtips. I feel them like they're feathers. I'm feet above the water. The people on the bridge are screaming, running. We go smooth under the span.

Then, immediately ahead of us, another bridge. This one is lower in the water.

"Fuck," I say, preparing to smash into it.

And the belly of the plane hits the top of the water. It bumps once, twice, three times, and each time, the water slows us. On the fifth time, we come to a halt. We're ten feet from the second bridge.

"Fucking fuck," shouts Finch, quite lost for any other words. "Fucking fuck, you fucking fucker. That was fucking incredible."

His cursing buoys me up. We are alive.

Water's pouring into our cockpit as we unstrap ourselves. We have time to lift the safety catch and step onto *Curlew*'s wing. I become aware of people cheering everywhere. The bridge ahead of us is filling with a crowd. Little riverboats are sailing toward us. Tombean Finch grabs me in a fierce hug. He's smaller than me but his arms are strong. His head is on my shoulder. I can feel his heart thump against my chest.

"You fucking fucker," he repeats. "Who taught you to fly a fucking plane?"

I feel laughter bubbling up in me.

"I don't know," I say.

Finch pulls my cheek toward his lips and kisses me.

I feel the imprint like a punch.

Water swirls around our ankles, quickly rising to our knees. Boatmen, laughing at our brilliance, help us to the shore. A crowd forms around us, slapping our backs, congratulating us.

"What happened?" someone asks, shoving a strange device in front of me. I'm startled, but Finch grabs hold of the device and speaks. We've been told not to mention the firefuel under any circumstances.

"The solar battery had a fault," he cries, excited. He slaps me on the back. "This lad brought us down on wind power alone. He saved my life and that's for sure."

The man with the device asks us for our names.

"Piper Crane," yells Tombean. "This brilliant pilot is Piper Crane." Finch tells the man that this is our first big training mission. At last I find my words.

"Tombean Finch saved my life too," I say. "He didn't give up on me, not for a second."

"You're heroes," says the man with the device.

"We won't be proper heroes till we've killed some Aylish," I reply, caught up in the joy of being alive.

The crowd starts roaring. There's a victory chant. Tombean and I are carried aloft. He tells me the weird device preserves voices for the radiobine. Kids are jumping up and down, trying to get a look at us. The boatmen put ropes around our plane. People on the bridge are helping them. They stop our wondrous *Curlew* from sinking into the river.

We're brought in through the palace gates. News is spreading about what we've done. We see Wing Commander Axby, hurrying to greet us. Our boys have all landed on the airfield up by the Brethren's Palace. Realizing we were missing, they were going to refuel and search. They saw the plane land from high up on the hill. Axby looks gray with relief. And also very, very angry.

"I saw you veer off course, Crane," he said. "Why did you do that?"

"I saw smoke coming from the Greensward, sir. I only veered by a percentage point."

"Were you given an order to do that?"

"No, sir. I was curious about the smoke."

"'Curious' nearly cost your lives."

Suddenly, I feel hot shame. What can I tell him? I wanted the Greensward people to be impressed with me? Stupid, foolish vanity. I hang my head.

"I'm sorry, sir."

Finch asks permission to speak. He tells Axby what we saw, the sprawling encampment under the trees. He describes the arrow, shot from a powerful crossbow into our tank.

"We were trying to gauge the size of the encampment, sir," says Finch. "We thought they may have been insurgents."

Axby nods quietly.

I feel the ache of adrenaline in every limb. I feel the imprint of Tombean's kiss. I will be scared to sleep tonight. I know what kind of dream might come. In my wretched and aberrant heart, I wish he'd kiss me again and again. I will destroy that thought, piece by piece, like all the others before it.

There's a group of men walking toward us and my heart almost stops when I realize that one of them is Brother Kite. We stand in formation, rigidly saluting him. Kite's our genius, our hero. We know how he's fighting to keep our firefuel planes in the air.

Axby apologizes for our unforgivable commotion. He is mortified. Kite looks us over, steely-eyed.

"Which of you is Piper Crane?" he asks.

"I am, Brother. This is Tombean Finch."

Kite takes us in. "Your reckless exploits are all over the radiobine. . . ."

I hang my head in shame.

"You've conducted yourselves like true sons of Thal," says Kite with something of a smile. "Wing Commander," he charges Axby, "give the whole squadron a night off to visit the Pink District."

There's jubilation at this. I break into a sweat of relief as Kite shakes our hands. I hear him thanking Axby.

"This is just the sort of thing we need," he says. "This will get the whole city excited about the Fireflies."

My heart soars with pride.

In the narrow alleys of the Pink District, my comrades laugh and joke, lewd and boisterous. Soon we're full of alcohol and the lads peel off into various Pink Houses. I prepare myself. It must be done. It's all part of being a man. I failed the first time, in Meadeville. I didn't like my Third Wife. She made me feel unaccountably depressed. But I will not fail again. Finch hands me his whiskey flask and I drink, hoping if I'm drunk enough, the girl won't care how badly I perform.

"I know a better place than this," says Finch quietly.

I look at him and suddenly, I understand. Everything fades out, as it did when I was landing the plane. There is just Finch. We give our comrades the slip.

I follow him down a different alley. I look at his shoulders, his muscular waist. I know what's going to happen. We have saved each other's lives.

Finch takes me to a doorway. A woman sits there in a pink veil. Finch says something to her that I can't hear. He gives her money and she offers him a key. We walk into near darkness, thick with stale tobacco smoke. I can see pink-and-black wallpaper, lit by a pink turbine tube. Finch unlocks a door and then we're kissing, kissing. My arms are strong around him. I feel him press himself against me. A sound comes out of my mouth. It feels better than flying. Tombean Finch saved my life. And who will see me in this secret darkness?

Thal will see. My life is in his hands. Thal. Kite. Thal.

Finch undoes my belt. I feel him grasping me. Another low moan comes unbidden from my mouth. I dreamed of this with—

Suddenly, I stop him.

"What's the matter?" asks Finch.

I'm pushing him away.

"What is it? Am I going too fast?"

I can see I have been pulled into a trap.

"We can go slowly, Piper. We have time. . . ."

I see Rye, lying in the compound, saying, *That boy loves another boy.*" I hear him telling me the Chrysalid House is open for all.

"This isn't a crime," says Finch softly. "It's not like they tell you. . . . There's plenty of soldiers like you and me. . . ."

Degenerate. Stumbling in the darkness, I do up my belt. *Definition of a Human Male.* Our desire must be for women only. And so it shall be. Women only.

"Piper . . . this is just another way to love."

I swear at him. I find the door and run.

I don't stop until I'm on a humpbacked bridge, overlooking a murky canal. Somewhere up ahead, this rank waterway must feed into the Isis, back into the light. I thank Thal for drawing me away from self-destruction. I will pray night and day to be spared from the dreams and the feelings that threaten to destroy me.

I have been misled by Tombean Finch.

He is no friend of mine.

I hear Rye's voice, as if he's standing at my back: *"That boy loves another boy."*

I quash it with an iron fist.

29 ✵ NIGHTINGALE

My head is upside down. I'm being carried over someone's shoulder. As my eyes open, I find myself staring through a black gauze. Instantly, I panic. I pull at it, trying to get it off, but it's tied tightly round my neck. I cry out. I can't breathe. The gauze is muffling me. The tighter I am held, the more I feel my lungs begin to scream. I thrash, tearing at the gauze, crying out. At last, I feel arms lifting me down, holding me, curbing my struggle with their easy strength. Someone pulls off the gauze. My papa.

"Breathe," he says.

"Papa . . ."

My panic calms, replaced by dread. We're on a bench, looking over the river. I know where he is taking me. Over the bridge to the Chrysalid House. As I look at him, I feel him shudder with a sob. His face is wet and red.

"I'm sorry," I whisper.

"You're not my Kaira. You no longer have a name."

Perhaps he cried like this when Mama died. His whole body shakes. I try to comfort him.

"I'm sorry."

"How has Thal done this?" he asks. "I don't understand how he could be so cruel. You're all I have. . . ." He holds me like he never wants to let me go.

The blackout drug is wearing off but my thoughts are still vaporous, like my head is full of dandelion clocks. I sit, breathing, letting the oxygen clear my mind.

"Are you taking me to the Chrysalid House?" I ask.

He nods, wiping the tears from his cheeks. "I told the others to go on ahead. I said I'd bring you in myself." Papa looks as if he'll break. "Keynes told me what you were. I didn't believe him."

"Papa, I don't want to be a chrysalid."

He curls up with woe, holding me. I realize the ache in my head will never go away. There is a lead band, pressing on my skull.

"Where were you going?" he asks.

"I don't know," I reply. "I was scared of Keynes. I just ran."

With a wrench, I remember Lark's lungs filling with water. Lark, drowning. Tears come tumbling down my face.

"What did you do to Keynes?" asks Papa. "The others had to take him away. You hurt his mind and he fell down in a heap. How did you do that?"

I try to explain: "When I'm upset or scared, emotion comes out of me. It feels like lightning."

Papa stands.

"That's strong songlight," he says. He grips my arm but he leaves off the suffocating gauze. We walk. Lark is dead, drowned in the sea. And I will go to the Chrysalid House. For a while Papa is silent and then he says:

"Your mother and I . . . we loved each other. Her last words to me were to care for you. So I've got the solution. You can be my Siren, Kaira."

My mouth falls open in dismay.

"I'll treat you just like I do now."

"No, Papa—"

"You can live in the house, in your own room. I won't lock you up. Nothing will change. You'll just help me with my work."

"I can't."

"You won't last as a chrysalid," he says. "You're not built for it. The work will kill you." His voice cracks.

We're walking through the busy dockside: wine merchants, corn merchants, fancy goods, boats being loaded and unloaded. No one pays us much attention—just an Inquisitor and his cull. The Chrysalid House is looming now. We only have to cross the next bridge and we're there.

I don't want Lark's death to be in vain. She was trying to help me, as Cassandra did.

"Why must we all die?" I ask.

"You won't die, as a Siren. Everything'll be the same."

I have to be firm, very firm and clear. "Listen to me, Papa. If you take me to the Chrysalid House, I'll choose death. I won't cooperate. Do you understand? I'll never be a Siren. I could never do this to another person."

"Unhumans are not people—"

"Yes we are. Keynes is a person, Radika Helms was a person. I am a person. We are all as human as you."

Papa looks at me dumbly. But these are my last moments and I'll tell him how I feel.

"I'm not unhuman," I say. "That word is a lie. I'm Kaira, the beloved child of Sol and Mia Kasey." The mention of my mother's name visibly affects him. "I know you love me, Papa. You sat by my bed when I was dying and you prayed. You can save me now. The Brethren have lied to you. There's no such thing as an unhuman. There's only me and you. And you must choose my freedom or my death."

I'm lying face down on my upturned boat. One leg is wrapped over the keel. I'm cold, so cold. I lie, unmoving, watching the waves, gray upon gray. All I do is float and breathe.

I feel as if I'm being held. Some force is around me. Slowly, I try to sit up, gripping the slippery boat. My belly's full of brine and it is sickening. My leg is thumping; the cold has turned me numb. I'm alive, but not for long, I think. I lift my head—and I get such a fright I almost fall into the sea. A man is sitting cross-legged on the keel. An Aylish man.

"Fuck," I say.

He's a luminescent visitor, like Nightingale. His hair is long. His eyes are dark. He's holding me in songlight and his uniform is blue.

"Try not to move too much," he says. "You'll slide into the sea." His accent is thick Aylish.

"Go drown."

"Don't waste your energy. My ship is on its way."

He's calm and concentrated, straight-backed, slim. I've seen his face before, looking down on me from his battleship, inflicting carnage on our men. I felt the wingbeats of his songlight. He was prying then and he's prying now. He wants inside my mind. So I show him the sinking transport ship. I show him the men scrambling aboard my boat, I let him see the helpless, drowning chrysalid. I hold out an image of the corpses on our quay.

"Aylish murderer," I say. "I saw you. You bombed our Listening Station. You sank our ship. Men died that day."

He acknowledges the truth of this. "I saw you too."

"Is that why you're saving me? Out of guilt?" I ask.

"I'm here because I heard a desperate cry of songlight. It blotted out all else. A cry for help, calling Lark," he says. "Is that your name?"

He heard Nightingale. That's why he's here. Nightingale called for help and she's saved me. I reach up, trying to find her.

My last memory coalesces. The pink door, a blue rose, our precarious hope of help. I remember Nightingale in that crowded street, trying to hold me, screaming my name. Did she find safety?

What happened to her? Nightingale . . .

"Don't try to send your songlight," says the Aylishman. "You need all your strength."

He's right. A swell tips the upturned boat and I almost lose my grip. I cling on to the keel but my fingers are so frozen they no longer work. Every muscle, every bone is sore. I'm so, so cold.

"You're certainly determined," he says. "When I found you, you were pulling yourself up. You were barely conscious, yet you clung on."

"I don't remember," I tell him.

"I sensed your harmony during the sea battle. I sensed another presence with you. I was pulled here by an extraordinary song. Is that Nightingale?"

"It's not fair of you to read me. . . ."

"I'm trying to distract you, to keep you alive."

They say that if you die of cold, it feels like you are floating. I feel that now, as if I'm tethered to this body by the thinnest silken thread and soon I'll dissipate into the air like mist. The sun is sinking, a blazing orange ball in the dark gray sky. The darkness will soon make it even colder. Perhaps I fall unconscious because next thing I know, the Aylishman is close, surrounding me with light, as Nightingale once did when I was going to jump into our barracks.

"Here's my ship," he says, and I twist, following his gaze. I see the Aylish battleship, blast marks on its side, the broken turbine mended with a trunk of wood. As it nears, his figure takes on a more substantial form. I see the azure of his shirt, an amber jewel hanging round his neck.

"We've been hiding on an island off the far north of your coast, mending our ship. You're lucky we were close. . . ."

Something breaks the water. White underbelly, black fins, a smile longer than my leg. The upturned boat bobs and sways in the disturbance. I cringe with fear.

"That thing wants me for its supper." I cling on desperately to the slippery keel.

I sense him trying to hear the creature's underwater song. Gala in Hel, is he *talking* to it? I feel his intense, nervy energy, his controlled intelligence, his passion. He's beaming on the orca like a light. I listen harder, deeper. There are thorns inside him too.

"Now you're reading me."

I'm caught. He doesn't exactly block me but I feel a strong sense of his privacy.

"She's in pain," he says. He's talking about the beast.

"Are you making excuses for that thing?"

"Your fishing hooks are tearing the inside of her mouth. I'll help her when the ship arrives."

"Just keep it off my fucking leg."

I like the way my swear takes him aback.

He starts asking me questions. "Where are you from?"

"Northaven."

"What's it like there?"

"Boring."

"Talk to me. I need to keep you conscious. How old are you?"

"None of your business."

"When did your songlight first appear?"

I try to answer but black dots are traveling across my eyes. I want to sleep, to let go of this body and drift away. The Torch encompasses me in his light, pouring his strength into my being. He feels me flinch away from him.

"I want you to live. I'm not your enemy, Lark."

"I never said that was my name."

"Then what may I call you?" He sees my mistrust. "It's not an act of treason to tell me your name."

"Elsa Crane."

He repeats it. It sounds strange in his accent. Elza Crenne . . .

"My name is Yan Zeru. But my true name is Kingfisher. As yours is Lark."

His ship is almost beside us. I see guns along its flanks; broken, twisted metal at the rear, where a Brightling cannon did its work.

"Forgive me if I leave you now," he says. "I'll be right back. Don't go anywhere. . . ."

He smiles at me, like that's a joke. He fades and disappears.

Without his presence, my body shakes. My bitten leg starts throbbing in pain. I concentrate on breathing. In and out, in and out. The ship is towering above me. There's a line of people on the deck now, peering down. I hear the crackle of their foreign voices.

As if my heart isn't hammering enough, the orca emerges, her belly rosy in the setting sun. Then a man climbs onto the prow, taking off his blue shirt. It's him, Yan Zeru. He dives—and I see that Kingfisher is the perfect name for him. He pierces the water with barely a sound. I gasp at the easy grace of it. But he's rash. As he rises, the orca is making straight for him. I watch in silence as she opens her deadly smile. Kingfisher, singing his trust, reaches his arm into her jaw. He snaps my two big fishing hooks with wire cutters. Carefully, he pulls them out. The people on the deck cheer. Kingfisher waves up at them. The creature emits a shattering vibration—which shakes me into pieces. She flips her tail and dives into the deep, leaving Kingfisher floating on the waves. He swims toward me, his hair trailing like seaweed, and lifts himself onto my boat.

My enemy. Neither of us speaks.

"I suppose you want me to thank you?" I ask.

"That would be normal and polite. But I understand that you're not at your best." A looped rope comes down. "May I lift you?"

I can barely nod. Yan Zeru puts my uninjured foot into the rope and then beside it, his own. I can hardly hold my weight up. I'm scared of falling and angry that I'm scared. He smells of the sea.

"Hold on to me."

I don't want to touch him. It feels like defeat, capitulation. He sees me hesitate and ties the rope around us both. He tugs and it begins to rise, away from my beloved boat. His heartbeat thuds. His arms and legs are iron with the effort of holding me. As we're pulled, twisting upward, I make the mistake of looking down. My giddiness spirals and dark spots crowd my vision.

"Just a few feet more. Stay with me." His arms wrap tighter round me. I can't pretend any courage. I am shuddering with fear.

As foreign strangers pull us on to the deck, my legs fail. I'm whirling through space as the dark spots take my vision. I feel Aylish hands upon me and I hear their voices as they carry me. Dizziness floats me. I pour fury on myself for being so weak, but my strength is spent and I drift away.

What in Hel's name did that to me? That mind-shattering cry. Lark . . .

What or who is Lark?

I try to sit up in my bed. Too soon. My head is splitting and my mind feels dense. That cry seemed both near and far away. Plaintive, desperate. I got a sense of distance; the song disturbed by water . . . The sea? Yet it felt close, the pain felt close. I've never encountered songlight like it.

I will find out who hurt me like this. I will track them down. I send my songlight out into the cityscape, searching as far and wide as I can. Need forces my mind into clarity. I sense other presences, suffering the same pain. I'm not the only person in Brightlinghelm who is reeling. Sirens have been floored—and one or two hidden Torches.

I slowly sit up and realize I am not alone. Starling Beech is getting to his feet, tractable and anxious. I assume that Kite has set him there to watch me.

"Have you been taking care of me?" I give him a vulnerable smile. I want this man in my pocket. "I'm very grateful, Starling. . . ."

I have a memory of him holding my hair out of the way as I spewed. I wonder if it will dent his adoration? From the ardent look of him, I don't think so. I realize with relief that my wig is in place and I am still unburdened by the lead band.

I put my feet on the cold floor. I let Starling see my bare legs, as if I'm unaware of my dishabille. I look into him, prying him open like a peapod. I make sure he feels my frailty, my delicate indebtedness, a sense that if he pleases me enough, I'll take him into this white bed and let him ride me over a rainbow. He's utterly distracted while I rifle through his mind.

I see myself stumbling from the council chamber. I'm falling, incapacitated. Kite steps back as I vomit on his uniform. He's disgusted. He barks an order to Starling.

"Take her to her rooms." Kite knows I'm being invaded by something stronger than myself—and he's afraid of it.

"Watch her," he tells Starling, shaken. "Remember everything she says. I want a full report."

"Yes, Brother, yes, of course." And slipping in my vomit, Starling lifts me to my rooms.

I retreat from his consciousness and he knows nothing of my intrusion. He bows and goes to tell Kite that I'm awake.

Kite—and the rest of them—saw me reduced to a wreck. Panic begins to set in. This is another proof of my weakness and Kite will use it against me. I have to turn it to my advantage. How?

I call my ladies. There's no time to lose. I need my wig styled, my teeth brushed, my body cleansed. I must have moisturizer, makeup, perfume—now.

"Faster," I yell at them. "I have to be perfection!" They work like machines.

Kite wanted me to influence Brother Drake but instead, I collapsed in the most public and humiliating way. I have let him down again. And what did Peregrine think?

My ladies work as I formulate a desperate course of action. My eyebrows, lashes, cheeks, lips, all are enhanced as I decide exactly what to say. As the veiled chrysalids work, the door clicks open. Kite never knocks. Why should he? Everything in here belongs to him. I quickly lie back on the bed, looking vulnerable, luxuriant. I let the sheets reveal the right amount of nakedness. I won't make it easy for him to abandon me.

He has my lead band in his hand. He puts it down beside my bed.

"What was it that hurt you?" he asks, enacting his concern.

I take a deep breath. "It was an assault," I reply. "The strongest force of songlight I've ever experienced. It almost shattered me."

"Who did this?" asks Kite.

I will let Kite's own logic lead him. "Who do you think?"

"The Aylish . . ." This is what Kite already suspects and it's easy to feed his hate.

"Undoubtedly," I lie.

"That same Torch who defeated you in battle?"

I mustn't appear weak. "No one voice could ever be that powerful," I assure him. "It was an attack by many."

He takes this in. "They banded together to hurt you?"

I nod, brave and vulnerable.

"Are your powers intact?"

I tell him that my mind is only bruised. Now for the real purpose of my plan: "If only you could tell Peregrine what those unhuman dogs have done to me. . . ."

Kite is taken aback. "Tell Peregrine you're a Torch?"

"Niccolas, don't you think he half suspects already?" This is true. And I am ready to take the risk. If Peregrine knows my true status, I am not alone. I am protected against Kite.

"I can't do that," says Kite. "He'll know that I've deceived him."

"But by attacking me," I urge, "the Aylish have reached right into our own council chamber. It's a direct act of aggression."

"Yes," he says, his inspiration dawning.

"Only the strength of my own songlight saved me. . . ."

I feel Kite's growing excitement. "This escalates the war. They've attacked the heart of our government. Peregrine will have to arm my planes."

I put my hand delicately over his. "I will do anything it takes to see the Aylish burn."

Kite considers his move. "I don't have to tell Peregrine that you're a Torch. I can tell him that the Aylish mind-twisted you because, as the only female, you were the weakest presence on the room."

"But—"

"You were unable to withstand them. It will have the same effect."

I don't press. Regretfully, I accept this.

I swing my legs onto the floor and arch my torso, stretching. Then I pretend it has made me dizzy. I lie back, exposed. It has the desired effect. My indisposition becomes of carnal interest to him. Weakened, I am making Kite feel strong. He puts a hand on my cheek, then lets it roam down to my breasts. I know my place, Brother Kite. It's underneath you. You will not send me to the Chrysalid House today.

Afterward, he locks the band around my skull and goes. I sit, breathing my determination. I've served Kite's lust for war. But for how long am I safe? I'm so weary of placating, flattering, cajoling, enticing him. I'm sick of him locking up my potency. My songlight is dying and in my heart, I know that Kite is growing tired of me. I must keep his need alive. I must convince him of my power. I know I must work fast.

If Kite is looking for a fresh Flower of Brightland, perhaps I need one first.

As my blank unbeings dress me, I think again about that cry.

"Lark . . ."

It wasn't an attack at all. It was full of pain and anguish. It was full of an emotion I have not felt for a lifetime: love. A powerful love, expressed in purest songlight. I would like to be so loved.

"Lark . . ."

I will find that powerful songlight. And I will have it for my own.

I send for my besotted Starling Beech.

"Did anyone else experience the onslaught that overpowered me?" I ask him. "Kite thinks it may have been an Aylish attack. Look in particular for anyone who may have used the word 'Lark.'"

Starling soon comes back with several names: people who collapsed, nauseous, experiencing head pain. One or two of them fainted, as I did. The most promising story is that of a young girl, who was taken in convulsions on the street. She was hysterically distressed. Passersby reported she was screaming "Lark."

"She's an Inquisitor's daughter," Starling tells me. "Her father's Siren collapsed at the girl's feet."

So this girl has songlight so strong that it can knock a Torch unconscious? I am awed.

"I want her brought to me, intact."

"The difficulty is, they've disappeared. The girl and her father; they've fled. The Siren has denied all knowledge of their escape."

"Where is he now?"

"In the Chrysalid House, being held on charges of aiding and abetting them."

"Starling," I grip his arm with the hint of a caress. "Take me to him."

I wear my most modest white dress, my wig styled under a veil. We take the new tram that runs from the airfield at the top of the palace complex, down the hill to the entrance gates. The final stop is the Chrysalid House. To any Torch, this place smells of death.

We walk in and Starling announces my name. Medics and workers gather into a greeting line. I stand, eyeing them all.

"The Flower of Brightland greets you," announces Starling.

I incline my head. They bow deeply and the chief surgeon comes forward. His name is Francis Ruppell. I've met Brother Ruppell a hundred times at the council table. He's one of Kite's favorites. Together, they conceived the whole system of the Chrysalid House. Ruppell runs it now. And he's the only other man who knows I am a Siren. At Kite's request, he acts as my personal doctor and locksmith. He's the man who invented the lock-in-skull technique for Sirens, and he knows just where to pierce the brain tissue in order to kill songlight, leaving enough sentience to follow simple orders. He's Brightland's top experimental surgeon. He and his henchmen took away my womb and I loathe him with every atom of my being.

"Sister Swan," he says obsequiously, "we're deeply honored by your visit."

I play my status. "I'm on our Great Brother's business. I wish to see the

Siren who was apprehended earlier."

"Nothing could delight me more."

Ruppell escorts us to a holding cell himself. Then he takes my hand and kisses it. "You are my finest work."

I smile bashfully, as if he's given me a compliment. I hate this villain like cancer. One day, I'll take his skin off with my peeling knife; I'll pull his eyeballs out with sugar tongs. But for now, it's expedient to have him on my side. I make sure my voice is velvet:

"I'll never forget how you humanized me."

I walk into the cell. A dusty, malodorous Siren kneels, clutching his dirty hat.

"Sister Swan," he utters, in deep veneration. His fingers are thin; his skin looks stretched. This man lives on scraps.

I ask about the girl.

"Kaira," he says. "Her name is Kaira Kasey."

He tells me she's a convalescent, a victim of the wasting fever. He tells me she's been kind to him. He wants her to be a Siren, like he is. He takes a book out of his horrid, crumpled jacket and hands it to me.

"These are her drawings," he says.

I open the book. I see a nurse as if from above, tending to a child in an iron lung. I see this same nurse pulling a girl through the clouds. I see a starlit city, houses made of glass, magnificent domes rising up behind them. There's a page of curious airships, hovering over a desert. And then a girl in a fishing boat, a village by the sea. In one image, this girl rises up above her boat, her hair blowing in the breeze. Swooping down to her is a beautifully rendered lark.

These images are pure and full of light. They're visionary. I feel a pang, as if I were sixteen again. Perhaps once, long ago, I had such radiance. I turn away from the groveling Siren because my throat is tight. I feel something pull at me, something that I thought was dead. These images are full of hope for something I can hardly name. Freedom.

229

I won't let Brother Ruppell destroy her in these rooms. I will risk every-thing to save this girl. And in return, she's going to work for me. This girl is going to be my songlight. She's going to keep me safe from Kite.

I call Starling. I put out my arm and let him support me. I tell him we must find Kaira Kasey.

The pathetic Siren wants to bargain with his life. He begs to have his band removed. In return for his freedom, he'll lead us to this Kaira; he will find the Inquisitor's daughter.

I would promise him the moon to get this girl.

I still can't believe it. It's a miracle. I love Papa so much I want to burst.

"I can't do it," he says.

He turns us away from the Chrysalid House, and, in a narrow alleyway, he takes the lead band off my skull. He throws it into a gutter with his nightstick and his keys. Then he holds me.

"I never believed this could happen," I say. Papa doesn't speak. He is shaking as if he can't believe it either. I hold him tight for a long time.

"I loved your mother," he says. "I love you."

"What are we going to do?" I ask him. "How will we escape?"

Papa can't collect his thoughts, as if the whole idea of escape is foreign. "All the city gates are closed," he says. "Everyone is being searched. . . ."

"But you're an Inquisitor," I say. "If we go fast, surely they'll let you through."

Papa doesn't seem to think that being an Inquisitor will help.

He goes into a cheap outfitter's shop and buys himself a long coat and scarf to cover his uniform. He notices how small my coat is. He buys me one that fits. At last, I look like a young woman, but Papa regards me as if I'm a stranger.

"Look at you," he says. "You're all grown up."

I'm coming to terms with this miracle. My father has saved me.

I cannot think of Lark. That pain is waiting, an avalanche waiting to fall. I must keep it frozen under the snow, far back in my mind. If it falls, I will collapse.

"I think the river's the best plan," I say. "Let's try our chances on a boat. But we need to go soon, before they start searching."

Papa nods but he doesn't speak. His great confidence seems broken. I tell him to get some money from his bank and he obeys me, as if he has no will of his own. We pass the city's big museum.

"Do you remember this place?" he asks. "I used to come here with your mother."

To my dismay, he goes inside.

"Are we waiting until nightfall?" I ask. "Is that your plan?"

He doesn't reply.

"Let's wait for the end of the working day," I say. "The streets will be crowded, better for us to slip away."

Papa is gazing at the exhibits. He seems far away, deep in his own thoughts. He walks through the entrance hall, to the Light People rooms.

"This war," he says. "It all comes down to the unhuman. That's why we fight. The unhuman is the core of all our sorrows. They're a blight upon the Earth." Papa is caught in the deadly threads of his old ideas.

"That's a lie, Papa," I say forcefully. "You know I'm not unhuman. You and Mama made me. I'm your girl."

We're standing in front of an ancient map of the world, the green-and-blue world, before the Age of Woe. Papa doesn't seem to be looking at it. He just stands, staring.

"We should try to get to the Greensward," I say as he wanders through the relics. "We can get a river bus out of the center and then we'll have to steal a boat." I force him to look at me. "We can get past the sentries in the dark. That's the best plan. We'll travel by night and hide out in the day. What do you think?"

"Yes."

"We're strong, Papa. We'll be all right."

"Yes," he says, but he walks away from me. "Your mother loved it here," he tells me, staring at a steel vehicle with a dummy family in the seats. They wear faded colors and peculiar hats.

"These people, they had everything. And they destroyed it. . . ."

Papa's shoulders are stooping like an old man's. What should I do? I wish for the thousandth time that I were as brave and strong as Lark.

Lark. Her name is like a cry inside me, melting the snow.

"Let's keep moving," I urge. "We should go."

But Papa wanders into a room of stuffed creatures. Striped horses, cats with fangs, things with scales and spikes, creatures so strange I can't describe them. They are old and faded, sagging at the edges. The fur is patchy; some of the spikes are falling off.

I mustn't think of Lark.

She's gone. She's drowned.

"In the early days," says Papa, "I once tracked down a whole nest of unhumans. They thought they could hide but the Sirens sniffed them out. We sent the lot of them to the Chrysalid House. I got a personal commendation from Brother Kite." His eyes roam over a troop of threadbare monkeys. "I did that, Kaira. I was proud."

"That's the past, Papa. We can start again now. We can start afresh."

He walks away from me, into a room of long-dead birds, trapped in glass cases, wings spread in a pretense of flight. I follow, heavy with distress. Birds, every faded color of the rainbow. One has a wingspan the length of Lark's boat.

"It's harder to catch people now," says Papa. "Most of the adults have been cleansed, or they have fled. It's just the nascents."

"What's a nascent?"

His voice is shaking. "An adolescent. A child. . . . Keynes is best at trapping them. He has all kinds of ruses. We have them in lead bands before they even know they're unhuman."

He looks down at me. His sobs come, big and shaking. He's falling apart in this room full of birds.

"Papa, stop. It will be different now." I try to draw him away.

"If you're human," he cries, "so are they. I'm nothing but a murderer. . . ."

"Stop this, right now," I tell him firmly. "People are noticing us, Papa. Let's *go*."

"This is my punishment," he says too loudly. "The gods have blighted the only thing I love."

"I'm not blighted," I say through gritted teeth. "I'm here and you can save me. You can save yourself." I'm pulling him toward the exit now. But one of the museum guards is talking to another and they begin to approach. Papa wipes the tears off his face.

"I'm a murderer!"

"It's the anniversary of my mother's death," I quickly say to the guards. "Papa used to come here with her, when she was alive. He's just upset."

"Sorry for your loss," says one of the guards, but he doesn't mean a word of it. He watches us, suspicious.

At last I get Papa out in the street again. The air is cool and night is falling. I lead him to the river as quickly as I can. The evening rush hour is starting to build and I hope we won't be noticed in the crowd.

"It's the shock," I say. "I've given you a shock and I'm sorry. There'll be time to come to terms with it when we've escaped."

"I deserve your hate."

"This is self-pity, Papa, and you'll get us both killed!"

My voice is raised and Papa blinks, as if my words have hit him like a slap. I lead him over the Palace Bridge, where there are queues of people on the esplanade, waiting for river buses to take them to the suburbs.

"We need a water taxi," says Papa soberly. "I'll spend some money on it—and we can get away."

Papa gets in the queue at the water taxi stand. He's coming back into himself at last and my anxiety begins to ebb. There are palace guards and Emissaries everywhere. We are almost at the head of the queue. I pray to Gala to guide us.

Then I see Cassandra.

She's standing by the palace gates.

I take a step closer. I must be mistaken. It's just someone who resembles her. But as I stare, she turns to look at me. It's her. I stand in disbelief. She sends me a quiet note of songlight.

"Kaira," she says. "I know you tried to find me. I had to stay silent, to keep us both safe. . . ."

That's her voice. She's there, a coat over her nurse's uniform.

"I thought you'd been taken," I whisper in songlight.

"I was rescued. Our people hid me. I can help you."

"Cassandra," I say. And I start moving toward her.

"Where are you going?" cries my papa. "Here's our boat."

I'm drawn to Cassandra, as if she's water in the desert. She's alive, my friend is alive and she'll help us. I can feel Papa coming after me.

"Kaira, come back!"

"Cassandra, where have you been?" I ask.

"It's a trap," yells my papa. "It's a classic Siren's trap!"

As soon as he says it, I know that it's true. I back away. Cassandra's face changes. Her expression loses its serenity. She becomes ugly. She becomes Keynes.

How has he masked himself to me? He has mind-twisted me, picking up on my deepest longings and presenting them as true.

"You walked right into it," he says.

Hands are grabbing me.

"Papa, run!" I yell.

Papa is fighting his own men. He's trying to get to me, but hands are forcing him down. As he cries my name, a bolt of electricity shoots into my back, paralyzing me. I fall to the ground, unable to move, rigid with pain. They'll kill me. Oh, Gala, they'll kill me. The last thing I see is Keynes. He leans over me, his eyes thrilling.

"I saved you," he says. "I saved you."

I wake to a turbine sound, an engine's hum, so different from my little fishing boat. Before I do anything, I unfurl my mind and send my song as far as I can.

"Nightingale . . . wherever you are, I'm safe. I pray to Gala you are too."

I wait, straining to hear a reply, but all I hear is the motion of the ship. I sit up on my elbows. I'm in a long room with rows of narrow bunks, low lit with bluish strips of turbine light. How long have I slept? Feels like days. I'm ravenous. I've got a raging thirst. I have to get home to help Nightingale, to save Rye. But where in the Sea of Sidon am I?

On my blanket lie some Aylish clothes. Black breeches and a blue, high-necked shirt: their uniform. I'm no traitor and I'd never put this on. But I realize that I'm only in some kind of foreign underwear. Who put me in this stuff?

Aylish bastards.

I see a shadow walking past the open door.

"Hey," I call. "Hey, Aylish! Where's my dress?"

Silence. And then a young man with soft cheeks and a long ponytail sticks his head around the door.

"You're awake." His voice is strangely high. "I'll get you food and drink," he says. I hear his footfalls, going and returning. He comes in, bringing a flask of water and some ship's biscuits.

"Where's my dress?" I ask.

"Eat something. Drink. You must be thirsty."

I look at him suspiciously, then I take the flask and glug it in one swallow, breathless with the fresh, quenching water. Before I start on the biscuits, I pick up the breeches.

"I can't wear these. I need my clothes."

"Your clothes are being dried. These are for you."

"I won't wear them. They're for men."

The young man laughs. He's wearing the same breeches and high-necked shirt.

"They're good enough for me," he says.

Gala, he's got breasts. . . . I realize it's a girl. That explains the high voice and the soft face.

"I thought you were a boy," I say.

She laughs again.

"I'm Renza Perch." Her smile is so open that I give her my name before I remember she's my enemy. She repeats it in her strange accent.

"You speak Brightling," I remark.

"Of course. During the occupation, we all had to learn it."

This makes me realize how little I know about the war. The *occupation?*

"Do Aylishmen bring their wives on ships?" I ask.

"Pardon?"

"Are you a First Wife or a Second?"

She looks at me, puzzled. "I'm a turbine engineer," she says.

I don't know what to say to this. The biscuits are damp and stale but I eat them anyway. I wonder how long this ship's been at sea.

"Do you feel well enough to get on deck?" asks Renza. "Torch Yan wants to see you when you wake."

Him. Torch Yan. The memory floods my consciousness of the way he held me in songlight, his presence keeping me alive. I roll his name around in my mind, mistrustful. Kingfisher.

I get out of the bed. My leg is all trussed up where the orca sank its teeth. I stand. The pain is bearable.

"How long have I been asleep?" I ask.

"A day and a night. Yan wanted you to rest."

"Is he your captain, then?" I ask.

"We don't have a captain. Yan's our Torch." She carries on before I can question this. "When he first heard you, he almost threw himself into the sea. He was quite transfixed. I mean, Yan's amazing, he has incredible songlight. But yours must be strong too. He guided the ship to you."

This girl knows I'm unhuman. And she's not recoiling. Weird.

"He healed you well, didn't he?" she chats as I dress. "I helped him stitch that wound. Then Yan held your leg and meditated on it. He was wiped out after. Honestly, I don't know how he does it. We all think he's brilliant." She sighs, as if Yan Zeru is some kind of genius.

"Is he a doctor?" I ask.

"No. His songlight tends toward healing. Not every Torch can heal. But Yan's exceptional."

The more I hear, the less I like him. Why, if his skill is healing, did he fire on our Listening Station? Those men screamed and burned. Why did he sail away, leaving our men to drown? These questions crowd my mind but I keep them all behind my teeth.

"It must be unthinkable being a Torch, where you come from," says Renza, with compassion. "No wonder you tried so hard to get away."

I look at her squarely. "If you pity me, Renza Perch, we will never get along."

She quiets then. It feels like an act of treason, pulling the Aylish shirt over my head, putting my feet into the breeches. My old seaworker's boots must be lying on the seabed. Renza finds me a pair of soft shoes. I slip them on and we go. I catch sight of myself in a mirror. I am taken aback. I look so like my brother.

Renza leads me past another dormitory and we climb a narrow staircase to the deck. Men and women are working together on the solar sails and turbines, all dressed the same in blue shirts and black breeches.

What am I doing here among these Aylish?

Nightingale.

Rye.

An urgency is throbbing in my heart. I have to get back. I have to get home.

But a distant coast is coming into view. Mountains, a wide river estuary.

"Where are we?" I ask, my heart sinking in dismay.

"We'll be docking in Caraquet soon," Renza tells me.

"Ayland?"

"Of course."

Gala in Hel. They've taken me to Ayland. . . . The panic is so great I can't form a single thought. I stare at the mountains, letting the shock sink in. How am I going to get back to Brightland?

"Yan's been in touch with Janella Andric; she's Caraquet's Circle Torch. She knows you're with us. You'll be well looked after."

What on earth is a Circle Torch? I don't like the sound of it one bit.

"I can't tell you how glad I am to get home," confides Renza as she leads me toward the prow. "We've crawled here. The ship's in a bad way. It's going to the shipyard to be fixed."

We pass a huge blast hole in the side of the deck. The interior of the ship is visible, a blackened melt.

"We hid in Brightling waters," Renza goes on. "Absolute sitting ducks. We had to go ashore to cut timber. We shaped pine shafts to mend the turbines and hauled them up on deck. I'm pretty proud of the results."

I look up at the repaired turbines, remembering how I saw the main one explode and fall, smashing into the bridge. The bridge still a ruin, tarpaulins pulled over it.

"Elsa."

I turn to see Yan Zeru in his azure shirt, the only one on this whole ship who wears a different color. His hair is loosely tied, the amber jewel glinting on his neck. His vivid eyes smile into me.

"Glad to see you on your feet."

I owe this man a debt. I'd be orca food without him. But somehow, seeing him so sure of his own brilliance, words of thanks stick in my throat. I don't say anything at all. There's another man approaching, broader, shorter, looking at me with suspicion.

"Elsa, this is Cazimir Cree, our navigator," Renza introduces us. "Caz, this is Elsa Crane."

I match Cree's suspicion with my own.

"How's your leg?" asks Yan Zeru. "Do you have much pain?"

"No."

"The wound was very clean," he says. "I don't think you'll be badly scarred."

Is he expecting my gratitude to gush?

"Thanks," I say. "But I have to get back home."

Cree laughs. "There's appreciation for you."

"I'm happy to make my own way," I assure him. "If you can spare me a lifeboat, I won't be any further trouble."

All three of them look at me, amazed.

"But you're safe here," says Renza.

How can I be safe in an enemy land?

"We went miles out of our way, in a damaged ship, to rescue you," adds Cree. "We've put our lives at risk to get you here."

"I just need my dress," I say, "and I'll go."

"Not many refugees are lucky enough to make it this far," says Cree in disbelief.

"I'm not a refugee, I'm a seaworker. Thank you, but I didn't choose to come and I need to get back."

Cree laughs again.

"Sure," he says. "Take a lifeboat, if that's what you want, and good luck to you. The current will take you straight to the ice lands."

I've clearly insulted him somehow.

"Caz," says Renza. "Give her a chance to explain herself. . . ."

I have to be careful. I need their help—but are they really expecting me to bare my soul and tell them everything?

"I'm sure it seems ungrateful and I'm sorry to be rude," I say firmly, "but I must go back to Brightland."

"So your people can destroy your brain in their Chrysalid House?" Cree's looking at me like I'm mad.

And I have nothing to say. Because he's right.

"I have to dock this ship without a bridge," he says, as if he's had enough of me. "Excuse me."

Cree walks away. Renza looks after him, troubled. She catches him up. I watch the easy way they have with one another, talking and listening. I can tell immediately that Cazimir Cree is Renza's man. But she's a turbine engineer and not a wife. Are they sex traitors, like Rye and me? And if they are, why does no one seem to care? They disappear into the ship.

"There's a lot for you to get used to, Lark," says the Aylish Torch.

I bridle as he uses my innermost name. I turn away from him toward the coast. And then I see the town. Smoke-blackened, cratered, bomb-ruined. Hardly a building still stands. Those that do are bullet-pocked with shattered windows. It has what's left of a large harbor and broken houses, falling up a hill. For a moment of horror, I think that some catastrophe has happened and I'm in a nightmare version of Northaven. It's a vision of the Underworld.

"Welcome to Caraquet," says Yan.

Even the trees have been destroyed. A shantytown of tents and makeshift buildings has sprung up amid the ruins. There are people living out of fishing boats.

"What happened here?"

"The Brightlings bombed it as they retreated. They left nothing behind. We're beginning to rebuild."

Brightland *retreated?* . . . I don't know what to say. I look at this wasteland, feeling a pang for Ma, for home. What if the Aylish do this to us?

As we draw closer, I see more signs of life. Children are playing on the devastated harbor front. There's a shipyard with workers crawling over a new ship. A man on the hill is hanging out laundry. People are rebuilding walls. I'm trying to piece it all together. There was an occupation and

Brightland has retreated. My mind is full of questions and the biggest one is Rye's: *What if the Brethren are lying to us about the war?* I turn to Yan, wanting to ask him who started this. Why are our people fighting? Why did we occupy Ayland? Didn't the Aylish destroy our colonies? But if I ask him anything, I'll reveal my ignorance. And I am mortally ashamed of it. I must stay silent and work out what I can.

"The occupation persists to the South," says Yan. "But we feel the tide is turning." Is he picking up the direction of my thoughts? I do my best to block him out, silently looking at the damaged town.

"This must be hard for you to take in. We know the Brethren don't tell you much. We know you're subject to propaganda."

What in Hel is propaganda? My hackles rise.

"I understand that you miss your home," says Yan, "but I hope you'll soon find many reasons to stay with us in Ayland."

"I need to get home."

"Why? Talk to me, Lark," he urges, his deep, striking eyes looking into mine. He's not just asking me to talk. He's asking me to join with him in songlight. It would be so easy to fall under the sway of his vivid gaze and easy, amber charm and share the terrible anxiety I feel for Nightingale and Rye. But I mustn't forget that this man is my enemy. His people killed my pa. I must be on my guard.

"Am I a prisoner here?" I ask him.

He looks at me, perturbed. "How can you think so? For the first time in your life, you're free. You'll be valued here. Your mind will be unmolested. And we can train you how to use it."

"Against my own people?"

"We are your people. You could reach your full potential, Lark. You have a most uncommon gift—"

"Please stop," I ask him. "Stop using that name. It isn't yours."

Yan is taken aback. "Forgive me," he says.

His words are piercing me. No one's ever called my songlight a gift before. It's a burden, a terrible secret. It's cleaved a rift between my brother and me. It's made me a stranger to everyone around me.

"Why are you set on going back to a place where you are persecuted?" he asks softly.

The ache in my heart forces out the truth. "I have two friends," I say. "I can't abandon them. Rye has been caught. And you heard Nightingale. She's in Brightlinghelm, surrounded by danger."

"That song I heard was in Brightlinghelm?"

"Yes."

He almost falls backward off the ship.

"Nightingale's precious," I tell him. "Her songlight has such a bright radiance. But it exhausts her being that way and she's often ill. I was helping her escape and now I don't know where she is."

I see real concern in the Aylishman's eyes.

"When we dock, come into the town. There's a Circle meeting in the morning and I think you should attend."

"What's a Circle meeting?" I ask.

"You'll see," says the Torch.

Evening is falling as we dock in the harbor. We hear the crowd cheering long before we land. I look down to see the quayside filling up with townspeople. The crew lines the bomb-damaged deck, waving down at them. The Aylish are coming out in force. They're not regimented into colors like Brightland people are, with elders and cadets in black, choirmaidens in white, widows in gray. They're a mishmash of clashing colors. Children are running alongside the ship, jumping in excitement.

"They're laying on a feast to celebrate our safe return," says Yan. "Janella Andric welcomes you. She's the Circle Torch."

He's communing with another Torch in broad daylight, with nothing to fear. So strange. So strange.

The smell of food wafts up. Fish is being cooked on outdoor griddles and my mouth begins to water. I see tavern keepers setting up barrels of beer and a group of musicians congregating to play. A drumbeat starts up, raucous, celebratory.

I think of Heron and his men, laying out the dead on Northaven's quay-side in the forbidding hush of our defeat. I'm with the victors in that battle now and it's hurting like a sore.

Yan is waving furiously at the people of Caraquet, smiling, blowing them kisses. I see a group of brightly dressed teenage girls, laughing up at him, shrieking with excitement: "Ze-ru! . . . Ze-ru! . . ." They're blowing kisses back, as if Yan Zeru is some kind of famed and incredible demigod. No wonder this man loves himself. The girls are still squealing as the gang-plank is lowered. Yan raises his arm, asking the town for quiet. The drums pause and silence falls. Yan speaks in Aylish. I don't understand his words. But my songlight senses what he means. He's happy to be home. But com-rades have died. I hear him list their names. His speech builds to a climax. He uses a word—*frelzi*. Everyone cheers, repeating it back—*frelzi*. I expect it means victory.

Renza is nearby and I ask her.

"It means freedom," she says.

I see pride and determination on her face. I lower my eyes, sweating with discomfort as the people of Caraquet, with one voice, standing in the ruins of their town, cry for freedom. I disappear inside myself, overwhelmed, as I'm taken onshore.

They don't fight for victory, like we do. They fight for freedom.

I'm conscious of Renza leading me through the crowd. Everyone wants to hug Yan Zeru. Women flirt with him; men shake his hand. I am wel-comed alongside him, mistaken for a member of the crew. An old woman kisses my cheeks and talks to me in Aylish. I nod, smiling. How can I tell her I'm a Brightling? Food is shoved into my hand, a delicious plate of fish and spiced rice. Yan is virtually being carried aloft. I watch him go and I sit, eating hungrily, trying not to be noticed. The food tastes so good after those stale ship's biscuits, and a smiling stranger hands me a frothing beer. I nod my thanks.

All round me the crew is talking loudly with the townsfolk. I listen to the foreign sound of Aylish. The crew is answering questions, telling stories, sharing their exploits. It strikes me that if this were Northaven, the crew would disappear into the barracks straightaway. There is such a separation between the military and the people. Our cadets are taken from us so young. I can't see the same distinction here. It feels like the battleship's crew and the townspeople have no division between them.

When everyone has eaten their fill, there is a ceremony in remembrance of the dead. I watch uncomfortably from a distance. At the end, the crew and the townspeople link arms in silence. Two strangers draw me to my feet, linking arms with me, as if I'm one of them. I bow my head. The dead deserve respect, enemies or not. When the ceremony is over, music starts up with an irresistible rhythm. A violka plays with an ache of pain and it draws out my emotion. I move farther away, unable to feel anything but lost. Beer is flowing freely and people begin to dance. I go beyond the crowd as the dancing takes hold. There is no one controlling it, no eldermen or Emissaries. Everyone just seems to let themselves go.

Strings of turbine lights cast a glow over the harbor. As I skirt the crowd, I see Renza and Cree, kissing in a doorway, joyful to be back home. No one is concerned that they wear no wedding bands.

Yan Zeru is dancing. My eyes rest on his slim figure and it comes as no surprise to see that he's as good at dancing as he is at everything else. His partner is a striking young woman with a dimpled smile who looks delighted to be with him. Her azure shirt is tied above her navel and her black breeches are so tight they could be sewn upon her legs. She too wears an amber jewel. I know immediately she's the local Torch that Yan has been communing with. And their closeness to each other is as plain as day. A circle forms around them—they're such a stunning couple and their pleasure in one another's company is contagious. I sense them communing in songlight as they dance. Each senses the other's next move and they twist and turn in a playful mockery of mutual desire. When the song ends, the crowd erupts into laughter and applause. I walk along the harbor, looking at the ships, leaving the Aylish behind, staring out to the dark sea. Would any of these boats get me back to Northaven?

I send my songlight up. "Rye. Nightingale. I'm coming back. I won't leave you. Please find a way to tell me you're all right." I close my eyes, forcing my concentration—and I am startled to hear a voice speaking in Brightling at my side.

"I should have introduced myself sooner. I'm Janella Andric. But you can call me Dove."

I turn to see the girl Yan was dancing with, glowing with perspiration, her dimples creasing with a friendly smile. "Kingfisher's told me all about you. Welcome to Caraquet, Lark."

Anger twists in me that Yan could so casually share my precious name. I'm damned if I'm calling her Dove or anything. I see Yan across the harbor, on the edge of the dancing, watching us thoughtfully. He turns away, drawn back to the dance by a couple of the adoring teenage girls.

"You were lucky that Kingfisher found you," says Janella. "He's one of our strongest Torches."

"I'm very grateful to everyone who's helped me," I say. "But I'm very tired. Is there somewhere quiet where I could be?"

"Of course." She immediately senses my discomfort. "This must be a lot to take in. We're not usually so rowdy. . . ."

As she leads me up a narrow street, an old woman passes us and grabs my arm, talking in Aylish.

"She wants to know if you're a refugee," Janella translates. "I told her you were a Torch. She welcomes you to Ayland."

The old woman kisses my cheek.

"Thank you," I say.

"The word for thanks is 'taka,'" Janella informs me.

"Taka," I say.

The old woman squeezes my hand and we continue on our way. It leaves me feeling shaken.

"Is it true Kingfisher dived off the ship and put his arm in an orca's mouth?" asks Janella.

"Yes," I say, reluctantly admitting it. "He did."

"He's an idiot," she says.

She loves him dearly, that's for sure. Some way up the hill, Janella opens a door. The room has a roof but not much else. A tarpaulin covers the blown-out hole where the window must have been. Janella lights a turbine lamp. There's a trundle bed in the corner, a shelf of belongings, and a small wooden table.

"These are my quarters," she says. "Please make yourself at home. You're welcome to use my bed. I expect I'll be up long into the night. Kingfisher and I have a lot to catch up on."

I'll bet you do, I think to myself.

I thank her for her kindness—and in truth, Janella is beaming goodwill and friendliness. But when she's gone, I breathe a sigh of relief to be alone. There is something in the way that she and Kingfisher danced that pierced me with a growing pain. I never got to dance with Rye, not once. And I've a gnawing feeling in my chest that it's too late. He'll be lying cocooned in bandages, no longer a man but a thing, a chrysalid. As I think this, pain consumes me. It feels as if it's eating me alive.

In the dim glow of the turbine lamp, I lie back, letting the loss run through me like the tide. For hours, it carries me.

He is gone. My love is gone. He is gone.

My best friend in the world is a piece of driftwood. It has borne me down-river, keeping me alive, hiding me from harm. But the time is coming when my wooden friend and I must part. I know I'm getting near the sea because I feel brine stinging my wounds. If I weren't so cold it would hurt like Hel. The river is slow-flowing here and I use the incoming tide to edge myself into a smaller channel. With the last of my strength, I let go of my loyal and stalwart driftwood. I use the rushes to pull myself toward the shore. When I reach it, I lie in the mud. I yank a water leech off my neck. I find more of them on my body, sucking my precious blood, and I don't rest until I've torn them from me. I'm hungry, wounded, mutilated, shivering with pain. I'm visibly unhuman to anyone who finds me. I have nothing. But I've achieved my aim. I'll die free.

I rest, my breath heaving, and I drift into a stupor. I'm aware of the sun, warming my body. Birdsong warbles on the edge of my consciousness and I hear buzzing insect clouds. I have strange, vivid dreams. In one, I hear a choir of mourners singing. I'm being carried through a wonderful city on a bier. I am a dead hero, my body is clean and beautiful, rose petals are falling all around me, maidens in white are singing my name. I'm trying to sit up, to tell the mourners that I'm still alive, but I can't move. They're going to put me in the ground. As they lay me in my grave, I try to rise, to find Elsa—and I awake to find myself sinking into the mud. I suck and slither, moving myself out, away from the river's edge, trying to find firmer ground. Clouds of biting flies buzz around my face. What a mess.

I don't want to die. I don't want to be caught. I want to yell with sorrow and rage. The pain in my skull is fucking unbearable. When I find hard ground, I sit in the long rays of the declining sun, aching from head to toe. I pry at the lead band but I fear that if it comes off now, my scalp will come with it. It's torturous, but this band is part of me until I can find a way to get rid of it. I see a bird, a sandpiper, staring at me. I pick up a handful of gravel and throw it. Fuck off.

This anger will kill me if I'm not careful.

Gala, I'm hungry. I look down at myself: leech-bitten, unshaven, sunburned, scabbed, ragged, muddy, blood-caked. I feel my hair, standing up in clumps. I must look like a madman. I stand, dizzily, and begin to walk. These fucking flies will blind me. I wipe them from my eyes and make my way through the tall rushes. It's slow progress. I come across a duck's nest and eat the eggs, swallowing them down, one by one. The little shit-wing can lay some more.

The ground becomes more solid. By the direction of the setting sun, I think I'm heading south. I go on and on, finding myself on a narrow path. Rushes grow high on either side. On the skyline, I see a small turbine whirring, silhouetted in the twilight sky. I head for it. I must calm myself. I must try to bury this anger and think clearly. I need food and water. I need shoes, a doctor. I need Elsa Crane. *Don't think of her, idiot. The grief will send you mad.*

Perhaps I'm mad already. Maybe I need to be mad to survive. I twist some rushes together and make myself a crown. I work until it sits tight on my head, hiding the lead band, fanning outward like a demented sun. I might look like a madman but I won't look like a Torch.

Hunger draws me toward the turbine, and, as darkness falls, I leave the reed marshes behind and approach a small farm. I can smell the pigs before I see them. This flat, muddy landscape with its saltgrass is an ideal place for them. I hear them snorting and snuffling. They're in a long, tumbledown sty. A low light is on in the farmhouse. What a dump: dirty, peeling paint, a broken cart by the door, a boarded-up window. There's a pile of pigshit a mile high. Poverty rules here. I see a woman moving about inside. Gala, she's serving food. My mouth starts watering uncontrollably. I lean over the sty wall to see if I can share what's in the pigs' trough, but it's bare; pigs don't leave leftovers. The runts start squealing.

"Shush," I pointlessly command them. "Shut your fucking snouts."

A dog starts barking up by the house. It sees me and almost yanks out its chain. A man appears at the window, suspicion in his eyes. This farm is right at the end of the estuary. I bet I'm not the first runaway who's washed up here. I crouch down by the sty wall. The door opens and I see the shadow of a big man cast in a beam of light.

"Hey—who's there?"

The farmer walks forward. I see the shadow of a carving knife disappearing behind his back.

"Come and have some food with us, friend . . . ," he offers.

The clown must think I was born yesterday. I can see his wife peering at the window. I swear she's loading a rifle.

"I've got a roast in here. And fresh water. I can help you. Whatever you've done, you're safe with us."

I see him bend to unchain his dog and I run, helter-skelter, as a madman would. I hear a blast behind me—and a bullet lands in the mud a few feet away. The farmer's wife isn't wasting any time.

"You won't escape," yells the farmer. "There's plenty of your kind buried in the salt flats. I'll feed you to my fucking pigs. . . ."

I see a raised walkway over the marsh. At the end of it, open water. Rather than die here, I'll throw myself into the sea. I run on, cursing the weakness in my legs. The dog's barks are getting closer. Ahead of me, over the incoming tide, the walkway turns into a long jetty. Tied to the jetty is a small boat. Gala, if I can get to it, this boat will save my life.

Usually I can sprint like the wind, but my legs are like jelly. The mutt is closing in on me. As I turn around to face it, something wild takes hold of my mind. I won't go down without a fight. I yell out all my rage, running toward the dog. As it leaps for me, I grab it. It takes a chunk out of my shoulder—and I fling it into the sea. But the farmer is on the jetty now. It shakes with each thud of his heavy boots.

"You can't get away," he calls. "You're fucked. My boat is padlocked."

I hope this is a bluff. I get to the end of the jetty and see a small, open fishing boat. Two fishing lines, a bait box, a tiny sail. In the distance his wife is following, reloading the rifle. I jump into the boat.

"You're an unhuman, aren't you?" says the farmer, getting closer. "Did you think those fucking reeds would hide your band?"

He's big, fed on the same slop as his pigs. His muscles are bursting through his jerkin but his gut is like a huge sack, drooping with years of cheap beer. Perhaps his weight might help me. I crouch low in his boat. He tries a different tack.

"I can see you're just a lad. Come on out now and I won't hurt you. . . ."

The boat is tethered with a thick leather strap, padlocked, as he said.

The gun blasts. The bullet almost takes the farmer's head off, embedding itself in the raised post at the end of the jetty.

"What the fuck are you doing?" he yells at his wife. "You almost fucking killed me."

"I was aiming for the boat," she cries.

"D'you want to put a hole in it? Useless fucking sow."

I half think he's going to leave me where I am until he's beaten up his wife, but he stands over me.

"You're a cadet, aren't you? I get a lot of them."

I stare at him, silent.

"Are you not going to talk to me, Unhuman?"

"Give me your boat and let me go," I say.

"Tell you what, I'm going to roast you for my supper." I see the glint of his knife. He wants to jump on top of me and gut me.

"I'm going to bleed you like a pig."

He puts one foot in the air, but I spring forward and grab his ankle. I pull as hard as I can. He's completely unbalanced. The boat rocks dangerously—and the big bastard falls into the water. His arm is still raised, holding the knife. I grab his wrist and while the shock of the water weakens him, I take it. I start hacking at the leather strap. BOOM—another shot from the gun whistles past me.

The farmer is splashing, yelling. The leather's hard but his knife is frighteningly sharp. I hear his wife running down the jetty. That fucking dog is with her. To my dismay, the water is shallow. The farmer finds his footing. I hear a library of swears and curses. He stands in the water and comes at me again. He's going to tip the whole boat on its side. I grip the knife as hard as I can. In the darkness, I throw myself and plunge it. I've aimed too high—but his flesh slurps. Gala. Gala. I have stabbed him through the eye. Disgust sends me reeling. He falls backward into the water, a look of shock on his face. Within seconds, he's dead. I am left gripping the gory knife.

His wife is staring at me, the wet dog baring its teeth at her side. An age passes with each of my breaths. She has the rifle aimed at me.

"Is he dead?" she asks.

I nod. My second murder.

The dog growls. I can't get away. At this range, she won't miss. Her husband's corpse floats to the surface, a great gray walrus in the dark. I think how it will haunt me in my dreams. She looks at it.

"Shut your growling," she says to the dog. "He's gone."

She straightens her back. She lowers the gun. Her eyes hold mine.

"Get out of here," she says.

Someone shakes me out of a deep, dreamless sleep.

"I hate to disturb you, but the Circle will be starting soon. Kingfisher thinks you should be there."

Andric. Janella Andric. Ayland. I'm in Ayland.

I want Rye. My whole body aches for everything we could have been.

If I can't save him, I can at least help Nightingale. How long is it since I left her on that street outside the Pink House? Did they take her in? Are they protecting her there? Is she safe from that Siren? Or did the unthinkable happen—was she caught? I have to find out. My anxiety for her fills me with intent. If these Aylish won't take me home, I'll steal one of their boats. I'm a good enough sailor to navigate their currents.

"There's some water to wash and a bit of breakfast," says Janella. "I'll wait outside and we'll go as soon as you're ready."

I thank her. Sunshine is peeping round the shutters. And I feel my hope begin to return. Today, I'm going to get home.

I eat the breakfast—hot porridge and a delicious bowl of cherries. It revives me. I take the bandages off my leg and have a good look at the wound. The orca's tooth marks have been stitched. Did he do that, Kingfisher? The wound is closed but it will leave a jagged scar. Needlework is certainly not his finest skill. It looks like a child did it and I'll make sure I tell him so.

The fresh morning air revives me further as Janella walks me to the harbor, telling me the history of the village. It used to be a trading town.

"Before the war there were often Brightling ships in the harbor. There used to be good relations between our people," she says.

Does she sense the level of my ignorance? Is she subtly trying to fill me in? I see another ship moored beside the broken battleship. It must have come in during the night. This one is brand new, smaller, faster, high solar sails and a rack of spinning turbines. It's flying the Aylish flag but it isn't painted blue. It's bright white. There are no heavy guns or missile launchers, no weapons visible. This is not a warship. I speak my thoughts unguardedly.

"I've never seen such a beautiful ship. . . ."

"That's the *Aileron Blue*," says Janella. "She's something else, isn't she?" Janella walks me toward a large, circular building with a brand-new roof. "This was the first building we repaired when the Brightlings left."

I nod, as if I know all about it. I let her chat on. Her posting to Caraquet is for two years, she says, and she is nearly finished here. She'll soon be going to Reem, to take up a position in the Central Circle House with Sorze Separelli, Ayland's most eminent Torch. It's a great privilege to serve in this way, and she tells me how thrilled she is. I smile and nod. Caraquet is part of the Great Network, she says, and she communicates all of the town's decisions with the central Circle House in Reem. She seems keen to tell me that in Ayland the people have a say on matters of local and national importance. I'm not sure what she means by any of it. All I know is that this young woman can read and write, she's living with songlight, doing a man's job and she's free to choose her own lover. If I stayed here, I could have this life.

The thought goes right through me like a honeyed knife.

The roof of the big round building is new—but the foundations look very, very old. There's a spiral pattern on each stone.

"There's been a Circle House here since the Age of Woe," Janella tells me. "In the Traveling Time, people would congregate here, coming from many miles around, and, eventually, the town sprang up. It's where we meet, the chamber where all our decisions are made. It's my role, as the serving Torch, to share our thinking with my counterpart in Reem."

"Like an Emissary?"

She doesn't understand.

"We have an Emissary," I explain, "who communicates with Brightlinghelm. He gives us orders and tells us what to do."

She looks at me, quite horrified. "I serve people. I don't tell them what to do."

Suddenly, it strikes me what this place might be. A malign ring, like we used to have in Brightland before Great Brother Peregrine swept them all away. They were riven with corruption, controlled by evil unhum—

I stop myself. But even so, if this is a malign ring, I must be on my guard.

"We're conducting the meeting in your language this morning," Janella informs me. "But if there's anything you're unclear about, please just ask."

"Taka," I say, in my one word of Aylish.

Inside the round building, everything is simple wood and stone. It's full of benches, placed in concentric circles. There's a space in the center and I see thirty or so people standing there. One of them is Yan Zeru.

"G'morning," he says, coming to greet us. I recognize some of the battle-ship's crew—Renza and Cazimir Cree. There's also a white-haired woman dressed in a pale blue jacket. She bows at me.

"Elsa," says Yan. "This is Eminence Alize. She's one of our most experienced negotiators, from Reem. Alize, this is Elsa Crane."

"It's my ship you see in the harbor, Elsa," says the white-haired woman, coming forward to greet me. "I've come downriver from our capital to pick up my crew."

She has a kind of natural authority, like Sergeant Redshank, borne of age and long experience. Her sleeves are pushed up, like a craftsman's, and one of her hands is missing. She must be a veteran. She catches me glancing at her short forearm as I return her polite bow.

"You're noticing my souvenir from Montsan Beach?" she asks with a wide smile.

"I'm sorry," I mutter, not knowing what to say.

"Don't apologize; you weren't responsible." Her cropped hair falls like snowflakes round her face. "Do you feel rested?" she asks.

"Yes," I say.

Alize offers me a seat, gesturing as if her hand is still there. We sit in a circle, gazing at each other. Yan Zeru introduces me to the people I don't know but I'm so keyed up I forget their names immediately. These people are all so confident and well schooled. Surely I must be in an invisible trap—and all of a sudden these Aylish will turn on me, behaving like the barbaric horde from our mural in Northaven. Their courtesy is weird. Why would the people who killed my pa conduct their meeting in Brightling, a language forced upon them in an occupation? These Aylish tore my family apart. I want to know how my father died. What if Pa's remains are here, in this town, lying in the fields outside? Rye's question is more insistent than ever. *What if the Brethren have lied about the war?*

"Torch Yan tells me you'd like to return to Brightland," proffers Alize in a gentle tone.

"Yes," I say. "Yes, as soon as possible."

"May I ask why?"

"There are people I can't leave."

"Can you tell us about them?"

Might this woman be the key to getting back home?

"I have two friends," I begin. "They're Torches like me, Nightingale and Rye."

"I heard Nightingale at sea," Yan cuts in. "An extraordinary, powerful song, like nothing I've ever experienced."

"She's in Brightlinghelm," I say. "She's been living in terrible danger. I was with her in songlight as she tried to escape, but . . ."

I'm suddenly aware that Janella has her eyes closed. She's communing with someone.

"Who else is in this room that I can't see?" I ask.

Janella blinks her eyes open. "Sorze Separelli," she says. "He's our strongest enabling Torch in Reem. I'm communing with him. I told you, that's my role."

I clam up. "I'm not sharing my business with strangers in Reem," I say.

They all seem put out.

"Our discussions in the Circle are open," says Cree. "What happens here is everybody's business."

"Not if it puts my friends in danger."

"Elsa, forgive us," says Yan. "The fellowship we're used to must seem very strange to you."

"Torch Janella," says Alize, "suggest to Separelli that we need a closed Circle."

Janella communicates this. "He's withdrawn," she says.

These people are my enemies. I can't forget a lifetime of a hate just because they wash my dress and feed me some nice fish.

"Please take me to Northaven or let me have a boat," I plead. "My mother and my husband will think that I am dead."

Alize looks at me in surprise. "You're young to be married?"

"We're all married. It's our duty. We must provide sons for the Brethren."

"You seem a little angry about that," remarks Alize, picking up on my resentment.

I shrug. "I'm luckier than some. Heron Mikane's a decent enough man."

I hear several intakes of breath.

Alize stands and moves away from the circle, as if I've slapped her.

"Mikane? You're married to Mikane?" Her eyes are full of horror.

"I'm . . . I'm his Second Wife."

"I knew we couldn't trust her!" cries Cree.

Alize leans on a bench, steadying herself.

Kingfisher looks at me as if I have betrayed him. "You didn't give me your married name. . . ."

"I didn't think to." And I realize why. I didn't give my married name because my marriage isn't real. It's a pretense of marriage, nothing more. But how can I tell these Aylish that in Brightland, a girl's only choice is to marry or to run?

"The name Mikane is an insult here," says Alize in a low voice. All her friendliness has gone, as if the mention of Heron has plunged the sun into the sea.

"We're only just wed. Neither of us had a choice."

"You can't possibly go back," says Yan. "That man has killed hundreds of

Torches like you. He's a vile and heartless monster to our kind."

"That can't be true," I say.

I am filled with a horrible foreboding. I think of Heron's mural, the warrior hero, standing on a pile of Aylish dead—and its real meaning comes home to me. I think of the curtains that Chaffinch made, the buildings of Montsan burning in a sea of orange flames. What has Heron done here?

Alize comes back to the circle. Her color is slowly returning. She sits, her eyes locked on mine. "I suppose the Brethren have told you he's a hero."

I don't know what to say to this. I feel hot shame and I don't know why.

"How much do you know about the true state of the war?" asks Alize.

I look down at the floor. This is what I'm dreading. They'll see how lumpen and ignorant I am.

"I know your people killed my pa."

Alize sits back. "I'm very sorry for your loss," she says.

"Do you know how it started?" asks Kingfisher.

"You . . . the Aylish destroyed our colonies. You massacred women and children in cold blood."

Kingfisher and Alize look at one another.

"The war began because the Brethren tried to persecute our Torches," says Kingfisher. "They used their trading colonies as bases to terrorize our population. We resisted."

I look up at him. He's telling the truth. Alize continues.

"Brightland has tried to take our land and impose its culture on us for over fifteen years. But we will not give up our Torches. They're our sons and daughters, friends and neighbors. And we call that genocide—a crime worthy of the Light People."

Rye knew we were being lied to. He knew it.

"This is too much too soon," says Janella. "It's unfair on Elsa. She can't process all this. You know what it's like for refugees. It takes time."

"I'm not a refugee," I cry. "I understand what you've told me—but nothing changes my need to go home. Please help me!"

"We will try," says Alize, "but first, you can help me. Tell me, what's your true opinion of Heron Mikane? As his wife you must know him as well as anyone."

This question throws me.

"Heron? I hardly know him at all. "

Alize is waiting for a proper response. Whatever Heron has done, he helped me when I needed him. I owe him my truth. The Aylish are silent, waiting—and the words come to me.

"From the moment I first saw him, Heron Mikane struck me as a man who belongs to Death." The silence changes shape, as if no one was expecting me to say this. Alize sits forward as I continue.

"I say this not just because he's burned and scarred," I begin. "He only has one eye; he's lost an ear—"

Alize breathes out, as if this is the least that Mikane deserves.

"I say it because he's so weary of life. He gave a speech when he buried his men"—I eye Kingfisher—"men that you drowned when you sank our transport ship. He said Death has marked him as her own. And in everything he does, it's like he's only waiting to be wrapped up in a shroud. It mortified him, being forced to marry. He hasn't taken me, or Chaffinch, his First Wife. I think he only married us to save us being sent to the front."

"Sent to the front?" Renza interjects. "I thought Brightling women weren't allowed to fight?"

"Not to fight. As Third Wives . . . comfort girls." I can't look any of them in the eye. I feel Renza exhale and I bow my head in shame for my countrymen.

Alize coaxes me. "What else can you tell us?"

I want them to see Mikane as he is.

"We were married before I'd said ten words to him—but he's treated me respectfully. I've seen his kindness, to people like John Jenkins—a soldier who has lost his mind—and to Gailee Roberts, my friend who's always been trampled on. He has no interest in being powerful in the town. They gave him a medal and he shoved it into his pocket, saying it belonged to the dead. There's always a smoke in his hand. He drinks. He's loyal to his men but I've never heard him say one good word about fighting or glory or anything he's done in the war. He hates Wheeler, our Emissary from Brightlinghelm, but as for hating Torches, you can't be right." I look up, my eyes on Kingfisher's. "I know what that kind of hatred is like," I say. "And I don't sense it in Heron Mikane."

"Does he know what you are?" asks Alize.

"I don't think so. But I was trying to find a safe house for Nightingale in Brightlinghelm. I asked Heron for his help. And he gave it."

There's a silence as they take in my words. I feel another wave of anxiety. Ma will think I'm dead. She'll be underwater with her grief and she is all alone. I have to get back.

"Is it your free choice to return to your home?" asks Alize.

"Yes," I say without hesitation.

"Please don't waste your future—" starts Kingfisher.

"If you can't take me, I will steal a boat and go."

Alize is quietly regarding me, as if she's thinking something through.

"Elsa," she begins. "I'm here on a special mission. My ship is not a warship, yet I'm sailing into conflict. I've asked for volunteers and these brave men and women have agreed to be my crew. We're seeking a dialogue with your leaders. We want to find a bloodless resolution to this war. We know that it's unlikely we'll survive, but . . ."

She's speaking too quickly. There's too much to take in. Yan and Renza and Cree are all part of her crew?

"We're offering your leaders peace."

That word won't sink in. What does she mean, peace?

"This war is destroying everything," continues Alize with feeling. She has her short forearm tight against her chest as if her lost hand is pressing on her heart. "It has to end."

"Take me with you," I beg.

Cree objects straightaway. "She doesn't know what she's asking. We need to get to Brightlinghelm. Northaven's in the opposite direction. It's a backwater—a waste of time and our resources."

Alize quiets him with a gesture.

"Elsa," she says, "I want to tell you about our mission. I want you to listen carefully so you truly understand. . . ."

"Eminence, be advised—" says Cree, trying to halt her.

"She has to know what's at stake." Alize has fire in her eyes and Cree backs down.

"We've known for some time that your leaders are breaking the First Law. They're developing firefuel planes. Yan Zeru has confirmed this."

I look up at Kingfisher in surprise. How does he know that? The only thing I know about planes is that Piper is likely to die in one. Is this Aylishman some kind of spy?

Alize carries on. "We know that Niccolas Kite is planning to destroy Reem, as soon as his planes are ready. So, we've been developing a firefuel missile to protect ourselves. Our Circle Houses throughout the land recently voted to strike at Brightlinghelm. Our missiles will be fired from ships and they'll destroy your city from afar. We won't even hear your people scream."

I feel the blood draining from my face.

"However, some of us insisted that before we strike, we must offer the Brightling people a chance to come to terms. The mission of the *Aileron Blue* is to end this war in peace, not in mutual catastrophic violence."

I'm trying to fathom why I feel so strangely moved. It's not just that she's describing momentous events, painting a terrifying future in my mind. I'm moved because she's not concealing anything. She's speaking to me as an adult, an equal, as if I'm worth something.

Alize takes in a breath. "We know that sailing straight to Brightlinghelm is fraught with danger. Our unarmed ship of peace might count for nothing and we'll probably be fired upon as soon as we are seen." She turns to Cree. "But suppose we land in a small town, having saved a young woman from the sea, returning her to her legendary husband . . . ?"

Cree begins to see her thinking.

"It's a strong gesture of goodwill," he says. "And the people of Northaven could arrange us safe passage to Brightlinghelm."

"You're risking Elsa's life," cries Yan. "Coming back on an Aylish ship? They'll be highly suspicious. You'd be putting her in peril—"

"I can speak for myself," I say. I look at Alize, wanting to talk as she does, from the heart. My throat is tight. I stand. And in the middle of their circle, I speak.

"My people chant for victory," I tell the Aylish. "But I don't think it's victory we want. We want our fathers and our brothers home." I try to put the tangle of my feelings into words. "It's hard to talk, without condemning myself as a traitor because I've been taught my whole life that you're my enemies. All we hear is *death to the Aylish, death to the Aylish.*" I pause for breath. "It's true that I'm ignorant. And the truth that I've been told is shifting under me like sinking sand. So I'm puzzling a lot of things. My friend Rye Tern once asked me who our real enemy was. And that question keeps going through my mind. They took Rye to the Chrysalid House—" I force myself on, swallowing the pain—"because in Brightland we can be destroyed for any kind of difference. Rye knew the Aylish weren't his foes. He knew our enemy was the Brethren." I look at Alize, taking in her soft white hair, her owl-like eyes. "I dream of peace, but peace isn't possible for us—because even if the war ends, our lives will still be full of violence."

Alize crosses the circle. She sits by me.

"Peace might be a dream but if the war ends, there's only you and the Brethren. Peace will weaken them. That's why they're so anxious to prolong the war."

I'm thinking of a pot full of slowly boiling frogs.

"Without the war," I say, "maybe we'd find the right way to protest." I look up to see Kingfisher gazing at me in concern.

"Don't make her a revolutionary, Alize," he warns. "They'll kill her straightaway."

"Elsa, we'll return you to Northaven, if you still desire it," says Alize. "And if you consent, we'll use the gesture to begin a dialogue with Brightlinghelm."

"I want my country to be free," I say. "And that can only happen if there's peace. So take me home. And I will help."

Alize grips my hands in hers. "You are a very brave young woman."

Janella asks me if she can communicate what's passed to Sorze Separelli, her counterpart in Reem. I agree to it without a pause.

"Please tell him we'd like to make landfall at Northaven," Alize instructs her. "If the Circles agree."

Janella closes her eyes. The Circle House holds her in silence. I sense the potency of her concentration and I wonder at Ayland's power lines of songlight, its intricate circular web of communication. It makes the radiobine look like an old-fashioned toy. We wait to hear Separelli's reply and at last Janella opens her eyes.

"It's passed by a small majority," she says.

"Well, then," says Alize. "Let's lose no time. We'll sail with the tide."

Alize walks me down to the harbor. She offers to give me a tour of the ship but, thanking her, I stay on land. I look around, wanting to retain something of the atmosphere. This land is the grave of my father. Yet it's the only place I've ever been where people have known what I am and accepted me. I imagine how Nightingale might flourish here, how she wouldn't have to be afraid. And I think, with a knife-blade of regret, how different things would have been if Rye and I had run. Could we have made it to these shores? We might be together, like Renza and Cree, kissing in a doorway carelessly.

I see Yan Zeru on the deck, staring down at me, like he's assessing me in a different light. Janella taps him on the shoulder and they talk. Something of deep import passes between them. As I climb the gangplank, they embrace—but when Kingfisher tries to kiss her, Janella tilts her head to one side and moves away, as if she has the measure of him. I like her for that.

As she passes me, I hold out my hand.

"Taka for everything," I say. "Goodbye."

To my surprise, she takes me in her arms. "In Aylish we never say goodbye. Our word is 'amou'—I'll see you again."

"Amou," I say.

"Be safe, Lark," she whispers. And somehow, I don't mind her using my songlight name. Kingfisher watches Janella go—until he's distracted by a group of teenage girls who have come to wave him off. He flirts a farewell to them, blowing extravagant kisses. This man is an azure butterfly.

"You shouldn't come," I say to him. "If my people find out what you are, they'll break you on a wheel."

"What if your life needs saving again?" he asks with a breezy grin.

"I'm serious."

"Far too serious," he remarks.

I do as Janella did and walk away.

As we head out to sea, I find my bunk. I look back on the broken shore of Caraquet and I find that the pain has shifted in my heart. The tide has turned. I'm no longer consumed with grief for Rye and my dead father. I'm doing something. In that Circle House, I was listened to, I was respected. It's crushing to realize that I have never known that. Today, *I spoke.*

The weight in my heart is easing and the honeyed knife slides out. I grasp it in my mind. I will need it as a weapon if I'm going to fight for peace. Rye knew that his enemy was the Brethren. And only in peace will the Brethren fall. If I can't save Rye, I will at least avenge him. I will do what I can to bring down the Brethren. That is what I want. That is what I'm fighting for.

I can speak.

I will speak.

As the mountains of Ayland recede, Renza comes in with my dress, clean and pressed. I thank her but I don't put it on. In the space of a day, everything has changed. I feel like it belongs to another girl.

Cassandra is with me. She has her warm arms around me. I'm so happy to see her.

"Cassandra," I whisper. "You're here."

"I'm going to teach you how to fly," she says.

She's here.

I find myself floating. Everything is white. I turn in the air and I can see my body lying down below. I am pale as a ghost, lying in a white bed. A woman sits beside me, glorious hair cascading down her back. She holds my hand and dabs my brow with an icy cloth. Something isn't right.

"Cassandra?" I say, and my voice comes out of my mouth, sticky, thirsty, dry.

I can see cuts on my temples; patches of my hair have been shaved off.

I fall like a brick back into my body.

My head is thumping, stinging sore. My eyes won't focus. The woman beside me is a blur in white. I put my fingers up to where the pain is worst. There are thin wounds above my temples.

I cry out: "What's been done to me? Cassandra!"

I remember then. I remember Cassandra's face becoming Keynes, the charged electric bolt tearing through my back. This isn't a dream; it's a waking nightmare. I'm trying to sit up. Then I hear a voice as smooth as silk.

"All's well. You're fine."

The woman in white is a powerful presence, but without my spectacles I'm struggling to see. Lights jump and dazzle around her face, reflected from the diamond earrings that she wears. Her clothes are white. Perhaps she is a vision, a statue come to life. This can't be real because she looks like Sister Swan.

"You've been so brave. You never made a sound," she says.

"Where am I?"

"I was as gentle as could be when I put in the knife. I'm sorry if I hurt you."

What does she mean? My breath catches with panic.

"What's happened to me? Am I in the Chrysalid House?"

"You're in my chambers," says the velvet voice. "My man Starling brought you here."

My songlight. I let it fly, terrified it's been destroyed.

"Lark! Lark!" I cry inside.

I feel my songlight leap. It's there within me, whole, unscathed. But there is no reply.

Lark's gone. The wounds on my temples are hot with pain.

"You're my counterfeit chrysalid," soothes the figure. "I've had to make it look as though you've been transformed." She presses a cool cloth on my forehead. "I made the cuts myself. Then I stitched them so, so carefully. I made sure you didn't feel a thing."

"Why?"

"I had to. To save you."

White on white. I don't understand at all. My head is full of white, white fog.

"I can't see anything," I say. My voice sounds small.

"You poor dolly. Here." Her hand holds my spectacles. I put them on. And she comes into focus.

"I think you know my name." She smiles. It is a mural come to life, the most dazzling beauty I have ever seen.

"Sister Swan," I say.

She inclines her head, pleased that I know her. She gives me water and I drink. So much makeup. Like a mask. Her eyebrows are perfect charcoal lines. Her lips are cherry red. She walks across to a white marble table and returns with a mirror. Her dress flows around her like it's made of pouring milk. I can't believe I'm in her presence.

266

I try to sit up. She puts white pillows behind me. I'm in a cot, under a soft white quilt. The pillows are like clouds. Sister Swan shows me her handiwork with the little mirror. A wound runs over each of my temples, red and angry on my pallid skin.

"I kept you from the surgeons. They stick in scalpels, thin as skewers. There'd be nothing left of your songlight by now. You'd be mindless," she says. "And that's what everybody must believe."

The shock of my capture comes back. My papa, warning me too late.

"Where's my father?" I ask her.

She exhales and smiles a thin smile. "I'm afraid I couldn't save him."

"No . . . No . . ."

A wrench of grief. It twists into an anguished cry.

"He's alive, silly girl." Sister Swan shushes me. "Kite might come in. If he sees emotion on your face, he'll know that I have tricked him. He must think you're just a dummy. Your father's in jail and I will do my best to keep him from the firing wall."

How do I make sense of this?

"Where's Keynes?" I ask.

"Who's Keynes?" she replies.

"He's Papa's Siren."

"That awful creature?" Swan smiles. "He was dangerous to you. He's been disposed of. You needn't fear."

This disturbs me more than I can say.

"Is he dead?"

"Starling Beech took care of him. You must be so relieved."

"He's been killed?"

I'm feeling horror, not relief. Sister Swan seems bewildered by my shock. "Sometimes hard things must be done. Nettles must be grasped. Yes, that odious Siren is dead. He'll never trouble you again. Now wipe your eyes. We must get you on your feet."

Papa's jailed. Keynes is murdered. Lark is drowned, pulled into the darkness of the sea. Tears are falling, unbidden, down my face.

Sister Swan offers a white handkerchief. "I think you should be glad to be alive." She says this in a gentle tone but I feel her lack of patience. She doesn't want a crybaby.

I must preserve myself. She needs to see my gratitude.

"Thank you," I say. "For sparing me."

"Do you want to know why I did it?" she asks.

I nod.

"Listen," she says. She closes her eyes. I see a force of concentration. At first, there is just silence and the ticking of her clock. Then I hear . . . her songlight. It's as faint as breath, barely audible, a distant finger running round the rim of a glass. Her notes whine.

"Can you feel how constrained I am?" Sister Swan shocks me by peeling back her hair. She shows me the ugliness beneath her wig: the brutal lock, the lead cuff.

"You're a Siren?"

Papa's words come to me: *Sirens hate us. They'd kill us all in our beds.* I try to stop my heart from hammering.

Swan takes my hands in both of hers. "When I first came here, Niccolas Kite gave me a glass of sparkling champagne. In it was a sleeping draft. I woke up with his surgeon staring over me. I had no womb and this hated cuff was locked into my skull."

She speaks with a dreadful kind of lighthearted bitterness.

"Oh, Sister," I say.

"I kept you from the Chrysalid House because your songlight is so strong." Her eyes are shining with excitement. "I spared you so that you can be my voice."

"Your voice?"

"You're going to be my shield and my knife."

What does she mean? What does she want me for?

"I don't understand," I say.

Swan claps her hands. Some women enter. They are dressed entirely in white, with gauze over their faces.

"Get my dolly on her feet," orders Swan in a harsh voice. Then she turns to me. "I'm sorry to hurry you, but Kite often visits at this time. We have to have you ready."

The women come to help me out of bed, but I cringe from their touch. They are entirely blank. My blood turns cold.

"This is what I spared you from," says Swan. "This was going to be your fate."

I've only ever seen chrysalids at a distance, moving about their tasks with invisible faces. These women appall me. I am silent in my horror.

"Dress her!"

There was a mural on the wall in the Light People museum, near an exhibit of a man in outer space. It was of a great black star, with other stars and planets eddying toward it, as if the black star was slowly consuming them, sucking all their light and energy away. That's how these women make me feel.

"Do my ladies disturb you?" asks Sister Swan. "I suppose I've grown used to them. They're my constant companions. Brother Kite gifted them to me. He names them all for constellations. Lady Libra was an insurgent before, can you imagine?"

I feel like I can't breathe. Blanks. Their presence is an absence.

"That's Lady Orion, Lady Scorpio . . . We'll have to find a name for you."

"My name is Kaira Kasey," I tell her with as much firmness as I dare. I won't let her name me like one of these dark stars.

"Well," muses Swan, seeing my dismay. "You may keep your own name. It can be our secret. And it's right that you're different from the rest." She tries my name on her tongue, seeing if she like the taste. "Kaira . . ."

The ladies put me in a white dress. They sit me at a dressing table. I look small, crumpled, gray.

"You need some powder and some pink," says Swan. "He won't look at you for long but when he does, stare straight ahead. Empty your mind of everything."

She dusts and paints me like a dolly. I swear she is enjoying this. She seems so excited to have my company. I look at the chrysalids that surround her. I think how they must drain her.

I want to be with my papa on a riverboat, with Lark on the ocean, far away from here. I am finding it hard to hide my wretchedness but Sister Swan seems thrilled with me. She brushes out my hair, telling me how fine it is. I'm sure she's trying to be gentle but she pulls at my tender wounds.

"Does my father know that I'm alive?" I ask.

I feel a high, whining ring of glass and can tell immediately that I've aggravated her. I realize that I mustn't speak of him.

"It's better if he thinks you're dead," she says. "But you mustn't worry. I'm your family now." There is something chilling in her smile.

The door opens and she starts. Through the mirror, I see an Emissary.

"Brother Kite," he announces.

Sister Swan snatches off my glasses and my vision blurs. She whispers: "Be absolutely blank."

Brother Kite enters, smaller than his statues, neat as a beetle. Sister Swan often speaks of him on the radiobine. She tells us he is one of Brightland's greatest thinkers, Great Brother Peregrine's right hand. Swan glides toward him.

"May the gods shine light upon you."

Kite gives her no greeting. He's unbuttoning his jacket.

"What's between you and Harrier?" he asks.

"Brother Harrier? I hardly know the man."

"Then why is he acting like your champion? He's asking pointedly after your health—as if your inexplicable collapse was somehow down to me." This comes out in a strangled jealous tone. Swan looks bewildered. She's nervous.

"Is that your plan?" accuses Kite. "To save yourself by seducing Harrier?"

I don't know what any of this means. I slide down inside myself, hoping he won't notice me. Swan is in my eyeline. I can see her mind whirring, thinking on her feet. She's frightened of him.

"I've been cultivating Harrier," she says coolly. "And I've gained his trust. Haven't you noticed what a favorite he's become? He's in Peregrine's rooms at every hour. The old man is quite besotted."

She pours Kite a glass of tawny liquor, handing it to him. I notice that her fingernails are painted icy white.

"Harrier's an obstacle to you," purrs Swan. "If you let me mind-twist him, I'll clear him from your path."

She lays her cheek on Kite's shoulder, her finger pressing gently on his chest. Kite is still hot with jealousy.

"You failed to mind-twist Drake," he says. "You told me you could get him in my camp."

"I didn't get my opportunity. The Aylish attacked me."

"He's still stalling on my planes, refusing his support, playing both sides like the rattlesnake he is."

"Forget Drake," whispers Swan, soothing him. "I'll have Harrier agree to arm your planes. I'll get the whole council on your side, you'll see. . . ."

Kite's hand wraps around Swan's waist. His fingers twist into her flesh. Swan lets out a little gasp and I can see that her smile is a contortion of pretense. He's hurting her. In my distress, I drop the mirror I am holding and it smashes on the ground. Kite sees me.

"What's that?"

I look straight ahead like a hollow, empty shell.

"Careless little thing," says Swan. "It's fresh from the Chrysalid House. I wanted to choose a dolly of my own."

She orders a veiled lady to pick up all the glass. Kite examines me.

"I thought it needed looking after," Swan explains. "I can't have children, so I must have a doll."

There's a spike of accusation in her cherry smile. Kite examines my scars.

271

I stare straight ahead, unblinking. Inside, I turn myself into a massive fist.

"You'll soon tire of it," he says. "It's as ghastly as the rest."

He backs Swan toward her bedchamber. She sends me a glance that tells me this is what he's come here for; he takes her when he likes and she may never refuse him. Kite kicks the door shut with his gleaming boot. They've gone.

My panic comes in a great gush. Gala, help me. She wants me as her shield and her knife. She wants me to save her from that man.

How can I? I'm nothing but a crybaby and that man is a monster.

How can I stand up to him?

I make no sound. I go so far inside myself I see the stars of space. I feel unbearably alone. I can't believe this horrid, deathly room is now my life. Inside I howl, grieving for my papa, for my future, for my Lark.

Lark . . .

What does it matter if I use my songlight now? I am caught already.

I sing her name, as far as thought can take me.

"Lark . . ."

Her brave soul now drifts above the sea. I try to rise above this suffocating grief.

And then, like a miracle, I hear her.

"Nightingale?"

The *Aileron Blue* is so fast. We're cutting through the waves like a scythe. A hundred miles across the sea is nothing to this ship. I doze fitfully, and in the night, I hear her. At first I think I'm dreaming—but her cry persists. Her songlight soars.

"Lark . . ." Her pure, bright, aching note.

"Nightingale?"

She's free; she must have escaped. I rush up to the deck, hoping the clear starlit sky will help me hear her. At the prow of the ship, I send up my songlight as strongly as I can.

"Nightingale?"

Her emotion reaches me before I see her. Her joy that I'm alive makes it difficult to breathe. Then she's with me, on the deck. We hold each other's light and her presence becomes stronger. She really thought that I was dead.

She senses the motion of the ship, the speed, and her songlight curls into a question. I show her my story. I show her Yan Zeru, sitting on my wrecked boat.

"You called him to me," I tell her. "He heard your cries. You saved my life."

Nightingale gasps, becoming aware of my Aylish clothes. "The Aylish have you prisoner?"

"No," I quickly reassure her. "They thought I was a refugee, trying to escape. They came out of their way to rescue me. They . . . They're not anything like we thought."

I let her share my experience. I show her Renza Perch, laughing when I thought she was a boy. I show her Janella Andric, giving me her bed. I show her Kingfisher.

"I haven't had to hide myself," I tell her. "I'm a Torch here, not an unhuman. I spoke to them, Nightingale, in their Circle House. They're bringing me home."

Nightingale looks at me, uncomprehending. As our harmony strengthens, I realize how strange and pale she is. Her face is powdered. She's wearing a white dress far too big for her. Then I see the shaved patches of her hair, the thin red wounds on the sides of her skull. My breath catches in dread.

"Where are you?"

Nightingale doesn't know where to begin. I see her father crying in a room full of dead birds. I experience her horror as she's tricked by Keynes. I share the agony of the electric bolt. Then I see Sister Swan. I hear her faint, chilling song. She's a Siren.

"She cut your head with razorblades and stitched you up herself? That's mad, that's criminal!" I'm struggling to take it in.

"But I've still got my songlight. This is what she saved me from." Nightingale shows me the ghostly veiled women standing motionless in her white room. I share her revulsion.

"She says I'm to be her shield and her knife."

"Sister Swan wants your songlight," I realize in horror.

"I think she's desperate, Lark. She's a prisoner too. She must be so lonely. She has no one except these pitiful ladies."

"She kidnapped you!"

Nightingale is so warmhearted that I worry she can't see the bad in people. She's had a lifetime of making excuses for her father and now this ruthless, grasping woman wants to take advantage of her.

"It's not Sister Swan I'm afraid of," she says.

Nightingale shows me Brother Kite. I see his weak mouth and his hard eyes, full of jealous want. I see Swan fawning upon him. I see his hands groping her flesh. I turn away.

"Kite controls her."

"What does she want you for, Nightingale?"

"I don't know. But my papa's in jail," she says helplessly. "He's facing the firing wall. If Swan saves his life, I'll do anything she says."

I take this in. I want to tear down the palace walls and carry her outside. What can I say that will help her? All I can do is give her strength.

"Nightingale, you're strong and good. You'll survive this, I know you will. I'm coming back to Brightland. The Aylish are taking me to Northaven. They want to make peace—"

"Shush!" Nightingale stiffens in fear. "I hear them—Kite!"

She vanishes. I feel as if the deck has gone from under my feet.

A glow of dawn is creeping into the sky. I stand, staring at the waves, as the *Aileron Blue* cuts through them. On the far horizon is a jagged black line. We're already in sight of Brightland's coast, hurtling toward home. I suddenly feel overwhelmed by a horrible apprehension for Nightingale, for myself. I turn, my breath catching in panic—and I realize that I'm being watched. Kingfisher. He's standing on the bridge, looking out at me in concern. Could he see Nightingale? I immediately straighten myself up, pushing down my physical sense of dread. But he's already walking toward me.

"Elsa, what's happened? You look pale."

"I'm fine."

"Come onto the bridge."

I follow him because, in truth, I'm so afraid for Nightingale that I don't know what else to do. He sits me at a desk covered in documents.

"Is there something you need?" he asks.

My consternation must still be on my face. I don't know what to say to him. Nightingale has to be saved. Can I tell this Torch she's in the Brethren's Palace? What if I reveal that Sister Swan is a Siren? That must surely be a deeply held state secret. Would I be a traitor? I'm sinking in the ocean, way beyond my depth.

Yan pours me a glass of water. He puts it in my hand. "Talk to me."

He means in songlight. I look at him. Am I desperate enough to speak?

"I can't share this. You're Aylish. It isn't right." I drink and it revives me.

"Elsa," he says, "there's a bond between People of Song that goes beyond borders, beyond nationality. It's one of the reasons tyrants find us such a threat. And one of the reasons we use our powers so carefully. Whatever you tell me, it stays between the two of us, until you decide otherwise. Torches find it hard to lie to one another. It's difficult to hold things back."

"That's my worry," I say. "You'd tell every Torch from here to Reem." That long hair of his, those eyes . . . No wonder strong women like Janella Andric flush crimson in his presence. This man was made to be painted into pictures.

"You think me a real wisp, don't you?" he says.

"A what?"

"I don't need songlight to have gauged your opinion. You think me insubstantial and unsound."

He's put his finger on it.

"Look," I say. "You saved my life, as you keep reminding me. I'm aware how much I owe you."

"It's not a debt. I promise I won't intrude on you," he says. "But I want you to see who I am." His songlight is inviting me. I hesitate.

"We're taught that the Aylish are all thought-stealers and mind-twisters," I say.

"Those things are forbidden by our very highest laws. The only time I've ever forced myself into another mind is in battle. And I was defending myself."

I remember how afraid I was when Nightingale first came. It's such an act of intimacy, to join in songlight. For Rye and me, it was as natural as breathing.

I look at the man in front of me.

"Who named you Kingfisher?" I ask in songlight. "They should have named you Peacock."

I feel his mind opening in a smile and before I quite know how, I find myself one with him. I am seeing Kingfisher's memory through his eyes, as if the separation between us is of no consequence. I see snowcapped mountains, green trees around a lake. I am climbing an overhanging rock. A ragged girl is watching him—it feels like she is watching me. I realize it's Janella Andric, aged about thirteen, dirty, barefoot. I'm going to impress her. I want to make her smile. I reach the edge and look down. Too late to turn back. I have to do it now. I dive, feeling the shock of the water. I cut through it, as soundless as an arrow. In that deep blue, I see a fish, stunned by my sudden presence. I come to the surface with the fish in my hand. Janella Andric is leaping up and down. She is crying, laughing.

I look at Kingfisher, trying to comprehend how he has shared himself so vividly. Perhaps it's his physical closeness—or perhaps that's just the way it is in Ayland.

"Diving into that lake felt like I was washing things away. It was like being reborn," he says.

"Reborn from what?" I ask.

A pause. Then a jumble of images hits me. I am a long-legged boy, sitting in dirt. I am living in a squalid hut with lots of other children. I'm ravenous. There isn't enough food and fleas are biting me. I work with all the older children, pushing trolleys full of rocks in a huge quarry. My hands are cut and calloused. There are guards with whips. Gala, they are Brightling guards. I see a woman through a fence, a band around her skull. My mother. I call to her. She sees me.

"Yan," she says. "Yan."

She comes to the fence and tries to reach for me. Her arms are skeletal. As she's pulled away, she's telling me she loves me. She tells me to be strong. I see Brightling soldiers, watchtowers, Emissaries carrying whips. I am screaming for her: "Mother!"

I draw my songlight back into myself. Kingfisher looks down, the memory still raw. We did that to him, us, the Brightlings. A Brightling soldier pulled his mother from that fence.

"I grew up in a labor camp," he says. "When your armies first invaded, they rounded up all the People of Song. My mother was a Circle Torch, so they came for our whole family. They . . ."

This is still too painful for him to say.

"You don't have to tell me," I assure him.

"Brightland's surgeons came here. They used our people to hone their skills for the Chrysalid House. I escaped from that camp when I was twelve. Janella got me out."

"What happened to your mother?" I ask.

By his silence, I know that she is dead.

"Why are you on a mission for peace?" I ask. "If that had been done to me, I'd be eaten up with hate. Why aren't you fighting us?"

Another slew of images, far more recent. He's on the battleship. He fires. He knows the accuracy of his aim because his consciousness is filled with the agony of burning men. Our burning men.

"The wrong people die in wars," he says. "It's not your people who should die, it's your leaders. Your leaders must be held to account."

He shows me one final image. It's hazy, incomplete, as if he saw it at the very limit of his powers: Sister Swan, her face contorted. Kingfisher is joined in songlight with her but it's not a harmony. It is the very opposite.

"I have you, spy."

They're struggling. Sister Swan attacks him, viciously forcing her way in. He fights back. Their environment shimmers, from a ship's deck to some kind of a control room. Light floods in through a long window and Yan sees a plane landing with a roar of firefuel. I feel a horrible sensation, as Sister Swan reaches into his memories and draws out his precious mountain lake. She grasps his name.

"Kingfisher."

He lets her go when he becomes aware of Kite. Kite is yelling at Swan, a lead band in his hand. I share the horror that Kingfisher feels, as he perceives the lock in Swan's skull. I feel his disgust, his hatred for Kite. This is

278

his enemy. This is the man who took his childhood and killed his mother.

"You want to destroy Brother Kite," I realize.

"Peace will destroy him," he replies.

Kingfisher knows that Swan is a Siren. He's already seen it for himself. Why am I holding back? I decide to share everything, as he has.

"This must go no further," I urge.

Kingfisher puts a hand upon his heart and I feel the gravity of his vow.

"Nightingale is in the Brethren's Palace." It comes rushing out in words and images. I show him the cuts on Nightingale's head, the ghostly white-clad women, her cloying mistress. He takes it in, a revelation.

"What does Swan want her for?"

"I don't know. But somebody must save her. Please take me with you to Brightlinghelm."

At that moment, Alize comes in, wearing a dress uniform.

"Good morning, Elsa." She smiles, preoccupied. I become aware of the growing dawn and I remember the task of the day. A silhouette of our coast is drawing nearer.

"Good morning," I say.

Alize looks to Kingfisher. "Are our terms ready?"

"The documents are all here. The Circle in Reem has approved them by the narrowest margin."

"How narrow?"

"Separelli used his deciding vote."

"Then we mustn't fail. Can you still reach him?"

Kingfisher shakes his head. "We're far beyond my range." He gathers up the papers he's been working on and hands them to Alize. I look in awe at his neat handwriting, illegible to me. Alize thanks him and begins to read. I see laughter lines in the corners of her eyes and deep frown lines on her brow. She's not as old as I first thought—perhaps a few years older than Ma—but this woman has *lived*.

"Elsa wants to come with us to Brightlinghelm," says Kingfisher. He gives no details, sharing nothing, as I asked.

"My friend needs help," I say.

Alize looks at me long and hard, as if she knows I'm not going to like what she has to say.

"Elsa, once we return you to Northaven, you'll belong to Heron Mikane. You understand? We can't interfere with Brightland's customs. You're your husband's property."

"But—"

"Your association with us makes you vulnerable already. Once we're ashore, we mustn't show you any undue attention. We'll try to keep you safe—but our mission must come first. If we get a passage to Brightling-helm, I'm almost certain we'll be leaving you behind."

I nod, suddenly realizing my lot. This is what I've given up by choosing to return. I will be nothing but Heron's Second Wife.

Alize is not without sympathy. "We're dancing on a tightrope. The narrow approval we have for this mission may shrink away to nothing."

Kingfisher senses my deep dismay as he takes me out onto the deck. "If I get to the Brethren's Palace alive, I'll do everything within my power to help your friend," he says.

I thank him. Northaven is visible now, its distant turbines in the rosy dawn. Kingfisher drinks it in.

"Don't be fooled by how pretty it is," I warn him. "It's an ugly town. Ugly things happen there. There's a gallows. People die. Everyone's afraid."

Kingfisher says something unexpected. "There's another Torch, isn't there."

I look at him, puzzled. "In Northaven?"

"I can hear him. A discord with a broken song . . ."

"Do you mean John Jenkins?"

Far away, I hear his jittery and senseless song, blowing dissonantly on the wind. Kingfisher's upset by it.

"Madness is close to us," he says. "When we cannot be ourselves, when we cannot exist as we should, madness can take root. I worry for you, going back to a place where you have no release, where you can never be yourself. I can't imagine how you've survived. I've teased you for being serious, Lark, but I don't know if I would've had your strength."

This leaves me raw. "Rye Tern gave me strength," I tell him.

I sense Kingfisher's songlight, forming a question. "Tell me," he is saying. He turns and leads me to a cell-like room on one side of the bridge. His kit bag is unopened on the bed. He clearly hasn't slept.

"You should rest," I say, backing away.

"We won't be able to use our songlight once we land. Talk to me."

He pulls the chair out from his tiny work desk and I sit, putting my hand out, touching his books and papers, as if the words inside them might somehow work their way under my skin.

I show him Rye. It hurts me to do it. I show him how precious our harmony was. I share our last meeting on the beach, when we decided to run, to try to find a different, better life. Then I show him Rye's beaten body, the lead band forced onto his head. I show him the shaming post, Emissary Wheeler baying; I show him how I threw dirt on the boy I loved and called him an unhuman.

"I didn't stand up for him. I couldn't rescue him." I'm crying like a child. "I don't have any courage," I confess painfully. "I'm a coward."

I find myself held, not in songlight but in two human arms.

For a moment, I let myself go. I let myself be comforted. His compassion hits me like a shock, this Aylishman, this stranger. He whispers my songlight name and I don't mind him using it.

"Lark . . ."

I draw myself away and go. I walk out on the deck, shattered by his kindness, dizzy with the loss. I breathe Rye's name as Brightland gets closer. Rye. Rye. I will find him—or avenge him. That is my new vow—that is what I want.

The ship slows as we near the coast. Alize calls the whole crew out on the deck. We watch Renza and Cree raise the white flag of peace. We must be visible from the town by now. What are my countrymen thinking? Are they aiming the mortar guns already? I pray we're still out of range.

"You weren't ordered to come on this mission," says Alize, as if she's talking to each person individually. "You volunteered, all of you. That deeply impresses me. We all know the risks so I won't dwell on them. We're here for what we believe in: freedom and peace."

Alize doesn't talk of valor or triumph or any of the usual things. She simply links arms with the two crew members on either side of her and says: "In our difference lies our strength." I get the feeling these men and women would follow her into a fiery pit. The whole crew is linking arms. Renza and Kingfisher take hold of me. We stand, in silence.

The silence lasts for a minute or two and then everyone goes about their business. But the feeling on deck is different. It's as if everyone is a Torch, as if we can all sense each other because we're all feeling the same way. I'm in a whirlwind of confusion because, for the first time in my life, I feel like I belong.

Renza helps me put my dress back on and, in the mirror, I see a lowly Brightling girl. I'm not ready to go back. I try to prepare myself, but as I walk across the deck, foreboding creeps up my chest.

I approach Alize, pointing at our cliffs.

"There are gun placements on the headland there, and there. Keep your ship back," I warn her. "Don't bring it into our harbor. There's too much hate. Take me ashore in a landing craft. There'll be more chance that I'm seen—and our mortar guns might hold their fire."

Alize is thoughtful at this. "Thank you."

She orders the ship to anchor, a landing craft to be lowered.

"Only four of us will go," she decides. "Yan, Cazimir, ready yourselves."

Is she seriously thinking of taking a Torch to Northaven?

"Yan Zeru shouldn't go," I say.

He objects at once. Of course he should go.

"There's nothing more vile to my people than an Aylish Torch," I tell him. "If they find out what you are, they'll kill you."

"Then we won't tell them."

"Yan has to come," says Alize. "He can communicate with the sensitives on board. If we walk into an ambush, he can save the ship."

"The sensitives?" I ask.

"Many people are sensitive to songlight, even if they're not Torches," Alize informs me. "Renza is a sensitive; I'm a sensitive myself. Surely you must have felt that sensitivity, even in Brightland?"

This is another revelation. I think again about the occasional strands of songlight that I hear, pushed down into the recesses of people's beings. Northaven might be full of sensitives and I would never know.

"At least take that azure blue off," I say to Kingfisher. "You need to look the same as everybody else."

He strips off his shirt in front of me and swaps it with one of his ship-mates.

"Does that satisfy you?" he asks.

I don't want to be affected by the sight of his lean flesh. But I am. I see Rye standing underneath my window in the night, looking up at me, his face a helpless mix of love and pain. Later on the beach, under the stars, I take off his torn shirt and kiss his flesh.

I turn away, discomfited.

Alize and Cazimir are already in the landing craft. Kingfisher helps me down, curious at my distress. Does he think I've been dazzled by his marvelous shape? To his credit, he puts my consternation down to leaving the ship.

"Are you sure about this?" His songlight surrounds me in concern. "We can keep you aboard and take you back to Ayland. Just say the word."

I shake my head, knowing that without me, their plan to land in Northaven will fail. I might be the lynchpin between war and peace.

Undiminished by his plain blue shirt, Kingfisher waves up at his ship-mates, pressing his fist against his heart. "Amou!" he cries. The landing craft speeds over the waves and we soon leave the *Aileron Blue* behind. My last chance to use my songlight has gone.

"Alize," I say. "If you have an ally in the town . . . my instinct says it's Heron Mikane."

She sees that I'm in earnest.

"We already have an ally in the town. It's you."

I take her words and cherish them.

As we approach the harbor, I see men running to the quay, armed with rifles and crossbows, taking positions behind the harbor wall. I stand in my dress and raise my arm, hoping they will see me before they shoot. I see Mrs. Sweeney running out of her front door, aiming her husband's gun, most likely relishing the thought of Aylish blood. I wave frantically at her, calling her name, expecting to feel bullets ripping through me. Slowly, she lowers her rifle.

"Hold your fire!" she yells.

There's a figure running down the hill. Ma. I'm too far away to hear but I know what she's shouting:

"Elsa! Elsa!"

I try to count the days since I've been gone—three, maybe four? Long enough to break my ma's strong, Greensward heart. Heron Mikane comes out of the Oystercatcher Inn. Greening and the Elders move forward, armed. I look at Gyles Syker as he pins me in his sights. As we come in to moor, Heron stands like a threadbare shield between me and a horde of rifles. My heart is hammering as Yan secures the boat. I can't call him Kingfisher here. It feels dangerous even to think of his songlight name.

Ma takes my hand and helps me out. For a moment, I'm blind to everything except her arms. She says my name over and over.

"I'm all right. I'm all right."

"I thought you were dead."

"They rescued me."

"Elsa," says Heron as Ma releases me. He looks past us to the Aylish, something stirring within him, rising to the surface of a very dark lake. Not hatred, no.

He whispers: "Can we trust them?"

"Yes," I whisper in reply.

I notice Elder Greening, his lips pursed like a cat's arse. I see Chaffinch running down the hill, half-amazed. I see Hoopoe Guinea approaching and Gailee, her eyes brimming tears of joy. Mrs. Sweeney pats my back.

"Sidon be praised," I hear her say.

I speak up, hoping my voice won't wobble like a child's. "My boat capsized," I say as loudly as I can. "I was clinging to the wreck. These Aylish saw me and they saved my life."

Heron's eye is on Alize. I've never seen him at such a loss. Alize meets his gaze and I see the same conflict on her face too. Slowly, Heron holds out his hand to help her ashore. There is a pause. Then Alize grips his hand with her good one. She steps out of the boat. They assess each other's scars and missing bits.

"Commander Mikane," she says. She lets go of his hand as if it's caused her pain.

Yan and Cazimir climb out and join her. Cazimir is looking at our mural, taking in the insult of the monstrous Aylish horde. Alize walks forward, showing no fear. She's as cool as a snow fox. She addresses the whole town.

"My name is Drew Alize. I am leading a diplomatic mission. Our ship is not a fighting vessel and we fly the white flag of peace. Our mission is to find a resolution to the conflict between us. Three nights ago we saw this young woman clinging to her upturned boat. She was very close to death. My comrade, Yan Zeru, rescued her. Being saved by the Aylish was hard for her to bear. She's very loyal to her home. I told Elsa Mikane truthfully, our aspiration is to end this war. We ask you to send this message to your leaders in Brightlinghelm. We can meet them there or parley with them here. We ask only that you respect our flag of peace."

Alize gets icy silence from the elders. But Heron shouts:

"Will you lay down your guns?"

One or two still have fingers twitching on their triggers, but they obey him. Syker is the last to lower his rifle.

Ma can't hold herself back. "Thank you," she says, "I owe you a debt." She hugs Alize, then she goes to Yan. I think she's about to hug him too but she shakes his hand and Cazimir's too. There are some shocked intakes of breath. Elder Greening is livid.

"Peace?" asks Heron, his eye on Alize. "Why should we believe you?"

Alize holds his gaze. "We must have an end to this."

Heron considers these simple words. And slowly he nods in agreement.

"Greening," he orders. "Wire the Brethren as they ask and Northaven might just be the town that ends this war."

There are a few shouts and cheers at this, but the majority of the towns-folk are silent with mistrust.

Greening walks to meet Alize, his face mask of hate. "I've no doubt this is an Aylish trick—a stratagem. But I'll send to Brightlinghelm, as is my duty. Your crew remains on your ship. If it comes any closer, we'll fire. You and these male subordinates must remain under guard in our hall." He looks at Yan and Cazimir with contempt, as if, by allowing a woman to lead them, they are not fully men.

Greening barks his order. "They'll stay in the hall, under guard."

Heron's eye is growing brighter and his back straightens, as if the whole energy of his being is catching alight with the idea of peace. I see him meet Ma's gaze. Her face is radiant with hope.

"You're welcome in my home," he says to Alize. "No guards are neces-sary, Greening."

"I've given my order as an elderman," says Greening, bristling at being undermined. "We will keep our enemies under guard."

The two men are at loggerheads. But Alize keeps her cool.

"We've brought some fine brandy. Perhaps we can begin by sharing it in your hall?"

Heron accepts this, bowing to her diplomacy. "I'll show you the way," he says politely.

I'm about to follow him when Elder Greening stops me.

"You bring the enemy into our town?" he snarls under his breath. "Get back to your home, girl. I'll see to it you never go on the sea again."

I'm diminished. I am in my place.

Kingfisher eyes me as he passes, shocked to see how lowly I am.

I remain with my mother. Soon, we're surrounded by a crowd of women and girls. Their questions bear me away up the hill toward my home. Home. Home.

PART 5

✦

I'm out of bed, pacing Swan's white rooms in the gray dawn light, trying to assess my strength. I spent the night in the white cot, aching for my papa. He'll face the firing wall for aiding my escape. His fellow Inquisitors will see him as a traitor. What can I do for him?

The door to Sister Swan's bedchamber clicks open and I freeze. It's Kite. He has a lead band in his hand. He puts it in his jacket. He stands in front of Swan's mirror, adjusts his crotch, and goes. I haven't moved. I haven't breathed.

I feel a strange sensation, the humming of a thousand crystal glasses, growing louder in pitch until I fear they'll smash. I'm being surrounded by brittle songlight. Kite has freed his Siren and I am being summoned. I peer into Sister Swan's bedchamber and she smiles at me, her eyes sparkling. Her ladies are working her wig into a sculpt.

"I thought you'd be tired," she says. "I was going to let you sleep."

"I'm too grateful to sleep," I say. "I'm so happy to be here with you."

Sister Swan walks toward me in a barely existent lace nightgown, her gaze penetrating.

"You're trying to save your father and you're saying what you think I want to hear."

My face falls. She has read me like a book. I gaze up at her.

"You must never lie to me, Kaira. Do you understand? If you lie, I will discard you like rubbish and throw you to your fate."

She gives me this threat with a kind and lovely smile. It scrambles me with fear.

"I'm sick of hatred and mistrust," she says, "but it is everywhere around me. I want things to be different with you. I want to trust you."

"I won't lie to you, Sister."

"There's something pure and true in you, Kaira. I couldn't bear it if you let me down."

"I'll try not to. I promise I won't lie. I'm worried for my papa, that's all."

I must stay strong and open. I mustn't think of Lark.

I realize that her eyes have many colors in them, like the pebbles at the bottom of a pool. She's different today, more vivid. I feel her flex her songlight. No longer constrained and discordant, it winds itself around me like the spirals of her sculpted wig.

"Kite has freed me. He wants my service." She smiles, sharing her liberty with me. "None of the Brethren know what I am. I am a secret."

I know I have to let her in. She'll want free rein in all the corners of my being. I feel her inch toward my mind. I rapidly draw Lark and Cassandra deep into my underthoughts, burying them in the dark.

Swan sighs herself into me. She looks around, moving past my fears for Papa, uncovering Ishbella and the spindly tree outside my room, pausing for a glance at Keynes. I show her lots of tedious sights, polishing boots, ironing shirts. I want her to believe my life is drab—but she finds some fragments of Northaven that I have failed to hide. She puts herself right in my senses and listens to the sea. It's as if we're both on Bailey's Strand.

"You love this place. Where is it?"

"I'm not sure of its name."

Swan strokes my face. "Withholding truth is another form of lying."

I pile rocks on top of Lark and Cassandra, keeping them in sea caves underground.

"It's Northaven," I confess. "Where Lark drowned. It upsets me."

"Lark?"

The tendrils tighten around me. She wants to know everything. I keep myself steady.

"Sister, I owe you my life. I want to serve you. How may I begin?"

Swan takes in a deep breath of fresh Northaven air. Then suddenly we're back in the reality of her white and stifling rooms.

"You're right. We've very little time and you have much to learn. But I want to show you who I am. I want you to love me, Kaira. Join with me. I want you to understand my plight. . . ."

She's ordering me to love her. Her songlight unfurls, inviting me in. I step into her memories, trying not to flood them with too much light. I know how overwhelming I can be, and I follow Cassandra's instruction to use my songlight as gently as steam. Swan's memories are powdery. Her ability to share them is not very strong—or perhaps she's keeping them under gauzy veils and only revealing what she wants me to see.

She shows me her childhood in Fort Abundance, which I know about from the radiobine. But as I watch her father drag her down to a water tank, I know that she's showing me something no one's ever seen. Her own father wanted her dead when he found out she was a Torch. I gasp with horror at his cruelty and feel a strange connection with her. I was always terrified that this was what Papa would do to me. Swan draws me on, toward a moment of acute desperation. I see her as a girl my age, begging Kite to spare her, promising him everything, her body and her soul, if he will let her keep her songlight. I see how Kite uses her. Swan doesn't spare me. Then I see a surgeon leaning over her, drawing out a key.

"Perfection," he says.

It's so horrific that a cry comes out of me. I hold Sister Swan in my arms, as I would hold Lark. She stiffens, as if no one has ever held her in sympathy before.

"Oh, Sister," I say. "Oh, Sister!" It takes her aback.

"What a sensitive dolly you are," she says. "You'll have to learn to control yourself."

But my compassion affects her and I feel her starting to unwind.

I see Swan's determination to survive. I feel her loneliness as Kite locks her in her rooms. I see how he controls her light. She doesn't show me everything. At her core, there is a dense midnight pool of closely guarded underthoughts. She's hiding things that haunt her in the night. She comes close to the present now. I see her humiliated, failing Kite. Her songlight is tarnishing, weakening from solitary confinement and increasing lack of use. Swan seems much older than her twenty-two years.

My papa always said that Sirens didn't last.

"Kite is searching for a Siren to replace me," she says. "If he finds a face that pleases him, he will get rid of me."

We part. I wipe my eyes, overpowered by the spikes and angles of her loveless life.

"What would you have me do?" I ask.

Swan takes my hands. "Your songlight is going to act as mine. Between us, we are everything Kite wants."

I feel a visceral disgust for Kite, having seen how he has treated her, and the thought of doing his bidding makes me sick. But I want to help her. I see how Swan's light has been warped by years of fear and threat. It isn't hatred that she feels for Kite. It's something far more painful, like a dress made out of thorns. It's obsession. She moves away from me in body and mind, standing at her mirror, preparing for her day. She's let me see enough.

"It's time for your first task."

Sister Swan snaps her fingers and orders her ladies to put a white gauze over my face. My skin shrinks from their pallid touch. It's like being waited upon by the dead.

"I'm going to teach you how to plant a thought," says Swan, leading me out through a set of glass doors into a leafy courtyard.

"Isn't that mind-twisting?" I ask, dismayed.

"It's politics," she breezily replies. "This is what I have to do in order to maintain my privilege as Flower of Brightland."

We walk across the courtyard and out into a large, grassy square. It looks bright and hazy through my gauze. It's filled with white rosebushes, a fountain in the middle. The sun shines across its perfect lawns.

"This is my favorite place to sit." Swan speaks to me in songlight but I'm far too nervous to reply. There are Emissaries and Inquisitors, soldiers and guards everywhere. At one side is a refectory with some outdoor tables. We secrete ourselves under the leaves of an old willow tree.

"You're going to begin with Starling Beech," Swan instructs me, showing me a skinny underling who's sitting with tea and toast, filling in a series of reports.

"Send your songlight into him," she urges. "Plant a thought in his mind that will make him spill his tea."

To invade another like this is dreadful. It's wrong. "What kind of thought?" I ask.

"That's up to you." She's smiling in encouragement. "He's quite unguarded. Plant an idea or a vision—something that will give him a surprise. See if you can make him spill it down his uniform." Swan giggles, as if this will be fun. I hardly dare voice my extreme reluctance. It feels like a criminal act to me.

"Mind-twisting is interdicted," I remind her.

I sense her frustration. Her songlight whines to a screech, angered at my misgivings.

"It's not interdicted if I say so."

"But—"

"I saved your life," she reminds me. "And now I'm teaching you a very special skill. Make Starling spill his tea."

Through the veil of willow leaves, I concentrate on the man at the table. I hear the toast crunching in his mouth as I steal my way into his consciousness. His mind is like a sharpened pencil with a chewed and bitten end: neat but nervous. Rules make him feel safe. I sneak further, past his neatly stacked agendas, to the dusty, unlit corners of his past. I catch neglected wisps of memory, floating like thin cobwebs. He holds each failure like a wound. At his core, Starling Beech is afraid. He's afraid of spiders, moths, his mother, losing, choirmaidens, the dark, chaos, the Aylish, and, most of all, Brother Kite. I feel his ache for Sister Swan. He adores her. He wants to protect her, cherish her and—I recoil from a morass of his physical desires that are absolutely not my business.

All of this is private. I have wormed my way into Starling Beech like a thought-thief. I can see him as a boy, pinning dead beetles into a case. I watch him sip his tea, holding the cup with his fingertips. He's remembering how his mother used to hit him when he slurped.

Swan is growing impatient. "It's a simple instruction. I know you can do it."

I focus on my task. I sit in Starling's retinas and find the pathways through to his brain. I wait until he lifts his cup—and I make a moth flap about his face. It isn't there, of course—but he startles, jerks backward, and a big splash of tea lands on his chest.

"Perfect." Swan laughs gleefully. "You see? That wasn't hard, was it?"

"No," I agree.

She kisses me, delighted, as if I'm her pet.

Starling wipes his uniform, looking for the moth. He stands, knocking his toast to the floor, unsettled, puzzled, and disturbed.

"I wish I had longer to teach you the craft," enthuses Swan, leading me out of our willow hiding place and back toward her rooms. "But we have no time to lose."

It feels horrible to have abused Starling Beech but Swan is delighted. My heart is hammering at what she might make me do next.

Back in her rooms, Swan claps her hands. The blank, spectral ladies take their positions behind her. Swan places me at the head of the formation.

"You must try to walk without that awful limp."

"But one of my legs is weaker than the other," I explain.

"You can't draw attention to yourself by being imperfect. Make an effort."

We set off down a long corridor and before we get to the end of it my hip is aching with the strain. It would help if Swan led us more sedately, but her pace is fast and she makes no concessions. Endless corridors, cloistered courtyards. Doors open into rooms I dare not look into. My sight is shrouded with the gauze. Swan instructs me in songlight as we walk.

"When we get into the council chamber, you'll see Great Brother Peregrine and all the other councillors. I want you to focus on a man called Harrier."

"Brother Harrier?" I ask.

She shows me an image of a handsome man with a beard.

"I've seen him," I tell her. My hip is aching raw. Everyone bows and scrapes and gets out of our way.

"My stepmother Ishbella and I once met Brother Harrier in the market as we queued for potatoes."

"Why on earth was he in your dreary marketplace?" queries Swan.

"He often comes into the city. He's just about the only councillor who ever leaves the palace. He walked right up to us and talked to all the women in queue. He joked with us and made us laugh and then he asked about our rations."

"Why did he care about your rations?"

"He asked if it was easy to feed our families. Did we think the Brethren could do more? Later that day we heard him on the radiobine, calling for rations to be increased."

Swan takes this in.

"Harrier's going to be your target," she tells me. "So you'd better not be sentimental. I want no shilly-shallying about mind-twisting being interdicted. You're going to put a simple idea in his head," Swan instructs me. "Just like you did with Starling Beech."

My protest has nowhere to go. It dissipates into the most terrible stress.

"What idea?" I ask.

"Kite is right. Make him believe it in his heart. Kite is right."

"Right about what?" My nerves are jangling.

"Show him a plane high in the sky. Show him bombs falling on Reem. Then show him flags, waving in victory. And repeat: Kite is right. Kite is right."

The crystal whine of her songlight surges as she chants. I feel its instability.

I follow Swan through a great hallway and up a wide, intimidating flight of stairs. Her dress billows like a ship in sail. I can't do it. I have to slow down. My hand instinctively grabs for the stone banister.

"Please," I beg in songlight. "Wait."

Swan slows—just enough for me to climb unaided. At the top, I'm so breathless I worry I will faint. She turns, concerned for me.

"You'll be all right, Little Dolly. You'll be wonderful at this. You're stronger than you know."

Her words of kindness fluster me almost as much as her threats.

"I always like to make an entrance," she says. "Speed is part of mystique. Are you ready?"

I nod, forcing my breath under control.

"You'll be magnificent," she says.

Guards open an enormous pair of doors and Swan glides noiselessly through them. I follow with her bevy of silent swans, trying not to stand out like a duck. The white-clad ladies fan out around the room. I stand in the shadows with them, hoping not to be noticed.

The council chamber is the most opulent room I have ever seen. Tapestries, windows of stained glass, a long table of dark wood. Each of the chairs is red—apart from Swan's, which is purest white. Brother Peregrine sits at the head. Kite is at his side. The councillors rise as we ladies enter. Sister Swan accepts this mark of courtesy by giving a deep, graceful curtsy.

Through the white gauze I see that Brother Harrier is opposite. I recognize his broad shoulders, his thick hair, his beard. I sense his deep laughter. He has an air of easy power, as if this great table is nothing special to him.

Kite and Peregrine are talking heatedly but I don't listen to a word they say. I am focused on my task.

I enter Harrier's mind, feeling his blood rush round me. I sense his pity for Sister Swan, his rage at Kite. I sense his hope in Peregrine, his need for Peregrine to take his side. I sense something bright beneath all his flaws. I don't know what to call it. This man has a core of light. He's here for something greater than himself. It's precious to him. I see his vision of the city and beyond, of Brightland in all its beauty, stretching out into forest and mountain. I see a vision where people are unafraid, where they have enough to eat, where no one is downtrodden. The Chrysalid House is burning and I see crowds of people in this council room, ordinary men and women, speaking freely. I see Kite, hanging from a noose.

I am so shocked, I hardly dare open my eyes. This man wants everything to change. His mind is a revelation to me. The fact that someone on the council feels this way lifts me, thrills me with hope. But I am forgetting myself. I am nothing but a flapping moth, serving the light that is Sister Swan.

I cannot do what she has asked. I can't abuse this man. Swan shoots me a glance. Her band is off. As I am reading Harrier, she is reading me. She can see me wavering. She pins a little image in my mind: my father, blind-folded, standing at a firing wall.

She need say nothing more. I concentrate on Harrier. I am a shallow trickster in his mind, an untrained peddler of lies.

"Kite is right," I urge. "Kite is right."

We have been preparing all day for a feast to feed the elders and the Aylish. In the heat of the afternoon, Mrs. Sweeney is dicing up stewing lamb and Ma is searing it in a huge pan. Hoopoe is making a heap of floury dumplings. Chaffinch sits in a corner with Tinamou Syker, cutting up a hill of string beans.

"Is it right," asks Chaffinch, "to be cooking for these people? Isn't it treasonous to our dead men?"

"Not if they've come to make peace," I tell her as patiently as I can.

"I'd have thrown myself in the sea rather than set foot on an Aylish ship," sneers Tinamou.

"Then you'd be dead," I point out.

Gailee is peeling spuds with her ma. "D'you think they mean it, about peace?" she asks, hardly daring to hope.

"If you believe that, you're a fool," says Tinamou with certainty.

"Don't you want this war to end?" I snap. "Your own brother's fighting and so's mine."

I'm so angry that I'm here, stuck in this kitchen. I should be in that hall with the Aylish. I'm the reason that they came. My teeth are clenched in sore frustration. Ma smooths my feathers, saying we must trust the people in the hall to do the right thing.

"That's right," agrees Hoopoe. "We should leave the business of war and peace up to the men."

"They're not men, though, are they?" says Chaffinch. "They're all under the thumb of that witchy, beaten-up woman. She might be mind-twisting our men to do exactly what the Aylish want."

"Alize is no mind-twister," I say.

"How would you know?" pounces Tinamou.

"I never got any sense she was mind-twisting me."

"Well, they're clever about it, aren't they?" puts forward Mrs. Sweeney. "They don't make it obvious. That's why they're so dangerous."

"You'd like her," I tell her. "You of all people. Alize reminds me of you. If you sat down and shared a dram or two with her, I swear you'd end up laughing."

Mrs. Sweeney shakes her head at my wrongness, wiping lamb blood off her fingers.

Tinamou keeps pressing. She's heard there's an unhuman on every Aylish ship. "Where's theirs? Is it that one-handed woman or one of those shifty men?"

"How would I know?" I say. "They were nice to me and friendly, but they're not fools. I'm a Brightling. They know how we feel about unhumans."

"What if they've worked on your mind, though, Elsa?" speculates Hoopoe. "They might have done, the way you're fighting their corner."

"They saved my life is all."

"Just be careful. Don't be too comradely about them when Elder Greening questions you." Hoopoe says this lightly enough but I sense her heavy warning. I peel and chop, my color rising.

"Go and get us some water from the pump, my love," requests Ma, realizing I'm better off elsewhere. I decide it's best not to say another word.

Gailee follows me. We go to the pump, which lies under the serene, impenetrable face of Sister Swan. I think of Nightingale, pulled in that woman's undertow.

"Everything's tense and taut," says Gailee, looking down at the Elders' Hall. "The town is full of charge, like before a storm." She feels the same foreboding I do.

"I can feel something coming," she says. "It's been coming since they took the Third Wives."

"How do you mean?"

"John Jenkins seems to sense it. He feels a lot of stuff like that. It's like we're all sizing each other up, wondering if we'll dare take sides."

Gailee has always had an intuition. It suddenly occurs to me that she might be a sensitive. If only I could bring it up with her. She seems older, more self-assured.

"How is John Jenkins?" I ask her.

"A little better," she replies. "Sometimes he's lucid—a sweet, shy man. Nela and I have both grown fond of him. And you were right about singing—music comforts him. But then he has these awful waking nightmares and there's nothing we can do. They'll send him back to fight soon and it's wrong. It's so wrong, Elsa."

"I'm praying to Gala that the Aylish will bring peace."

Galilee nods. I'm about to return to the house when she stops me. She looks as if she's wrestling with herself and suddenly a story comes pouring out of her.

"Your ma was so upset when you went missing," she says. "We all were. The search went on day and night. Your ma, she was in bits, Elsa." My heart aches for all Curl has suffered.

"Anyway, she got drunk with Mrs. Sweeney the night they found the flotsam from your boat. They sat outside and your ma was saying very fiery words about the way things are run, in hearing of the elders. Mrs. Sweeney got worried and sent for Heron Mikane. He virtually carried your mother home. I was sitting outside with John—he likes to sit on our front step, looking at the stars. Anyway, your husband passed us, helping your mother up the hill. I was so upset for her, I followed them a way. I was going to give my condolences but suddenly, in the shadows . . . they held each other. Like, not a hug. Heron and your ma, they clung to one another."

I don't like the way this is going.

"She kissed him," says Gailee guardedly. "Like, a full-blazing kiss. And Heron kissed her back."

My feet shift slightly. I am blushing with discomfort.

"Gailee, it's none of our business," I say.

"But he's your *husband*. . . ."

I let this sink in. I remember how Heron looked at my mother when she first brought me to his house. I remember how he said her name: "Curlew Crane." I see him turn the carving that she made over in his hands.

It's strange to think of Ma as a woman with feelings and desires like that. She's always been only my ma, Pa's widow, her life as gray as the misty sea, her light hidden by her widow's veil.

"Heron's not my husband, not truly."

"Of course he is."

"It's a forced marriage, like your own. We've never shared a bed. Not me, nor Chaffinch."

"Do you think I've shared a bed with John?" she asks. "It doesn't make a jot of difference. We're bound to those men for life. Anything else is adultery."

Her words give me chills.

"I'll talk to Ma."

Gailee looks relieved. "I don't judge her, Elsa. But there's some monstrous people in this town," she says. "They're neighborly one day and the next, they'll cut you into bits."

She takes the pail of water from me, carrying it back into the house.

I try to take in what she's said. I think of Ma with Heron. I'm sure he was sweet on her before he went away to war. And I'm sure she never noticed him then. She had a husband, little children. And she loved my pa. But eight years have gone by since Pa died and everything has changed. Why shouldn't two people who have known such loss find happiness together?

In my mind, I see windblown corpses swinging from the gibbet. Adulterers.

As I shudder with the thought, Mrs. Greening comes up the lane, sweating into her expensive dress. She stops, trying to get her breath, eyeing me with unconcealed dislike. I can tell she knows what's happening in the Elders' Hall and I am pierced with an angry longing to be there. But I playact at being a good Second Wife.

"We're cooking up a fine feast for everyone, Mrs. Greening," I say, in what I hope is a friendly way.

"That's typical," she puffs. "Our enemies for all these years and some folk are fool enough to cook for them."

Ma comes out, ignoring this barely veiled insult.

"How d'you do, Mrs. Greening?" she asks politely. "What news from our elders?"

All the other women are spilling out behind Ma, eager to hear what's happening. Mrs. Greening pulls herself up to her full height.

"Ely telegrammed the palace for instructions from the Brethren. He has just now received a reply, from Great Brother Peregrine himself."

"Well?" asks Hoopoe.

"The Aylish are invited to Brightlinghelm in terms most cordial. Their ship's to get an escort later on today."

I feel a huge relief. Bringing me to Northaven has worked for them. Ma's face is flushed with hope. "So Great Brother Peregrine is willing to talk peace?"

"It's a diplomatic invitation, yes."

The news takes hold among the women in an instant. The idea that peace is possible lifts and floats like the delicious smell of cooking.

"Well, isn't that a miracle of Gala?" says Ma, laughing. "That seems like hope indeed, for all our sons."

But Mrs. Greening's lips are pursed. "If you believe a word of it. Personally, I don't. This is a clever Aylish ploy, using a foolish girl to make their landfall here."

Ma ignores this. "Are they all coming up to Heron's house to dine?"

I could kick her. Why doesn't she call him Commander Mikane?

"Ely has ordered the Aylish not to leave the hall."

"Oh?" Ma is disappointed.

"But Heron Mikane stood up. And in direct opposition to my husband, he's insisted on hosting the Aylish. That commander woman accepted his arrant invitation. And her crafty, long-haired boot-boys followed suit."

Ma takes Mrs. Greening in stride. "Well, we'll help make the visitors and the elders welcome, though it will be a bit of a squeeze up there."

"Don't bother. The elders won't come. And they say that any man who attends is risking arrest."

"For what?"

"Collaborating with the enemy."

Ma is shocked. Anxiety is pressing on my ribs.

"But our Great Brother is showing them diplomacy," she points out. "Should we not do the same?"

"Take your food to Mikane's house if you will," finishes Mrs. Greening. "It won't be wanted in the hall." She turns on her heel and clacks down the lane.

Chaffinch looks at me like her foot's trapped in a snare. She looks at Curl with a spark of anger. And she runs off after her mother.

40 ✳   SWAN

It's a success. My dolly is superb. The whole council table is galvanized in the debate. Kite argues for arming and deploying his Fireflies with all his might. I have my gaze focused on Harrier—and Harrier is unable to articulate any objection.

"The threat from Ayland is indeed grave. And Kite," he says, grimacing through his degenerate beard, "may be right."

Peregrine looks surprised. He regards Harrier, almost disappointed.

"Then I must consider the matter very carefully."

It's a step closer to agreement. Kite shoots me a glance, impressed at my easy success. I thrill to take the credit for my dolly's quiet power.

At that moment, a messenger enters with a telegram. Peregrine reads it and his expression changes.

"Forgive me, Brothers. I must attend to this."

Peregrine goes and Kite follows, presumably to ram home his argument.

The meeting breaks up and Harrier leaves with a look of deep disquiet on his face. My Kaira's shaking like a mouse. I send a wisp of songlight up to reassure her.

"Wonderful, dolly," I tell her. "Well done."

I send the rest of my ladies back to my rooms and bring my dolly out into the palace grounds for her next lesson—mind-twisting from afar—but as soon as we're alone, she half collapses, trembling. I'm shocked by her reckless display of distress.

"What's this? I ask her. "You should be pleased with yourself."

"It's wrong," she cries. "I did Brother Harrier a terrible wrong. Please don't ask me to do that again." Her breath is catching. Her face is red and all screwed up.

"Control yourself," I command her. A troop of guards is approaching and her display of emotion is dangerous.

Kaira forces herself into stillness. I wait until the guards have saluted me and passed. She looks tired, fragile under the gauze. Perhaps I've pressed her into service too soon.

"You'll get used to it," I tell her. "And next time, it will be easier."

I take her to a bench. I must never treat her like the others. I must never hit her or shake her, never pinch her or deny her food. I must treat her like the treasure she is. I explain that it's what Kite wants and we must do his work.

"The alternative lies over there."

I turn her to face the Chrysalid House. It does the trick. I feel her recover. With every breath, she grows more and more determined.

"You're so kind to me, Sister," she says. "I'm sorry that I got upset."

It's a peculiar thrill, being with someone so full of emotion. She's mine, mine to cherish, my very own. I feel a rush of care for her, a warm glow to hear her call me Sister. This is the first time in my adult life I've had a confidante, a friend. This sweet dolly has cried on my behalf. She put her arms around me in compassion. The thought fills me with lightness, a brightness.

"I'll learn, I promise," she says.

I kiss her darling little hand. And then I turn to business.

"What did you see in Harrier's mind?" I ask. "I need every drop of information. There is power in every secret I unearth."

My dolly's vision clouds. "Oh . . . He was full of last night's drinking."

"And?"

"He doesn't much care for Brother Kite."

"Tell me what he wants and don't keep anything back. I won't let you hide it."

Sometimes, firmness is the only way. Kaira's eyes hit the ground.

"Harrier cares a lot about us, the people. He wants us to have better lives. He feels that change is in the air. He thinks that we— He thinks that people can't go on."

"But this is Brightlinghelm."

"Yes—"

"It's the foremost city in the world. The people live in a blessed land."

"Oh?" Kaira seems surprised. "I suppose it might seem that way in the palace."

"What do you mean?"

"Life in the city is much harder."

"How?"

Kaira looks at me, puzzled by my question. "Don't you know there isn't enough food?"

I stare at her, uncomprehending.

"Our rations have been cut again and again. Yet there's so much here in the palace. Starling Beech put more butter on his toast than my papa would get for a week. People are hungry. Harrier thinks that all our wealth is being wasted on the war."

"Wasted?" I'm astonished to hear this. It's seditious.

"He thinks the people want change."

"If people are hungry, it's the fault of the Aylish," I explain. "That's why we must win. When Kite triumphs, all the riches of Ayland will be ours and no one will go hungry."

I wait to hear Kaira's thought but she's silent, afraid to speak it.

I press her. "Tell me what else you saw."

"He'd like to see a different kind of government."

I leap on this. "Is he plotting against Peregrine?"

"No, he's grown fond of Peregrine," she says. "They disagree about a lot, but Harrier keeps telling Peregrine the truth. He thinks Peregrine could lay foundations for a different kind of future."

"What future?"

"Harrier would like a world where no one has the right to tell another person how to live. In his mind, the council chamber is full of ordinary people, deciding things together."

I want to laugh at the thought of this, but Kaira turns her face away, staring at the city.

"Sister," she asks, "what if Harrier is right?"

Slowly, I realize what has happened.

"He has infected you," I inform her. "When you enter someone's thoughts, you must be very careful not to be infected by what you find."

"I haven't been infected. I'm just asking, if Harrier might be right?" Her look is so ardent, so expectant. This is troubling.

"You mustn't get swayed by anyone's vision, no matter how strong and forthright it appears. You must never forget who your master is."

Kaira gazes at me in surprise. "I don't have a master," she says simply. "I have a mistress. I'm your voice, not Kite's. I work for you."

Kaira speaks as if this is obvious, but it hits me like a revelation. She is here for me.

Her expression changes as she sees someone over my shoulder. She speaks in songlight. "He's coming near."

I turn to see Kite approaching. His lips are pressed into a hard, thin line. I stand, gracefully bowing my head. My dolly instinctively does the same.

"I hope you're satisfied with my success," I say, giving him a pretty smile.

Kite takes me by the arm and wordlessly pulls me away. I see where we're heading and my blood runs cold. He's taking me to the Chrysalid House.

"My dolly—" I protest.

"Leave the damn thing there."

Kite pulls me on. I worry for my dolly. Will she know how to behave? Will she give herself away?

We walk at a breathless pace.

"What news from Peregrine?" I ask, trying to be breezy. "Do you need my counsel?"

"No. The time for that is past."

"Did you see how well I bent Brother Harrier to your righteous cause?"

"I'm not concerned with Harrier."

The Chrysalid House soon fills my horizon. Guards see us coming. They open the great doors. My dread deepens. What does he want me for? As we enter, I see a flurry of personnel forming a greeting line.

"Keep your flummery," Kite barks as Surgeon Ruppell grovels in attendance.

Kite marches me past the scurrying crowd and pulls me through a metal door. He slams it shut.

It's an interrogation hall. The walls in here are lined with lead. Dark red turbine lights, tables and chairs nailed to the floor, chains hanging from the roof. Panic seizes me. Why has he brought me here?

"An Aylish ship has landed in Northaven," he tells me in clipped tones. "A diplomatic mission, wanting to talk peace."

"Peace?"

"Peregrine's ordered them safe passage. He intends to negotiate."

"Negotiate?" I'm stricken with disbelief. "It's unthinkable. . . ."

The Aylish killed my family. Negotiation is a betrayal of everything I've suffered.

"Damn his peace." Kite spits his words out. "May Thal damn him. There can never be peace—only victory."

"Yes, victory," I cry in agreement, grasping his arms.

"Peace is a contagion," he says. "One small germ and the idea will spread."

"These peace talks mustn't happen," I say, immediately knowing how to please him. "They must fail before they start."

"Of course they must fail." He raises his voice impatiently.

I must think quicker. I must meet his anger with subtlety, with a plan.

"We will derail them," I assure him. "But you can't be seen to be the saboteur."

My mind is whirring. Kite waits for more.

"How many ships in the Aylish party?" I ask.

"One. It flies the flag of peace."

"Why Northaven? Why this unheard-of place?"

"They found a girl, lost at sea. Turns out she's a wife of Heron Mikane."

This is significant. A girl lost at sea.

I take two deep breaths, remembering the Aylish Torch who bested me on the battleship. His name comes up from my guts in a gob of fury: King-fisher. I remember his songlight constricting mine, humiliating me in front of Kite. I could feel that bastard's pity.

"Send an Emissary to Northaven," I tell Kite. "Make sure he's loyal to you alone. He must tell the Aylish there is one condition for the talks. Insist their Torch is kept behind."

"For what?" he asks.

"If you truly want to sabotage the talks, you'll snuff the torchlight out."

"Murder their Torch?"

"You can blame the act on the ignorant people of Northaven."

Kite likes the idea. He nods, turning it over in his mind. "Ayland will be outraged."

I have pleased him, thank Gala.

"Without their Torch, the Aylish can't communicate with Reem," he calculates. "Their parliament won't know that talks have failed. We'll have a perfect window to attack." Kite presses himself against me. Guileful behavior has always excited him. "Rather than peace," he says, "we will rain down war."

He pushes me back so I am lying on the table. His excitement is sharpening into desire. I know not to invite him. I know not to move an inch.

"It's treachery to talk of peace." Kite's breath is rising.

"You're right. It's treachery."

"Peregrine's shown his hand by offering to negotiate. He's a traitor."

I know that my agreement is required—but it is hard to give. "Yes. He's a traitor."

Kite's voice quiets to a whisper. "Zara, you know what must be done. . . ."

He wants me to peer into his mind. In an instant, I see the terrible thing he has plotted. It's there, in the air between us, in the taut stillness that we hold. I can see the murder he's given form to in the dark hours of the night. I feel his secret longing to kill his master, his mentor, his Brother Peregrine.

"It's time that Brightland had a better leader," he whispers, full of zeal. "One who has the courage to win the war we started."

I know I should agree with him at once, but I am full of horror. I say nothing. My silence grows like a pool of blood.

"Well?"

"It's murder," I whisper.

"It's for the good of Brightland."

Now I know why he's brought me here, to this place of horror. If I refuse to be his accomplice, I am signing my own death warrant. I'm in the Chrysalid House to plot an assassination—or to die. Waves of terror are running through my body and, damn him, I can't think straight when I'm pinned to the table. I try to collect myself, playing for time.

"How will you do it?" I ask, trying to keep the softness in my voice.

"By the fairest and most subtle hand. It must be swift, invisible. Tonight."

He puts a phial of poison by my side.

Me. He wants me to do it. He will not sully his own hand.

"The Council is dining to discuss the talks," he says. "I'll stay absent with my troops. You'll have a free hand."

Kite has made me do some dreadful things. He has corrupted me into his rankest aide. But this? Not a single word comes to save me. My mind is blank.

He grips me harder. "Speak!"

"No one hates the Aylish more than I . . . but to murder Peregrine?"

"Death is waiting for him anyway." Kite is losing patience with me. "You know we need strong leadership. You've whispered it to me in the night. You've told me how much you long to be elevated at my side. Now is your chance."

I think of the old man and a rush of hot, inarticulate emotion confounds me.

"Niccolas, I can't poison Peregrine. Find another way."

His grip is like iron. "Are you refusing?"

I say nothing. I'm too afraid to speak. But Kite knows my silence is resistance. He releases me abruptly.

"Very well," he says. "I respect your choice."

"I will help you in any other way," I breathe. "You are my idol and I live to serve you."

"I feared that this would happen," he says, tidying himself.

"You'll be our leader," I reassure him. "Very soon all obstacles against you will fall away."

"I've sensed your growing cowardice for a while."

Kite goes to the door. I am dizzy as I stand. As he turns to me, I see a flicker of something almost like regret.

"I'm going straight to the radiobine room. I'll tell Brightland of my sorrow as I discovered exactly what you are. An unhuman, hiding in plain sight, deceiving us all—a serpent, not a flower."

"Kite— Don't!" I am on my feet, flying toward him.

"This is the last time you'll let me down. You'll never leave these rooms again."

The door is closing. I grab the handle and scream his name:

"KITE!"

But it's too late. The thick door locks behind him. I bang on it with my fists. The turbine lights flicker and buzz.

"KITE!"

My throat is tight with terror. I feel the ghosts come alive in the room, where so many unhumans have screamed before me.

"KITE!"

I slowly turn, looking at my prison.

On the table, he has left the phial of poison.

I feel an overwhelming urge to run, to force my weakened leg to work. In my mind, I'm sprinting down the lawns, across the parade ground, over the walls, onto the esplanade. If I were Lark, I'd dive into the river and escape. I feel a longing to send my songlight up to join with her, to ask her what to do—but, Gala, I can't. Somewhere close by, my papa needs saving.

I turn my face slowly, inch by inch, until it's facing a high building at the back of the palace complex. The prison. If my papa's still alive, that's where he'll be. I can explain to Sister Swan that it would be an act of love to reprieve him. She's spent too long in her dreadful isolation and I don't think she realizes that love is born by doing things for others. With each act of generosity, love expands. Nobody has taught her this. But I learned it first from Cassandra and then from Lark.

I must not fall into Swan's dark heart. I must teach her how to love.

"What have we here?" It's a voice that sounds like cake.

I glaze my eyes, remembering that I'm a lifeless doll, a toy. An old man is peering at my face. My heart turns upside down and I fix my eyes upon his chest. I see a row of medals and some crumbs caught in his uniform. It's Great Brother Peregrine. "You must belong to Sister Swan," he says. "I wonder why she's left you here?"

He pulls his fingers down his beard. He's really peering hard. "Gala," he says. "You're just a child."

Peregrine sighs, turning to Brother Harrier, who walks up beside him.

"I don't need to go to the Chrysalid House," he says. "This creature tells me all I need to know about the work we do there."

I am a creature.

"Kite's gone ahead of us," says Harrier. "Bending Ruppell's ear to his cause, no doubt."

Peregrine considers. "I won't chase them. Tell Kite and Ruppell to meet me in my library. I'll return this female to Sister Swan."

I am a thing.

Harrier walks swiftly on. Peregrine regards me.

"Come," he orders. And I follow him.

Brother Peregrine walks me toward an old, domed building. I try to keep my gait as steady as I can but I've worked my hip into a sore fatigue. Peregrine turns round.

"Are you lame?" he asks.

I don't reply, of course.

"She's put spectacles on you. Is your sight defective?"

I gaze at the inside of my veil.

"Why has she chosen to keep such a thing?" Peregrine asks himself. He walks around me, studying me. "She has more compassion than I gave her credit for. . . ."

He continues on, passing the domed building. It is ancient, neglected, weather-damaged. I have seen it from our park. It lies like a relic between the palace and the towering new Temple of Thal. I know what it is: the ancient temple of Gala.

Peregrine stops by the doors. They lie open, rotting off their hinges. He turns from the path, as if on a whim, and looks at me again.

"Come," he says to me. And we enter the temple.

Inside, sun cascades from a jagged hole in the dome. Creepers are growing down through it. The floor spreads out, a perfect circle of cool marble, cracked with age. Light falls dappled, like waves running over shallow sands. Pillars are carved like living trees. Stone animals are caught as if in motion. I almost gasp at the beauty of the place. It has been empty for a long time. A drip of water is the only sound. On the altar, Gala sits, mighty, ageless. Her expressive sandstone face is worn with time and one great arm is lost. Her breasts are swollen, her belly huge, pregnant with creation, and on her knee, held like a toy, sits Thal, the god of war.

Peregrine looks up at the mighty statue, his white hair like thistledown. I feel the intensity of his emotion grow, a storm of anger and contempt, held in him lifelong.

"My mother was your servant," he says, addressing Creation. "You were all she could see. She had me chained to her knee as you have Thal, holding his power, his brilliance in check, blaming him for all the folly of our ancestors. I could see what you were, Gala—nothing but a superstition, infantilizing us, holding back our progress. . . ." He exhales. The storm in him is receding and I see his shoulders bow.

"And yet," he says, "here I am, seeking you."

His voice sounds pained. It echoes into the statue's space. Peregrine remains, his head bent, breathing heavily.

Time slows to a drip of water.

I imagine I'm climbing Gala's massive sandstone leg. I imagine that it's warm, like flesh. I put my arms around her belly and I imagine that I'm crawling to the top. I can hear the heartbeat of her baby, Creation. I curl up over her heart. I hear the rising and falling of her breath. It sounds like the waves, crashing on the shore. I can almost feel them running over the marble floor.

I think of the waves on Bailey's Strand, where I first saw Lark. I think of her, breaking her heart about her lost boy, Rye. My feelings flow into Gala's stone. Could I, even in front of Peregrine himself, send my songlight out to my friend? I'm desperate to find out how she is. It feels freeing, audacious, gloriously bold. I swear Gala herself is egging me on.

I rise up, searching for Lark's songlight. I give myself up to our harmony. I find her setting a table. She senses me. She goes out into her garden and we hold each other wordlessly. I feel the sensation of joining with her. She hears the drip of the water in the temple. She sees the immense statue, the old man in front of it, his head bent. It's dangerous for her. It's dangerous for me. Neither of us speaks. But I feel the strength flowing between us.

The Aylish are coming to make peace.

I ask Gala to protect us. Gala, keep us safe. Gala, you're the tide, you're Lark, you're me and this old man, you're life on Earth. Gala, hold us in your living stone. We're yours.

I open my eyes and Lark has gone. The old man is looking down at me. And his expression is quite different. He lifts my veil.

"There," he says. And with his dry and wrinkled thumb, he wipes away my tears.

I must not lift my eyes to him.

He runs a finger along the fresh scar on my temple, regarding me as an enigma.

"Could it be reversible?" he muses. "The human brain is so easy to harm, so hard to heal. Who could fix this? No surgeon I know. And all our powerful Torches are snuffed out, so we have no one who can light the way." A sigh shudders through him. It's as if he's in an underworld of his own making. "This is my legacy, not peace, not prosperity. This wretchedness is what I'll be remembered for."

He replaces my veil and turns away, his shoulders bent. He walks toward the entrance doors and turns back to Gala.

"None of us is very far from death," he says to her. "And when we die, we die alone."

This is the loneliest thing I have ever heard.

"Come," he says. And once again, I follow.

As he leads me across the palace grounds, I think how hard it must be to be old, to be facing an inevitable end. No wonder Peregrine is thinking of his legacy. Lark says the Aylish are coming to make peace and I suddenly wonder if there's a way I can help her. I want to know what's in the old man's mind. Swan has taught me well. I concentrate upon him until I am seeing the world through his eyes. It feels natural, as if I should be there, as if nothing separates us.

Peregrine paces like an old mountain lion. He misses his youth, his vigor. He loves Harrier—but he trusts Kite. War and peace weigh upon him like a heavy set of scales.

I follow, silent and obedient, but in his mind, I plant the thought of a peaceful dawn. I think of a beam of sun, breaking through the clouds, and

I see Brother Peregrine turn his gaze toward it.

"Peace," he sighs. I hold back as more beams of light appear. His breathing swells. I think of Brother Harrier's vision of the city and beyond, of a Brightland stretching out into forest and mountain, where people are united, unafraid, where no one is downtrodden. I show Peregrine an image of the Chrysalid House on fire. I show him a crowd of people in his council room, ordinary men and women, speaking freely.

"Harrier," he says. "Harrier is right."

The mountain lion leads me into his palace. He pauses, looking up at the great statue of himself. I leave him, returning to my small, imperfect body.

Have I mind-twisted him? It doesn't feel like it. It feels as if he could reject what I have shown him with one shake of his mane. But he doesn't reject it. I sense his deep consideration as he climbs the long, intimidating staircase. He inhales, filling himself with strength, his fur warming in the golden sun. At the top, he licks his lips across his fangs.

"I still have some power yet."

I'm in the washhouse when I'm told our wing commander wants to see me. I put my uniform back on with haste, wondering what I've done wrong. How is he displeased with me? Our fleet has been in Brightlinghelm for three days now and I've flown each new training mission without incident. Today, we've been over the Isis, hitting floating targets that represent invading Aylish ships. Isias, my new gunner, only missed twice. Isias is a quiet man, like myself, and we returned to the palace airstrip ahead of time. But Wing Commander Axby had no praise for me.

I walk toward the hangar, passing the ground crew's mess. I can hear Finch, laughing and joking with his new colleagues. I keep my eyes straight ahead but he falls silent as I pass.

It's his own fault he's no longer a gunner. It could have been far worse for him and I hope he knows that. I've behaved exactly as a Brightling soldier should. I've shown restraint and leadership. I told Finch that I'd forget what happened in the hope he would reform himself. I said I wouldn't tell our seniors that he's an aberration—but I could never fly with him again. Finch was very quiet. He said he understood. He said he was mistaken.

"Mistaken in what?"

He paused. "In my behavior."

He thanked me for my understanding. I said how important it was that he should conform to the tenets of Great Brother Peregrine's *Definition of a Human Male*. His desire must be for women only, so he could make his family proud by repopulating Earth.

"Yes," he said.

I said I was sure he could change his nature.

"Can you change yours?" he asked, looking at me with a pointed gaze.

I dismissed him then.

I'm saving Finch and I wish that he could see that. I will change. It's just a matter of spending more time in a Pink House. But the thought of going to one depresses my spirits. The places have no dignity. Some humans are made to love no one and I must be one of them. I have moments of weakness, of course I do. When I think of his kiss—

It will pass. Thal will help me. And I will save Finch.

He'll not end like that boy in Rye Tern's prison yard.

Wing Commander Axby was surprised when I asked for a new gunner.

"I thought you and Finch were a great success," he said. "It isn't often one sees such a bond."

"But he's volatile, sir. I'm sorry but I need a steady hand."

Axby respected my wishes. He gave me Isias and bumped Finch down to serve with the ground crew.

"There's no place for volatility up in the air."

I pull my jacket straight and walk into the hangar. There's a group of men standing by my plane. I hardly dare believe my eyes. Brother Kite is at the fore. Brother Kite. Strength and wisdom sit in the strong contours of his face. I'm not sure that my voice will work.

"Brother." I click my heels and bow my head.

With a heartbeat of dismay, I realize he has Emissary Wheeler with him. I haven't seen Wheeler's face since I left Northaven. I nod at him politely and greet him with his name, but I am horribly reminded of how he battered Rye.

"Wheeler, this is the young rascal who landed his plane on the Isis," says Kite, putting his hand on my shoulder. "He has a very special talent."

A flush of delight creeps over my whole body.

"His commission was my gift," says Wheeler, self-satisfied.

Kite turns his gaze on me. "You're a native of Northaven?" he inquires.

"Yes, Brother."

"Where could you land your Firefly near the town?"

I don't even have to think. "Bailey's Strand. A mile of golden sand, a few minutes from our harbor."

"Could you take Emissary Wheeler and deliver him safely?"

My heart leaps with excitement at the thought of going home. Ma. I will tell her of this, and she will burst with pride.

"Providing the tide's out and the wind's not roaring."

"What about bringing him back?"

I glance at Wing Commander Axby. "If I had a spare battery, or double the fuel reserve. I'm sure it's possible."

"We don't want you landing on the Isis again. . . ." The corners of Kite's eyes are crinkling as if his smiles are rare. I will preserve this moment forever.

Men go to check the tidal charts and the weather reports. The ground crew fits my plane with everything we need.

I avoid Finch's eye as he helps with safety checks.

His touch—like a crucible, melting everything away.

I turn to Kite. His cool icon face. I see that he has drawn Wheeler aside and is speaking low, so only Wheeler can hear. These must be very special instructions. I hear the name Heron Mikane and something like "won't hinder us." I will work toward the day when Brother Kite whispers his trust in my ear like that.

As he parts from Wheeler I hear him say, "Leave Peregrine to me," and I know that I am at the very center of the world, witnessing great power.

As Finch helps Wheeler into the gunner's seat, I ask Kite what my instructions are. His eyes beam into me.

"Your hometown's been invaded. The Aylish have come by ship, bringing with them a fraudulent peace. How does that make you feel?"

I can't articulate my spinning dread and confusion. But Kite does not expect an answer.

"The Aylish mean nothing but harm, be assured of it. You must educate your people to the danger that they're in."

"Yes, Brother."

"Northaven must stay strong. Do you understand me? The Aylish must be thwarted, whatever it takes."

"The Aylish killed my father. And I will slay them," I tell him.

"You father would be proud of you."

In his strength, Kite will save me from myself. If I give him my heart, he will keep me true. I will tear it out of my chest and put it, bloody, in his hand.

"I belong to you and Brightland, Brother."

"Follow every instruction that your Emissary gives," he says.

I could take on the world. I could fly to the moon. I ascend to the sky on the wings of Kite's praise.

I think Wheeler is unprepared for the sensation of flight. I try to reassure him with some friendly remarks, but I soon see him vomiting into a bag. After that, he keeps his eyes shut.

The supper is ready; everything is done. I'm in the garden behind my husband's house and we're setting out tables and chairs for any townspeople who want to come. It's that golden time of day as the sun begins to set.

Nightingale has left me but I still feel our harmony humming through my core.

After a while, Curl comes out and puts her arm around me. We look at the harbor. Above us, the turbine blades are like burnished bronze, casting long shadows as they turn and turn.

"I have songlight, Ma. I'm a Torch."

I say this without thinking, the unsayable thing that's been stuck in my throat for so many years. I glance at her. Her face looks golden in the low sun, her eyes like smoldering ambers.

"I think I always knew," she says at last. "But when they took Rye, that's when I was sure."

I lean my head against her. "I have to leave Northaven," I say. "I can't stay here, I know that now."

"Then we'll go," she replies.

So much has passed between us, in so few words.

Ma looks at me, smiling. "Any more secrets you want to tell me?"

I meet her gaze. "What about you?" I ask pointedly. "You tell me yours."

She sighs out slowly. "Not today."

She's about to leave me. "You need to watch yourself, Ma," I warn. "You've been noticed."

I don't need to say Heron's name. Ma looks down, as if something precious to her is being damaged in the light.

"You're safe so far," I tell her. "But don't let them hang you for adultery."

She's angry.

"It's new," she says. "So new we haven't even spoken of it yet." It takes a while for her to steady her breath. "I've done nothing wrong and neither's he."

"I know that," I assure her.

The sun is turning fiery red.

"Warning understood," she says. And she heads indoors, shaken.

I look down at the Elders' Hall. Feeling my exclusion, I send a note to Kingfisher in the shape of a question. One note comes back:

"Don't."

He doesn't want to use songlight—for my own protection. But it angers me. I brought him here. I'm part of this.

"Is cooking your dinner all that I'm good for?"

He hears me. But I'm not expecting any reply.

Inside, the table is laid, the lamps are lit; the house is clean. It went downhill in the time I was in Ayland, due to Chaffinch being such a slattern. She comes running in as I return from the garden.

"Heron's bringing the Aylish. Sergeant Redshank is coming too."

"I'm glad of it," I say.

She's nervous, edgy. "My pa won't come. He called Heron a traitor and Heron came down on him with a firestorm of swearing. There's bad blood between them now. And where do I stand in that?" She's hot and flushed. I pour her water and she drinks.

"We should support Heron, Chaffie."

"Why?" She flexes her fingers like dainty little talons. "I was proud to be gifted as his wife. And I offered myself freely. But Heron Mikane is not a real man."

"He needs our loyalty," I press.

"He's not been loyal to us. Sometimes I wonder if he's loyal to anyone. He despises Leland Wheeler; he holds the elders in contempt. Is he even loyal to Brightland?"

I'm shocked at this. "He gave his body and soul to Brightland. Of course he's loyal. Don't you want peace?" I ask vehemently.

Ma interrupts us, coming in with a steaming lamb stew. There's a burning heat to her that isn't only from the stove.

"There's discord in the village," she says. "And perhaps it's up to us women to turn it into harmony." She puts the stew on the hearth to keep it warm. "Chaffinch, go down and invite your mother."

"My *mother?*"

"If the elders have forbidden men to come, we must invite women. Hoopoe Guinea and Mrs. Sweeney are coming. Invite your mother. Heron will be glad you've done it, trust me."

"He's not Heron to you; he's Commander Mikane," says Chaffinch peevishly.

Ma almost loses patience. "I've known him since he was a spotty boy," she snaps. "And I've known you since you were pooping in your pants, so don't pull your airs and graces on me."

Chaffinch crumbles then, brittle, close to tears. Curl draws in her breath, instantly regretting her outburst.

"I don't mean to raise my voice," she says. "There's just so much at stake. The eyes of all Brightland will be on us tonight. . . ."

"There might be peace, Chaffinch," I urge her. "It all depends on what we do."

Chaffinch looks unmoved. Ma tries a different tack.

"Great Brother Peregrine wants these talks," she says. "Do you think he'll be happy if your father scuppers them before they start? Keep his position safe. If your father won't come, your mother must."

Chaffinch mulls this. She bites her lip and looks at Ma resentfully. Without a word, she goes.

But when the diners arrive, her mother is with them.

Swan comes back to her rooms at sundown, pale and drawn. I can smell Kite on her, as if every blood cell in her body is secreting fear. She looks exhausted. She doesn't meet my eye and her mind is now impenetrable under her lead band. Kite has locked her light away. I bring her water to drink.

"You should rest, Sister," I suggest.

"There's no time."

She gets to her feet and has her ladies dress her in one white dress after another, rejecting them all.

"What happened in the Chrysalid House?" I ask.

"Nothing."

"Did Brother Kite do something to upset you?"

"No."

She looks defeated. I feel a wave of revulsion for him. It turns into hatred as it crashes on the shore. He's hurt her, broken her; something has changed. Swan sees my concern and she smiles a wan smile.

"Sweet Kaira," she says, brushing my face with her startling nails. "I have another little task for you. The most subtle thing in the world." She takes a deep breath. "All you have to do is put the color yellow in Brother Peregrine's mind."

What on earth is she talking about?

"Yellow?"

"Yes," she instructs. "Sweet lemon yellow."

"Why?"

"No reason."

Sister Swan moves restlessly away.

"What's the point, if there's no reason?"

This is some intrigue of Kite's. She wants to employ me in his service.

"What harm can yellow do?" she asks. "It's the color of sunshine and daffodils and all things nice. You must trust me and the reason will come clear."

I look her straight in the eye. "I do trust you. And you can trust me. What's it for?"

Her irritation shimmers like her jewels. "I saved you," she shrills. "I saved you from damnation and you'll do what I say."

I nod, saying nothing. The nerves in her neck are pulled taut. She turns her back on me, regarding herself in a mirror. She is wearing layers and layers of frothy white organza.

"Take this nightmare off," she shouts at her ladies. "Bring me the snow-moth damask." They follow her instructions. A dress is brought, so vast and heavy it takes three of them to carry it. A fourth lady brings a set of steps and the dress is lowered over Swan's head. It spreads out around her like a falling avalanche.

"Take it off!" Her voice is a shriek. "How dare you put me into this! Take it away."

Her ladies wordlessly obey. "Bring me the satin with the plunging back. I want my arms on show. I need to look vulnerable."

The snow-moth damask is removed and a dress that looks like a wisp of smoke is brought. Swan steps into it. She looks youthful, slender, and so, so sad.

"You look lovely," I assure her.

She raises her eyes to mine and I see that she's in torment.

"Is it a very special dinner?" I ask.

"No," she replies airily. "Peregrine dines with his council every week. It's quite routine. I choose the menu and my ladies always serve."

I'm aware of a faint, whining dissonance under her lead band, as if a hive of hornets is swarming in her mind. A knock on the door makes her start.

"I can't have you at the table, you understand that. But you'll be close by, thinking of yellow."

"Is something bad going to happen?" I ask.

"It's just a dinner party," she snaps. "I've asked you kindly for your help and all you do is undermine my love. If this is how it's going to be, I don't want you anymore."

The look in her eyes is so ruthless that I take a step back. I stare at her, silent with distress.

Starling Beech enters and almost gasps. Sister Swan's bare arms glow in the whiteness of the room. Truly, she looks like a goddess.

"The table is ready," he manages to say. Swan turns away from me and approaches him.

"Starling . . ." She whispers his name like a love word. "I want you to do me a small service. The Inquisitor who was arrested with my dolly . . . put a hold on any orders for his execution."

I feel my heart lurch. This is so swift and unexpected. My papa's life is spared. Starling nods, besotted. "Consider it done," he says, and goes.

"Thank you." I want to throw my arms around her neck but she stops me, holding me apart.

"Your papa's safe," she says. "For now."

It is a threat then, not an act of love. I understand. She will do Kite's will come hell or high water. Her subjugation is deeply ingrained—and she will make me serve him too.

"Yellow, lovely lemon yellow." She smiles. "Plant it in the mind of our dear, beloved leader."

Lark said that I was clever. She said I must survive this, any way I can.

I reach up on my toes and kiss Swan's perfect cheek.

"You have my word, Sister," I say.

Swan inhales sharply, revealing a momentary beam of pain. "I knew you wouldn't let me down."

Swan pulls the gauze over my face, as if she doesn't want to see my eyes. And as we leave the rooms, I become, once more, a blank.

45 ✳ LARK

Heron's garden is full. It turns out so many people want to come that we have to borrow more tables from our neighbors and set them out. Families share their food, buoyed up by Peregrine's approval of the peace talks. People have come in spite of the eldermen, as if Heron's defiance has given them permission. A few of his men, including Hamid and Jenkins, sit outside with the townspeople and their children. Gailee and Mrs. Roberts are dishing out stew and serving it with bread.

Inside, Ma and I make sure that everybody's glass is kept topped up. We're feeding the three Aylish, Chaffinch—who sits at Heron's side and doesn't lift a finger—Mrs. Greening, Soldier Wright, Mr. Malting, Sergeant Redshank, Hoopoe Guinea, and Mrs. Sweeney.

Syker, Forbe, and the eldermen have stoutly refused to come.

At the table, two conversations are going on at once. One is about roundball. Sergeant Redshank is old enough to remember when games were still played between our nations. The rest of the table is talking about Brightling and Aylish food. Everyone is trying as hard as they can to keep away from the subject of war.

Kingfisher is quiet, listening. He looks small and ordinary, as if all his energy is going into hiding his true nature. As I serve the vegetables, I wonder how much it costs me to hide mine. Perhaps on the ship, my light was brighter too. But here in my own home, I feel invisible and my lips are glued tight shut.

Kingfisher watches me as I serve the other end of the table. I've been trying to avoid his gaze but now I raise my eyes to meet his and the energy between us grows intense.

"You'll go to Brightlinghelm soon." My songlight comes out of me unbidden. "What if I never see you again?"

My notes are simple and direct. Kingfisher's expression changes. I notice

Chaffinch staring at us. I turn away and Kingfisher busies himself with his food.

I go into the kitchen. Gailee and Mrs. Roberts are coming in and out of the garden. I see Nela out there, sitting with John Jenkins. He's eating quietly. He seems calmer.

I understand how madness lurks for every Torch. Perhaps, when there's nowhere for our flame to burn, we consume ourselves from the inside out.

I step outside and look up to the sky, longing to reach for Nightingale—and in the last rays of sun, I see a golden insect, a beautiful thing like a dragonfly. It's too big to be an insect. It's a plane.

It's a breathtaking sight. A hush falls over the garden as the glittering plane circles lower. We watch in awe as it veers over the headland and disappears. All the children set off running, chasing it. I feel a strong urge to follow them, when I hear Ma's voice calling me back.

"We need beer, Elsa!"

I go inside and grab a jug. As I fill the glasses, I whisper in my husband's ear: "A plane is landing on the beach."

Heron nods, thanking me. I look at Kingfisher and in songlight, I tell him the same thing.

Mrs. Sweeney's sitting opposite Kingfisher and I can tell she's curious about him. As I fill her glass, I hear her.

"Do you have a wife or two tucked away, young man?"

"No," he says, "my heart is free." He flashes her a smile. "Are you single?"

Mrs. Sweeney laughs. "Hoopoe would choose you a wife quick enough."

"I might keep him for myself," says Hoopoe, coolly sipping her wine—and everyone laughs. Kingfisher is abashed but Alize sits forward, intrigued.

"Are you a matchmaker?" she asks.

"It's one of my duties as choirmother."

"So how does it work?" asks Alize. "How do you find a good match? For example, how did you put this happy couple together?" She indicates Heron and Chaffinch.

Chaffinch gives an awkward smile and Heron says nothing at all. Hoopoe is put on the spot.

"Well," she begins, "marriage isn't just about a woman and a man, it's about a community. We have to think of what's best for the whole village."

"It must be a very delicate business," says Alize, intrigued.

Hoopoe warms to her interest. "It's like putting magnets together. We want them to stick. We don't always get things right but it's a serious endeavor, I can tell you."

"And you have to choose Second Wives as well?" asks Alize.

"Oh no, the returning men choose their own Second Wife. The First Wife is his prize from the town. The Second, much lower in standing, is only for his pleasure."

I suddenly find everyone looking at me, like they're weighing me up as an object of pleasure. My eyes hit the floor. I put the jug on the table and start clearing empty plates. When I look up, Kingfisher's eyes are upon me again. There's a fire of compassion in them. He, who throws kisses from ships to young, adoring girls, will never know what it's like to be auctioned like a toy. My eyes blaze my defiance.

"I have had love," I say in songlight. "I have known bliss. Don't you dare pity me."

Kingfisher locks his eyes on mine as if he has so many things to say. I break away, taking my plates to the sink. When I come back, Alize and Hoopoe are still deep in discourse.

"You're a skilled negotiator," points out Alize. "How would you begin to negotiate a peace?"

Mrs. Greening humphs, almost a laugh. But Hoopoe takes the question seriously.

"I never could," she says. "That's quite beyond my power."

"I feel the same way," admits Alize. "And yet it must be done. Imagine it like matchmaking. Where would you begin?"

Hoopoe thinks. All eyes are on her.

"We begin by laying all the pieces out on the table. Each girl has the positives and negatives around her, and each man the same."

"So you'd do that for the Brightlings and the Aylish?" asks Alize.

"I suppose we would."

Ma comes in from the kitchen with a steaming tray. She sets it on the table. "We have an apple cake to serve. It's a Northaven favorite."

"I swear Curl Crane's is the best in all of Brightland," says Heron, glancing up at her, admiration in his eye. Chaffinch's jaw twitches.

"Do you bake?" Hoopoe asks Alize.

"What a silly question," sneers Mrs. Greening. "In Ayland, I'm sure it's only men who bake." She intends this as an insult to Cazimir and Kingfisher. But Cazimir is smiling.

"You must give us your recipe, Mrs. Crane."

Ma shakes her head and smiles. "My apple cake's a state secret."

"I used to bake," says Alize. "Not much good at it now." She raises her missing hand.

"How did that happen?" inquires Mrs. Sweeney, looking at the stump, as if she's been dying to ask the question all day along.

Alize leaves a pause. "At the battle of Montsan Beach."

Heron's eyes meet hers. His color drains. There's a silence so lengthy I hear beetles in the woodwork crawl.

"You should talk about it," says Kingfisher. "It's there between you, sitting like a beast."

"That's right," says Heron in a low voice. "We should talk, here, with food and wine between us, so it doesn't rear its head in Brightlinghelm."

Alize glares at him. "You want to talk about how I lost my hand?"

"I do." The candles shine on Heron's scars. The silence in the rest of the room is profound. Ma and I stand like statues with the empty plates.

"We had a weapon you couldn't match. We knew it," Heron begins. He exhales, as if something dark is crawling out of him. "A flamethrower. Brother Kite's first experiment with firefuel. I had no care that he was breaking the First Law. I had one order—win. We set our force on Montsan Beach—the perfect base for an assault on Reem—and we waited for you."

"One of our academies is there," says Alize. "Where our Torches are trained."

The Brightlings virtually recoil at the word.

My eyes go straight to Kingfisher. Is it where he trained? He shakes his head. But he knows this story and he looks somber with a deep-held grief.

"It's a hallowed place for us," says Alize. "Our children lived there."

"Unhumans," says Mrs. Greening.

"Children," stresses Alize. "Adolescents, unarmed and barely protected. It was a trap. It was a massacre." The words come out of her like they're birthed in fire and blood.

I'm witnessing something private and ugly, something brave.

"I want you to know," says Heron slowly and softly, "it was my idea to land at that place, to make battle there. I put it to Kite and he said it had good logic. The River Montsan would lead us up to Reem and I knew we would prevail. To defeat you, I didn't care who or what was lost. It never occurred to me to find out what that building was."

"They were burned alive," says Alize. "Two hundred of our children."

Heron hangs his head. A wave of sickness comes upon me. I didn't know this. I didn't know. I can feel Mrs. Greening fidget in her seat. Maybe she knew. Maybe, when she told Chaffinch to make those ugly curtains, she knew there were children burning in the towers. Children like Nightingale and me.

"That burning chemical you used," says Alize, trying to remain calm, "nothing put it out; no water was enough. It was so fierce it burned on the surface of the sea. There was nothing we could do."

"We knew that. And we knew how hard you'd try."

"My daughter was in there." Alize has to stop. The silence in the room is taut with her pain. She forces herself on. "She was thirteen. I tried to get to her. I carried on one-handed, till my comrades pulled me back."

Her grief is shocking and sudden. She cannot control it. Cazimir grips her arm. She tries to put her mental armor back but it has gone and she is bare.

"Gala," cries Heron in anguish. "Why are you here? How can you be seeking peace? Why don't you run me through?"

"Why are *you* here, Mikane?" she counters. "Why have you welcomed us? When Montsan fell, you were the commander who was poised to win."

I want the answer to this question too. Quietly, it comes.

"I was near enough to hear the screams. When your ships were still blazing, I walked down on the beach. I walked among the dead. You could smell the burning flesh for miles. Amid the carnage, I saw a figure. On her bony face, a grin. I knew her for Death. It was her victory, her triumph. She was thanking me. I knew in that moment that I hadn't served my country. I was only serving Death. Death has had me ever since."

Alize nods. For her, death is no more than he deserves. Her tears are running silent, in tribute to her child. "My hair went white when they told me the news."

Heron has no composure left. Words are wrenched out of him.

"I found out what that place was when it was too late," he whispers. "These burns are the result." His scarred head is bowed. "I'm sorry."

I've heard that remorse can kill a man but I never believed it until now. Heron has been letting himself die since Montsan Beach. Maybe Curl Crane is the only thread still tying him to Earth.

Alize looks up at Kingfisher. I sense that she wants to know for sure if Heron's speaking true. Kingfisher meets her eye and subtly, he nods.

Then something utterly remarkable: Alize puts her forearm across the table. Heron takes it, like it's a hand. They both stand. Something is releasing in both of them. It flows out of them. It goes on and on. None of us know how this moment will end but it feels as if this simple gesture, full of courage and anguish, this is how peace should be made. Alize leans across the table and presses her forehead against Heron's.

334

"Death has had us all."

Mrs. Greening starts to panic. I feel her breathing rise. I get an image like a magpie, caught on a limed twig. She's going to start flapping. I can feel Redshank coming apart as every heroic tale he has ever believed is being consumed in the flames of Montsan. And then, beside me, my mother starts to sing.

It's one of her songs from the Greensward, not a Northaven song. It's a sweet song to Gala, a children's song, a lullaby. I remember it from when I was tiny. It doesn't intrude on Heron and Alize. It adds to the moment. It seems to say that all children are with Gala. Gala holds them all. I know she is singing for the children of Montsan. Slowly, Heron and Alize part. Alize brushes the tears off her face. She holds out her hand, the living one, to Redshank. He grasps it. Heron offers his hand to Cazimir Cree.

All around the table people grasp each other's hands. Alize holds out her forearm to Mrs. Sweeney. Chaffinch looks at Cazimir's proffered hand. Slowly, she takes it. Only Mrs. Greening remains in her seat, her hands clasped tightly in her lap. Kingfisher is holding out his hand to me. I put down my dishes and walk forward. I take it. And I take Heron's, loving him for the pain of his remorse. I hold them both together. The song ends. As the final note dies away, it's almost like the light in the room returns to normal.

It's then that Heron notices Ma. Now that it's over, he suddenly hears what she's done. Standing there, with dishes in her hands and her simple lullaby, she's sealed the peace between the Brightlings and the Aylish.

There's something about the quiet knock on Heron's door that gives me a bad feeling. It's not bold nor strong. It's the kind of knock a shadow-man would make. Kingfisher's shoulders stiffen. He senses danger straight-away. His eyes meet Alize's and the Aylish stand. Heron strides over and opens his door.

"Emissary Wheeler," he says. "Come in."

I see Wheeler narrowing his eyes at our overcrowded house. Bastard.

"Why don't you come out?" he asks.

Heron looks round at Alize. She nods at him slowly and we all file out. Heron introduces the Aylish, one by one, and Wheeler says nothing, his face like a brick.

"There's food left," says Heron, trying his best to be polite. "Would you care to eat with us?"

"I'm here with orders from the Brethren," says the brick.

My foreboding is so strong it makes my knees go weak. But when Ma steps outside ahead of me, her face lights up.

"Piper!" she cries.

Piper steps into the light. He's the pilot that he always longed to be, so handsome I could weep. Ma embraces him full-heartedly. He accepts her affection but quickly steps back, as if her love is somehow out of place. I feel a rush of sorrow for the rift between us.

"So it was you, flying?" I ask warmly. "I saw your plane from the garden. It's beautiful, Piper."

Maybe he's changed, no longer the green boy who sold his friend to the Chrysalid House. Maybe there's a way that things could heal. Above all, maybe he has news of Rye. For a moment I am full of hope. But Piper is unsmiling.

"How is it possible you're cooking for the Aylish?"

Ma looks disappointed. "They saved Elsa's life," she explains. "Your sister would have drowned if they hadn't rescued her."

Piper looks at me, hostile. "So it's you?" he accuses. "You brought them to our town?"

Suddenly I'm afraid. *He knows what I am.* He could reveal me with a single word. *Unhuman.*

People are spilling round the side of the house from the garden; Heron's men, our neighbors. The crowd is growing.

"We're grateful that Peregrine has agreed to meet us," Alize tells Wheeler in her most diplomatic tone. "And we thank you for bringing his instructions in person."

"You must leave Northaven immediately," Wheeler tells her coldly. "Our coastal guards are ready to escort your ship to Brightlinghelm."

"That's a request I am happy to comply with," says Alize, refusing to be cowed. "The sooner we get around a table, the sooner we can look toward ending this war."

Hope ripples through the crowd. But without another word, Wheeler turns his back on the Aylish and leads the way down to the harbor. Ma follows, keeping close to Piper. It pains me how Piper is avoiding her gaze.

Heron gestures to Alize to accompany him and I walk behind them with Kingfisher. I use my songlight to give him a warning.

"Under his jacket, that man Wheeler has a scorpion's tail. Don't trust him."

"We knew this would be dangerous," he replies.

As we walk on, curious faces stare out of doorways and join the throng.

"I don't want to leave you here," confesses Kingfisher, as if he's been holding the thought for a long time. "I wish more than ever that you'd stayed in Caraquet."

I glance at him, playing a bravado I don't feel. "It isn't me who needs protecting."

In truth, I'm hurting sore at the thought of him going. He's been a bright melody in my life. And I will miss his vibrant color.

Down at the harbor, the coastal guard are in their boats, waiting to escort the Aylish back to the *Aileron Blue*. The crowd swells in force to watch this historic sight. I see that some faces are filled with hope; others are tight with hatred and suspicion. I see Mozen Tern, shoulders hunched, looking mean as a raven. I walk past him, proud to be with the Aylish.

When we get to the quayside, Alize turns to Mikane. "Commander, why don't you bring your wives and come with us?"

I immediately know that she is trying to keep me safe—and it thrills me that she's trying. But Wheeler has heard and he cuts in before Heron can reply.

"Heron Mikane is not coming. He's no longer a commander and he has no place at the negotiating table."

This is news to everyone. Chaffinch looks appalled.

"No longer a commander?" asks Heron, puzzled. "How so?"

"You resigned," Wheeler tells him.

"I tried to resign a year ago and Peregrine wouldn't hear of it."

"Brother Kite approved your resignation today. You no longer have military or diplomatic standing, so your presence in Brightlinghelm won't be required."

Heron eyes Wheeler, digesting this. I wish he'd punch him in his smug-ugly face.

"It seems I must stay here," says Heron regretfully to Alize. "And yet I have a yearning to see Brightlinghelm again."

"Amou," says Alize, using the Aylish word. "I hope we meet again."

Both have been changed by their encounter and the well of emotion is still deep between them. Nothing more needs to be said.

The Aylish prepare to board. "Thank you for bringing me home," I say to Alize, and I put my arms around her. I don't give a damn what people think.

Cree is shaking hands with Soldier Wright and Sergeant Redshank.

Hoopoe and Mrs. Sweeney are wishing Kingfisher farewell. I swear he's giving them his most dazzling smile.

"If I ever need a wife . . . ," he says with charm—and the women cackle with laughter.

Wheeler is impervious to this genuine goodwill. But the townspeople see. I notice Gailee with John Jenkins. They're deeply moved, as if we're all witnessing something momentous. I look to see if Piper's been affected, but he has his fists clenched, looking daggers at me.

Piper, don't.

Wheeler takes a position in front of the Aylish craft with the eldermen at his side. I notice that Syker and Forbe are armed.

"If peace is to be made," he cries, "it must be made fairly. The Brethren require you to give up your Torch."

Panic seizes me—"No, no, no," I cry in songlight—and I sense Kingfisher's deep dismay.

"Our culture won't allow an unhuman at our table. Yours must remain here for the duration of the talks." Wheeler's voice rings out sharp against the slates and flagstones.

Alize keeps her calm. "My comrades are all human, as you can see, and we'll remain together, as our culture demands."

"That order can't have come from Peregrine," cries Heron, outraged. "It goes against the whole tone of his telegram. His invitation was cordial and clear. Has Niccolas Kite sent you to sabotage this peace?" he demands angrily.

Wheeler is wrong-footed. I don't think he expected Heron to be so public and so blunt.

"There'll be no talks if the Aylish bring an unhuman," he says, implacable.

I flash a streak of songlight to Kingfisher, showing him an image of Wheeler at the shaming post, reveling in his dominion over Rye. "Don't give yourself away," I warn. "This man hates our kind."

Sergeant Redshank pushes through the crowd and faces Wheeler. His voice is raised on purpose so that all can hear.

"You've known me many years, Leland Wheeler, and I can tell you these Aylish come in good will. What's passed here tonight makes me believe that peace is possible. Mikane and Alize spoke from the heart about Montsan Beach. They made a real and proper reconciliation. There's no place here for hatred and mistrust. Let all the Aylish leave in peace."

That's the most I've ever heard Sergeant Redshank say in my whole life. He's liked and well respected in the town and his words resonate throughout the crowd.

"Are you giving me an order, Redshank?" asks Wheeler sneeringly.

"We have green shoots of peace here in Northaven," cries Heron in his battlefield voice. "They could spread throughout two nations."

I can almost smell Wheeler's hunger for violence. In his eyes I see drops of blood falling in a darkened room. I know this man means harm.

"If you fail to comply," he threatens Alize, "we'll give you ten minutes to get back to your ship. Then we'll fire our mortar guns."

Alize looks at him, sorrowful. "So be it."

She heads for the landing craft as the crowd turns vocal. Waves of frustrated hope clamor against a riptide of prejudice and hate.

Kingfisher takes Alize aside, blocking my songlight warnings.

"Let me stay," he offers with quiet urgency. "We've got safe passage to Brightlinghelm. It's more than we ever thought we would achieve. The mission must come first."

"Our strength's in our fellowship," insists Alize. "I won't leave you."

"Go without me," he presses. "Keep the rest of the crew safe."

And Kingfisher, risk-seeking, reckless, orca-diving fool, steps forward.

"I'm the Torch," he cries. "And I would never use my songlight to make a false peace."

"No, no, no." My songlight cry gains in intensity.

Alize sees Kingfisher's determination. She turns to Wheeler. "We'll comply with your demand for the sake of peace. But mistreating our comrade will have grave repercussions."

Wheeler bows, smug and silent. This chills me even further.

Heron courteously helps Alize into the boat.

"There's some mischief at work," I hear him say quietly. "But Peregrine is genuine, I have no doubt. He'll soon send for your Torch. Meanwhile, I'll protect him with my life."

Alize nods, thanking Heron, clasping his hand. Then she turns her wise, perceptive eyes on me.

"Elsa, amou."

"I'll see you again, in a time of peace," I reply.

Cree speeds the landing craft out of the harbor. Three Brightling military boats accompany it. We watch until they're gone.

Kingfisher is alone now, in his plain Aylish blue. I see John Jenkins on the edge of my vision, looking at him with fascination. Wheeler's staring at him too, lust for violence quickening his blood.

"Yan, my home is yours," Heron offers. "I hope you'll be my guest."

But Wheeler wastes no time. Before Kingfisher can reply, the scorpion reveals his sting.

"Take the unhuman to the jailhouse," he orders.

"You just gave your word no harm would come to him," I cry.

"Keep your wife on her leash, Mikane."

"She speaks the truth and I agree with her. You gave your word." I rejoice at Heron's support. It makes me feel bolder and I meet Wheeler's eye. *Double, triple bastard.*

"The mind-twister must be kept underground where he can't use his powers. Those are my orders, and I will do my duty." Wheeler nods at Syker and Forbe, who come for Kingfisher.

"Over my dead body," says Heron, stopping them.

Kingfisher puts himself between them. "No violence," he says. "I'll come."

"Don't trust him, Yan, he's a torturer!"

My cry hurts my throat and I realize with horror that I haven't used my songlight. The whole town has heard.

"Hold your tongue, Elsa," demands my brother, in a cry as painful as my own. "You're shaming our family."

Piper has the word behind his teeth. *Unhuman.*

Wheeler's gaze falls on me, twisted with contempt. "We have an Aylish-lover here."

I look at Piper's face and I know the blow will come. His next sentence will give me away. I think of Rye, broken at the shaming post; Nightingale, trapped and misused; her friend Cassandra, lost to time. I won't cower, waiting to be caught.

"Sir, my sister, she's . . ."

I won't let him say it.

"Don't do it, Piper," I entreat in a low voice. "You did it to Rye and it destroyed him. In your soul, it's destroying you. Don't do it to me."

I see Piper struggle with himself. "Elsa is . . ."

I won't let him decide my fate. I'll take it in my own hands. It feels like I am leaping into a deep blue lake.

"Yan Zeru is not unhuman," I tell the whole town. "He has songlight. He's a Torch. And so am I."

I feel an odd relief. The terrible secret is out. There are audible gasps, a cry from Chaffinch and a broken whisper from my ma.

"Elsa, no . . ."

I feel Kingfisher move closer to me. Some of my neighbors look pained; others would kill me on the spot. My anguished voice rises up to the blades of the turbine towers.

"Why must I be destroyed for it?" I ask. "I'm a daughter of this town. I'm a part of you, like Rye Tern. Why must you kill your own children?"

I see Gailee's eyes upon me, full of comprehension. I see a dawning understanding on Hoopoe Guinea's face. Wheeler addresses his flock.

"This girl has lured the Aylish here, intending to destroy us."

"You said that about Rye Tern," yells my ma. "It was a lie then and it's a lie now. You're mean and murderous, Wheeler. You set us against each other every time you come. You took our girls to be Third Wives and probably raped them all on the ship."

My heart leaps with pride at everything she's said, but to my utter shock, Piper puts his hand over my mother's mouth.

"This must be contained, sir," he warns. "We can't give them an excuse to riot."

So my brother's picked his side. He belongs to Wheeler.

"Lock up the unhumans," cries Wheeler. "Anyone who helps them knows the consequence."

"I learned one thing as a solider," cries Heron, "and that's when a battle is worth fighting. I'm telling you now, this battle is for peace—and that's worth dying for. I said I'd protect Yan Zeru with my life—and I'll do the same for Elsa Crane."

I love him at that moment, like my pa. Wright, Hamid, Jenkins—they all come to Heron's side. I see Mr. Malting come running to protect me. The crowd surges.

Curl is struggling to get to me but Piper pulls her away.

"What are you doing?" he asks her. "Where's your loyalty?"

Syker fires his gun above the crowd. "Take another step and you're dead," he shouts.

Silence falls. Forbe and the eldermen point their rifles. Elder Haines grabs me. Forbe puts his gun in Kingfisher's back.

"Let them go," says Heron calmly, coming toward us. But Forbe doesn't move and Syker aims his rifle, stopping Heron in his tracks.

"Come to your senses, Mikane," he says. "That girl has twisted your mind and one day you'll thank me."

Heron is halted as the eldermen drag us away. But the crowd is heaving with discontent. More rifle shots are fired and people start screaming. I turn to see Heron and Syker, wrestling each other for the gun. I hear shouts of support coming from the crowd, yells of agreement—and cries of outrage, calling for us to be hanged.

I hear Ma crying: "Elsa, Elsa!" I see Piper, holding her back.

The eldermen pull us toward the jail. Kingfisher has his arms raised. He isn't resisting them—but I send up a flare of anguish, my anger ripping into the night sky.

I can hear Kingfisher's bright whisper on the wind: "Stay calm. There'll be a time to fight. Stay calm."

Elder Haines is twisting my arm off. A cry of pain comes out of me—

And I see an image in a flash. Nightingale. She has heard me.

"LARK!"

"They have me," I tell her. "They know I'm a Torch."

"LARK!"

She's horrified to see me caught. Kingfisher stumbles, his eyes closing at the force of her. Her song is like an explosion of light:

"LARK!"

I see two of the elders running ahead to open the jailhouse door. It's called "the tank" because it floods when the tide is high and the wretches inside must sit upon a ledge until the water ebbs backs down again. The walls are thick and solid and, by reputation, no unhuman can sing through them. This is where they held Rye.

I feel Nightingale's anguish. I tell her I'm all right. She knows it's a lie. I tell her to stay brave—and I stumble down a flight of slippery stone steps. I lie at the bottom, winded. Our connection is lost.

It's dark. A stench of rust and rotting seaweed. I crawl into a corner as Greening and Wheeler send Forbe back into the fray with his gun. Kingfisher seems shaken as Wheeler forces him down the stairs. He can hardly find his footing. Nightingale has stunned him with her powerful songlight. How can I stop this? How can I help him?

Piper appears at the top of the staircase.

"The crowd is angry," he says. "Mikane is stirring them—we can't contain them without resort to violence. Sir, you could calm things." I can hear gunshots in the distance.

"Tell Redshank to arm the cadets," orders Wheeler.

Piper sees the knife glinting in Wheeler's hand. "What will you do?" he asks anxiously.

"They're going to kill us, Piper," I yell.

Piper dithers at the top of the stairs, looking at me, stunned.

"I've given you an order," yells the Emissary. And my spineless brother runs outside.

"Don't hesitate," says Greening to Wheeler. "Do what you came here for."

My eyes meet Kingfisher's. The thick walls still allow our songlight to each other.

"Peregrine doesn't want you dead, I'm sure of it," I tell him. "I saw it, in the temple of Gala with Nightingale. He was preparing to make peace."

Kingfisher has recovered his composure. He faces his assassins. "Make sure you have Peregrine's approval of before you do such a reckless thing," he says to Wheeler. "My death will bring war for years to come and history will lay it at your door."

"Are you trying to mind-twist me?"

"Kite won't own this action," Kingfisher warns him. "He won't protect you. Kite will throw you to the dogs."

With a swift and graceless twist, Wheeler brings the knife to Kingfisher's throat. "Peregrine's day is all but done," he says. "I'm fighting for the winning side."

Kingfisher moves quicker than light and Wheeler lands upon the floor. How has he done that?

Wheeler stands clumsily and comes at him again. Kingfisher springs out of his way, kicking him down to his knees. For the first time, I realize that Yan Zeru is a fighter. Haines comes at him now. Kingfisher holds off both of them, lithe on his feet, twisting, turning, using his opponent's weight, sending Haines onto his back.

If that's what you learn at Torch School, then I want to go.

I race up the stairs. There is one man in the town who can help us. I send an arrow of songlight through the grille in the door. And I feel it land in a cacophony.

"John Jenkins," I say, bright and loud and clear. "Tell Heron to come. They're going to kill us both."

Then I see Greening, blade out, behind Kingfisher. I feel as if I'm lifted by my own scream. I jump down the stairs and throw myself at Greening. His knife splits my hand with a white-hot pain, but I won't let him kill my azure friend. I bash Greening's arm against the wall and his knife falls through the grille, into the sea. Someone whacks me between the shoulders. I hear the thud of my head on the wall and before I even feel the pain, everything goes black.

Venison with all the trimmings. Peregrine's last dinner is underway.

Kite's place at the table is empty. He wants no spot of guilt on his pristine suit. My bare arms are shivering. I can't muster any of my usual sparkling charm, and every forkful has to be forced down. But the councilmen barely notice. I'm there for decoration only, like the flowers on the table. As the wine flows, they talk the business of our state. Peace must be prepared for. I watch my ladies as they serve, unhuman under the gauze.

The stench of the Chrysalid House is lingering in my cortex: blood, gray matter, and despair. I won't have them needle the songlight out of my brain and wrap it in a cocoon. I won't be like one of these gauzed specters. I won't die there. I won't die.

So Peregrine must.

That's the covenant I've made with Kite. He's reprieved me until tomorrow. But if Peregrine still lives . . . I die. I want to throw myself on the mercy of these men but I have deceived them all for years and if they knew my truth, they'd shrink from me as the Siren that I am.

I want to turn the poison on Kite. But how? When? How can I escape this?

Peregrine has no idea that I'm the serpent in the flower. He makes preparations for talks with the Aylish, unaware that his peace is already spiked.

"We must anticipate every condition they will ask," he tells his Brethren.

I know he loves a lemon-coated almond.

The sweet tang will hide the taste of poison.

I prepared it carefully. One is enough.

Harrier is talking about the economic benefits of peace. "They're worth all the concessions we must make."

What if I threw myself on Harrier's mercy? Would he accept my loyalty and my service? No. He'd abhor me as unhuman and throw me into jail.

My dolly is nearby in an anteroom. I want her out of sight, so she may do her task. Yellow. She'll make the old man drool for lemon yellow.

Why have I agreed to this?

When the time comes, I won't do it. I won't be able. When my ladies serve the sugared almonds I will throw the platter to the floor.

Yet the old fool wants peace. Traitor.

"They'll want us to abandon our remaining coastal colonies," anticipates Peregrine. My ears prick up at this. "That'll be their first demand."

"It's out of the question," I say.

The men turn and look at me. Peregrine is solicitous. He smiles indulgently.

"We all know how you lost your family, Zara. The colonies have been the scene of much bitter fighting. We won't concede them immediately but we must be open to restoring Aylish lands in exchange for our continental trading routes. There are lands beyond Ayland that we have lost access to."

I hear Kite, as if he's hissing in my ear: *What crime is it, when the old man would dare to make peace with the Aylish?*

I mutter an apology. "Forgive me, I spoke from the heart."

"You remind us all how hard it will be to reach an accord," says our Great Brother. "There's visceral hatred on both sides."

The clock ticks on, through the main course and dessert.

The almonds will come with the coffee.

Without Kite's iron presence, the evening becomes more convivial. During dessert, Harrier does a very amusing impression of my master. We're allowed to laugh because Peregrine laughs. And when the darkness nags at me, I force it down, away.

Could I confess to my dolly? Could I share this horrible plight? I know she senses the choking quagmire I am sinking in.

But what could she do, that frail child?

Kite would kill her too.

I must keep her at arm's length from now on. She's nothing but a tool. Loving her is a mistake and it will only weaken me.

When Kite is in power, he will exalt me at his side.

The coffee arrives.

Lady Orion brings in the sugared almonds. She's been told to start with Peregrine. One yellow almond sits near the top. I half hope that Kaira's refused to do my bidding. She could tell that the whole enterprise was rank.

But at that moment, her songlight comes howling through me, churning me, blinding me, even under the lead band.

"LARK!"

I grip the table. How dare she.

"LARK!"

"Take those back," I cry out to Lady Orion. "We don't want them!"

She walks away, taking the almonds.

"LARK!"

My cortex screams. My chair scrapes as I stand.

"Has something upset you, my dear?" inquires Peregrine.

"I'm sorry," I splutter. "Please excuse me for a moment. . . ."

I go into the anteroom.

Kaira is on her feet, coming toward me, tears swimming in her eyes, imploring me in songlight.

"What are you *doing*?" I hiss.

The images she's sending me are brilliant, so dazzling I cannot see. She's not concerned with Peregrine or Kite.

I see a girl being forced across a town square. "Save her," she cries in desperate songlight.

"This must wait. It must wait until later."

Kaira shakes her head. "They're going to kill her."

"Stop now or I'll cuff you with a lead band."

"They've taken the Aylishman prisoner in Northaven. Tell Peregrine. You can stop them. LARK!"

My whole cortex jars. She'll make me retch.

"How dare you put your friend before me. You are putting me in peril!"

"LARK!"

I almost sink to my knees as the pain sears through me. Damn her. She loves this Lark far more than she will ever care for me. One of my ladies is standing by the window. I grab her white scarf. Kaira's voice chokes as I gag her.

"If you don't shut up, I will knock you out."

Kaira steadies her breathing. Her eyes are huge with unspoken distress as I pull the gauze down over her face.

"Take her back to my rooms," I say to Lady Libra. "Get her out of my sight."

As Swan gags me, I smell something sickly on her hands. Her lead band cannot hide the opalescent drop I see, falling from a phial onto a single yellow almond.

Peregrine.

I have been sitting in this room, filling his mind with sweet lemon. Suddenly I know how she has used me. I know what she has done. Our Great Brother is her victim.

I'm too horrified to speak. Truly, I wonder if she's mad.

She instructs one of her ladies to lead me out. The creature takes me by the wrist and I don't resist her clammy touch. We go.

I don't think I can live another day of this.

Lark . . .

I try to reach her in Northaven but there is raw silence. I pray to Gala: save her.

The palace corridors are deserted. We move like phantoms.

I am powerless. I am already dead.

The white-clad automaton brings me to Swan's rooms. It lifts my gauze, removes the gag. It does what Swan's instructed.

I will never look these ladies in the face, for fear they'll suck me into their dead eyes.

Then I catch myself. Surely my fear makes this woman more unhuman. Why am I treating her like a thing? She and I are one and the same. She's still a person, no matter what's been done to her.

"Thank you," I say.

I resolve to look at her, to talk to her as if she is still there. But it's hard to lift my eyes, to look into that dreadful gauze.

I look at her hands first. Human hands. Poignant that they're lifeless now. Lifeless yet alive.

There's a tattoo on her lower arm. A stork, one long leg raised.

She has a smell I remember.

I peer through the gauze at her face. I stand.

A hospital bed, a neat uniform, a blue-and-white nurse's hat.

She saved my life; she taught me what I was.

Those hands are hers.

"Cassandra . . . ?"

Her name means nothing to her now. I watch as she moves to the window, unblinking, unthinking.

It is monstrous.

A wave of rage comes upon me, rushing up the river with all the waters of the ocean, and it crashes over Brightlinghelm. My anger destroys the Brethren's Palace and it floods the Chrysalid House. It sweeps Kite and his armies into the sea.

Cassandra.

When I walk back into the banqueting hall, I see that Peregrine has sent the councillors away. The platter of almonds is at his side, half demolished.

My heart falls though the floor and tumbles down, down, down into Hel.

"You had the almonds?"

"Your lady tried to take them but you know how much I love them."

The yellow one is gone. Who ate it? Peregrine? Harrier? Surgeon Ruppell? There is no antidote. One of these men won't live to see the dawn.

I tried to stop it. It's out of my hands.

"Zara," says Peregrine, offering me the seat next to his. "I'd like to speak with you, alone."

This is the last thing I want. He needs to go. He should make his peace with Thal.

"Forgive me, Great Brother. I have a new dolly from the Chrysalid House. She isn't strong. I must put her to bed."

"I won't keep you for long."

I sit with him as my ladies clear the table.

"I believe I met your doll earlier today."

"I chose her myself," I tell him, my head bowed.

"I respect your compassion," says our Great Brother, with uncommon gentleness. I look up at him. Instantly, I want to lay myself open, to tell him what I am. But that is Peregrine's special skill. He can draw secrets out without any songlight. He is the father we all want to have. We love him so much we don't see how he's debasing us and taking all our freedom. We forgive him for climbing to power on death and division.

"Kite is an eminently able man," he begins. "Together we've transformed Brightland into a mighty force. There's much good in that transformation, but in his zeal for change, Kite has become increasingly cruel. I've seen him tightening his hold on you and I can't bear to watch it anymore."

I have nothing to lose. I will be frank.

"You know, don't you? You know that I'm a Siren?"

Peregrine's eyes shine in the lamplight. "I think I've always known. . . ."

This opens a tinderbox of questions. And he might be dead before he answers them. I let him speak, uninterrupted.

"I'm going to resolve this war with Ayland. Harrier is right. We can't win without a catastrophic loss of life. As well as his weapons of fire, Kite is developing a poisonous gas, an invisible killer of every living thing that breathes. It's his plan to drop it from his planes and murder the citizens of Reem by stealth. As warcraft, it's beneath contempt. And the Aylish will take spectacular revenge. The Light People have shown us which way it's going to go."

His gnarled hands wrap themselves round mine.

"I know that Kite is trying to thwart this peace," he says. "My spies inform me that it's his intention to attempt a coup. He's seeking support from the armed forces. So tonight, I'm having him arrested and imprisoned."

I am amazed to death. His instinct hasn't failed him. He spotted the snake slithering in the grass.

"Great Brother, I wish you had told me sooner."

"I had to act quickly. Better for no one to know until it's done. I'm having Kite removed from power. He'll be stripped of his titles and tried for treason." Peregrine pauses. "Justice will then decide his fate."

If he's eaten that almond, the venom will soon start burning through his stomach wall.

"Why are you telling me this?" I ask. "You know I'm Kite's creature."

"I'm fond of you, my dear. Even as a Siren, you never lost your radiance. Under that lead band, I'm aware of your daughterly heart."

A wave of bitterness sweeps over me.

"You let Kite use me. You saw what he did. You never spoke. You never made him stop."

"Divide and rule," he says. "That is the statecraft I have lived by. Pit one councillor against another and control them from above. I've put man against woman, human against unhuman, Brightling against Aylish. In my youth it seemed like wisdom. Every time I sowed division, my power would rise. But it's not wisdom. It's tyranny."

"Kite's the tyrant," I tell him. "The threat of the Chrysalid House has been upon me every day."

Peregrine pauses, as if feeling a twinge of indigestion. A deep sigh comes from within him.

"We needed to cull the unhumans," he tells me. "People of Song were a corrupt elite. I believed they could be excised, eliminated from our race." He sighs again. "I was wrong. The persecution is going to stop. My next edict is for a change in policy. By the time the Aylish ship is escorted into Brightlinghelm, we'll be demolishing the Chrysalid House."

I look at him, stunned, trying to take this in.

"That doll of yours, that child . . ." He shakes his head. "It's an abhorrent thing we do."

"What will happen to me, as a Siren?" I ask.

"As soon as Kite is jailed, I'll take his key and free you. No one will ever wear a Siren's band again." He puts his hand up to my wig and with his fingers, he traces the metal band. "Zara," he says. "I hope you can forgive me."

Suddenly, I'm crushed.

To my consternation, I start sobbing like a child.

I am the one who is unforgivable.

The old fool. Why didn't he say all this before?

It is too late, far too late.

His arms are wrapped around me. He's comforting me, holding me like my father never did. And I am his murderer.

"I love you very well, my dear. Don't cry." When my sobbing ebbs, he lets me go and stands.

"Tomorrow is a new day." He smiles, patting my hand. "We look to a better future."

I sit at the table and watch him walk toward the door. He stops and holds his guts.

"Peregrine?"

He turns and sees my deep concern.

"Too much fine food . . ."

His suffering begins.

I could tell him. I could confess.

But he is dying anyway.

I hear myself say: "I hope you will sleep well."

And the old man bows his head and goes.

The first thing I'm aware of is the pain in my hand. I'm cold. I open my eyes to the gloom. Then I feel his songlight. Kingfisher has my bleeding hand in his.

"What are you doing?" I ask.

"Slowing down the flow of blood," he says. "We need it to congeal. I made a tourniquet from my belt. Tell me if it gets too painful."

This must be what he did when the orca bit my leg. I feel how his concentrated light is numbing the pain.

"Are you healing me?"

He shakes his head. "Your own body is healing you. I can only encourage what it does by itself."

I hear waves rumbling beneath us. The tide is coming in. I breathe with it, letting Kingfisher work. His dark hair falls forward; his plain blue shirt is torn. He's bleeding too.

"You got hurt. . . ."

"You saved my life," he says simply. "That man was going to grab me from behind and cut my throat."

"Where have they gone?"

He shakes his head. "They argued about my fate. I think they want assurances from Brother Kite before they murder me."

He looks up at the door and the light catches his eyes. They have flecks of amber in them, like his jewel.

"I expect they'll do it with a gun," he muses. "A bullet through my unhuman Aylish head."

Time holds us on the edge of an abyss.

"We're not going to die here," I say, but he can feel my apprehension thudding with my heart.

What if this is it, and my life ends here—eighteen years old, shot, stabbed, or smothered in a dungeon?

His lips are a really beautiful shape.

"How do we get out?" I ask.

Kingfisher picks up Wheeler's knife. I see it glinting in his hand. "All we can do is fight."

"I'm ready," I reply.

"Lark, what you did, the way you spoke . . ."

I don't want to hear what he has to say. There's more important business on my mind. I reach up and kiss him.

He kisses me back. Sweet, so sweet. Like water in the desert. We drink our fill and then I let him go.

"You understand that's just in case we die?" I assure him.

He smiles. "Are you using me, Elsa Crane?"

"You know I am. You're like a Second Wife, made for my pleasure."

Kingfisher laughs a low laugh, shocked at me, I think.

"You know my heart's not mine to give," I say. "And I can see that yours belongs to no one but yourself."

He laughs again, bashfully. "You think me selfish, on top of all my other sins?"

"Not even Janella Andric has a hold on you."

"Janella won't have me," he says. And half of me believes him.

"Wise woman."

Our eyes meet. My whole body has come to life and I'm filled with curiosity for his touch. My good hand feels the slim contours of his back, and I want to draw him down into another kiss. But Rye comes into my mind again and I sit up.

I see a single chair, salt-rust, slime. "Rye was here when they beat and tortured him."

Kingfisher's breathing changes.

"I won't stop looking for him, Yan. I won't give up hope."

Kingfisher nods, making no reply. He passes me the knife. He puts it in my good hand. "Use it. When you must."

He loosens the tourniquet. My circulation flows and a searing pain pumps into my hand with the blood.

"I'll tell you about Janella," he begins. And I feel something in him falling open, some painful secret he holds tight. He's about to speak—when a key turns in the door upstairs. We're both immediately on our feet, alert.

The murder party has arrived.

Kingfisher puts his finger to his lips. He leaps up the stairs and crouches, just inside the door. There's nowhere I can hide. My life rushes past: I'm playing with my brother in the sand. Pa lifts me down into his boat. I'm with Gailee, singing in the choir; I'm hauling up a lobster pot, bathed in Rye's songlight. I see a girl in spectacles, standing on the beach. I'm speaking in the Circle House. Alize and Heron have their arms clasped in peace. I see my brother put his hand over Ma's mouth.

There's a shaft of light as the door opens. Kingfisher springs. I see two silhouettes, fighting on the stairs—then I realize who it is.

"Stop! Stop!" I cry.

"Easy, easy," warns Heron.

They almost fall, the pair of them.

"Mikane," says Kingfisher, grasping Heron. My legs are so weak with relief that I can hardly walk toward them.

"Quickly," says Heron, reaching down to help me. "We're taking a boat. Yan, I'll get you back to your people. Elsa, you'll go too."

Heron notices my wound. "What's this?"

"Nothing," I lie.

"She saved my life," says Yan.

Heron looks at me and nods, as if he might have known.

He brings us out into the jailhouse. I see his men, tying up the guards. Elder Haines is trussed and gagged.

"Where's my ma?" I ask him.

"With your brother."

Heron offers Kingfisher a gun. Kingfisher declines it, in favor of a knife.

"Where's Wheeler?"

"In the Elders' Hall. He'll be back."

To my amazement, Gailee is there. John Jenkins is showing her how to hold and fire a gun. He looks at me, his songlight trying to form a question. I nod my thanks—and he nods back. As I get my bearings, I see Mr. Malting arming both his wives; I see neighbors and seaworkers preparing for a fight.

Gailee finds a box of bandages. She quickly wraps one round my hand and stuffs my pockets with extra rolls.

"Make sure you keep it clean," she says.

I thank her.

"We have to break out as quickly as we came," Heron instructs us. He's so calm, so resolute. I can see why men follow him into fire. "Wheeler knows we're trying to get to the quayside and he'll do anything to stop us. He's trying to enlist the cadets—but Redshank's on our side and he won't arm them. Their wrangling will buy us a moment of time."

"The harbor barrier," I say. "They'll try to stop us from taking a boat."

Heron looks grim at the thought of this.

"Go," says Soldier Wright. "We'll cover you."

These people know I am a Torch—and they are here, saving me. I never dreamed that this was possible. As I pass, I see the look in Gailee's eyes.

"Stay alive," she says.

"You too."

Something extraordinary is happening.

We are no longer powerless.

As we leave the jailhouse, Heron's men and our supporters come pouring out, surrounding us. I see John Jenkins, clear in his determination, returning the fire that comes at us from across the square. Perhaps the fight makes sense to him at last.

Heron shields us and we run. I pull Kingfisher toward the harbor. We weave our way behind shop stalls, sheltering behind the communal laundry.

Suddenly, I halt. I see Piper in a storehouse, pleading with my mother.

"I was trying to protect you," I hear him say.

"Ma," I cry. "Come with us." I slip Kingfisher's hand and run toward her.

"Elsa, stay back!" she cries.

She comes running toward me—I hear a shot—it flings her backwards and she falls.

Wheeler is by the statue of Peregrine, aiming at me. Ma has taken the bullet. She writhes. I think I start screaming.

"Cease fire! Cease fire!" yells Piper. "Cease fire!"

Heron runs at Wheeler like a bull. He lifts him off his feet, his knife plunging through Wheeler's breast. He lets the Emissary fall, and with an easy swipe, he cuts his throat. Wheeler is dead before he hits the ground.

The gunfire silences; the fighting stops. All eyes are on Heron, shocked at his easy, practiced violence. He stands in a growing pool of Wheeler's blood.

"Hold your fire," yells my brother—and we both dash to Ma. The wound is in her shoulder, red and ugly. Blood is soaking her gray widow's dress. I cradle her as she breathes her pain.

"Heron," she manages to say—and I realize that her gaze is fixed on him.

Heron is standing in the open, careless of his safety, looking down at Wheeler's corpse, as if Death has tricked him into one more kill.

In the weird silence, he realizes the eyes of the town are upon him.

"Wheeler came here to murder," he says. "He has set us against each other. Now he's paid." He drops his knife. "No more violence."

"You're finished, Mikane," yells Syker. "You're a common murderer."

Sergeant Redshank moves forward, trying to keep the peace. "We must all live with whatever happens here. For the children's sake, let's lay our weapons down."

His words carry weight—people begin to lower their weapons—but Chaffinch pays no heed. I see her running, a rock in her hand. Wracked with rejection, she hurls it at Heron. It hits him on the temple, drawing blood.

"Aylish-loving traitor!" she cries.

It's a battle cry. As Syker takes aim, Soldier Hamid rushes to protect Heron, pulling him down behind the statue of Peregrine. A hail of rifle fire begins—and our Great Brother's effigy is peppered with bullets.

We try to get Ma behind a pile of crates but there's an explosion nearby and the storehouse behind us ignites in flames. The harbor seems a million miles away.

The medal on Piper's uniform glints in the flames as he grabs Ma's hand. "You need a doctor," he says. "I can fly you to Brightlinghelm."

"He gagged you, Ma; he shut you up," I say, unable to conquer my disgust.

Ma is fighting to stay conscious. Her voice is low and full of pain as she draws Piper close. "I thought it would be safer if you loved Peregrine . . . I told you that your pa believed in him. But your pa never did. He mistrusted all the Brethren. And now your nature has been twisted to their will. I should have taught you better. . . ."

Piper shakes his head at her words, uncomprehending.

"I can save you," he says desperately. "Come with me to Brightlinghelm."

Ma implores us both. "My children . . . we must have peace." She sinks back, insensible. All the color is draining from her face. I look at Piper and he looks at me. He doesn't need to say the word; I know what he is thinking. The prejudice goes deep in him. *Unhuman.*

"Curl!" cries Heron. He's risking his life, trying to get to us. Through the smoke I see Kingfisher crawling toward us. He sees the growing bloodstain on Ma's shoulder.

"If we get her somewhere safe," he says, "I can treat the wound."

Piper's face is ugly with hate. "Get your hands off her, Aylish."

I put myself in front of him.

"He can help her. Wake up, Piper," I warn. "Before you kill everyone who loves you."

Piper stares at me like a statue. My words have hit home. I feel a reply stirring in him—then Forbe grabs me from behind.

"Here," he yells. "The unhumans!"

I struggle. A chaos of bodies converges on us. The pain in my injured hand roars. In the other, I grip the knife and slash. With a yell of pain, Forbe twists it from my hand. I see John Jenkins coming toward us, armed.

"Let her be," he says. His songlight is making a sharp, clear chord.

"Jenkins," says Forbe dismissively. "You fucking brainsick coward."

Jenkins fires. I reel backward, suddenly released, and Forbe falls to the ground. Piper is fighting with Mr. Malting. I get the sense he's torn—he doesn't want to fight—but Mr. Malting sees him as Wheeler's boy and he won't let him go. Gailee, Nela, and Soldier Wright are covering our escape with gunfire. I see Heron and Kingfisher carrying my ma away, and I run after them. In seconds, we have reached the harbor.

My heart sinks. Eldermen are guarding the entrance to the quay with guns raised. The harbor barrier has been drawn across. Our escape is cut off. Heron stares ahead in deep dismay. We won't get past those men unless we kill them all.

I glance behind me and see Syker lift John Jenkins on his bayonet. As Jenkins writhes on the spike, my legs go from under me. I see the look on Gailee's face and my whole instinct is to run to her.

Then Mrs. Sweeney appears at my side.

"This way," she says.

For a second I wonder whose side she's on—but as she grabs my hand, I instinctively know she's going to help. Her concern for Ma is evident.

Mrs. Sweeney ushers us through her parlor, out into her tiny yard. Her house forms part of the harbor wall and the back of it opens straight onto the sea. There's an old boat waiting, turbine whirring in the wind. It's her husband's, as dilapidated as the man himself.

"Her battery should take you a fair few miles," says Mrs. Sweeney. "But she's not fast. You'll be in trouble if they follow you. You can't use any light. You must trust your knowledge, Elsa, to steer clear of the rocks."

I thank her with a wordless hug, but Kingfisher is looking at the boat in dismay.

"We'll never catch my ship," he says. I fear he's speaking true—but there's no time to think.

Heron lifts Ma into the boat and lays her down. Her dress is red and soaking now. I give Kingfisher the bandages and he kneels at her side, packing the wound, stanching the blood. Mrs. Sweeney puts a bundle of blankets into my arms. I am expecting Heron to steer us away—but suddenly he stiffens, looking up into the village.

In the flames of the spreading fire, I see a cohort of boys, screaming with fear and hatred as they charge. Greening has armed the cadets. Heron's supporters are faced with terrified fourteen-year-olds, their own sons and brothers. They refuse to fire on them. Wright and Hamid raise their arms, surrendering. Malting and the others follow suit.

"Heron, we must leave," I urge.

But Heron is staring at something else.

"Can't you see her?" he says. "She's there, on the harbor wall, mocking me."

Heron is ashen. He sees Death.

"I can't come with you," he says to me. And he tries to leave the boat.

I stand in his way. "What are you talking about?" I ask in frustration. "You killed Wheeler. They'll hang you if you stay."

But Heron's demon is waiting. Her bony fingers beckon him.

"Your mother's life's in the balance," he says. "If I come, I will bring Death."

I see how deeply the war scars run into Heron's mind. He's not so very different from John Jenkins. I won't let him succumb to this despair. My voice comes out of me, fierce and determined.

"You saved me. You saved Yan. You brought us life. You bring hope. And people have died so that you can leave."

I turn him to face me, forcing him from his terrible vision. "This fight is bigger than you. It's bigger than Northaven. Can't you see? We're shaking off the Brethren."

He suddenly seems to see it.

"Your mother," he begins, and his throat chokes.

"Heron," I say, "I divorce you. Now sit in the boat."

Heron sits, collecting himself. I take command of the vessel and the battery springs to life. I help Mrs. Sweeney loose the ropes.

"You should come with us," I tell her. "They'll arrest you for helping."

"I'll tell them you forced me at knifepoint," she says.

I hear shouts coming from the harbor wall. "Here, they're here!"

Mrs. Sweeney steps back.

"May Sidon keep you safe," she says.

Rifles fire as the eldermen and the cadets come running down the wall. As Mrs. Sweeney turns for the cover of her house, a bullet gets her in the back.

"No!" I cry.

I reach out, trying to grab her. Bullets rain upon the water—Heron pulls me down. And Mrs. Sweeney slips into the sea.

Death is with us, to the last.

Wheeler's bloodless corpse. Find myself staring at it as the elderwomen clean him up.

Who do I report to? How do I proceed?

I saw them firing at the boat. I was screaming her name when the blow fell.

Ma.

No idea who hit me. Might have a concussion. Must stand, must get to my feet. I think a rib is cracked. That must be what is causing this pain around my heart.

Wheeler's mouth is open and his eyes stare up, like one of Elsa's fish. I see other bodies, prone and dead. Gyles Syker is nearby, exhorting sea-workers to chase the traitors' boat. They're hurrying to reopen the harbor barrier. Floodlights are turned upon the bay. I hear our mortar guns, firing overhead.

They are firing cannons at a fishing boat.

Elsa.

"What are you doing?" I yell at Syker. "Tell those guns to stop!"

He pays me no heed, as if he is our leader now that Wheeler's dead.

The eldermen are rounding people up. I see Marcus Wright and Mr. Malting sitting back to back in cuffs. The warehouse is burning to the ground.

Ma.

Mrs. Greening passes me with a bucket and a cloth, drenched in Wheeler's blood. She empties the gore into the harbor. I suddenly feel vomit in my throat and I am sick in plain sight. I tighten my guts, trying to keep it down—but I retch till there's nothing left. Mrs. Greening helps me to my feet.

"Poor boy," she says. "I'd be sick too, if I was in your family. You're the one good apple, Piper Crane."

I can't form any words.

"Your sister, you could tell she wasn't one of us," she goes on. "Even your father was full of wrong-thinking."

"What do you mean?" I ask. *Is this woman insulting my pa?*

"He objected when Ely was made elderman. And he found fault with every edict. We were glad when he was drafted. But you, his brave son, you have a commendation from Brother Kite himself."

A voice comes up from the heart of me. I hear it over the roar of the flames.

Wake up. Before you kill everyone who loves you.

Rye tried to tell me. Finch tried to tell me.

Elsa has told me.

Ma.

I turn away, afraid I'll push Mrs. Greening and her bucket into the sea.

Where's Redshank? Sergeant Redshank will explain. I'll ask him why Commander Mikane sided with the Aylish. Why was the Hero of Montsan fighting on their side?

Ma.

The world is spinning. *Nothing I believe in is real.*

Did Kite lie to me? Was Wheeler lying? I have held Elsa's secret like a shame. When she said she was unhuman, why didn't everyone recoil? I need to find Redshank. I'll find Sergeant Redshank and ask him these things. Have they all lied?

Redshank will put his hand on my shoulder and say, *Well, my lad, it's probably best if we don't think of it. Our job is just to do the best we can.*

Ma.

There are people all around me but I walk through them, seeing nothing. Gailee Roberts is sobbing over a dead soldier but I don't feel a thing.

"Airman, help us tie these damned insurgents," calls a voice.

But I move on.

The airman is not here.

I wash my head in a trough and my thoughts start to come clear.

My own free thoughts.

I've had them in a wrestling hold for so long that I don't know what to do with them.

Tombean Finch . . .

I put my hand up to feel the imprint of his kiss.

It's just another way to love, he said. He wanted me to be free.

Rye.

I walk toward the barracks, seeking absolution. I need to ask Redshank if I did the right thing. But I know already I was wrong. I feel my crime like a knife wound in my soul.

A corpse lies at the entrance to the barracks. The street comes up to meet me. I find myself on my hands and knees. Sergeant Redshank is before me, dead.

I lie down next to him, holding him.

"He was with the traitors," says a junior cadet, a boy with dirty knees, guarding the gates with a real gun. "He sided with the insurgent Mikane."

If they have killed Sergeant Redshank, they are wrong. That's all I know. I curl up and howl silently. If I had songlight it would hit the moon.

I don't know how long I lie there, holding him. Black smoke is billowing over the town, filling my lungs with dust and ash. The mortar guns fall silent. Syker and his men are swearing as they round their neighbors up. Someone is cuffing Hoopoe Guinea.

This is madness.

Redshank, tell me what to do.

I close my eyes, trying to turn the clock back to this morning—and when I open them again, I see a figure walking toward me. Ely Greening. He looks down.

"Come now, Crane," he says. "It's a terrible thing. Redshank was clearly mind-twisted. This talk of peace was nothing but an Aylish stratagem. They came here to unleash anarchy and chaos."

This morning, I would have believed him. Now I know what he is. A liar.

Wheeler brought this disaster. And I flew him here.

Greening pulls me to my feet. "We'll take care of Redshank, young man," he says. "You must take Wheeler's body back to Brightlinghelm and tell them exactly what's happened in Northaven."

"Yes, sir, I will," I say, playing my role like a good airman.

"I'm sorry to say your own sister was part of it." Greening is shaking his head. "You must publicly disown her as soon as you can."

"Yes, sir, I will."

"I'm sorry for your mother, boy. I always thought Curlew Crane had sense but perhaps she was mind-twisted too."

It's on the tip of my tongue to tell him what I think. But I am cleverer than that. I live in a world of liars and the only people telling me the truth are gone.

Ma.

I'll take Wheeler's corpse and I'll lay it at Kite's feet.

I'll find out if Kite's a liar too. And when I know the scale of all the lies, I will make myself a sword of truth.

In the sky, everything is clear. Flight is natural to me, as if I'm a bird. And in the air, when I'm climbing and falling, turning in the wind, all things are simple and I'll know what to do.

I'll find the life that I should live.

And if it's short, then so be it.

I watch Swan as she paces, waiting for news. Cassandra is standing by the window with empty eyes, her spirit locked like a chrysalid inside her.

I have always been held back by fear.

People tell me that I'm strong, that my songlight is extraordinary. I have never believed it until now.

I breathe in my power.

Swan thinks that she can use me? No. From this time onward, I will be using Swan. The silence is terrible as she paces. She must feel the judgment in my gaze, for she turns to me, something honest searing out of her.

"I sent the almonds back," she cries. "I sent them back—but he ate them anyway. How was I to stop it? I was with you, dealing with your hysterical cries."

Is she really trying to shift the blame to me?

"Look at you," she accuses, "you're shining with a pure, untarnished light. All you've known is goodness and love. You couldn't begin to understand me."

I understand her better than she thinks. She is the most selfish person I have ever met. And if she thinks I am her dolly, she is making a mistake.

There's a low knock at the door. Starling Beech comes in, respectfully delivering his news. Great Brother Peregrine is dead. Sister Swan's presence is required.

I get a sense of her falling through space with nothing to cling to. She turns away from me, clutching her sides. She falls and falls. Her legs give way. She makes no sound, landing on her dark, black lake.

The Emissary rushes to her side. He asks if there's anything that he can do. She puts out her arm and clings to him. I see her slowly recovering her strength, as if she's feeding on his mute devotion.

This palace will be full of cobras now, fighting to be king of snakes. There is only one honest man: Harrier, who carries a vision in his mind of a land where people matter. He wants to see the Chrysalid House in flames.

I'm going to help him. That is my first task.

I use my songlight to search him out. Swan was going to teach me how to mind-twist from a distance. I will forgo her lesson and work it out myself. I find the center of emotion in the palace. A large room full of books where an old man has just died in pain. Harrier is with him, horrified and shocked. I see him take the old man's hand.

"We were too late," he says.

If Harrier stays here, Kite will kill him. He is in Kite's way and Kite will have no obstacle. I want this man to live. It is imperative that Harrier survives. I sneak through his dark curls into his bent head and plant an image there. An image of fleeing, of saving himself, of hiding in the city, so he can fight from a place of safety.

Harrier sits very still, emptying his mind of everything but the thoughts I give him. I show him cobras slithering toward him. Kite has the army and the air force in his hand. I show him the gates of the palace, the bridge into the Pink District. A house with a blue rose on the door where he can hide.

"Well, then," he says to Peregrine. "I must leave you." And he kisses his pallid, papery hand. There are feet marching toward the door. Guards burst their way in.

"I'm praying!" he yells at them, with such force that they stop where they stand. "Where's your respect for the dead? Get out!"

Seeing Peregrine's corpse and feeling Harrier's authority, they back away. As soon as they've gone, Harrier picks up his walking cane and opens the window. He looks at the ivy-clad walls and sighs, thanking Gala that Peregrine's rooms are close enough to the ground. Swinging his one good leg over the sill, he goes.

I blink back into my own reality. Swan is still clutching the Emissary's puny arms. I see her incredible will to survive. By the time the Starling leaves, his heart belongs entirely to Swan and she's almost herself again, repossessing her brittle splendor.

She was once a girl like me. Kite has pushed her into that black lake and held her face down under the water. I walk toward her, resolute. My will to survive is as strong as her own.

"Let me help you," I say. I bring her powder and very gently, I dab it on her face.

"The murder isn't yours," I say. "It's Kite's."

She looks at me, ashamed at my knowledge. Tears stream down her face, making rivers in the powder. I will make this woman love me. I will save us both.

"I'm your sister," I tell her, "not your judge."

I'm doing what I do best, steering the boat, steadying her as she dances through the cannon fire. My special skill. I cannot use the sail, as it will make us visible, but with the turbines facing windward and the battery at full power, we're soon beyond the headland, out of range of their mortar guns.

On Bailey's Strand, I see a crowd of children. They ran out of Heron's garden following the plane, what seems like a lifetime ago. They must have been down here playing ever since. They have lit a bonfire and they're guarding my brother's plane, keeping it safe from sea monsters, no doubt. Its mirror-like surface glints in the flames; it's a thing of startling beauty. The children play on, unaware of how their parents in the village have torn themselves apart. The tide creeps up toward them.

Kingfisher is bent over my mother, his hands upon her wound. Heron is at the stern, his gaze on the sea behind us. I try not to think about his demon, grinning in the breeze, coming after us over the waves.

Ma flickers into consciousness.

"Where's Piper?" she asks me in a whisper.

"He chose his side, Ma. We left him behind," I tell her.

Every word causes her pain. "You must forgive him, Elsa."

I don't want to upset her so I nod. But I can't reply.

Ma feels the motion of the sea. "Are we fugitives?" she asks.

"Yes," I reply.

Heron silently takes her hand.

"How am I, Doctor?" she asks, looking up at Kingfisher.

"You're strong," he tells her. "But we must get you somewhere safe."

"I know where we must go," says Ma.

"Where?" asks Heron.

"Brightlinghelm. We must get there somehow. We have a battle to fight, Mikane."

Heron sees that she's in earnest and he nods. The ex-commander cannot find his words.

I see the relief on Kingfisher's face. "Brightlinghelm. My mission cannot fail."

I try to smile at Ma. "I always wanted to go."

Curl smiles back, drifting on her pain.

The moon goes behind thick clouds, covering our escape. Perhaps Heron's demon will lose her way.

In the darkness, I reach up to Nightingale, to tell her I'm alive.

And within a breath, she is beside me in the boat.

We share the confusion of events. She sees Kingfisher, pouring his songlight into Ma's wound. She knows immediately how close we came to death and what passed between us in the prison cell. I show her Heron slicing Wheeler's throat, Mrs. Sweeney dying in the sea. She sees what has been done to Ma.

"Oh, Lark . . ."

She feels what I am suffering.

Then she shows me a drop of poison falling into sweet lemon yellow. I see Swan, sitting at a banquet, shimmering in white. Then I see Cassandra, an empty and unliving wraith.

"Nightingale . . ." I share her pain. But Nightingale does not despair.

"I looked into her eyes," she tells me, "and for the longest time, I could see no light. But then I got a sense of who she is, of Cassandra. In truth, I don't think it's possible to kill a human soul. I think somewhere, at her core, she's undiminished. Deep inside, Cassandra is still there. I'm going to find her, Lark."

I feel her determination not to give up and it inspires me, filling me with light.

In Nightingale's reality, I hear a prayer, being incanted in a low male voice.

"Where are you now?" I ask her. "Is it safe to be communing with me?"

"I don't care," she says.

I sense no fear in her. This is a different Nightingale, stronger, bolder.

"I want you with me, Lark. You have to witness this." And I join with her in songlight, letting myself travel.

Nightingale shows me a ghostly scene through the gauze she wears over her face. She's at Swan's side in a dimly lit chamber. There are books from floor to ceiling and a canopied bed, draped in rich green velvet. On it, a corpse has been laid out.

Peregrine.

The room is full of men. A gray priest of Thal drones the prayer. I see Kite and the Council of Brethren. They eye each other in mistrust as Swan lays a single white lily on Peregrine's chest.

"Who could have done such a terrible thing?" she asks in counterfeit grief.

Kite speaks coolly. "I think it's obvious who did this. Brother Harrier has fled, like a thief in the night. I've been suspicious of him for some time," he says. "He wormed his way into Peregrine's affections and used his position to murder our Great Brother."

In our harmony we watch as not one of the councillors dares to disagree.

Kite comes forward to the corpse. He takes the ring of state from Peregrine's cold finger and puts it on his own colder one. He breathes in, trying the fit of his power.

"A new era," simpers Swan. And I feel a deep disgust for her.

"An era of victory," says her master. "My era."

Nightingale shows me how Swan was forced—but there are no excuses for what she has done. She's a murderer. She curtsies in front of Kite, making her submission clear. She gives him his new title.

"I will serve you always, Great Brother Kite."

Kite lifts Swan's face. And weighs her fate in the balance. He decides to kiss her. And Nightingale closes her eyes.

When she opens them, she is with us once more in the boat.

Kingfisher can sense her, I am sure of it.

"My friend Nightingale is with me," I tell them all. "She's in the Brethren's Palace. She has shown me that Peregrine is dead. Kite is our Great Brother now."

The news lands. Heron slowly shakes his head. "Then peace will surely fail."

Kingfisher's voice is grave. "Are my comrades sailing to their deaths?"

The coast is dark ahead of us. There is no light to guide us. Not a single star is out. It seems to me that the evil is too great, that we cannot fight it. We are one small boat against the tide.

But Nightingale's strength is kindling. "There is a light," she says, catching my thoughts. "The light is Harrier. It's Heron Mikane. The Aylish ship. It's you, Lark."

I take her meaning. "It's Drew Alize and Kingfisher," I say. "It's the people of Northhaven, who risked everything to help us. It's my mother. It's you, Nightingale. The light is us." We hold each other in the brightest light we can. "We have to do more than survive," I say. "Fate has put us where we are and we must dare to act."

Nightingale agrees. "I can help the Aylish. When their ship gets to Brightlinghelm, I'll find a way to warn them." Her fortitude flows through me. "You may be a fugitive, Lark, but you are free."

Frelzi. Freedom. That is what we're fighting for.

Ma drifts in Heron's arms as the moon draws us south. Kingfisher's head is bent, filling her with warmth and strength.

I'm leaving my home, an outlaw, a Torch. I'm leaving with nothing but the dress I stand in. My heart is sorrowing for Rye. But I have my mother, Kingfisher, and Mikane. I have my songlight. I have Nightingale.

In this small boat, I have all that I need.

"We're coming to you, Nightingale," I say.

ACKNOWLEDGMENTS

Thanks to John Wyndham, whose cold-war novel *The Chrysalids* inspired me to think about the far distant future, when I was in my teens. It has stayed with me ever since.

Thanks to Matt Charman, who believed I could write this strange story of telepaths for the screen. When I told him it had to be written in prose, he kept on believing I could do it. Thanks, Matt, for listening to all those early chapters and for never losing faith.

Thanks to all at Binocular: Annelie Simmons, Elena Hamilton, and especially Josh Fasulo, for long days spent weaving story. You have been game-changing collaborators and one novel became a trilogy because of the work we did together. Thanks also to Annelie Simmons for her pertinent questions about what the *Songlight* world would look like.

I'd like to thank Martin Biltcliffe, Nuala Buffini, Fiona Buffini, Andrée Molyneux, Isabel Lloyd, Sam Jones, Hugh Williams, Bridie Biltcliffe, Joe Biltcliffe, and Maya Gannon for reading early drafts and for their thoughtful notes and loving support. Novel-writing is a solitary business and I never felt alone.

I'd like to thank St John Donald at United Agents for reading, listening, and wholeheartedly supporting my efforts to write this story. Thanks to him also for supporting my sabbatical from writing drama. I will be back, I promise!

This novel spent a year and a half sitting in a digital drawer. Thank you to Anwen Hooson at Bird for encouraging me to finish it and for the incredible job she did in finding the right publishers.

Thank you to Allison Hellegers at Simola for sterling work in finding *Songlight* a home in the USA.

Massive thanks to my US editor, Tara Weikum, at HarperCollins, for believing in the book and for such carefully considered notes and encouragement.

A huge thank you also to my UK editor, Alice Swan, at Faber. Alice, when we met, I had a strong feeling that under your guidance the novel would only get better. You haven't proved me wrong.

Finally, Martin Biltcliffe, most generous of men, you have been on this journey with me every step of the way. My loving thanks.